AUG 3 2005

NOVELS BY DAVID POYER

THE CIVIL WAR AT SEA

A Country of Our Own
Fire on the Waters

TALES OF THE MODERN NAVY

The Command
Black Storm
China Sea
Tomahawk
The Passage
The Circle
The Gulf
The Med

THE HEMLOCK COUNTY NOVELS

Winter Light
Thunder on the Mountain
As the Wolf Loves Winter
Winter in the Heart
The Dead of Winter

TILLER GALLOWAY

Down to a Sunless Sea
Louisiana Blue
Bahamas Blue
Hatteras Blue

OTHER NOVELS

The Only Thing to Fear
Stepfather Bank
The Return of Philo T. McGiffin
Star Seed
The Shiloh Project
White Continent

THAT
ANVIL OF
OUR SOULS

A *NOVEL OF THE* MONITOR *AND*

THE MERRIMACK

DAVID POYER

SIMON & SCHUSTER

NEW YORK   LONDON   TORONTO   SYDNEY

SIMON & SCHUSTER
Rockefeller Center
1230 Avenue of the Americas
New York, NY 10020

SIMON & SCHUSTER and colophon are registered trademarks
of Simon & Schuster, Inc.

For information about special discounts for bulk purchases,
please contact Simon & Schuster Special Sales at
1-800-456-6798 or business@simonandschuster.com.

Book design by Ellen R. Sasahara

Manufactured in the United States of America

1   3   5   7   9   10   8   6   4   2

Library of Congress Cataloging-in-Publication Data

Poyer, David.
That anvil of our souls : a novel of the Monitor and the Merrimack / David Poyer.
        p. cm.
1. United States—History—Civil War, 1861–1865—Fiction. 2. Merrimack
(Frigate)—Fiction. 3. Monitor (Ironclad)—Fiction. I. Title.

PS3566.O978T47 2005
813'.54—dc22   2005042616

ISBN-13: 978-0-684-87135-6
ISBN-10:   0-684-87135-1

ACKNOWLEDGMENTS

Ex nihilo nihil fit. For this book I owe thanks to Steve Boyer, Alan B. Flanders, Howard Fuller, Herb Gilliland, Eleanor Smith Gordon, Sandra Y. Johnson, Lawrence Jones, Edison McDaniels, Alan W. Mitchell, Tara Parsons, Rocco J. Pierri, Naia Elizabeth Poyer, Ellen R. Sasahara, Isolde C. Sauer, Jay Schmidt, William N. Still Jr., Jo Taylor, John G. Zimmerman, and many other individuals who gave unstintingly of their time and expertise.

Thanks also to Jan Hilley of the Manuscript Department Staff, The New-York Historical Society Library, James Cheevers at the U.S. Naval Academy Museum, Katrina Boston at the Newsome House Museum and Cultural Center, Carol Hanson and David Johnson of The Casemate Museum at Fort Monroe, Alice Haynes of The Marshall W. Butt Library at the Portsmouth Naval Shipyard Museum, Michael Crawford and Mark Hayes of the Naval Historical Center (Early History Branch), Jean-Michel Brunner of the Musée National de la Marine, Palais de Chaillot, The Navy Department Library, Bob Holcombe and Bruce Smith of the Port Columbus Civil War Naval Center, Ivan T. Luke and the United States Coast Guard Barque *Eagle,* Mary Catalfamo, Gary LaValley, and Jennifer Bryan of the Nimitz Library Special Collections and Archives Division, U.S. Naval Academy Library, John V. Quarstein of the Virginia War Museum, Sandra Scoville and Paula Mills of the Eastern Shore Public Library, John Coski and The Museum of the Confederacy, Susan Berg, Mary Ann Cleary, Kim Gove, Josh Graml, Lester Webber, and Kathy Williamson of The Mariner's Museum, Jeff Johnston of the Monitor National Marine Sanctuary, Mike Cobb and Barbara Boyer of the Hampton History Museum, Cora M. Reid and Sherin Henderson of the Peabody Collection at Hampton University, Gail Nicula of the Joint Forces Staff College Library, Sylvia Weedman of The Bostonian Society Library, Kay Peninger of St. John's Church, Richmond, Robert Hitchings of the Sargeant Memorial Room, Kirn

Memorial Library, Norfolk, and Burt Altman of Special Collections, Florida State University Libraries.

Above all my gratitude to two remarkable women: Marysue Rucci, editor of these several volumes, and Lenore Hart, wife, best friend, and first reader.

As always, all errors, shortcomings, and debatable interpretations are my own.

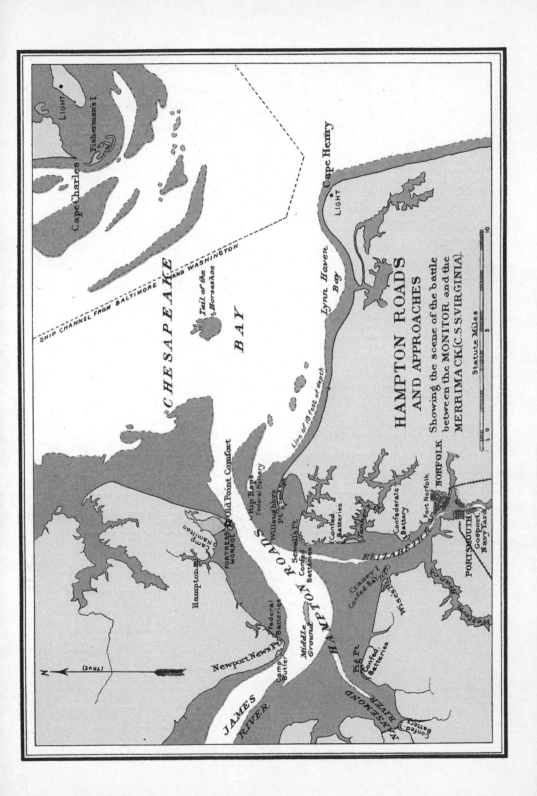

HAMPTON ROADS
AND APPROACHES

Showing the scene of the battle
between the MONITOR and the
MERRIMACK (C.S.S.VIRGINIA).

CONTENTS

———◆———

I

A MATTER OF THE FIRST NECESSITY.

September 1861–January 1862. *1*

II

THAT FERVOUR OF SCRAPING THE BONE,
OF KNAPPING THE FLINT.

December 1861–February 1862. *57*

III

THAT ANVIL WHEREIN IS HAMMERED OUR SOULS.

January 1862–March 7, 1862. *181*

IV

THE CLANGOR OF THAT BLACKSMITH'S FRAY.

March 8–9, 1862. *277*

V

THE FEAST OF FIRE.

March–June 1862. *361*

Part I

A MATTER OF THE FIRST NECESSITY.

September 1861–January 1862.

———◆———

1

A Residence on Fifth ♦ Introduction to Personages of Importance ♦
The Southern Bug-bear ♦ Advice from Men of Wealth and Influence ♦
At the Delamater Ironworks ♦ 95 Franklin Street ♦ Impromptu Examination
in Gearing Design ♦ Rejection of a Long-Cherished Scroll

MR. Theodorus Hubbard. Responding to the invitation of Mr. Micah Eaker. Theo gave the butler his card, stripping off his dripping mackintosh, glancing resentfully around the interior of 372 Fifth Avenue, New York City, to which the note waiting at his hotel that afternoon had invited him.

Theo Hubbard was no larger than a boy. But he'd never let his size confine the scope of his dreams. At twenty-six he'd already earned the confidence of the engineer in chief of the Navy. At the moment he was in civilian clothes, a rumpled brown suit of only modest quality. His lips were firm, his blue eyes determined, his small chin smooth-shaven. For once his hands were free of coal dust and machine grease, though not, he suspected, for long considering what his orders laid out to accomplish over the next ninety days.

—You are expected. If you will follow me, sir.

The room into which he was shown from the chill of an October afternoon had been decorated by someone of taste. Lavender moiré draperies puddled to a figured carpet. Gold-on-cream wallpaper glowed beneath glass torchieres. A black leather settee stood between the front windows, and a huge fireplace mirror reflected prints of the Hudson Valley. A fire crackled on the grate, its reddish heart well nourished, he saw, by a good draft. By the finest Pennsylvania anthracite too, by the smell. Three men in black broadcloth stood around it, holding segars.

—Mister Theodorus Hubbard, the butler announced. The paneled door closed softly.

—Mister Hubbard. I am Micah Eaker. Thank you for responding to my note.

A rubicund old gentleman with white chin-tuft. His grip was dry, glance sharp. —I had not expected so young a man.

—The Navy considers me old enough for my responsibilities, sir.

—I am sure you will prove up to the mark. My own boy is in the naval service too; in North Carolina, I believe. Though we do not correspond just now.

—I have met an Eaker.

—We must compare notes. But now let me introduce you to two very good friends of mine. Mister G. L. Barnes, in the employ of Mister Griswold, of Albany. And this is Mister Cornelius Bushnell. Gentlemen, may I present Theodorus Hubbard. Engineer Hubbard has been noticed in the papers both at Fort Sumter and at Gosport, and more recently in the battle at Hatteras.

Theo shook hands, his natural bumptiousness daunted. Barnes was unknown to him, but John A. Griswold was a major industrialist and very well connected politically—specifically with the former governor of New York and current secretary of state, William Seward. And Cornelius Scranton Bushnell was probably the most influential man in Connecticut . . . grocery magnate, railroad tycoon, industrialist. They looked down at him as Eaker suggested he help himself to a segar, that whiskey was on the side table, that they all might be more comfortable seated.

—Well, sir. It seems appropriate to congratulate you, Bushnell began. Tall and self-assured, with upper lip shaven and a dark beard brushing his stock. —I am given to understand the chief engineer has put you in charge of our ironclad project. The counterbalance to that great Southern bug-bear, the *Merrimack*.

—Thank you, sir, but it may prove no bug-bear. And I believe Captain Ericsson would claim the distinction of being in charge.

They chuckled. —I'm sure he would, but as the Navy's representative you will be responsible for a good deal of the construction. As such, we thought our views might be helpful.

—I should be very glad to hear them.

Old Eaker said, —Before we begin, boys, you might like to know Hubbard here is from Gideon Welles's hometown.

—From Hartford, eh? Do you know the secretary, Mr. Hubbard?

—I have had the pleasure of corresponding with him.

Theo didn't add that it had been in the form of a letter to the then editor of the *Hartford Times*. From his first startle he was beginning to feel more comfortable. This was the sort of personal examination wealthy, powerful men liked to have with underlings. Which was fine with him.

One day he intended to be one of them.

Theodorus Coggswell Hubbard had been born on a farm in Weatogue. At twelve he'd walked to Hartford and signed on as a machinery oiler at the Hanbury cotton mill. Hard work, respectful address, and natural ability made him assistant foreman at fifteen, foreman at sixteen, and journeyman machinist and head of loom maintenance at seventeen. On his eighteenth birthday he applied to the best school he could afford, living on his savings as he completed his education.

When he graduated, the largest toolmaker in town hired him as a master machinist. When the company failed in '55, a notice in the *Courant* of a board to hire steam engineers in government service caught his eye.

He'd taken the next morning's train to Washington, changing at New Haven, New York, and Philadelphia, sitting up all night on a hard bench seat. The questions were practical ones, easily answered by anyone who'd run a stationary engine. He was assigned as third assistant engineer in the old paddle wheeler *Susquehanna*. He went from there to first assistant in *Mississippi* after her return from shelling the Chinese at Pei Ho, then to *Owanee* as first engineer. He'd been about to resign and seek a position in engine design when the war had come.

Clever men with vision, such as Drake and Morse and Rockefeller, were changing the face of the country. America would bring the world wheels of steel and wings of bronze, nerved by electricity and powered by steam. Men like Cyrus McCormick, Eli Whitney, and Joseph Henry were famous and rich. Theo Hubbard wanted these things with the desperation of a man born poor and nearing thirty.

He had one more reason for bidding farewell to the ocean waves. There were no applicants for the position at present, but he had no doubt of his eligibility for marriage should a suitable candidate appear.

Barnes said vigorously, —A fine figure of a man, Welles. Sees to the heart of a matter.

When the others murmured agreement, Bushnell took up the thread. —When I presented Captain Ericsson's proposal, he saw at once how revolutionary it was. My own plan looked unimaginative beside it. But we have ironmaking capacity for both and for many more.

—Quite so, said Barnes. Then, to Theo, —Now you, sir, are a protégé, one might say, of Mister Isherwood. Not so?

—I work for the chief engineer.

—Who has great confidence in you. You're a loyal employee.

—My previous masters have thought so.

—And your opinion of him?

Theo hesitated, searching the hard faces. Poker would be a child's game to these shrewd financiers, lobbyists, political fixers. —We worked together, trying to save *Merrimack* in Norfolk. His "Experiments in Steam Engineering" is a masterpiece. I'm proud to follow where he leads.

—Well said.

—Quite so.

Eaker patted his shoulder. —Well, sir, you leave no doubt where you stand. Let us inquire further. You have seen considerable service afloat. What is your opinion of Captain Ericsson's design? Not so much as to its buildability but as to its . . . seaworthiness?

They were all eyeing him now. Theo said, —I've only seen sketches. There are many good points. But I cannot say I've fully matured my opinion.

—Really?

—Yes sir. I only arrived in the City today. I was preparing to report to Captain Ericsson this evening when your note arrived.

Barnes said, —And so you shall; we shall not keep you. We wish you the best of luck in your new post, sir. And to assist you in your efforts . . .

The envelope was of heavy, calendared, expensive paper. Theo accepted it with raised eyebrows. —What is this, sir?

Old Eaker murmured, —A letter of credit, sir, on Eaker and Callowell—my firm—for the sum of two thousand dollars. The Union is in peril, sir. While young stalwarts like my son defend her with their lives, it is only meet we older patriots defend her with our purses. You may draw on it for any expenditure you think fit to advance the cause or make your own efforts easier.

Theo found himself stammering. —I must say . . . as I think fit . . . You will require an accounting?

—I do not think that will be necessary, Eaker said gravely.

—Only a word of caution, Bushnell put in.

—A caution, sir? Theo fingered the envelope, still in shock. Two thousand was what a first engineer drew a year.

—Rather let us call it advice. Barnes glanced at the others. —Well-meant counsel from those inclined to be your friends. That is, if you have any brief from the chief engineer or the chief constructor or any other quarter to frustrate Captain Ericsson's efforts in the country's defense, you may find your career prospects shortened. If, on the other hand, you lend him your full assistance, and he meets with the success we expect, you will find them much enhanced. Other opportunities will beckon after the insurrection is put down next summer. Aid him with your seagoing expertise. And let us know—confidentially, of course—if you should foresee any problems.

Theo stood with gloves in one hand, the envelope in the other. Should he tell them he didn't need threats or rewards to do his duty? Or simply bow and withdraw? One would give him a moment's satisfaction. The other, not only two thousand dollars to spend as he wished, but preferment in business when peace returned. These were powerful men. The sort he'd always planned to serve . . . and to become.

He said quietly, —My orders are to assist Mister Ericsson in any way possible. Of course I will give him the benefit of my experience, such as it is.

And that must have struck just the right note, for all three nodded. —Quite so, quite so, old Eaker said. He raised his voice. —Parkinson! Show our new friend to the door.

A locofoco flared in the dark, then was applied to a short pipe. Theo gazed up at the shadows of great brick chimneys, brewing with a woolen tangle of smoke and steam; serrated factory rooves; a great crane that flung its arms wide above the gray North River, an iron scarecrow loftier than the highest steeple in Hartford. The lamp at the gate lit a red pennant that flapped endlessly in the breeze.

The Cornelius H. Delamater Ironworks was the largest steam engine manufactory in the New World. It had provided the propeller and boilers for the first screw-propelled warship, *Princeton*, and dominated the growing market for screw-propelled merchant ships. They'd built Ericsson's radical caloric-propelled ship, driven not by steam but by heated air. It hadn't worked very well, but only a genius could conceive of replacing steam itself. Hubbard was standing on Thirteenth; the works spanned six hundred feet all the way to Fourteenth.

A steam whistle shrieked, and hundreds of men hurried toward him, grease-stained, exhausted-looking, thoughts intent no doubt on beef and potatoes and beer. Quitting time, and well after dark. Delamater must be laying on extra hours.

Inquiring where he might find John Ericsson, he was told the engineer wasn't there. He maintained an office at his home, 95 Franklin Street.

Twenty minutes later, after a brisk walk through gaslit downtown, Hubbard was shown into an upstairs room by a cowed-looking housekeeper. The inventor of the steam fire engine, the screw propeller, and the forced-draft blower sat in rolled-up shirtsleeves at an enormous drafting table. His balding head was bent under an intense light and considerable heat from large oil lamps with polished reflectors.

—What the hell do you want?

The inventor barked the words without turning his head. His Swedish accent was overlaid with Scots. Stocky, with bearded cheeks but clean upper lip, his forehead was as broad and his expression as determined as any physiognomist could wish. The nib continued to scratch, noting calculations with incredible rapidity on a sheet of foolscap, then moving back to specify the length of a lever arm.

—Sir, I am ordered to assist you in the construction of your steam battery.

—And who the devil are you?

—First Engineer Theodorus Hubbard, United States Navy. He extended his gloved hand, but the man waved it off impatiently.

—I am no schoolmaster, sir. Why does the Navy insist on sending me dolts to instruct? I have no time. Good day.

—I'm not here for instruction. Mister Isherwood feels I may be of service in lightening your load.

For the first time Ericsson looked at him, blinking reddened, pouchy eyes. He obviously hadn't slept for a long time. His shirt was ink-stained, his hands and fingers black. It looked as if he'd wiped his pen on his forehead. —Isherwood, eh? You one of his minions?

—I'm a naval engineer.

—A machinery oiler, you mean. Ericsson nodded at the diagram. —No doubt you can drive a steam engine once it is explained to you. But only those familiar with mathematics can understand my construction. If you don't know the calculus, you had better go back to your stoking.

Stung, Theo transferred his attention from the irascible tyrant to the diagram before him. And was struck speechless.

Pinned out under the artificial brilliance was a drawing of such elegance, purity of style, and, yes, beauty that for a moment his dazzled eye saw a work of art rather than an abstraction of machinery. He searched in vain for clutter or clumsiness, for the usual contrivances lesser designers employed to cram machinery within the confines of a hull. All was simplicity, efficiency, direct action. Most amazing, Ericsson had been sketching it freehand. No pencilled tracings lay about. He was drawing direct to manufacturing diagram, and doing his calculations as he drew. The brain before him was accomplishing the work of four men simultaneously.

The Swede was smiling contemptuously. Theo cleared his throat. —It seems to be . . . the rotating gear for a gun cupola.

Ericsson hoisted heavy eyebrows. —A naval officer in here yesterday identified it as the works of a coffee grinder. Anything strike you as interesting about it?

Theo gave it several seconds' more examination. The terrific weight of the iron cupola, or turret, had been dealt with in an unusual way. In other proposals, such as Coles's sketch in *Blackwood's*, the weight rested on the bottom edge, supported on balls or friction rollers. This drawing showed a ring but no bearings. Instead a central spindle supported the entire massive assembly, guns, men, and armor, transmitting the weight downward through an iron pedestal to the keel. He pointed this out, and the inventor nodded. —The advantage?

—Less friction. Thus, a smaller drive engine. Less mechanical advantage necessary in the cogwheel train. A greater speed of rotation?

—What strikes you as the weak point of such a system?

This threw him for a moment; he was not used to hearing any mechanical contrivance described as a "system," a word usually reserved for philosophical reflections. He finally pointed to the gear train. —I should say it lies in the possibility of a bending moment developing. Should the craft take a steep roll—

—This wedge assembly raises or lowers the turret. In heavy seas it would be lowered, to rest on the bronze base ring.

—I see that. But if, when jacked up on the spindle, it should be struck by a heavy shot, could it not jam? I should look into the centros and clearances on these cycloidal gears.

They discussed mating and generating surfaces, pitch angle and backlash. The arrangement seemed unimpeachable, and at last Theo said, —It is brilliant in its conception and extremely interesting in its arrangements.

—It merely derives from the circumstances.

—How do you mean, sir, only derives? The whole concept of your craft seems to me quite novel and original.

Ericsson rubbed his eyes. The glare was making Theo's own water; he could not imagine how the man endured it. The inventor said through gritted teeth, —Is this world composed only of imbeciles? The *Merrimack* has progressed so far, no structure of large dimensions can be completed in time to meet her. On the other hand, the heavy armor all observers report means only the largest guns will be of any use against her. The waters of the Southern rivers are shallow. They are also narrow, making it difficult to return fire from along the banks by maneuvering to present a broadside. We are thus driven to a small craft mounting heavy guns, of shallow draft, with a rotating turret. It is all so obvious I only had to explain it to the Navy board three times.

Theo did not like being called dolt and imbecile, but restrained his anger. The man was under terrific strain. —As I understand it, you have only ninety days to produce this marvel, along with hull, driving machinery, internal arrangements. In a navy yard this would scarcely suffice to begin the planning. But you have promised the vessel in that time.

—Good, you know of the time limitation in the contract. Are you aware we also had to post bond that it will be invulnerable to enemy shot? We will not be paid in full until it passes that test. If it does not, all monies advanced for construction must be refunded within thirty days.

Theo thought of the men he'd met at Eaker's. He wondered at their daring and envied their ability to wager such vast sums. Either they were selfless patriots, or immense profits were in the offing. —That is a shameful reservation.

—I should not have signed it had we not already ordered the materials. Well, my battery will do all they require. I personally feel it will render nugatory the present superiority of England and France over this country. But *speed* is of the essence. I am dividing the work among three leading establishments. The Novelty Ironworks, on the far side of Manhattan, is tooling up for the turret and associated machinery; they have the only steam-powered presses capable of forming heavy plate to a circular section. Rowland laid the hull-keel at Continental today. Unfortunately I had no time to attend. And Mister Delamater is building the engines, also of my design.

—The chief engineer has high regard for all these companies, especially Novelty. He worked there early in his career.

—Then he may not be as pedestrian as I have assumed.

—Mister Isherwood is not a pedestrian man, sir. Though he is no universal genius like yourself.

He'd heard the old inventor was not insusceptible to flattery. He regarded it not as an emollient but as his due. But Ericsson still sounded suspicious. —Yet he's trying to push the Bureau's design. So far my supporters have managed to hold out for the genuine article, the only truly invulnerable floating battery.

Theo remembered his meeting with some of those "supporters" at Eaker's. Somehow Ericsson had managed to engineer not only machines, but a political-industrial lobby of considerable influence. —It is a most ingenious ship.

—Not a "ship," sir. It is a *fighting machine*. Impregnable. Irresistible. Unsinkable. Ericsson spied the housekeeper lurking on the landing and shouted for coffee. —So you're here to assist me. How?

—In whatever capacity you wish. I have some ability in drafting.

—Mister MacCord does the working drawings. He nodded behind him, and Theo, looking over what he saw now was another drafting board, realized an assistant had overheard the entire conversation.

—Then if you wish me to hoof them back and forth, I will gladly do that. Whatever you like. I believe in your vision and will do all in my power to assist you in its realization. And the Navy is paying my salary. You need furnish nothing in that direction.

Ericsson cocked his head. —Can you do without sleep?

—That is one thing one learns in an engine room. I will sleep no more in the next ninety days than you.

The engineer looked skeptical. He said slowly, drawing a pen through a wiper: —You *might* be young enough to train. If you are capable of checking a calculation for any errors fatigue may interpolate, I can put you to use. As well as in carrying instructions to the various contractors. Ensuring plans are being carried out to specifications.

—It will be my honor to work under you, sir.

A frosty, remote grimace. —Perhaps we shall give you a trial. Coffee, Hubble? I confess I need a cup.

—Hubbard, sir. I would be honored to take one with you, Captain.

Ericsson included MacCord in the invitation; he and Theo exchanged cool bows. As they gulped the bitter brew, and Ericsson began explaining his time line for construction, Theo recalled his own scroll, reposing within his coat. He too thought the Navy hidebound, unwilling to step into the nineteenth century. Perhaps the great man's backers would be interested in another new machine of war. And thinking of them, he remembered their confidential charge, and cleared his throat.

—I will be happy also to give you the benefit of my experience, sir.

Ericsson looked up sharply. —What do you mean?

—I have spent years at sea; have been through storms and so forth. I could look over the design from that aspect.

—That will not be required. Matters of buoyancy and stress can be foreseen better from the viewpoint of the experienced engineer than from the untutored guesses of seamen.

—Then let me ask your indulgence in one thing more, sir.

Feeling perhaps the moment was not right, yet unable to resist, Theo brought it out into the light. Conscious suddenly of the erasures and inkblots, false starts, conjectures unsupported by calculation, he unrolled it at waist level.

Ericsson scooted his stool back from it. —This would be . . . ?

—It is a . . . submersible boat. Powered by a liquid fuel derived from petroleum oil.

This time Ericsson's smile was hawkish, contemptuous, his eyes sliding from the very sight of the document. —I have no desire to be subjected to amateurish fantasies, sir. Nor with your pretense to knowledge of the mysterious ways of the sea. Let us deal with realities. We must build the machine by January 12. *My* machine. Just as I have drawn it. A race against time. If we lose, the Confederates will rule the waves. Is that quite clear?

—Of course, sir. But I thought certain ideas—

Ericsson's attention was back in the board. Dipping his pen, he began etching in a watertight door. —Let me make myself plain, Hobart. Or whatever your name is. *Ideas* are not required of you. You are here to help me save the Union. Shall we confine our relations to that, sir?

Meekly, Theo agreed.

2

Saint John's Church, Richmond, in the Rain ♦ An Empire of Death and Pain
♦ The Consolations of the Spirit ♦ An Outburst of Despair ♦ The Golden Bath
of Laudanum ♦ Visit from the Reverend Doctor Minnigerode
♦ Ladies of the Circle ♦ The Sentiments of People of Our Class
♦ The Duty of a Daughter

THE rain. That was what she'd always and evermore remember past the frozen horror of this endless September day. It fell endlessly from lowering clouds. Soaking the clapboards of the old church. Chilling those who stood gathered around the opening in the black Virginia earth. Running down the worn leaning stones around them till they seemed to stir and heave within the brick wall that circled them like embracing arms which could never close.

—Thou knowest, Lord, the secrets of our hearts; shut not thy merciful ears to our prayer; but spare us, Lord most holy, O God most mighty, O holy and merciful Saviour; thou most worthy Judge eternal, suffer us not, at our last hour, for any pains of death, to fall from thee.

In the churchyard of Saint John's, Richmond, Catherine Bowen Wythe Claiborne hugged herself as she gazed into the open grave of her infant daughter. The mysterious process in her heart that played like complex music through every waking moment, whispering endlessly of this and that concern or aspiration, had gone silent for the first time since she'd become conscious of it as a child. In the face of this unutterable it did not speak. Nor could any communication reach her. She stood under the pouring rain, in the huddle of black cloth and pale faces around the muddy verge.

The little girl had lived for two days, weakened by her difficult passage into this world. That cruel travail from which her mother still trembled as she leaned on the arms of those around her. The rector of Saint John's had baptized little Elfair before she died. He stood now in the old Wythe plot, water running off his hat, his square concerned red face lowered to the book he read from. She felt the pressure of her mother's hand and, on her other arm, that of her father's.

A rattle, a clatter of stones on wood. Catherine flinched and felt her mother's fingers tighten. Stared unbelieving at dirt lying like a dung stain across the clean white wood.

—Forasmuch as it hath pleased Almighty God, in his wise providence, to take out of this world the soul of our deceased sister, we therefore commit her body to the ground; earth to earth, ashes to ashes, dust to dust; looking for the general Resurrection in the last day, and the life of the world to come, through our Lord Jesus Christ; at whose second coming in glorious majesty to judge the world, the earth and the sea shall give up their dead; and the corruptible bodies of those who sleep in him shall be changed, and made like unto his own glorious body; according to the mighty working whereby he is able to subdue all things unto himself.

The ritual words went on, solemn and high. She could feel them trying to catch her. But they slipped off like fingernails on ice. They could not touch her. Neither the body which still bled nor the heart which had so mysteriously abstracted itself.

She swayed, eyes sealed, over the abyss into which her child had vanished. Gone, yet *where*? Lost little girl, who'd reached her tiny arms out to her as she died? She bit her lips till they split, till she tasted the salt of mingled blood and tears.

—My fault, she muttered beneath the priest's words, the murmur of the rain. And felt her mother's grip tighten again as she whispered beneath the black tulle of mourning.

—Nothing you could have done, Cathery.

—I should have stayed in Norfolk. And had a doctor. Not a midwife.

—No doctor could have saved her. God called her. She's home.

Catherine screamed softly inside her head. —Her home's here. With me.

From the right her father shook her. —We buried one when he was four, and another when she was twelve. Count yourself lucky, child.

The pastor intoned, —I heard a voice from heaven saying unto me, Write, From henceforth blessed are the dead who die in the Lord: even so saith the Spirit; for they rest from their labours.

Catherine said, so loud the priest faltered, —*She* never labored. She never knew her own name or got to play. She never got to *play*.

—Hush, her mother hissed. —Quiet!

—What need had He for such a *little* child? She clawed a breath, hating the very air. —No, Mother. I can't pretend God wanted her or that she's with the angels. She's dead and cold, and you're burying her in the ground. O, my precious little child.

She began to rock, easing the pit between heart and loins where her very life had been torn out. The priest read faster, not looking up. Around her the others moved their lips too, asking for a kingdom of God on earth and bread and forgiveness and deliverance. But His kingdom was here already, and it was not deliverance but an empire of death and pain for the smallest and most helpless of His creatures.

Then she saw the faces, so white, and the Reverend Doctor's shocked eyes, and realized she'd said it aloud. So she said it again. Her voice rising to a scream against the rain and the heartlessness of brick and marble and an open hole.

—She's gone and God took her. Goddamn Him. Goddamn Him forever.

When she rose up out of the mists of the swoon or spell, she was back at Wythe's Rest. The rambling rose-brick pile on Church Hill she'd grown up in, met Ker in, the house they'd been married in. She was lying on the fainting couch in the parlour. She heard the crackle of a fire, the Reverend's voice from back in the kitchen.

When she opened her eyes, Dr. Lassiter was standing over her, holding her wrist in one hand, his watch in the other. Her first thought was, O my

God, they've taken her from me. Little Rob stood at the far side of the room. Her heart twisted at the sight of his face, so drawn and so frightened. She held out her other hand, and he came running and buried his face in her lap.

—Where's Sister?

—We won't see Sister anymore.

She felt her mother's expectant glance but couldn't add any lies about heaven. Or say anything else but hold his shaggy head and feel his tears on her hands.

Lassiter leaned, and she tasted the hot bitterness of alcohol and opium. She almost spat it out, then gave in to her mother's urging. She lay back, exhausted, weak, feeling as if those hours of torment were about to begin again. Why could he not have given surcease from pain then? Oh, he had not been there. The midwife instead. The best in town, the ladies said. How hard she'd fought when they took the child away. Quite torn her nails.

—Her husband? the doctor was asking.

—In England, for the government.

—A pity. She lives here, then?

—In Norfolk. She came home for her confinement, of course.

The clink of payment exchanging hands. The bitterness on her tongue grew, and she realized suddenly she couldn't feel the pain. It was still there, but she couldn't feel it. The black hole grew and grew until it ate her and she was no more.

—It is so dreadful. And Ker will be so sad.

—Have you met him? The sea hero? He is taking such a toll on the enemy.

—So many of our men are away. The Judge says only iron resolution will bring us out safe from this war.

The words floated without meaning. She lay in a bathe of warmth, like honey all over her body. She drifted in this golden fluid for years. Then, very gradually, she felt it seep away and the cold creep back. She lay without opening her eyes, remembering.

Dr. Taylor, back in Norfolk, had warned her. She'd had a hard time with little Rob, and though she'd feared to think of its being so bad again, there was nothing to be done. A woman had certain duties, and chief of them was the bearing and rearing of the next generation.

A dark concerned face, hands bearing a platter. —I don't want anything, Aunt Lily, she muttered. Her lips were so dry. She licked clotted blood inside her mouth. She must have bitten them through. As if from centuries back she remembered the grave. Screaming at the priest. She had ought to feel ashamed. A lady did not lose control of herself. But something else in her breast, deeper, did not care. It told her she had as much right to scream as any animal being crushed in a trap has a right to shriek out its despair and its protest.

Another black face, this time her Betsey. The girl shoved the plate at her. —Miz Catherine. You got to eat this here soup your mamma made for you.

She turned her face from the girl.

The next day Reverend Minnigerode came from Saint Paul's, but Catherine would not receive him. Her mother apologized and said she was unwell. After he left she lay by the window and watched rain drip from the eaves.

Later that morning the voices of ladies drifted through the house. Her mother's circle. They swept in carrying cakes and pies in gloved hands, and offloaded them to a clumsily curtseying Betsey as they told Catherine she must pull herself together for the sake of her young one.

—You mustn't give up, Mrs. Harrison told her. A short, acerbic woman who was always there when work needed to be done. —God gives us these trials to test us.

—Then I've failed His test.

—Others have endured as much. And so must you.

—It's true. We all suffer, Catherine said. Betsey looked at her strangely, setting the tea tray down. —But must we therefore bow, and scrape, and magnify Him who torments us? It seems to me quite wrong. I do not wish to offend.

The ladies shifted on their chairs. —What was her name, honey? old Mrs. Crenshaw creaked. —Tell me her name.

—Elfair.

—I'm going to bring you a little chair.

—A what?

—A little chair. You put it by your hearthstone. That'll be Elfair's when she comes to visit. It's what I did when I lost my little Todie. And it did ease my heart.

When they left, she lay without speaking for hours. Looking up at the gray sky and thinking of nothing at all.

All over the world He tore children from mothers, parents from children, husbands from wives. For such a King did a subject owe obedience, respect, and praise? For such a Kingdom did one pray?

Her mother sat down beside her. —I made you tea and toast. The way you like it, almost burnt so it's crunchy. And Aunt Polly's plum jam sent all the way from Vicksburg.

She didn't answer. And after a time her mother added, —You have to write to your husband. He'll be worried, not hearing from you. Ker knows the date of your confinement.

She didn't answer, and after a time her mother said briskly, —It doesn't need to be long. Just a note. But you must write it. It is your duty, Cathery. You've always done what you had to do. Ever since you were little. I know this is not easy. I miss the little girl too.

—Is it my duty, Mamma?

—It is, darling.

She felt her mother's fingers twining with hers. After a moment Mrs. Wythe went on. —I'll tell you what I've learned, Cathery girl. Life is a train of sacrifices and trials and disappointments. Only so very rarely do we get what we desire. There is no changing it. All we can do is endure. Can you do that?

—I don't know.

—There must be no more outbursts. Do you understand? Whatever we may think in the privacy of our hearts, people of our class do not voice such sentiments.

So many words came to her tongue she could select none to say. At last she only whispered, —No, Mamma.

—There, you are being sensible. Her mother patted her wrist as if she were six again. —All you need do is scratch out a little note. Then I'll give you some more medicine, and you can sleep. You must stay here with us, at home, for as long as you can. You can get well here.

She didn't answer, and after a time she heard the click of knitting needles. She blinked, the world dissolving into tears; then resolving again into a cutting blade that seemed to section her heart.

—Bring me the paper and the inkwell, Betsey, she said at last. —Then help me sit up.

3

◆

Discipline Aboard U.S.S. *Cumberland* ◆ Advice on the Development of
Character, with Reference to the Shortcomings of the Negro Race ◆ History
of an Escapee ◆ Man-o'-War's Day ◆ A Venture Ashore ◆ Observations by
a Volunteer Officer ◆ The Grand Contraband Camp ◆ Ten Dollars, Free
Whiskey, and Great Personal Gain ◆ Speaking His Mind and
the Consequences Thereof

M INDLESS rage is not the answer, my dear fellow. The reflecting
mind alone can deal with the world as it is. The officer, a
delicate-wristed young fellow from up north, paced back and
forth before the tableau at his feet.

A dozen strong hands held the one he addressed facedown on holy-
stoned pine. He lay gambreled; wrists lashed together, arms made to embrace the legs, a gun-swab thrust through between the bent knees. He
wore bell-bottomed trousers, woolen blouse, and heavy square-toed brogans. His flat cap lay on the deck. A scrap of paper peeked out of it, fluttering in the wind. He did not speak, only blinked. His breath came in
spasms around a rag bound so tight he was close to losing consciousness.
His dragged-up sleeves revealed massive forearms, white-scarred knuckles,
pads of palm flesh like leather padding.

The lieutenant prodded him with a toe. —He is of a size, is he not?
But as Emerson says, no virtue goes with size. He has given trouble before, has he not?

—Yes sor. Contrary 's Dick's hatband he be. 'Spect that's why 'is old ship got rid of him.

The officer tilted his head at the boatswain. —I beg your pardon?

—Like twelve dead men, but he don't seem to get n'any good of her.

—I have not observed one of his race as gun-captain before.

The boatswain slapped his colt into his palm. —I don't like her neither, sor. But he seem to know the gun business.

—I see. And where is he from?

—Cullie don't niver tell, sor. Some says as he's an escaped slave.

—You don't say? Very well then. Let that count in his favor. This time. The officer gestured dramatically. Declaimed to the winter sky, —Today, unbind the captive; So only are ye unbound. Lift up a people from the dust. Trump of their rescue, sound!

The sailors stared ovalmouthed. Finally the boatswain ventured, —Ye say to unbind 'im, sor?

—Yes, Boats. He prodded the prisoner again with the boot-toe. —But I warn you, Quarter Gunner. Restrain your passions, or you will find yourself on the hog chain. My sympathies are with your people. Striving upward against the foul Southrons' tyranny. Yet Quashee has much to learn of self-control before he may count himself equal to the more advanced race.

Stripped so roughly of harsh manila his wrists flamed with rope burn, Calpurnius Hanks, steerage officer, United States Navy, stood rubbing them as the grouping dispersed, dissolved back into the routine of a cold fall day aboard the sloop of war U.S.S. *Cumberland*, anchored off the low coast of Virginia. When he was sure they were gone, he lifted his eyes. Touched the worn deerhide pouch that hung at his neck. Gazed after the insolently sauntering officer, the boatswain trotting at his heels. But his face betrayed nothing. Slack jawed, still suffused with blood, it might have been that of a creature that neither thought nor felt anything at all.

Calpurnius Hanks was not his real name. He'd gone through so many in his journey from frightened child to grown man. He didn't know his age, nor his birthday, nor how to read, nor write, nor cipher. But that did not mean he dwelt in ignorance. For he also knew things those around him did not.

What it felt like to punch a knife into another's flesh.

The meaning of iron and the speech of powder.

What it was like to *be chosen*.

Chosen, dreading it . . . yet not knowing what he had been marked out *for*. That was the shit of it. The twisted root-crone telling him enough to dread but not enough to understand.

You is the split twig.

From starboard came a shout and rumble as a nine-inch Dahlgren rolled into battery. He stared blankly, rubbing at a short beard so tightly curled it almost corkscrewed back into the skin.

Red clay country, where worn hills lay rounded like sleeping women. Mama leaving in the cold gray, but you got to stay snuggled close to Baba. Ash-pone and peas and the sizzle of fat meat. The littluns squatting naked, eating with their hands from the ground. At Christmas the Junkanoo men clattering their bones from door to door, the children laughing and shouting behind them.

Didn't know then you was owned. That you yourself and your mother and all those child faces belonged to the ghosts up in the dark house by the river.

He'd lived and labored there for twenty-three years, then one day set out to follow the drinking gourd through night and rain. Hiding during the day, creeping thicket and wood and stream in starlight and moon. Carrying a dream in his head of going back someday to buy them out: his mother, three sisters, two brothers. His father he'd never known, some nameless field hand called in to quicken a brood mare against the next crop.

But the North was no land of milk and honey. And the navy had always taken the colored man to hoist and mend and cook and serve. Before the rebellion he'd voyaged to Africa. Seen firsthand the land from which his grandparents had been sold. Smelled the nauseating reek of a captured slaver's 'tween-decks. And known then there was no going back. Words a preacher had shouted out one day said themselves in his inside ear. Stranger, in a strange land.

He'd thought once slavery was something you could run from. Freedom, something to run toward. But he'd never found it and didn't think now he ever would. As long as there was white and black, there'd be slaves. In one form or another.

One night he'd gone to the root woman, asking about his family back in Georgia, but instead found something else in the hut with them. A thing that looked out of the fire with eyes made of coals. Something that studied him now always from behind, that ducked out of sight no matter how fast he turned.

She'd said two paths lay ahead. On one lay all the sons and daughters of Africa in this land, dead and burning. And on the other fork, singing hosannas of Jubilee. Two times ahead, two roads to Time. He himself would see it cut the feather, burning stronger than red oak lye.

Rubbing his burning wrists, he looked with unmoving face on a flag that did not yet stand for freedom.

Up till dinner time the day had passed in the routine of a man of war. The night had been cold. With no heat on the berthing deck the men hugged every inch of their blankets. At the reveille bugle he'd risen quickly and dressed, rolling and stowing his hammock before a tin cup of government whiskey shot life into stiffened limbs.

Pans of warm coffee and hard bread. Before dawn grayed they were topside, swabbing and stoning barefooted in the cold. The men bitched and moaned of chilblains. Then rolled-down bell-bottoms and brogans without socks, tugging a comb through his hair. The executive officer, stitching through the ranks with cold efficiency, jerking his head at those he found too dirty for his liking. After that, gun drill. Each day Captain Radford had one gun fire three rounds as he stood by, watch in hand. Today was his crew's turn. When the commander nodded icily, pocketing his timepiece without a word, Hanks felt the rest of the day would go well. He set his boys to clean and reload with a fresh charge against need.

At eleven bells another half gill of whiskey. The hands standing patiently behind the rope, watching the holy ritual of grog, each stepping forward as his name was called. At twelve bells the ship knocked off work and divided into messes. Had he been white, he'd have eaten with his gun crew. He might have messed with the steerage officers—as a quarter-gunner he ranked with them—but had been advised this too would not be appropriate.

So he'd been on his way below to the makeshift mess of the blacks aboard. The officers' orderlies, the few other seaman of sable hue. When without warning the routine was interrupted. At the top of the compan-ionway Lieutenant Selfridge, the gunnery officer, told him he'd be going ashore with Mr. Randall. They'd shove off from the port-side boarding-ladder at one bell. He was to wash face and hands, put on Sunday jumper, neckerchief, and inspection cap. Draw a revolver and gear, though he'd need no powder or ball.

This left no time for dinner, but that wasn't why he felt apprehensive. Selfridge hadn't told him why he was wanted or why he had to look his best. He drew the revolver and belt, then went to change his blouse. Along with the embroidered cap he pulled from his seabag a varnished canvas jacket against spray and rain. Topside again, the cutter was waiting, and he stepped in ahead of Randall; the senior boarded last, and they shoved off and made for shore.

They sat in the stern-boards, facing the rowers. Strange, to watch other men bending and straightening to push him over the water. Was this how Marster Ingram had felt looking out over his fields under the Georgia sun? A grayhearted comber spattered him with salt cold. A sailor coughed into his sleeve, shielding his face from the bitter wind. A rope's end whistled, and he straightened with a jerk. The blue shore rose from the gray. To the east Cal made out the ramparts of Fort Monroe. Ahead, bare beach. As they made up on it the coxswain altered course. They ran along the shore toward the shipping anchored under the fort. Till then there were no more trees, just the stripped bristle of fields and a bereft-looking earthwork battery with a flag whipping in the breeze.

They made up at a wharf of green lumber already splitting and warp-ing. A party of workmen unloading a lighter gazed at him. Randall swung himself up and made his way shoreward. He glanced back. —Gunner?

—Yes sah.

He'd not touched mother earth for six months. The damp sandy wagon-road felt deeply wrong beneath his boots. Yielding. Untrustwor-thy. Randall too, ahead of him, rolled and swayed as if braced against a heavy sea. Cal snapped his fingers and spat. Luck placated, he hoped, he followed to where a mounted trooper in a smart kepi and bright leather gauntlets held the reins of two more restive-looking animals.

Randall, turning, noticed his hesitation. —What is it, Gunner?

He cleared his throat, knowing you couldn't explain to a white man how it felt to be back on slave territory. The dread, like lead cored along the marrows of your bones. That your face told nothing of your praying to whatever saint or loa was listening, to keep you from what waited in the shadows under the trees.

—Ain't never been on no horse before, sah. Thass all.

The acting master raised his eyebrows but made no remark. He returned the broad-sweeped salute of the horseman, who barked suddenly, —Off the *Cumberland,* sir? To the Grand Camp?

—Acting Master Augustus Randall, U.S. Navy, at your service.

—First Lieutenant Golusha Wethrell, U.S. Volunteers. Been waiting for you.

—I fear there was a misunderstanding about the time. My apologies to you and to your commanding officer.

Randall swung himself into the saddle, and both eyed Hanks. —Looks like ye brought the biggest dog in the boneyard, the army man observed.

Cal had watched Randall and now tried to imitate his fluid grace. Unfortunately he put the wrong foot into the stirrup, and halfway up faced the choice of either mounting backward or substituting one brogan for the other while his weight was still on it. The horse snorted and danced beneath him. The others laughed as Cal struggled. He seemed to be a great distance from the ground. But by leaning across the saddle and shaking his foot free he was able at last to swing his leg over the beast's rump and grope for the reins. He yanked savagely, and the horse whimpered as the bit sawed at its mouth. —Fuckin bitch, he muttered to it.

Meanwhile Wethrell had been speaking to Randall. —I confess uneasiness about the matter. We are neither Negro catchers nor Negro stealers. But they just keep coming, and we can't give 'em back to their owners—they'd just put them to digging on the rebel forts. So they squat, and steal, eat army rations, and make trouble.

—As my commander may have informed yours, we will be very short-handed when our current crew comes up for discharge. We have received a number from various vessels—the gunner here is one—but we would do well to fill out our complement.

—The more you take, the better, far as I'm concerned. Ought to ship 'em all to Hayti and have done with 'em.

They wheeled and were off, and Cal kicked the horse in the ribs and hung on.

He heard the camp before they reached it. Yelling, then groaning. A breathless silence, then a hollow noise as of someone striking a tree with a log, succeeded by even louder shouting from many voices, white and black alike.

—Welcome to Slabtown, said the Army officer in a dry tone. —Though some uses that to mean the part over against the fort. This here section used to be Hampton, before the fracas at Big Bethel, and Magruder burnin' them out. All the secesh skedaddled. Now look at it.

They rode down out of the tree line into the stink of smoke and shit, and Cal caught his breath.

A sizeable and prosperous village had stood here not long past. Tall chimneys over gaping basements and the charred remnants of fallen walls attested to that. But nearly all had been burned, smashed into drifts of scorched brick and charred beams. Gardens and lawns churned into mud and strewn with broken crockery and flindered furniture. He'd seen drear landscapes, but this was the most desolate, a wilderness of ruin pervaded by the seared scent of fire. As they rode on, between the still-intact brick street-pavings grew a hotchpotch of rail-and-brush lean-tos, discarded Sibley tents, and makeshift huts run up from Soponica boxes, driftwood, scavenged brick, burlap, and looted windows. Women in shapeless drabs and head rags called in high voices like the cawing of crows, and a gut-puckering miasma blew from the open trenches they squatted over.

Contrabands, the army called these people; short for contraband of war. Run off from the plantations, streaming toward Fort Monroe for protection. He'd never realized there were so many. Hundreds, perhaps thousands; more black faces than he'd ever seen at once. Women in muddy shirtwaists and skirts, balancing laundry on their skulls African fashion or bent grinding hominy on hand-stones. Children in jute sacks with ragged holes for arms and head. Cal's back prickled. He remembered how jute felt against bare skin. Snow-haired old men in ragged homespun, scraps of cast-off uniforms. One creature in utter tatters was writhing its way like a very dirty ball rolling through the mud. Almost everyone was smoking, clay pipes or corncobs or crude twists. This he understood. Smoking was a privilege denied slaves. Moving through them in no order, white soldiers toted muskets muzzle-first over their shoulders like shovels. They sauntered toward the meeting of the roads where a struggling ring shouted and thrust and shoved, waving handfuls of shinplasters aloft.

Facing each other, two men with bloody faces squared off. Cal stood awkwardly in the saddle to see. Their hands were tied behind them. They were wearing what looked like dark aprons.

The combatants, for such they seemed to be, lowered their faces, churned their legs, and charged. The hollow *clock* of wood striking wood came again. A moment later they staggered back.

Sickened, he realized the sound was heads colliding with all the strength of their respective owners. It must have been going on for some time now, for against their skin, as he rode closer, he saw gore running down their faces and chests. That was what he'd taken for aprons. Both were now pulled back into the crowd, into knots of their supporters. Whiskey flasks tilted over their mouths. They sucked hungrily. Then were shoved back into the ring.

Cheers and shouts crescendoed as they staggered to and fro, then launched themselves again. But this time instead of the sickening collision, they missed, stumbling to a halt paces past each other, peering about through blood and matted spongy hair like charging, blind bulls, mad with rage and befuddled with drink and addled wits.

A gray-mustached trooper ran up and popped to a rigid brace. —What is the meaning of this, Sergeant O'Leary? Wethrell sounded annoyed rather than angry.

—Sure, an' 'tis just a little head-buttin' contest, sor. Give 'em a dollar, fuckin niggers'll do anything.

—Clear them goddamn fools out of there. Prop that hogshead on end. Call the darkeys together. The bucks only, we just want the cocks.

Pushed roughly aside, the combatants reeled from the ring. Soldiers began drifting away, arguing about who owed what. Settling bets with blows and displays of bayonets. Many staggered, obviously drunk. Cal thought it slipshod, not good order. He half-dismounted, half-fell from the horse, which shied. A wide-eyed child whose pants were held up by one suspender pinned with a rusty nail stood frozen. Cal dropped the reins into his hand. —Hold this.

—Who hey is you, mister?

—A sailor. U.S. Navy.

—You is? And dey gives you a *gun*? His eyes fawned on the revolver butt, and he reached a hand.

—Don't touch that, boy.

—Puncie my name. Not *boy*.

—Don't touch that, Puncie.

—Hey, Ro! Dis heah darkey say he be in de nayby! Think dey lets us go?

The boys dissolved in helpless laughter, but he caught the admiration in their eyes. It straightened him as he followed Randall pushing through the crowd, as if through some thick fluid that only gradually parted before their forward motion. The Army officer lifted his arms for silence, for attention.

—Men of the Grand Contraband Camp, hello. The colonel has asked me to announce rations will be delayed until tomorrow. Also, we have a guest who wishes to address you, Acting Master Randall of the United States Navy. Master Randall.

Randall, arms behind the tail of his coat, launched into praise of the robust physiques and evident intelligence of those gathered round, and their courage in leaving their treasonous masters to strike out on their own destinies. He went on to how much they owed the Union, which was feeding their wives and children, mothers and aged fathers. He moved to the advantages to be gained should they volunteer for service aboard the vessels whose topmasts they saw standing out beyond their camp. Guarding those now in their shelter, and standing ready to intercept any privateers attempting to come down from Richmond.

Randall pointed out that if they wished to advance themselves and serve the flag, they could not do so in the Army. But the Navy had never barred men of color. They had served heroically in the War of Independence, the War of 1812, and their sacrifices and competence had won a good name among their seagoing brethren. He had been commissioned by Flag Officer Goldsborough, commander of the fleet anchored in Hampton Roads, to enlist the most quick-witted and fit among the contrabands.

—Many freemen already serve with us, Randall declaimed. —Landsmen are paid twelve dollars a month, ordinary seamen fourteen, seamen eighteen dollars per month. They receive three free meals a day, living accommodations, and immediate medical attention should they fall ill. Also to be mentioned is prize money, paid share and share alike; in many cases sailors have earned hundreds of dollars for their participation in capturing enemy ships.

—Nowhere else will your race find such ample rewards for hard work and good conduct. You will be rated either as boys or as landsmen according to age and capabilities. If there are skilled sailors or watermen among you, we may be able to do better. It is true those currently in the condition of fugitive slave cannot receive full wages. Their payment is limited to ten dollars per month. Nonetheless all the other benefits apply to those who step forward now for this glorious opportunity.

Black faces listened in silence. Even Cal couldn't tell what they were thinking. These were ex-slaves. No, by the law they were still slaves, though their masters had temporarily lost use of their labor due to their adherence to the rebel cause.

Randall went on, seeing they were not yet swayed. —Promotions are possible to the brave and efficient, and those who display conspicuous valor. Here with us—he pointed to Hanks, who started—is one of my best men, rated as a petty officer; that is what the eagle means upon his sleeve. Step up, Gunner. Look at this frame, boys. When he joined us, he was near dead from ague and fever. Hardtack and navy beans, healthy sea air and manly effort made him what you see today. Quarter-Gunner, step up here. Let them hear from you what it is like with other stout hearts aboard our bulwark of oak.

Randall dropped to the ground and jerked his chin at the hogshead. —Get on up there, he snapped.

Hanks ascended with a hitch and jump. Men slapped their thighs, exclaiming with astonishment at his leap. He looked down on circling faces. At Wethrell's, at Randall's, at Sergeant O'Leary's, contemptuous and closed. Among the coloreds they looked pasty, unwholesome, as if some vital element had been bleached out.

—Go ahead, lad, Randall said. —Tell 'em the good news.

He pitched his voice and hollered, —It's true, you can enlist.

Someone called, —Will they sure enough give us a mess o' vittles?

—Rations is white biscuit and salt pork. Beans and duff on Sundays. It ain't over plentiful, but it's better'n pone and fatback.

—Don't forget the grog, Randall said. —That will appeal.

—And grog, Cal told them. They looked confused. —Half a gill of whiskey twice a day. Not good as what Marster drinks up at the Great House, but better than the squeezings you makes in the corner.

—What they pay you there, nigger?

—I gets eighteen dollar a month.

—Say you "gets" it. Does you *see* it?

He glanced at Randall. —I draws what the paymaster lets me. Some every payday, but you don't gets all your pay till your enlistment's up. Got you a woman you stepped over de broom with, you can make her out 'n allotment. So she gets somethin' every month whether you thinks to send it or not.

—How is de navy? Good work? Easy?

For answer he held up his hands. The broken, missing nails. The heavy callus. —Sailor work ain't for no house niggers. Not for no eye servants, neither.

They murmured, understanding this.

He went on, gathering volume. —You gone work from crack o' day to when de fust star shine. Some of you gone break your ribs when the bars comes outen the drumhead. Or drown fallin off the cutter. Mist' Randall here says, promote you for valor in action. Not saying it won't never happen, but that ain't much of what you be seeing. Most of it just plain old work. Some of it busy work too.

—Hanks.

He didn't look down, kept his face to the sea of listening faces. —Takes a lot to keep a ship running. Painting. Polishing. Cooking. I serves on the guns, but y'all probly be serving on the small-arms crew.

Means you fight with swords and pistols. Boarding the other fellow. Fighting him off when he tries to board you. You more likely get shot an' your collardbones busted than to get rich. Or you fights fires and cut away your fallen spars. No, it ain't easy, and the white sailors they been known to throw gun chocks at you.

—Hanks!

—Just tellin how it is, sah. They men, not chilluns.

Randall looked apoplectic, but a stir had started. Men were pushing forward. —I done sailt oyster-pungies on the Bay fifteen year, one called up. —That get me a seaman's rating?

—Maybe a landsman, brother, but don't count on it. Likely start you as a boy, third class. And another thing. He raised his voice again. —Lissen good! If you signs up, ain't no way they going to know your real name or whether you run off or freeman. Say you is a freeman, you makes four dollars more a month.

—What you say, brother? Tell us straight. We ought to join up or not?

—I can't tell you dat. You wants to be free, you runned away from Marster. Now you gots to make up your own minds.

—No one said anything about freedom here, the Army officer said uneasily.

—Freedom, slavery, be like two snakes in the road, Cal told them. —One layin' with his head pointing north, the other snake lookin' south. But they both full of poison, and they both bite dumb-ass niggers don't keep they heads about them and study on what they is doing.

Now O'Leary was dragging at his arm, and Cal finally jumped off the cask and Randall was shouting, —So there you have it, from the horse's mouth. Any stout young fellow interested in United States service, now's your chance. First month in advance, ten dollars on the barrel head here and now when you sign! Free whiskey twice a day, and get rich capturing Southern ships! You'll have an hour to gather your things and say your farewells, then we'll head out to your new home on the briny deep. To Cal he muttered, —You will pay for this insolence.

He thought of protesting they'd never believe promises without the salt of witness, but slave habit won and he looked at the ground. Randall took out a piece of paper and began putting down names and taking X's as several men crowded close. Others stood a few paces off, talking about it. The first volunteer was youthful, lanky, nearly as tall as Cal. Randall had him open his mouth, felt his biceps, smelled his breath, cupped his balls.

—Well, you seem sound. Name?

—Asberry Rollins.

—Age?

—Twenty-four.

—Residence?

—Up near Toano, in James City County.

—Owner?

—Marster's a captain in the rebel service. His name is Kendall, Marse John Kendall. No, wait a minute—I is a freedman—

He gave Cal a shamefaced look. Hanks turned away, disgusted. He'd told, and they still hadn't the sense to listen.

They got six. On the way back, the whites leading the little snaffle on their horses, the new men began to sing.

> *Wake up, snakes, pelicans, and secesh'ners!*
> *Don't yer hear us comin?*
> *Wake up, I tell yer! Git up, Jefferson!*
> *Bobolition's a comin-*
> *Bob-o-lish un!*

Randall touched his reins to move close to Cal, who was getting the hang of steering his mount and even starting to enjoy it. Even though it felt every moment he was going to fall off. —You won't keep that crow much longer if you go on as you are, Hanks.

—Sah. They done signed up, dint they?

—You know what I'm talking about. We'll discuss this when we get back.

The sloop lifted above the dunes, and the men behind them shouted admiringly. She did look lovely in the afternoon light, riding easily to her anchors, flag streaming in the wind. But on the row out, the new recruits stopped singing. Every man jack was too busy retching violently over the side.

4

---◆---

Richmond in Gray ◆ Presentation of a Less than Commendatory Letter
to Captain Franklin Buchanan, C.S.N. ◆ Revenge Against the Yankee ◆
Captain William H. Norris, Signal Corps, CSA ◆ Richmond by Night ◆
The First Necessity ◆ On Special Service ◆
Such an Obstacle Must Be Removed

L IEUTENANT H. Lomax Minter, the clerk read from the card
tossed on his desk. Sniffled, and blotted his nose with a none too
clean handkerchief. —Oh, yes. The gentleman we sent to England
at the outset of the year. Some time since we met. But always a delight.

Minter lifted his chin. He had long red-blond hair and bright green eyes.
His cheeks were cleanly shaven, unusual in an epoch of beards. —Will you
send my card in to the Commodore?

—I will permit myself that pleasure, sir. And may I say that is the most
finely tailored set of full dress ever seen in this office? Truly "the glass of
fashion and the mould of form." Will you have a seat, sir?

Minter did not take a chair. His sword jingled as he paced the office,
wheeling impatiently, cocked hat tucked under one arm. He looked into
the hallway. A young woman in shirtwaist—apparently they were employing them for file clerks—nearly collided with him, carrying an arm-
load of papers bound in red ribbon. He caught a flash of dark, slightly
protruding eyes, quickly dropped. He turned away to the window, looking over the low skyline. Back straight, hands locked behind him.

To one used to London brick and stone the Queen City of the James's wooden houses, its hilly, lurching, unpaved streets, looked makeshift and dingy. But tremendously overcrowded and tremendously active, the focus of the war effort of a virile and determined new nation. The sky was palled with coal smoke. The lanes and alleys below this upper window thronged with limping wounded, strutting officeholders, chinquapin women, colored draymen, and Union parolees awaiting exchange. Minter sucked deeply of its raw air, chafing at the wait. He wanted battle. To strike down the mudsills and traitors hammering at the gates of the Southland. This war could not last long. Those who hungered to win glory would have to do so soon.

Unfortunately his efforts in that direction had not gone well thus far. Due to no failure of his own but to the interference of those less deserving. Opportunists and half-traitors who had set themselves between him and the enemy. He'd nearly succeeded in England. But his command had been snatched from him by a cunning schemer who'd frittered away every opportunity to actually damage the Union. This time he must succeed.

And, one day soon, requite the coward who'd insulted him.

Quoddy put his head back into the room. —Lieutenant Minter?

He cleared his throat. Glimpsed himself for a moment as the girl in the corridor might have seen him. *Implacable as grim Mars himself, Lomax Minter brushed flaming hair back from a fair and spotless young brow.*

He turned from the window to confront his fate.

Commodore Franklin Buchanan did not glance up when he announced himself, nor rise from behind the oaken desk. The old man's beaky nose was red and chafed-looking, but there was no note of spirits in the air. His voice came hoarse. —Quoddy, ask Mr. Tidball to step in for this interview. Lieutenant Minter. You have a communication for me.

Face heating, Lomax slid the sealed envelope from his blouse. He stood as the old man scanned it, then handed it to the slight, fastidious chief clerk of the Department. It surprised him to find Franklin Buchanan chief of the Bureau of Orders and Detail. When he'd left the country, Buchanan had been trying to regain the commission in the federal navy he'd resigned after Sumter. Who would appoint a waverer, a trimmer, to such a responsible position?

Tidball returned the letter without comment. Buchanan laid it aside, flattening it so that he could still read it. Leaned back. Pursed his lips. Then sneezed so vehemently that the bushy white hair at his temples flew out.

—Sir, may I speak? Lomax asked.

Buchanan burst out, beak buried in an embroidered handkerchief, —You may, sir. I should like much to hear your explanation of these matters.

—Claiborne is no Confederate.

—He is not?

Just in time, Lomax bit back what he'd always considered proof of his enemy's cowardice, that it had taken him months to make up his mind to join the new government. Not the tack to take with Buchanan, who'd hung in irons even longer. —No, sir. Merely an opportunist who hopes for rapid advancement in a new service. The right offer and he would follow renegades like Farragut over to the enemy.

—Quoddy tells me there have been words between you and Claiborne. Even, I understand, a challenge.

Minter said hotly, —The duel was interrupted, sir. But if I may be permitted? It would have been better for our revolution had I been let to blow a ball through him.

Buchanan looked interested, or perhaps only entertained. He flicked the letter. —Yet he was your official superior aboard a man-o'-war. He states here that as such he could not overlook disobedience and disrespect, much less an inclination to precipitate action in delicate situations. To what is he referring?

—To my urging the crew to open fire on Boston during the raid on the navy yard.

—You urged him to fire on the city itself?

—I did, sir.

Buchanan frowned past him at the chief clerk. —Well, young sir. I confess I am rather taken aback. Would that not have been a gross violation of the usages of war?

—Sir, it is not without precedent. I need only mention Carthage.

—Carthage, yes; I take your point. But this is after all the nineteenth century—

—That cradle of abolitionism brought us this war. Its pious apostles are determined to bring us free love, women in trowsers, and Negro equality at the business end of a Sharps. The usages of war can obtain only when both parties respect them. Only when we bring home to the Yankees that war means invasion and destruction of their own territory, and not ours alone, will their cowardly hearts turn from their loathsome and inhuman aims.

Buchanan glanced at Tidball again, but his expression did not seem that of one who disapproves of what he hears. The old commodore had a reputation for being something of a fire-eater himself. —And his response?

—To threaten me with a pistol; to confine me below; and to put me ashore in Bermuda. No gentleman will speak ill of those not present, yet I have already said all to his face. I doubt his loyalty, his courage, and . . . I shall not speak of his relations with his monkey.

—You believe such to be . . . unnatural? Tidball murmured. Lomax neither answered nor acknowledged him; he was speaking to the commodore and did not intend to be drawn off.

Buchanan blew his nose again, cleared his throat loudly, and leaned to spit into a vessel by his desk. When all passages were clear, he said less hoarsely but with a dismissive gesture, —We will not discuss your captain's moral character. So far as I am concerned, men are too prone to make their own depraved natures the test of the rectitude of others.

Lomax could not believe what he was hearing. —Are you speaking of *me*, sir?

Buchanan said with perfect coolness, —Far from it, sir. If you will construe my words, you will see they redound to your credit rather than in any other direction. He flicked the foolscap again. —You say Claiborne cherishes a personal animosity. Yet he states here you are a capable sea officer and recommends your continued employment in the Service. Only advising that, for the sake of prudence, you be placed under the supervision of cooler heads.

Lomax seized the pommel of his weapon. —Sir, the decision is yours. Does our country, at the present juncture of our glorious struggle, need cool heads and lukewarm prudence? Or does it cry out for bold, true, loyal knights determined to conquer or die? Give me a vessel of war in a theatre where the enemy is present in force. When you do so, you will hear again the name of Lomax Minter.

The old man nodded. —Your sentiments do you credit, sir. I for one have never considered audacity a shortcoming in a young officer. And in fact I have considered closely where you might best be employed. I regret I am not presently in a position to gazette you for command. We have too few ships, as you well know. But are you prepared for dangerous service?

—I am *eager* for such, sir.

—We shall see. Mr. Tidball, if you please.

—What is this? Minter fingered the card the clerk had handed over.

—I desire you to report to Captain William Norris, a staff officer with General Magruder, presently in town at the address given.

—An army man?

—Just so.

—May I ask what sort of assignment you have in mind, sir?

—That is for Norris to tell you, sir. I will say that an order from him should be regarded in the same light as one from me or, for that matter, as from the secretary himself.

Lomax thought of asking what sort of naval service required the intermediary of a land officer; but looking at Tidball's departing back, the smooth pink of Buchanan's lowered bald spot, and the snapped fingers to which Quoddy immediately opened the door, he knew he'd been dismissed. Dangerous service. Not a command, but a chance to strike the enemy. One, perhaps, that he could make into what he desired above all.

He bowed and withdrew.

Captain William H. Norris, of the Confederate signal corps, was soft-spoken, well dressed, and strongly framed. His face was square, his nose straight, and his jaw solid under a close-trimmed brown beard. His piercing blue eyes uttered absolute determination. Minter had found him in at the Exchange Hotel. They met in the bar, as Norris put it, to "draw the wine of life." Before they had sat thirty minutes—he in uniform, Norris in a well-cut sack coat, vest, and bowler—Lomax learned his new acquaintance had been brought up in Baltimore, had family ties in Virginia, and had read law at Yale. He'd gone to San Francisco during the Gold Rush, then acted as judge advocate with the Pacific Squadron until he married the daughter of the U.S. consul to Chile and came back east. Like so many other Marylanders he had rallied to the South even though the bayonets of Ben Butler's occupation troops kept his home state pinned to the Union.

—And you, Minter, Norris said courteously over a fine cognac, —Are a Mississippian, I am given to understand.

—Like you, sir, my family was originally from Virginia. Fauquier County. But we've been out there since the thirties.

—Indeed? Then you may know the Hackleys. Old Joe Hackley? Brandon Hackley? Norris coughed, dabbed at his eyes. —Damn it, everyone in these diggings has got such bad colds this winter. It's only peach brandy and honey gets me through some days.

They discussed the Hackleys, then the Embrys, and the Clatterbucks, and eventually traced out a cousin of Minter's and friend of Norris's who was now in the Eleventh Virginia Infantry. —And your father? Norris asked. —A naval man like yourself?

—No, sir. He was a well-respected broker in the Delta.

—Slaves?

He bit back a hot reply. —No, sir. Cotton.

—You said he *was* a broker. His present occupation? If I may ask without offense, which I do not intend to give.

—None taken, sir. Unfortunately, my father trusted a Yankee. Extended credit during the Panic to one he considered a friend. But Mister Eaton suddenly declared bankruptcy.

—Eaton being the one he trusted?

Minter went on bitterly, —*He* is still in business and doing very well, I hear, once he unsaddled those inconvenient debts. My father lost everything—business, servants, our land, our home. I was at sea when he turned a pistol on himself.

—He left you with nothing?

—Save honor, sir. Which I regard as the highest patrimony he could have given me.

—*Et haec olim meminisse juvabit.*

Lomax lifted his glass, assuming this to mean something like rest in peace. Norris went on, shaking his head, —You have the reputation of a firebrand. I see now why the commodore admires your dash. Which is saying something. He is the true cavalier, *sans peur et sans reproche.*

Lomax considered what he was about to say. It might not reflect well on Buchanan, but the more he thought about it, the more he suspected the old man had in fact offered a veiled affront in his remark about moral rectitude. —Yet—and I do not mean this in any way other than as an observation of fact—it remains that he *did* not come over directly upon the news of Sumter or Lincoln's call for militia to crush us.

For just a moment, from under the urbane bonhomie, he caught a flickered glance, a glimpse of what might be a very different and much less affable man. The next moment it was gone, so completely he was no longer sure he'd seen it. Norris lifted his glass imperturbably. —I will take the liberty to remind you, in kindly tones, that his situation and yours differ.

—How so?

—It is a *peculiar* relation we Marylanders hold to our brothers. Being forced to struggle through enemy lines to reach the colors, we are in a distinctive degree isolated from firesides and friends. Loving them deeply as does any true Southron, we must yet part from them to defend the higher right. Perhaps that may be offered in expiation of a certain hesitancy at the brink? *A tout hasard,* he has the confidence of your navy secretary and of our president—that "very noblest Roman of them all." And such a record in Mexico, and China! No, I regard Franklin Buchanan as one of our most splendid acquisitions. You may be proud he thinks of you as one of our young Nelsons.

For the first time the conversation had neared the compass of his assignment, and the needle of his attention swung immediately. —He said that to you?

—A note, received just before you were sent to me. A recommendation not easily come by.

Norris tapped his breast pocket and then with the same motion plucked a silver-chased half-hunter from his vest. The twitched-back coat also revealed, Lomax noted, the curving walnut handle of a Colt's pattern revolver. —Well, sir, eight bells, as you naval gentlemen would say. Have you another engagement this evening?

—I have not.

—Perhaps you would do me the honor of sharing an early supper and then going downtown. It may be we shall meet some friends there. Who knows?

They had a fairly good chop there at the hotel, with a decent port and a segar apiece. Once downtown they stopped at the New York Saloon for a little something. The saloon was packed, but Norris did not see anyone he knew, and after two or three whiskies they continued on.

Lomax was impressed by the change in the city. Before the war Richmond had been nothing more than an overgrown tobacco town. Now it was corner to corner with lager houses, billiard rooms, faro hells, oyster cellars, small hostelries, and dram shops ("inlets," Norris called them), every one of which was so busy that soldiers and civilian workers stood on line in the muddy roadway. Norris lifted his hat to lean gentlemen in frock coats and stovepipe hats. He introduced members of the provisional Congress and ironmakers, horse dealers, and even a general of artillery, though Minter didn't catch his name. Not one addressed Norris as anything but an equal. Lomax began to understand that the rather junior rank of army captain might not convey his acquaintance's gravity in the new state. They went to Sandy Craig's and had more drinks, then descended to an oyster cellar for succulent Lynnhavens dripping with their own liquor and schooners of foaming Dutch lager.

By now he was losing his bearings. He trailed the swaggering figure before him as the winter night darkened and silent Negroes went from post to post lighting gas lamps. But they only illuminated the main streets. From these rivers of light stretched pitch-dark tributaries from which flowed laughter and music and now and then the thumps and screams of someone being beaten. His breath danced white as steam before his lips.

Asked if he was an Odd Fellow, Lomax shook his head. Norris took him into the club anyway. There they had more whiskies. The captain was explaining the intricacies of a mechanical baking machine he had invented when a man coughed so near his glass that Minter had to strike him in the face. They were ejected more or less forcibly and staggered through dark and mud toward a place on Cary Street where Norris said they might see some women.

They did indeed, but they were all occupied. Neither officer wanted to wait in line with common soldiers, so they went to a dram shop to get warm instead. Several drinks later they staggered out on their way to Alice Hardgrove's on Fifteenth Street. Lomax had a memory later of reeling into an alley to relieve himself, then hearing after moments of blessed relief drunken protests from the dark. A form started up, beating at its clothes and cursing so menacingly he drew his sword. But the straps tangled in the skirts of his overcoat, and he would have tripped himself into the mire and piss if not for Norris's grip. Then an interminable march through freezing cold and another house, brightly lit as a church at midnight service. Only the women there were acolytes of a more ancient order. He was swiftly caressed, undressed, and mistressed violently as on a galloping horse until he sobbed out his spasm. Unceremoniously uncorked, reclothed, and reunited with a red-faced Norris, he was processed out the door again with the businesslike efficiency of a Lancashire woolen factory.

Now it was long after the curfew and they were reeling down another muddy street who knew where in the dark, maybe Butchertown, and the stars whirled above the house fronts and he slapped off a hand that groped for his purse and drew his sword and swept it round in a star-glittering circle. The shadows scattered and voices cried out, one of them Norris's, and he allowed himself to be taken in hand and led down steps into light again, and in the fire-warmth and sweat-warmth more whiskey burned down his gullet and voices shouted out a song he'd heard snatches of at the railroad station. This time he caught the words, and he roared it out with them, mugs hammering on the trestle tables, the flushed sweat-streaming faces of soldiers staring with lustrous fixed eyes.

> *Shoulder to shoulder, son and sire!*
> *All, call all! To the Feast of Fire!*
> *Mother and maiden, and child and slave,*
> *A common triumph or a single Grave!*

Norris leaned close, speaking through the din. —Are you all right, Henry?

—I prefer Lomax. Henry I do not care for. And I'm so drunk I can't tell my ass from a shotgun.

—I am most damnably sotted myself, I fear. But a draft of calomel and oil will soon set us straight.

The thought of such a dose clapped his stomach against his gullet, made him feel like disgorging as so many others obviously had on this dirt floor. He gagged as Norris clapped him on the back, taking it for a choking fit. Lomax threw the captain's arm off and lifted the mug high. —To the U—to the U—damn it, to the C.S. Navy. May all Yankee scum be nine miles into Hell before they know they're dead.

The soldiers roared back, cursing Lincoln and Stanton and McClellan. Lomax was filled with sudden hot pride. He clawed sentimental tears from his face. —These are the chaps to win a war with, he bawled toward his companion.

—Yet there are union sympathizers still among us.

—Do you think so? he said, reeling on the bench as a bearded oldster across from them sneezed wildly again and again, then leaned to blow his nose out on the dirt, first one nostril, then the other.

—I know it. I have seen their smearings on our walls, leaving their testimonials to be revealed with the light of day. "The scorpion of secession has stung itself." And worse. It is a problem of our character, I fear.

—Of *our* character?

Norris said, —We Southrons are fools. *C'est-à-dire*, such fools as believe everyone else to be as noble and sincere as ourselves. Admirable, you might say. Unfortunately it leaves us open to any liar who may scheme to outwit us, or lead some ingrate to betray our glorious cause.

—I can't think any of us would do that, he said, but then gripped his mug in sudden hatred, recalling one who already had. The fastest clipper on the seas, her captain too craven to turn his guns on the enemy. He'd have left Boston in flames and the dread of stern War in the heart of every greedy, sanctimonious, nose-talking New Englander.

Norris's lips brushed his ear. —Know what our first nesheshety is?

—Our what?

—Our first *ne-cess-i-ty*. According to your navy. Mister Secretary Mallory.

—Ships, I suppose. No, men. No, officers of honor and probity and aud—he hiccuped—*audacity*.

Buchanan had called him audacious. He smiled with pride and nearly fell off the bench.

His mouth against Lomax's ear, the captain murmured, —The *first ne-*

cessity is a weapon the Yankees cannot stand against. Invulnerable. Irresistible. So proof against anything they possess, they will be swept aside like chaff. So potent it will end this war.

Through numb lips Lomax murmured, —There is no such.

—There will be soon.

—What is it?

—An ironclad steamer.

He struggled to form words with a wooden tongue. —I have heard tell of it. Thought it was a rumor.

—She is a-building in Norfolk. And someone is telling the federals every clamp and screw that goes into her.

For a moment he sat still, not so fuddled he could mistake the man's meaning. —Should we discuss this here?

Norris glanced around the crowded basement, at the distorted candleshadows that leapt and danced on rough brick. —Nowhere better, my boy. There is a spy aboard her. A betrayer of his country who must suffer the penalty a Judas deserves.

—What are you asking?

—Join her company. But with open ears and an untrusting eye. Do your duty. But also: Observe. Deduce. Find our spy, our traitor. Force the truth from his bosom. Nail him to the counter. And when you are certain, kill him.

He stared openmouthed at blue eyes around which the room spun in great huge circles he was powerless to stop. —Who *are* you? he murmured.

—There is a special service. A small circle of great spirit and devotion, serving our country not only at the front, but in the shadows as well.

—A special service. He stared into the challenging eyes. No longer drunken but sharp with demanding intelligence.

—Up to the challenge, Minter? Will you join us in this business, to defend and secure forever the sacred soil of the South?

He didn't even need to answer. Just to join his hand with Norris's under the table's rough dripping planks.

5

A Snowy Day in Boston Harbor ♦ Welcome to Fort Warren ♦ The Brotherhood of Aesclepius ♦ An Accidental Wounding ♦ The Engine of One's Fate

O
UT of the boat, rebs. Form up, two lines. Put it in the bag, damn you! No talking!

The lowered bayonets of their guard underlined the order convincingly, Alphaeus Steele thought. Stamping his feet on the planks, he clutched his overcoat to his throat. Shoulders hunched, shaking in the milling, windblown snow, he blinked up at the battlements of what might be home for a long time.

Or where he died, kicking at the end of a rope. If Secretary Seward made his threats good.

George's Island, Massachusetts, on a wintry January morn. The prisoners had been pulled from snug beds at the Oregon House long before dawn. Now they huddled on the fort's pier, shuddering in the crackling cold and watching full day light the wintry sea. The mile-long pull through the choppy waters of Hull Gut in an open boat had been sheer freezing misery.

Fortunately, he'd managed to organize a dram of apple sass as they'd mustered in the lobby. The desk clerk had been an older fellow, one who understood what a stimulant could mean to one of their years.

For Alphaeus Foster Steele, M.D., late of the United States Navy and for the last eight months of the Confederate Navy Medical Corps, was no longer young. And he feared he was growing rather stout. He needed glasses to read or even, of late, to conjure the time from his watch. A beautiful four-ounce Howard his mother had given him before she died. Which a Yankee had "confiscated," along with his wallet and his surgeon's pocket case, when they'd landed in Maine after their raider had gone down. His boots were still damp from days in the cutter, his hat was missing, and he had not a thread of clothes other than what he stood in. He also had a bandage round his head; a splinter from one of U.S.S. *Potomac's* shells had aerated his scalp as he operated during the engagement.

But at least they were alive.

Alive but dangling in the hands of a federal government bitterly vengeful over the millions of dollars of damage C.S.S. *Maryland* had cost New England shipowners. The Boston papers said Seward intended to try every officer and man of the most dreaded raider ever to put to sea. He was convening a military tribunal and would charge them all as pirates.

Shaking his mind off that unpleasant subject, he peered up through the snow at a frowning granite battlement, dark embrasures scattered across its face. The mournful moaning was the sea-wind whistling in those apertures. More guns were visible above a high parapet. Smoke poured from tall brick chimneys, and a huge Stars and Stripes rippled endlessly in the icy wind. A slush-and-gravel road led upward from the pier. It passed between a massive granite guardhouse and a toy-soldier sentry box. Then, still rising, crossed a drawbridge before reaching a sally port. Within was what looked to be a deserted parade ground. Around stretched a gray waste of winter sea, and far to the eastward the cream glimmer of rocky islets. And over all, the descending pall of a New England winter.

—All right, get moving, the guard bawled. Slowly, unwillingly, the bowed, coughing men began trudging toward their prison.

Some hours later he and Mr. Dulcett, Count Osowinski, Mr. Shepherd, Mr. Bertram, and Mr. Kinkaid gathered in a spacious but icy casemate they were given to understand would be their berthing area, mess room, and gathering place all in one. The wind whistled through open loopholes. A flickering coal-fire barely cut the stony chilliness of the granite walls. Their captain they had not seen for some days. Ironed, as they had not been, he'd been transported separately, with his own guard, and was now in solitary confinement. The exec, of course, was dead, killed in their last savage engagement with the sloop of war that had pursued them for so long. The next senior, Osowinski, was feverish and unwell. Steele had prescribed strict dieting and purges; he had considered operating but had decided to let nature abide her time. Very few penetrations of the skull, in his experience, resulted in the recovery of the patient over the long term.

They were sitting on the narrow iron bedsteads—hospital beds, Steele judged, or the garrison's bunk beds—set directly on the stone-cold blocks of the floor when the sentry shouted through the grate. A lock rattled. They rose as a sergeant entered.

—In line, in line. At attention. Can that one not rise?

Steele said placatingly, —Count Osowinski is suffering from wound fever.

—If he's alive, I want him on his feet, said the sergeant. Kinkaid and Bertram helped him up, and he stood shakily, pale, knees buckling.

—Colonel Justin Dimick, United States Army.

A white-bearded, elderly officer, trailed by another whose shoulder straps, Steele noted, bore the green backing of medical staff. The colonel locked his hands behind him and looked around sternly. —Gentlemen. I am commander of Fort Warren. This is Doctor Frothingham. Are these all the officers from your craft?

He was looking at Steele. As the eldest present, he cleared his throat. —Those remaining, yes sir. The rest were killed in the battle or in the subsequent days adrift. However, our captain has been separated from us. May we ask where he is? And the rest of our men?

—Your crew is being confined separately in the North Bastion. Young Master Prioleau is being sent back to England due to his tender years. The pirate captain Claiborne is being held in close confinement. His servant is with him.

Dimick went on to outline in spare sentences the circumstances of their imprisonment. Valuables, money, liquor, pocketknives, and writing implements must be deposited with an officer of the fort. There would be no visitors, no mail, and no parole ashore. All prisoners would be locked in between sunset and sunrise. They would be marched to the cookhouse at eight and again at noon to pick up their two meals. They would be allowed to walk out on the terreplein between two and two-thirty each day, weather permitting. Any departure from the southern bastion or attempt at escape would be met with deadly force. He could not advise them of their ultimate disposition; such was beyond his ken. He would execute his orders as they were received.

Dulcett cleared his throat. The youngest, his voice broke as he essayed, —If we may not receive mail, sir, may we beg the privilege of sending it? To relieve the apprehensions of our families. And to purchase additional rations?

—And stimulants, Steele added. —So necessary in inclement weather to continued health.

—There will be no mail in or out. As to rations, you will be limited to those provided.

Kinkaid said angrily, his Philadelphia accent marking him out among the Southerners, —I believe it is the custom, Colonel, to treat prisoners of war with rather more liberality.

Dimick cocked his full beard, like a vindictive Father Christmas. —But you are not prisoners of war. You are rebels and criminals, awaiting tribunals for treason, piracy, and murder. Accustom yourselves to that, and our relations will run smoothly. Test me, and you will regret lifting your hand against your country.

The commander ran his eye along them again, then nodded to the sergeant. Keys jingled, and the door clashed closed.

The officer in the green sash remained behind. He said to Steele, —Are you the medical man?

He bowed. —I have the honor to be a devotee of Aesclepius. Alphaeus Steele. Of Maryland, sir.

Frothingham put out his hand, and after a moment Steele grasped it. —Your wound, sir; I trust it is not serious?

—Merely a flap of scalp. I directed a fisherman to sew it and so far have no complaints to make of his skill.

—I am happy to hear it. A Marylander, eh? Do you know Mister Lawrence Sangston?

—I have not the pleasure, though I am acquainted with his family. Steele hesitated, not sure how questions about other prisoners might be taken. —I had heard you held Mister Mason and Mister Slidell here.

—Until their late release, yes; they and their secretaries were in Quarters Seven. I did not care much for Slidell. Frothingham shook his head. —But to the business at hand. First I suppose I should examine Mister Osowinski. A count, you say? How interesting.

After a close examination Frothingham ordered Osowinski taken to Bastion D. He asked Steele to come too. They followed the stretcher-bearers along shadowy corridors to a dank infirmary lit by candles and a single barred window high up in the stone. After seeing the Pole to a cot Frothingham took Steele along to the enlisted quarters where they held sick call for the raider's crew. Afterward the Union doctor led him on a short tour of the fort turned prison. Four companies of volunteers garrisoned it, drawn, he said, from the best families of the city.

The tour complete, Frothingham invited him into a physician's office next door to the infirmary. An orderly stoked a coal-fire as he gestured to an upholstered chair. —Will you light the calumet with me, Doctor?

Steele accepted a curiously made little segar and lit it at the wall lamp. His gaze lingered on a dark bottle. Taking the hint, Frothingham poured out a generous mug of what proved to be gin.

Not Steele's favored tipple, but this was not an occasion to be discriminating. —Thank you, sir, he said, raising it in salute. —I will tell you I have not felt so cold since once I took the twigging cure in a Swedish establishment. I fear indeed I have not yet recovered from four days on the open sea.

Frothingham urged from him the tale of their long pursuit by the Yankee man-o'-war and the final battle, which had ended with the sinking of the Confederate cruiser and the destruction by fire of her enemy. Following which, both crews had set out in company in the boats for the closest shore. Another mug coaxed a recap of their raiding career, beginning with their takeover of the former opium clipper off the coast of Madeira.

Frothingham chuckled over their assumption of ladies' dresses as a ruse de guerre, but the smile vanished as Steele's tale spun on. When it was done he said, —It is your attack on Boston, I fear, that has most incensed the authorities.

—I can understand that sentiment. However, the navy yard was a lawful target of war.

The army physician waggled his boots before the fire. Not looking at him, he said, —As a border stater, sir, has it perhaps crossed your mind that you have made the wrong choice in this unfortunate rebellion? Especially now that your home state has decided to remain loyal?

Steele cleared his throat, turning over how he should answer this. Amicable though he seemed, Frothingham might have been ordered to sound out his loyalty. —Perhaps it is my age speaking, but I will not pretend to be an ardent advocate of sanguinary war, even for the highest of goals—which do not seem, forgive me, to accurately describe the aims of either side in this conflict. With Tibullus: *Quis furor est atram bellis accersere Mortem.*

—Hear, hear. Frothingham raised his gin. —Then you would consider taking the oath of allegiance? Do that, and most likely you will be released at once.

Steele shook his head. —Unfortunately, sir, I am too old to change my colors again. I hope those who govern us will soon weary of this waste of blood and treasure. But having made my choice, I will remain with my compatriots.

—You speak as if both sides were equally at fault. Yet it was the South that wanted this war.

Steele said courteously but with emphasis, —No sir; never *wanted* it, sir. If we had desired it, we should have been better prepared at its outbreak.

—Then why did Beauregard trigger the first shot?

—There is an ancient principle, I am given to understand, that holds the aggressor is not he who strikes the first blow but he who makes the striking necessary. Sumter was only the recognition that hostilities had begun.

—Well, let us not argue, Frothingham said. —As you are technically a noncombatant, Doctor, and do not strike me as dangerous or untrustworthy— Steele bowed in his chair —I may be able to procure some amelioration of your personal conditions of incarceration. Especially if you are willing to assist in the care of your fellow prisoners.

—I am at your disposal, Doctor.

—You will allow me to refresh your embrocation?

—With all my heart, sir. A most serviceable gin. Though I confess I should find a brandy more warming, given the glacial conditions.

—Perhaps I can find some if that is what you prefer. There is also a decent whiskey I can order from the city at three dollars the gallon.

They were discussing changes in atmospheric conditions as the cause of lockjaw when a rapid knock interrupted them. Two soldiers bore a third between them, a youth whose lips bent anxiously, whose eyes searched here and there as if gazing on some ghastly scene invisible to those around him. The physicians stood, taking in the blood dripping on the flagstones. —How did it happen? Frothingham asked.

—Accidental discharge, sir. He was leaning on his musket, on sentry duty.

Alphaeus stood back courteously but then saw the other was hanging back too, looking embarrassed.

—Sir? You will examine?

—You are the surgeon, sir. I am not.

Ah, Alphaeus thought. So that is how it stands. —You do not have a surgeon at the fort?

—Unfortunately not.

—And to take him ashore in this weather . . .

—There's none in Hull either. Frothingham struggled with himself, then bowed. —I should be very glad if you would take charge of the case.

The orderly cleared the table. The soldiers helped their friend up on to it, then retreated to stand along the wall.

Bending over the wounded soldier, Alphaeus saw by the moist, pallid skin, the thready pulse, and the glossy fixity of his pupils that he was already in shock. He asked Frothingham to prepare a drink of whiskey, water, and morphine, and to find him an apron or smock. As the spoon clinked, stirring, he stroked the boy's cheek. —Can you hear me, my lad?

—I can, sir.

Steele noted the thick speech, the tardiness of his answer, the way he sighed and seemed to forget from time to time to breathe. —Can you tell me where the ball went in?

—Under my armpit. Jim was funnin with me. I'm sorry—

—Don't worry about that now. What weapon were you carrying? And the type of ball?

The lad whispered an old smoothbore; they hadn't got their Springfields yet. Steele held the glass to his lips and made sure he swallowed all the mixture. He refilled with neat whiskey and administered this dose to himself. Then he bent close again, noting the smooth curve of the youth's neck with compassion and tenderness. —Now listen to me. You are hurt, but we shall do our best to help. Doctor Frothingham and I will put you to sleep. Then we will see what we can do.

When he turned, the medical orderly was proffering a tray on which were a brown bottle, a linen napkin, and a sponge. Steele twisted the cloth into a cone, poured a teaspoonful of the evanescing fluid onto the sponge, and stuffed it up into the apex.

When it hovered over the boy's face, the frightened eyes sought his own. Steele smiled and winked. He brought the cone down. Only the faintest of struggles as the vapor took hold, quelled by the orderly's grip. When he saw the eyes sink closed, felt the jaw relax, and heard the breathing become noisy, he let the cone go.

The patient slept. Steele rested his hand for a moment on the uninjured shoulder, feeling the relaxed sinew and muscle. Amazed anew at the magic slumber, unknown at the beginning of his medical career. Another triumph of science. Yet with the wonder he felt anger. The smooth-faced lad was another victim, not even of battle but of sheer accident. How many more would this savage war claim?

He turned back to find Frothingham laying out instruments. Bullet forceps, bone file, scissors, saw, scalpels, probes, tenaculums, and a selection of needles. He took up a probe-pointed bistoury. Tested the edge on his thumb. Then quickly slit the boy's blouse, the blade whipping through the cloth with a sure speed that made the attendant flinch and mutter under his breath.

—Comment, Fanning? Frothingham said sharply to the orderly.

—Nothing, sir. Sorry, sir.

Alphaeus sliced off the boy's shirt next, and last his rather soiled flannels. The narrow-ribbed, freckled chest rose and fell. Boyish nipples peaked in the cold air. Steele examined each removed layer of clothing, then laid it aside for later reference. He placed his ear to the bare breast, listening closely. He ran the tips of his fingers over trunk and shoulder, the front of the chest, the left side, the neck, then down to the flat stomach whose light hairs glistened wetly in the lamplight. Then he retraced his course, pressing his fingers firmly here and there, working them into the masses of muscle.

—You are searching for the bullet, Frothingham said.

—I am, sir.

—After dealing with the antiphlogistic tendencies of the immediate effect of the wound.

—In the inferior animals the various portions of the body are not tied together by the cords of nervous sympathies, Steele explained. —In man, however, an exquisitely sensitive system is susceptible to both physiological and pathological impressions. I administered morphine to jugulate the tendency to congestion and, hence, inflammation. Its action is superior to opium and exhibits none of the latter's tendencies to habituation and vice. Raise his arm, if you please.

The boy's comrades had pressed rags into the wound. Steele tore them free, and a gush of blood spurted onto his apron.

—Roll him on his side, he told the attendant. —Bring that lantern closer.

With the patient's arm raised, the aperture where the ball had entered was clearly visible. The clothing had absorbed most of the powder-smut. The flesh was depressed and already purpling around the entry wound. Blood was pumping out steadily, bright red. Steele frowned as he noticed bubbles in it, a trace of froth.

Bending to look along the trunk, he visualized the course of the bullet. He didn't see an exit wound. Since all three layers of clothes showed the same penetration hole, the ball was probably still embedded.

—Hold him quite still, he told the two men. Then he inserted his index finger and began working it in. He felt the smooth channel the bullet had made, slick with blood.

Face distracted, he murmured, —This nervous shock is Nature's salutary response to wounding. The heart no longer distends the vessels with blood. Within minutes, in those of sound constitution, a fibrinious secretion forms. This natural hemostasis stops up the loss, avoiding the dangers of hemorrhage and the filling up of the tissues with extravasated blood. Unless, of course, a major artery is severed. But I see that seldom with round balls. They seem to slide around such vessels without damaging them.

—Interesting, Frothingham said. —Can you feel the projectile?

Alphaeus shook his head after a moment; his attention was on the sensations as his finger probed along. A surgeon's digit was the best diagnostic he owned. Searching deeper into the wound, he frowned. He felt spicules of bone. A rough surface that when forceped out proved to be the blackened, bloodied wad, driven in along with the ball.

But of that leaden messenger, not a sign.

He opened the wound further with a flick of the scalpel. Thrust his finger deeper, searching past the shattered edges of bone. Frothingham looked concerned. —We must not fear to patulate, Steele told him.

The boy's breathing was becoming labored. He concluded reluctantly that the ball was too deep to reach. It was either within the lung itself or had proceeded around it toward the opposite shoulder. It might even be lodged close to the heart, which would explain the rapidly fading pulse, the increasingly difficult respiration.

—Should you not ligate? Frothingham muttered.

—There's nothing yet to ligate, Doctor. This bleeding is mostly from inconsequential vessels close to the surface. I am concerned about what lies deeper.

Steele's arm was extended, his finger probing as deeply into the boy's rib cage as it was possible to reach. Past and through the muscle sheath of the *serratus anterior,* his middle joint was hooked over the ragged edges of the broken rib cage. His fingertips searched the emptiness of the pulmonary cavity; he could neither reach nor feel the slick surface of the pleura, of the lung itself.

The orderly murmured, —The bleeding is becoming profuse.

Indeed it was, spraying out with each of the boy's increasingly agonized exhalations, soaking Steele's apron, dripping onto the stone floor.

He said, breathing harder, —Do you have any iron styptic? Persulphate of iron or perchlorate?

Frothingham didn't, so Steele sent the orderly out for snow. He now had his entire hand within the chest cavity. He could feel air whistling past it. —I very much fear the lungs are injured. That would explain the dyspnoea.

—I saw no haemoptysis.

—The military surgeon learns not to expect it with all lung injuries; nor to assume the lung is injured when blood is extravasated orally. There really is no one pathognomonic sign. It is evident, however, that our patient is sinking.

Indeed they all could hear the whoop of intake, the hiss and suck of exhalation. The case was turning difficult. He'd hoped the projectile might have missed the vital organs. For some reason round balls often did, skating around the rib cage and even the soft parts of the lung to come to rest on the far side from the entry. While miniés, entering at a higher velocity, smashed through muscle and bone and soft tissue in a more direct course. He was considering now that it might be best simply to close the wound, turn the boy on the wounded side, and leave the case to the *vis medicatrix naturae*. He did not like to leave projectiles unlocated, but further exploration would result only in more damage. Once certain areas were penetrated, the issue was out of the surgeon's hands. The lungs, the heart, the brain were impenetrable mysteries, and would always remain so. He glanced at the needles and asked Frothingham to thread a curved one of medium length.

—Snow, sir. The orderly presented a basin.

Steele was gathering up a handful preparatory to packing the wound when the boy gave a shuddering gasp. A little blood ran from his mouth, and he stopped breathing.

Sweated through, out of spirits at their failure to save the lad, he excused himself and went outside. He lit one of his host's segars, looking out over the empty parapets, the patch of brown grass at his feet where the orderly had scooped up snow. The banner that streamed in the icy wind.

Tears blurred his gaze. He dashed them away with the back of his hand. A sentry looked his way, but the bloodstained apron flapping at his waist must have explained his presence. The wind made him cough. He felt his clothing turn icy.

He was about to go back in when a figure atop the far parapet caught his eye, a hundred yards off. A greatcoated sentry followed it, ten paces behind.

It was Captain Claiborne. He recognized their commander's pointed imperial, the way he walked bent forward, hands clasped behind him. The distant pacer did not look up.

Simultaneously with the sight came the knock of hammers. Lowering his gaze, the old doctor observed men carrying boards out to the center of the parade ground, handing them up to where others spiked them in. It did not take long before his eye sorted out shape. Recognized the framework of beams going up. The black engine gradually rearing above the frozen earth.

Numbed by the freezing wind, Dr. Alphaeus Steele gazed up at the scaffold whereon he might die.

PART II

THAT FERVOUR OF
SCRAPING THE BONE,
OF KNAPPING THE FLINT.

————◆————

December 1861–February 1862.

6

Nomenclature of the Ten-Inch Dahlgren ♦ Return to the Grand Camp ♦
A Much-Anticipated Liaison Interrupted ♦ Enter Mouskko Goran ♦ A Lesson
in Moral Philosophy ♦ Tea with Mrs. Mary Peake, the Reverend Lewis
Lockwood, and Major General John E. Wool

S O you sees this shell, den? They measures it close fore they ships it
out to us. Got to be widin a tenth of a inch to fit in these guns. The
shell man—that is who?

—Dat is me, Petty Officer Hanks.

—That's right, Chubb. Every time you picks up a shell, you checks
this fuze hole. When the inspectors finds a shell ain't right, they chips a
morsel out right here. If you sees that, don't load that shell 'ceptin in a
emergency.

The rapt circle of dark visages surrounded him on the forecastle where
the pivot gun squatted, squinting up the James. *Cumberland* pitched to
her moorings in a brisky wind. The day was bright but cold, and they
huddled close for warmth as they listened. The purser wouldn't give the
contrabands a full issue. He said they didn't take care of their clothes like
white men would, so they went about shivering in dirty uniforms.

—Dewitt, tell me what you knows about this here gun.

—The U.S. Navy ten-inch Dahlgren smoothbore weighs twelve thousand pounds and fires shells and solid shot from ninety-seven to a hun-

dred and twenty-five pounds. Got a range of seventeen hundred and fifty yards at five degrees elevation.

—Peadle, the parts of the gun. Point to each one.

—Face, swell, neck, lip. Chase, curve of reinforce. Trunnions, reinforce sight-mass, breech sight-mass. Lock-piece, vent, and cascabel.

He and Mr. Randall had made a second trip man-catching at the camp; they were planning a third that afternoon. As the new hands reported aboard, Mr. Selfridge had put them under Hanks's command at the forward pivot gun. Replaced his white boys with Calistra and Lysander, Sundag and Asberry, Narcy and Sadrick and Ashduebal. Two were free, the rest escaped, loose chattel. Hardly any was unmarked by the lash, and two had felon holes in their ears. The crew called them the African Avengers, the Ethiopian Cannoneers, the Sable Shooters. The oldest, Chubb Johnson, was thirty, near as they could figure, squinch-eyed, copper-colored, with scrofula scars on features that suggested some New England overseer had gotten too close to his mother. Cal wanted the young ones. If he got them trained right, they'd maybe turn into sailors.

The downside was that they weren't gratifying down on the berth decks. He'd had to break up fights. Once, he'd turned a white man over to the master-at-arms, who'd given him a strange look, then smiled at the white boy. Who said, —Who appointed this uppity darkey boss man? And the master-at-arms had said, —He'll get his comeuppance. Don't worry your head about that. Both smiling at him, shaking their heads at this animal who had decided he was as good as they.

He was waiting by the ladder when Randall tapped him on the shoulder.

—Did you not hear me calling you, Hanks?

—No sir. I is maybe getting a lil deaf, sir. He was not, but as a slave he'd often found it useful to pretend not to hear what whites said in his presence.

—From the guns, no doubt. Randall glanced around as if making sure they couldn't be overheard. —I shan't be able to go to the camp with you today, Gunner.

—No sir?

—Pressing business elsewhere.

—Will you not be going ashore, sir?

—I shall. But you'll have to conduct your business alone. The Confederates are cooking up some sort of surprise for us. You know your way around by now, do you not? I have written you out an order in case there is any trouble with the army.

He handed it over and went forward, leaving Cal looking at the writing and wondering what it said, and also at the dollar note enclosed in it. It was the first time a white man had ever given him money. Oh, he had some of his own. Quite a bit, in fact. Two thousand dollars in gold from the attorney who'd tried to cheat and sell him and gotten a fiery death for his deserts. The problem was how to keep it. A sailor had no privacy. Even his hammock roll was subject to search and theft.

His fingertips brushed the compact weight of the money belt under his uniform, then shifted to the juju under his blouse. He showed the paper to the officer of the deck, who smiled loftily as he told him what it said. Not long after, he was being rowed toward shore.

The dollar served him well, as did the absence of supervision. A plug of Virginia's finest nestled in his cap. A tin cupful of what a sutler assured him was the identical corpse-reviving fluid generals whiskified on glowed in his belly. Next lay a *long* anticipated event. He swaggered along King Street, taking his time. Staring with contempt at the ragged scarecrow oldsters. Laughing at the kids. At last a passing laundrywoman caught his eye. He praised her, she insulted him, but with a spark in her eye. No, she ain't never had no truck with a sailor. No, she didn't live far. He followed her down a lane past shrieking children whose bare feet puckered with cold; past a black cat, staring from a stack of cut sticks. He stumbled on frozen, crooked mud, so hard to walk on after a smooth deck.

Her house was a slab shack. Slabs were waste wood, the curved outer sections of log cut off at the mill before they sawed planks. Strip off the bark, and you could lay it in courses and tie it with briar vine to make a roof; you could nail it to posts to make rough walls.

—It ain't much. But it ain't no slave shack, the woman said.

He bent through a door-curtain of negro-cloth. A smoky fire of straw and dried manure smoldered in a fireplace so gaping huge it was one wall.

Some massa's house once, chimbly all that was left. The shack smelled of old kush-cakes, dirty woman, and a grease lamp smoking in an iron bowl. Neither the smell nor the bugs that crepitated in the newspaper-glued walls made any never-mind to his stiffened poker. But he faltered as he realized a bundle of rags was actually a hideously twisted human being, watching them with flat eyes like slate buttons.

—Who that in the corner? What he doin here?

—Thass mah husband.

—Your husband?

—Oh, don't mind him. She chuckled. —He done run away one too many time. Last time Marster cotch him, dey put him 'tween de screws of de cotton press. He ain't gone trouble us none.

Cal unbuttoned his trowsers and his bow-yard sprang free. She threw herself on the pallet, chuckling, and drew back muddy skirts from immense thighs. From a beckoning yawn that drew him in like a tide-race.

He was setting to couch his lance when a hand snatched the curtain aside. He recognized the livid, bristling face after a moment's staredown as the gray-mustached sergeant, O'Leary.

—An' whut the hell be ye doin here, ye black jackeen?

—I gots a paper, Sergeant.

O'Leary scowled at it. Hanks, standing with his dick throbbing, the woman staring insolently from the pallet, realized O'Leary couldn't read it any more than he could.

—So you got a paper, *thurra mon dhiol;* every fuckin woolly-head in camp's got one. Don't mean a fart in Connemara. What ye after in Big Fairinda's shandrydan?

—Gettin my two bits 'worth. What it look like?

—I didn't sign up for to be sugar-titting black apes. Give all you animals back to your masters soon's they give up this secesh.

—Didn't ask for no sugar titting, Sergeant. Hanks grinned at the woman, who turned over massively, exposing immense jiggling hams that made him lick his lips. —Leastways not from you.

—Get out o' there, you imp o' darkness. Or ye'll get a brushing over ye'll not soon forget. O'Leary laid his hand on a revolver Cal had not noticed until then.

Hanks wasn't sure if a steerage officer saluted a sergeant. He didn't feel like saluting this one. He finished buttoning his fly, ten, eleven, twelve, thirteen, and only then said, watching the Irishman's face squeeze purple like a fisted tomato, —We still lacking crew. Figured to see what the latest arrivals looks like.

—Sure an' you're thinking to start a new crop between her legs, is you? Stick your peg in your pants an' get out of there. I want to talk to you. He withdrew and Cal heard him shouting hoarsely, as at dogs.

As he pushed his way out, children scattered, shrieking. They'd been watching through the chinks in the slabs. Angry but concealing it, Cal said, —What you want, Mister Sergeant? Seem hard to interrup a man at his jivin.

—You'll be needing to know something, darkey boy. This here's a white man's war, and we'll fight it.

—Navy thinks different.

—Far's I care they can put all ye shotty spalpeens on them ships, then sink 'em. But that brings me to me business. Which is, things'd go easier for you in this camp if there was anythin in it for anybody else.

The brogue was thick but the meaning clear: O'Leary wanted cut in. Hanks eyed his boots, knowing a sharp fighter would set them before he started anything. He figured he could throw this mick right over one of these shacks. The problem would be what happened after. —Ain't nothin I can rightly do for you, Sergeant, he said mildly. —Mister Randall, he never said nothing about no sweetenin for you. I kin ask him. About expenses, you might say.

—Niver mind, then. I'm thinkin ye'd best be gettin back to your ship.

—I'se here on orders, Sergeant. If you wants me off army land, you'll have to talk to somebody higher than me. Cal reached into his hat, bit a piece off the plug. Held it out, the wet end that his mouth had just closed around exposed. —Want a chew?

O'Leary slapped it to the dirt and strode off. He called over his shoulder, —All right, Sambo, you had your chance.

The two little boys who'd been following Cal, who seemed to catch up with him in minutes every time he came to camp and never let him out of their sight, were on the tobacco instantly, scuffling and punching each other. Cal got them up and made them split it down the middle. He bit into what he'd kept in his cheek, drawing juice, and swaggered round, intending to get back to his interrupted business. But when he pushed back in, Fairinda was gone, the pallet empty. Gone with his two bits, and the thing in the corner laughing at him with a silent wheeze.

Down the shabby dirt streets of the Grand Camp, nuts hurting with disappointed lust. Eyeing every woman who passed. There were more people and more shacks each time he returned. The old life of the white masters was gone, replaced by a more vibrant, noisier, crowded throng, dusky of face and shabby of raiment. Despite the snap in the air everyone was out. Hanks sneered at their raggedness, their furtive sidles. They still walked like slaves. On the way he was offered segars, whiskey, card games, cakes, pies, and the favors of more women. He made terms for later with a high yellow whose fixed wild grin foreshadowed untold pleasures. After some distance he rolled down Queen Street past the ruins of a brick church and toward the old courthouse, set on fire but not completely destroyed when the retreating Confederates had torched the town.

Several lads were already gathered around the recruiting handbill. One caught his eye. In loose pantaloons, lanky, but his coal-colored limbs looked well formed. Through a ragged shirt Cal caught sight of a deep chest. His lower face projected into jutting teeth. His head was covered by a red bandanna, corners knotted into wings that fluttered in the wind. His antic grin was forward and utterly bumptious. Hanks grabbed his arm, felt muscle solid as rock. —Where you get dese, darkey?

—Run de ferry sometimes, barge man, stevedoring up at Rocketts. Anythin on de water my marster rent me out for to do. The bandanna'd boy added, —Who is you? De driver?

—Ain't no damn driver. Hire you out, huh? They don't do that where I comes from.

—Sixteen dollar a month. Marster take ten and give me back six. He done turn down sebenteen hundred dollar for me last year.

—Uh huh, you is a valuable darkey. And where is dat? Rocketts?

—Rocketts? Down by Bloody Run. Billies Creek. *Richmond*, boy. Don't you knows dat? Rocketts to Shockoe, say de man; nickel and a nickel from lan to lan. He did a little step, a cut, wood-soled slave clogs scuffling in the mud.

Hanks ignored the dancing. —That where you is from?

—I borned at Doctor Eppes's. Charles City County, on the river. Ebry tub shall stand on its own bottom, dat what Marster Eppes say. So he send me for boatman, take ten and give me back six. Yassuh. He done turn down sebenteen hundred dollar for me.

—You say dat already. Boatman, huh? What dey calls you, darkey?

He put a finger up and twirled round under it and came down mock-fierce, showing his teeth. —I's Mouskko Goran. Mean as de tiger and shifty as de smoke, can't no man fix what ain't nebber been broke.

—So what you doing here, lebenteen-hundred-dollar Goran? Eatin army rations and spittin and lickin in Hampton?

—Marster done se-ceded from dese here U-nited States, Goran said. He grinned. —An' I hab done se-ceded from Marster. Yassah! Ebry tub shall stand on its own bottom.

Cal put out his hand, and Goran's joined it. He felt the hard callus of a workingman. Ran a hand over Goran's back and shoulders, and bent to feel his legs. Pointed to his mouth; Goran yawned obediently. —How long you been here, boy?

—'Bout a week. Come here to get me a erster boat and sell ersters to de sojers and get me rich, but I done los my stake. That Davis darkey says I stay here, I hab gots to go to work for de army diggin on de fort. We gets rations, but dey says dat Quartermaster Tallmedge puts de pay in his own pocket. Maybe you is got a better op-tunity in de nayby.

—An opportunity, but you got to be a man to take it.

Cal explained it to them all. When he'd answered their questions, calmed their fears, and sorted out the sick and old and hopeless moon-calves, he had three takers, including Goran. Not as many this time. They were thinning out; the army was putting the fit men to work on military construction, teamstering for the spring advance everyone knew was on its way. He made sure they knew he got one of every ten dollars the navy paid them. No white officer needed to know about that arrangement, and if they popped on him, they'd be off an easy billet on a clean wind-ship and shoveling coal in a stinking steamer. He told them to say good-bye to their womenfolk and be at the wharf at frog peep for the sundown boat.

When they were gone, he looked at the sun and figured he had two, three hours yet to kill. He grinned and spat. A picture of yellow thighs shaking, that crazy smile. He turned the corner and shambled to a stop.

O'Leary, swaggering down King Street with three boyos. Blue soldiers, and hard-looking cases. Carrying clubs and long sword-bayonets. They looked into each lane, stopped the children to bark questions. Cal stepped back into cover. To go back to the landing would put him athwart their course. He turned and walked hastily toward the courthouse, hoping to find some officer before the Irish caught up.

—There he is. Hoy! Sambo!

—Hold that big one up there. The monkey in the sailor suit. Hold that buck up!

A tug at his reefer-coat and an upturned face, one of the boys who'd followed him around the camp and once had tried to pick his pocket. Puncie, that was his name. —You comes wid us, Mister Hanks, he said urgently.

—Where we going at, boy?

—We gets to de freedom fort, you be safe dere.

Maybe so. O'Leary's shoulder hitters wouldn't follow him through the gates. Unfortunately those gates were over a mile away, and the road led through Camp Hamilton. He was trapped. He started to sweat. —Ain't no darkey going to make it alive running through a camp full of white sojers.

—Then foller us.

They were dragging him toward the courthouse. Looking back he saw the Irish cutting through the scragglety backyards, kicking down the stick fences. A woman carrying something under a cloth ducked out of a shack. They clubbed her aside and she screamed, beating her fists to her head, at a trayful of pies that lay bleeding red juice out on the dirt. The little boys tugged at him. He shook them off and ran up the steps, looking for a shovel, a club, anything to fight back with.

—Come in, sir, a pleasant voice called.

It had been a courtroom. The jury box was still there, and chairs for the audience, though most were broken. One wall was smoke-stained and buckled. The windows were broken or missing. Yet it had been swept and sanded, and thirty big-eyed, mop-headed children in hues from deepest black to palest yellow, boys on one side, girls on the other, sat gaping at him.

At the front stood a quivering-tense woman in a figured skirt and a blindingly white shirtwaist. Her face was thin but very beautiful. Her eyes were a soft brown, large and calm and steadier on his own than he was used to in a female. Her skin was a light coffee, her nose almost that of a white lady. She wore her hair up too, like a lady's. One of the smaller children sobbed in fright; she touched it, smiling in a sweet, grave manner. Her fingers were very thin, her wrist sticklike. —There's nothing to be afraid of, Daisy. Remember whose arms protect us. You, sir, will be . . . Sailor Hanks. Will you not take your cap off and join us?

She even sounded like a white missus, used the modulated singing notes they used to put you in your place. Only she sounded as if they were friends, though he'd only just laid eyes on her. He took off his flat hat. Held it in front of his crotch, the way slaves learned to in front of white ladies. —Yes'm. Calpurnius Hanks, ma'am.

No, she *wasn't* white. He didn't have to call her ma'am. But what *was* she? What were these littluns doing? It looked almost like a prayer meeting.

—You are interrupting our class, Brother Hanks. Or did you come to join us?

He threw a glance out the window. Through heat-crazed glass he saw the sergeant and his boyos checking out the street. He ducked quickly and felt his way to a vacant seat.

—Brother Josie, you may begin at the top of page three.

A very skinny boy with bushy hair, ill-fitting eyeglasses, and a worn old osnaburg coat that hung to his bare feet came up to the front. Taking a small green-bound book the woman drew from a fold in her skirt, the child began telling a story. Frowning, Hanks watched the boy's eyeballs jerk this way and that. The story was about a poor girl who went to collect a payment from a rich man who owed her mother a small amount of money for some laundry she'd done. The man, who was busy conducting an auction—Cal wondered what kind, what he was auctioning—pulled a bill from his pocket without looking and gave it to her. The girl was on her way home when she looked at it and saw that instead of a twenty-five-cent note it was for five dollars.

Suddenly he realized the boy, the child with the crooked eyeglasses, wasn't making this story up or telling something that had happened to him. Of course Hanks had seen people read before. The captain read the Articles of War each Sunday and sometimes a lesson from the Bible. But he'd never seen black lips form words above lines of print.

—Very well. Thank you, Joseah. Let us halt there for a moment. What then is the Christian thing to do?

Hanks waited. When none of the littluns spoke up, he said, —Sure is a stroke of luck, ain't it? Us darkeys can eat a long time on five dollars.

Eyes turned on him. With a quiet smile the woman said, —Our new classmate will interpret the passage for us.

—Sayin it be a stroke of luck for them, white man mess up like that. She best put that money right away where can't nobody see it. Take it home and give it to her mamma to buy up some cornmeal, grits, pork, molasses for the winter.

The woman started to speak, then turned aside to cough. He glanced at the young ones. They didn't act like anything was wrong, though the cough was agonized. When she was done and had wiped her mouth with a lacy handkerchief, she said gently, —But that five dollars is not really hers. Is it, Brother?

—It is now, Cal said. He heard a strangled chortle and frowned around. —What I say? True, ain't it? She got de money. That white man, he don't know they got it.

—The story does not specify the man is white, Brother.

—It say he rich, don't it?

Guffaws, unmuffled now. The woman said, —His color is not to the point here. The honest action is to return the note to its rightful owner and to explain the nature of the mistake.

—What, to that slave auctioneer? That devil got that money off auctioning darkeys. He probly goin to put her and her mamma up on that block next.

Now the whole class was laughing at him. He was getting angry and would have left except the Irish devils were probably still out there waiting. But the woman said kindly, —Brother Hanks. The Lord does not ask whether those we injure be white or black, or rich or poor. They are all our neighbors. Do you not see that if we are to expect others to treat us as their equals, we must show ourselves worthy of it? The only possible answer to hatred is love; to dishonesty, honesty; to cruelty, mercy.

He was about to point out that this was not his experience of life when she called the children to stand. Their voices joined, not very loud but inexpressibly sweet.

> *Firm as the earth thy gospel stands,*
> *My Lord, my Hope, my Trust;*
> *If I am found in Jesus' hands,*
> *My soul can n'er be lost.*
>
> *His honor is engaged to save*
> *The meanest of his sheep;*
> *All whom his heavenly Father gave*
> *His hands securely keep.*

Not long after, she dismissed what he now understood, astonished, was a kind of makeshift school *for colored*. It was the first time he'd ever seen such a thing. It was against every slave code he knew of, and he did not know what to think about it, or her. He peeked out again. O'Leary was still there, leaning against the porch post of a shabby saloon. But as Cal watched he shook his head, spat, and left, striding off up the street.

Beside him she said, —I do love Watt's hymns. And the children sing them with such beauty, I am hard put not to weep.

—Ma'am, I's sorry to interrupt your . . . prayer meeting here. If that is what it is.

She did not look at him. She was shuffling . . . *paper*. His eyes bulged again. No slave in the South had the right to own a sheet of paper, on pain of the whip. —That is all right, Brother. You are most likely closer to their way of thinking. They, and no doubt you, have been hardly used by a great evil. Which I myself, raised in the bosom of a loving family, have largely, though not completely, escaped. She flashed him a smile. —But they have fair capacities and a few rare talent. Given the sunlight of knowledge, they will astound all who behold them.

—You knows my name, but I doesn't know yours.

—I am Sister Mary Peake, Brother Hanks.

The curtsey so dumbfounded him he goggled before executing a stiff bow. For a moment he almost felt himself a gentleman being introduced to some fine lady, though it was really only to a tired-looking, fortyish woman who he now saw trembled with weakness, with cold, in a dusty, smoke-smelling room now empty of all but the two of them and the smallest girl, the one who'd sobbed in fear. She clung to her mother's skirts, looking up at him.

—This here's a school, he said.

—I have been conducting it for some years now.

—And the marsters. They been lettin you do this? In Virginia?

She smiled as if she knew something he didn't. —We have had the most powerful protection, Brother Hanks. *Divine* protection. It has shielded us from the vigilance of those conservators of the slave law. Or, when they interfered with us, enabled us to begin again. Now I have more scholars than ever before. If only my strength were equal to the challenge.

He didn't have anything to say. She dropped her eyes after a moment. —But perhaps even you doubt your strength at times, though that is hard to conceive.

—Oh, I doubts, Miz—Sister Peake. Not my strength. But what I gots to do.

—That is your soul within you struggling toward the light. Will you walk me home, Brother? And then you will perhaps come with me to tea at a friend's.

Again he stared, astonished, at her outstretched glove.

Cal Hanks sat sweating violently in an upholstered armchair, balancing a china cup and saucer and a tiny silver spoon on the knee of his trowsers. He had never used these implements before and was having trouble with them. With him in a parlour of a large frame building overlooking the beach were Mrs. Peake; a white parson from Massachusetts named Lockwood; Mr. Peake, so fair-haired and blue-eyed that Cal took him for white till he got a close look, who had said nothing thus far; and, last, an elderly, spar-straight, smooth-shaven soldier introduced as General Wool. Cal had heard this name before. It might be this was the man in charge of Fort Monroe. If so, a very important white man indeed, the most important he'd ever met, not excepting *Cumberland's* captain. With only the slightest hesitation the general, spare and erect in a beautifully cut uniform, had even touched his hand, though not actually shaken it.

He tried to take a sip without slurping or spilling hot tea down his chin. He succeeded, but when he put the cup back on the saucer, he couldn't get his finger out of the little handle hole. When he freed it at last, his hand was wet with tea and sweat, and he dangled it down where the others could not see and wiped it surreptitiously on the upholstery. For some time now the two white men had been discussing the Colored Question as if three of them weren't sitting right there. Only Mrs. Peake occasionally put in a word.

—So that in a way General Butler's ruling was no boon to us, the general was saying. —Though I admire it as a cunning product of the legal mind. I doubt any other man in the Republic but Benjamin Butler could have come up with it. Certainly no man in the Regular Army.

Mrs. Peake said softly to Cal, —He means the determination that fellow Christians seeking safety and freedom are not human beings attempting to win their liberty, but more like cattle that have wandered.

Wool cleared his throat. —It was the guile of the interpretation, Mrs. Peake, that impressed me, not *necessarily* its moral sagacity. That if the owners wanted them back, all they had to do was take the oath to the Union and they would be returned under the Fugitive Slave Act. If they asserted Virginia was no longer part of the United States, then the Fugitive Act could not apply to them, thus impaling them on the horns of a most uncomfortable dilemma.

—How sad, Mary Peake said. —That they should be *uncomfortable*.

Wool balanced his saucer on his knee. Seemed to consider taking his leave; then settled more firmly, as if for some reason he had to be here. —The policy as I have outlined it is the best General Butler and I have been able to come up with. Ship them north? Politically unacceptable. Return them to disloyal owners? Militarily unwise. So we keep them here until I can organize shipping to Hayti. But if they are to eat government bread, these people must work for it. Otherwise they are simply encumbrances, and most seem likely to remain so. These shacks they build—disgraceful. Not fit for human habitation.

Mrs. Peake said, —Perhaps you are not told, General, that those who *do* build well are evicted by your troops, who then claim the houses as their own.

Wool colored. Reverend Lockwood said seriously, —General, I beg to most respectfully disagree. They are not "encumbrances." Indeed, upon these colored refugees—I dislike the term "contrabands"—perhaps hinges the destiny of this Republic.

—This is hard to conceive, sir.

—Let me set forth my reasoning. First, I have gone among these people. I find them industrious and remarkably intelligent, considering their circumstances. Many are truly followers of our Saviour. But to proceed to arguments that may suit you better: Without their cooperation this rebellion cannot perhaps be suppressed.

—I fail to see that, Reverend.

—Consider that the economy and agriculture of the South depends upon its four millions of black bondsmen. Take that labor away, and the South cannot live. You have heard what these people were told by their masters. That the Yankee was eight feet high and ate slaves for breakfast; that we should plough them under for fertilizer or sell them south to Cuba. That they should realize we are their deliverers is above all what the Southern despotism fears. Word they are being kindly treated here would move rapidly through the mysterious channels by which they communicate.

The general did not look pleased. —You are advocating I foment servile rebellion, sir. "The Union as it was"—that is our sole aim in bringing the rebels to heel. General McClellan has made plain the line our military administration is to follow. We will not interfere with slaveowners in the lawful exercise of their rights. On the contrary, we are to crush with an iron fist any attempt at black insurrection.

—The Union as it was. Lockwood gestured broadly. —And all these thousands, they are to be . . . what? Returned to slavery once that Union is restored? All as it was, not a jot nor a tittle changed of that whole frightful system of control and torture, the crushing-out of the human spirit? That cannot be, General. The civilization of the age cries out against it. If this war changes anything, it *must* eradicate human bondage. God will not stay His wrath from us forever.

Wool said coldly, —Returned to their rightful owners, employed under a modified condition of servitude, or shipped overseas, as Mr. Lincoln and Mr. Seward favor. I lean to Central America myself, but it does not matter. That is not mine to decide.

—We are not asking for liberation tonight, General, came the soft voice again. —I know you are a benevolent man who rejoices in doing good. You will do all you can for the helpless who depend on your mercy. All I ask of you is permission.

Wool grimaced. —Your school again? It is best I simply not know about it, madam. The administration has established no policy. In its absence local law continues to govern. I am not without sympathy. I simply cannot commit myself on the subject.

Lockwood argued that official countenance of a school would be an advantage to any Union effort to enlist the help of the Negro in the zone of rebellion. The only possible beneficiaries of keeping a whole people in darkness and degradation were the slaveholders.

—All we need is your consent, General, put in the soft voice again.

Wool cleared his throat, whatever requirement to hear them out apparently satisfied. —Mrs. Peake, you must not tire yourself by sitting up so late. I will send you my regimental surgeon. You would do better to intermit your exhausting duties than take on more.

—I can no more evade my duty, General, than can you. She leaned forward, and Hanks saw how drawn her face had become. —As Job said in his trials, "All the days of my appointed time will I wait, till my change come."

Wool said unwillingly, —I can promise nothing beyond thinking on it.

—Will you give us your decision in the morning?

—And I had still hoped to speak to you about your medical service, which refuses even to see our people—

—Where have you put my sword, Lewis? In the general vicinity of my cap, I hope.

They all rose, Cal upsetting his teacup. Fortunately it was empty. Wool nodded to Cal, to Mr. Peake, and bowed a fraction of an inch to Mrs. Peake. He touched Lockwood's hand briefly, glanced once more at Cal, his expression troubled, and withdrew.

Mrs. Peake turned to him. —Brother Hanks, thank you for your presence.

He was surprised. —I didn't say hardly nothing.

—Oh, but you did. Your being here, *in uniform*, spoke more plainly than any words. Did you not see him glancing at it? Your very presence was a contradiction to those who say we have not their capabilities. *You* do not believe such a thing. She stretched out her hand to Lockwood. —And *I* know it is not true.

She took Hank's hand too, and he felt humbled. —We should so much like to see you again. If the General gives his permission, and I believe the Lord is moving his heart in that direction, it may be possible to convene an evening class as well. For adults.

—Adults?

—Yes, for the grown-ups. Do you read, Brother?

He muttered angrily, lowering his head, backing down the steps, —Marster never let us touch a book. Too late for me. I'll leave that to the littluns.

In the falling dusk he stood under the burgeoning stars. Wondering and fearing. Then a distant, heavy thud traveled to his ear, echoing out over the Roads. The evening gun from the fort. Meaning *Cumberland's* cutter would be lying at the wharf, his day's collection waiting for their sea daddy. He couldn't leave them to the white sailors. If they got hold of them, there'd be no harvest this day at all.

With a swinging, rolling stride he moved off into the gathering dark.

7

December in Portsmouth, Virginia ♦ Some Black, Misshapen Phoenix ♦
John H. Porter, Esq. ♦ Reporting to Lieutenant Jones ♦ Capabilities of the
Rebuilt *Merrimack* ♦ Shortage of an Essential Commodity ♦ Obstructions
in the Elizabeth ♦ The Yankee Cowardly by Nature

T HE straight-backed, green-eyed young officer stalked through the
crowd of rough workmen, black and white. They gave way,
touching caps. Henry Lomax Minter was in freshly brushed
blues, sword, and cocked hat, disdaining an overcoat though the wind
was sharp this overcast and blustery December morning.

The Federals had burnt and wrecked the Gosport Navy Yard on their
hasty departure the April previous. But the largest shipyard in the South
was back in production, and from the smoke and noise at the tributary
machinery works, business was going ahead at speed.

He'd taken a room on High Street. This morning a brisk walk across a
wooden bridge and then down Water Street had taken him to the gate.
Now he threaded between lofts and shop buildings of scorched brick, and
others hastily built of oak planks. Where the great ship houses had stood,
acres of charred timber and ash still stretched like the debris of a volcanic
eruption, and the reek of burning lingered beneath the smells of coal-
smoke and of incipient snow.

His orders—the overt ones from Buchanan, not the covert directive
from Norris, which of course had not been put to paper—directed him to

report to Lieutenant Catesby ap Roger Jones, the new battery's first lieutenant and executive officer. He knew Jones by reputation; the Service was not large, and he'd made it his business to find out about him and the state of affairs in Norfolk before leaving Richmond.

Jones—the "ap" was a Welsh idiom meaning "son of"—was Virginia born and well connected indeed. His mother was a Page, and Robert E. Lee was her first cousin. His father had been adjutant general of the U.S. Army, and his uncle a hero of New Orleans and the capture of Monterey, though later marked for dismissal by the Retirement Board due to his overfondness for young boys—at least that was the scuttlebutt in the fleet. Catesby himself had served since 1836, afloat and ashore. Jones had been working with John Mercer Brooke, the ordnance expert, on the ironclad conversion since its conception the previous summer.

Lomax's plan today was to look in and see how the reconstruction was progressing. Then he'd report to Jones and perhaps Brooke, if he was present, before calling on the shipyard commander.

The dry dock was a granite-lined crater that as he neared, as it opened beneath him, gradually revealed a presence so impressive he slowed to a halt, hardly believing what his sight portrayed.

He'd toured *Merrimack* not long after her launch. Six years before, the enormous two-decker had been the most powerful warship in America. First of a class of broad-shouldered titans built to defeat the heaviest British and French ships of the line. The first screw-propelled capital ships in the U.S. fleet. Their lofty quarter-galleried sterns, the glossy black ramparts of their towering sides, and their sky-piercing masts dominated any harbor they entered.

This . . . thing . . . that was being born of its remains, like some black misshapen phoenix, was like no craft he'd ever seen. Braced by heavy timbers, the lower hull stretched the length of the dock. Yet halfway from load line to gunwale a horizontal guillotine had cropped her, razed her, slicing away everything that to a seaman made a ship a ship. No stem. No sprit. No gunwales. No masts. It was like viewing the corpse of a lovely woman truncated at the waist.

He strolled toward the river, passing as he went a party of civilian sightseers. He recognized General Wise and his son John, but did not feel like intruding. Turning away, he gave his full attention to the colossus.

Atop what remained the workmen had stamped down a monstrous carapace of oaken balks. Beneath their swarming he made out a flat fore-deck, unpenetrated by hatch or companionway. Aft of it rose an even less seamanlike construction: an elongated pyramid of heavily bolted oak sloped up to a flat roof. The ends of this construction were smoothly rounded. Oval piercings, smaller than conventional gunports, indicated a not very numerous battery. At the stern, near the river, he looked down on another flat vee of oak and below it a huge two-bladed screw.

What would this thing look like afloat? He could not vision an answer.

At second look it struck him there was very little iron on this ironclad. Only a black, thinnish hide reached around the forward curve of the case-mate. As he watched, a team of four slave workmen strained to manhan-dle a plate into position with pry bars. It was twice a man's length but not quite a foot wide. They lanced it with long bolts, passing them through into the interior of the gun-house. Then hammered it down with mauls, the clang echoing off granite and brick.

He suddenly realized his was the only uniform in sight among ragged denims and patched coats, stocking caps and slouch hats and tight-wound scarves. The clatter of hammers and the shriek of saws rose over the gray river. A steam pump thudded, and far down at the bottom of the dock water glistened. He caught a passing mechanic by the sleeve and asked where he might find Lieutenant Jones. He was directed to a frame shed, its planks still pale from recent construction.

Five lamps burned, one at each corner. A betty lamp hissed overhead. Wood shavings curled on the floor, giving the air a resinous bite. A black-bearded, harried-looking fellow in a frock coat stood with two others at a table of planks and sawhorses. When Lomax introduced himself, the fel-low passed a hand across his brow before welcoming him.

—This gentleman is Mister Meads, our master carpenter. Mister Farmer, our master blacksmith. I am John Luke Porter, naval constructor in charge of the conversion.

Lomax bowed—not deeply, only what was due from a gentleman to honest and loyal workmen. Though it occurred as he straightened that any of these might not be.

Loyal, that is. An observant workman could gather all the information Norris had said the enemy were getting. He'd have to be alert. Suspect everyone until proven beyond doubt faithful to the Cause.

—Delighted, gentlemen. I am Lomax Minter, and I beg pardon for intruding. I was in search of Lieutenant Jones.

—You'll most likely find him at the commandant's quarters this time of day, Lieutenant. Mr. Porter nodded to the others; they gathered notebooks and calipers and left. —Can I be of assistance?

—I'm reporting in.

—I see. Porter scratched in his beard, looking harassed. —Well, you'll be wondering why we missed the November launch date. There have been setbacks. Each change introduces additional work, rework, more delay.

—Have there been many?

—Changes? Altogether too many. To the shield, hatches, ports, the armor. And each time—

—Who specifies these alterations?

Porter half-turned away, as if realizing he was speaking out of turn to someone he didn't know. —You should ask Lieutenant Jones that question. I was about to check on the stern tube. Care to accompany me?

Lomax debated. A tour in the company of the executive officer would be one thing. Crawling through it with one of the workmen quite another. —I believe I shall postpone that pleasure till after I check in.

Porter looked not quite happy with this decision, but bowed him out the door.

The quarters was of brick, smoke-stained but otherwise unharmed from the conflagration. He found Jones on the ground floor, going over letters with a writing assistant. Slight and balding, with a small graying beard, *Merrimack*'s exec welcomed him with faultless courtesy and a firm handshake. Lomax presented his orders. Jones asked him to sit a moment while he finished his business. Then, when the writer left, he limped to the sideboard and poured him a welcoming dram. Flourished his tumbler. —To the Cause.

—And the brave boys of Belmont and Ball's Bluff.

—And to "Bruin" Wilkes, who bids fair to do us more service than to our enemy.

Lomax smiled grimly. The impetuous Charles Wilkes, U.S.N., had seized two Confederate diplomats from a British mail steamer in international waters. The next mails from London could bring a declaration of war upon the North by the greatest sea power in history.

—Welcome aboard, Minter. You join myself and Mister Simms. I see, however, you were to report to Flag Officer Forrest first, our yard commander.

—I took the liberty of looking over the . . . experiment this morning.

—Rather a change from her previous incarnation, eh?

—Not as much a ship as some armored Leviathan. I confess doubt as to whether such a beast will be navigable. But if it has as much impact on the Yankees . . .

—Then we shall not have labored in vain. I sailed on her first voyage. A magnificent warship, though her engines did not seem well adapted. The crankshafts breaking and so forth. Nor was she as fast under sail as we'd hoped.

Jones outlined their progress. Since she'd been first scuttled and then set afire, the frigate had been undamaged below the waterline. Her hull was of the finest live oak and white oak, impervious to submersion. Secretary Mallory had not originally thought of her in connection with his ironclad plan. Chief Engineer Williamson had suggested using the hulk as the basis for a makeshift, while purpose-built ironclads were begun from the keel up.

Mallory had appointed a triumvirate to supervise the conversion. Gosport's naval constructor, Porter—Lomax remembered the harried man at the waterfront—would raise the wreck, cut it down, and rebuild it into a steam ram. Brooke would design its armor and guns with assistance from the Bureau of Ordnance and Hydrography. Williamson would oversee restoration of its engines and boilers. They were even less satisfactory now than ever, after having been ripped out for scrapping, hastily reassembled, then burned and submerged during the Union withdrawal.

While Williamson and Porter had been cutting her down and putting her engines into shape, Jones and Brooke had carried out firing tests at

Jamestown Island. The lieutenant said their first shots had shattered the originally planned armor, three layers of one-inch plate spiked into two feet of oak. Two layers of two-inch plate resisted much more stoutly.

Lomax said, —But I had understood—correct me if I'm wrong. I thought those tests showed all her armor quite ineffective.

Jones grinned. —We released that news for our federal readership.

—A *ruse de guerre;* I see. What armament do you plan? I notice she has not many piercings.

—It's cramped under that shield. Room for only ten guns. Two will be new seven-inch high-velocity rifles with reinforced breeches. Brooke has cast them at Tredegar, along with two of his six-inch model. We had hoped all her armament would be rifled, but due to the slowness of production, the remainder will be of her original battery.

—Not a heavy armament, considering what she carried before. Forty guns, was it not?

Jones smiled. —True, sir. But these new rifles will project a steel-tipped bolt capable of penetrating many inches of solid iron.

Minter said slowly, —They are your ironclad killers.

—Exactly so.

—Such as the Stevens battery?

—According to their newspapers, the Yankees are getting up several iron-plated vessels. It is of the utmost importance we get into action first. If we can, I believe we will break this blockade, gain foreign recognition, and conclude hostilities with an honorable peace this spring.

—End the war? With one ship?

—No such weapon has ever before taken the sea, Minter. I consider this the most important naval affair the country has to deal with. I neglected one "point," so to speak. She will also carry an iron ram-head below the waterline, so shaped as to be deadly at the faintest contact. We can sweep the Roads clean and extend our imperium to the mouth of the Bay. Such has been the focus of our efforts since July . . . but you will have no doubt noticed that unfortunately we're short an essential commodity.

—I had noticed her only partially armored state, if that is what you mean.

—She requires nearly a thousand tons of plate. So far we have only about three hundred in hand.

—Why so little? Lomax paid close attention now. He'd reasoned his way to the suspicion that no spy could remain content with reporting the progress of so dangerous a weapon. Sooner or later his masters would press him to interfere. To sabotage; or to less obvious methods of interference and delay till their own ironclads could take the waves, and the moment of advantage passed.

—Tredegar's first problem was obtaining the necessary metal, since imports from Pittsburgh had been cut off. General Thomas ripped up most of the rails of the Baltimore and Ohio. The War Department arranged for them to go to Richmond. The horsecar rails went into the furnaces as well. We shipped them three hundred tons of scrap from the yard here—old tooling, damaged guns, iron from the other ships the Yankees burned.

Jones explained the difficulties the Confederacy's ironworks had encountered fabricating armor plate of sufficient thickness. —First they had to rebuild their furnace doors to admit plate of this width. Then drill each section in such a way the first layer, laid fore and aft, aligned exactly with the second, laid vertically. This became especially exacting on the curved portions. I don't mind telling you it's caused me many a sleepless night.

Lomax said, —And the delays?

—Having to redrill when Porter changed the design? Yes.

—So *Porter* changed the design. Are you confident of his . . . abilities?

Jones waved away his implication. —Actually Brooke demanded most of the alterations. The steering, the gunports, the backing. Porter's no genius. He's botched jobs in the past. But we keep a close eye on him; and after all he's the only naval constructor we've got.

—In the yard?

—No, the South. He's the only one who stayed after Sumter. There's also a shortage of flatcars to get the iron to us. Until we receive it we are not fit to fight. The Yankees are not likely to wait until we're fully dressed. If one of theirs completes first, they'll sweep up the river and shell us into splinters in the dock.

—What of a crew?

—We have no orders yet in relation to one. I hear of good men anxious to ship, but there it is.

—It is of first importance, I should think, that they be prepared and drilled.

Jones ceased smiling. —I do not wish to give offense, but considering what I have had to take from Secretary Mallory, Commodore Forrest, and others, I do not require further spurring from any additional quarter. Particularly from those junior to me.

Lomax said, bowing slightly in his chair, —I had only intended to be of service, sir. Forgive me if I expressed myself with excessive warmth.

Jones nodded, though anger remained in his tightened lips. —I had thought of asking you to expedite the delivery of the material.

Lomax did not like the sound of this. Further, if he was to seek out whoever was furnishing information to the enemy, he could hardly do so while on the road between Norfolk and Richmond. —Sir, is that a proper concern for a fighting officer?

—We're useless without iron. We must have the remainder of it and very soon. Jones looked up. —Am I to understand you refuse the assignment?

—No sir. I only ask, is there no other? Involving the chance to inflict damage on the enemy? Surely you have others who can play at railroad clerk as well as I.

—Actually Forrest will have charge of you until commissioning as he commands the yard and you are not, strictly speaking, attached to the ship yet. I should add he expects to captain our new invention when she is finished. Perhaps you could ask him to let you take a look at the river.

The first lieutenant explained that Major General Benjamin Huger, pronounced "Hugee," had scuttled hulks and driven pilings to keep the enemy squadron off Fort Monroe from ascending the Elizabeth River. Once *Merrimack* was completed, she'd have to pass these obstructions to attack. They also had to be ready to react should the Yankees raid.

—I'm uneasy they've made no move yet, Jones concluded. —They must know what we're doing here. A few hot shot would put paid to our whole effort. Yet they've not even probed our defense.

Lomax said, —Easily explained. The Yankee is cowardly by nature. And as you said, he's waiting for his own ironclads.

—Cowardly? I'm not so sure of that, Jones said, still somewhat coldly. —They too have fire in their blood when it is up.

Lomax could not let this pass. —No sir. With all respect, that I cannot admit. Nor—begging your pardon, and ventured in the *most* friendly manner—do I believe any true Southron should lower himself to thinking it so.

—Only a fool underestimates his enemy, Lieutenant.

They glared at each other. At last Jones cleared his throat and stood. Lomax instantly rose too, adjusting the hang of his sword.

—Well, sir. Please convey my respects to the commodore. And do let me know what he decides.

Offering a sweeping bow, Minter withdrew.

8

Two Months of Incessant Travel ♦ Intense Activity at Bushwick Inlet ♦
The Envelope of Iron ♦ Airy Comments by a Yankee Caulker, Disputed
by Brooklyn Riveters ♦ Report to Captain Ericsson, Who Is Found
in Mixed Company ♦ An Evening on Broadway ♦ Unexpected Reunion
with a Former Heart Interest

THE ship house was a hundred feet high, perched where the East
River opened to Bushwick Inlet. Theo Hubbard heard the pulsat-
ing roar from blocks away. The sound of hundreds of men riveting, caulking, sawing, beating recalcitrant iron into a shape never taken
before. The shrill warnings of rivet boys hovered above the din like the
piping of sparrows. Close to it was deafening, and as his steps crunched
through new snow, wending around blowing dray horses and a gang of
frostbitten Irishmen unloading precut iron scantlings from wagons, he
pinched off a bit of the combed cotton he kept in his pocket and rammed
it into his ears.

In two months he'd grown familiar with the grounds of the Continental Ironworks, as well as the offices and shop floors of stamping mills,
gear-cutting establishments, chain works, and foundries throughout the
Empire State. New York was the only place in the country such a complex
and novel machine as Ericsson's could be fabricated. All the contractors
were either in Manhattan or upstate, with the exception of the rolling mill
of H. Abbott and Sons in Baltimore. Unsettling to think the one estab-

lishment that could roll armor plate was in a city unsafe to wander after dark in a blue uniform.

Only days after reporting in he'd realized the Consortium, as its owners called it, had promised more than they could deliver. It might have been barely possible to build a machine like this in ninety days, given complete plans, contractors instructed, and raw materials on hand. But Ericsson had not even begun the detailed drawings when time commenced to tick. As he and MacCord hunched over the drawing boards, Theo had taken on the contractors. From Schenectady to Long Island, Baltimore to Albany, he negotiated tolerances, selected materials, and browbeat owners into putting on night shifts. He'd gone for days at a time without touching a bed, nodding on the cars between one snowbound town and the next.

No one guarded the ship house, though he'd mentioned the matter to Mr. Rowland. Who seemed out of sorts, perhaps because he too had submitted an ironclad design, one of those the Board had rejected. Theo pushed the door open and ducked his head, nearly hurled back by the sheer volume of sound.

From grimy windows high in plank walls a washed-out light fell on a pointed oval of metal not unlike an enormous bathtub. The sides had risen since he'd last inspected. The deck was half beamed in, liced with caulkers inchworming along on their knees. Within the framework others swung rivet hammers, eye-aimed adzes, or ground away at foundry rust with sand and sacking. The air was chill, though stoves roared in the corners, screened and vented against errant sparks. Every breath was freighted: coal-smoke, cold iron, earth floor, tobacco, oakum, and fresh-sawed pine. Scores of workers streamed in and out of the shipway doors, carrying angle iron, planking, toolboxes, augers. They wore greasy wool jackets and peacoats, work gloves, woolen watch caps, rags tied around their ears. Their breaths puffed white clouds that drifted upward toward the cavernous roof.

Shears were lowering what he recognized as the anchor well casting. He'd seen it last as a specification, handed over to the Niagara Steam Forge Company in Buffalo. Ericsson had designed a protected anchoring contrivance so that men need not go on deck. Theo had suggested applying steam power, knowing how exhausting the work was and how few crew the craft would carry. This had been as brusquely dismissed as every other suggestion he'd put forward.

The ship house foreman, Grandy, was a bent old mechanician with white mustaches so long they curled around the point of his chin. They exchanged a few words, Grandy pointing out progress here and hitch there. They descended into the depths beneath the shipway and then, by means of plank steps covered with layer upon layer of tar and paint stains, up again till they stood within the gradually coalescing assemblage of iron and oak.

Theo gazed round, marveling at the translation of ink lines on tracing cloth, drawn beneath bright oil lamps by an aging man under great pressure, into a reality unlike anything yet seen under the sun.

The lower hull, of iron plate braced from within, was only half an inch thick. It was supposed to be strengthened by numerous heavy angle irons from Holdane and Company, but that dealer had consistently missed its promised delivery times. The gauges of his substitutes did not match, and this worried him, though his calculations had shown the strength would be equivalent to Ericsson's specifications.

He didn't like to bother the older engineer with such details. Each time word of shortages, late deliveries, or parts machined out of dimension reached the Swede, he groaned in obsessive despair. Muttered about shadowy forces conspiring to thwart his achievement. He would quiz Theo accusingly. On a good day he got called a "machinery oiler"; on the bad ones a "dolt," a "simpleton," even a "Bureau spy" or "Isherwood puppet." But Theo had had commanding officers worse. Considering the importance of what they were about, he could put up with complaints, grumbling, and the occasional insult.

Leaving the foreman at the transverse bulkhead, he climbed up out of the gap that waited to receive the engines, condenser, and turret machinery, up onto what would be the main deck.

What Ericsson called the "raft" was taking shape. Of solid oaken beams a foot square, it fit over the lower hull like a saucer inverted over a teacup. Overhangs at bow and stern protected the anchor-hoister, the rudder, and the huge four-bladed iron screw. Once the machinery was in, the flat deck would be plated with two layers of half-inch iron. A thicker skirting of several one-inch plates would run down along the edges to well below the waterline. He walked forward, worrying. The underlying framework had to be exact for its iron jacket to fit. And if one of his suppliers went on strike, he'd have to depend on the remaining firms to complete the armor.

The turret was a different matter. There were no backup firms for its complex and innovative rotating and control mechanisms. There, he was utterly dependent on Abbot, Novelty, and a Buffalo firm.

The piercing blast of a whistle. Grandy snapped closed a large repeater timepiece. The clatter stopped, and silence reverberated in the shed. Workers streamed down ladders and wriggled from beneath machinery mounts. Some were no more than ten, their smudged faces like soiled flowers amid the iron.

When Hubbard reached ground level, he found several workmen standing in a tight circle, warming their hands in the stream of hot air that came up from the roaring furnace and lighting dudeens with splinters they dipped into the coals as a boy labored at the foot bellows. —Ten-minute break, one said as he came up. He nodded and they made space for him.

—Navy, huh? one fellow asked him.

—Bureau of Steam Engineering.

—Wanta buy a poky ticket?

—No.

One blew on his blue hands. —Colder'n common, ain't it? Hey, you wouldn't be the skewpod designed this thing?

Theo said frostily, —I assist Mister Ericsson on this project.

The man spat tobacco juice into the sand under the furnace. —You tell him for me there ain't enough caulk in the wahld to keep this fuckin coffin afloat. The poor fuckin jack who rides this into the water better have him a puncheon to hang on to, she's going straight to th' bottom.

—Just oakum your damn hole, one of the others told him. —You old-line Down-Easters are gonna have to find a different way to trowser your dollars. We're iron men, he told Theo. —Mister Rowland got us in here to rivet up the aqueduct and kept us on to build your battery, or whatever it is.

—Ain't a proper boat a-tall, the caulker said primly. —Government got financeered big on this contraption.

—There's been iron ships before and they floated.

—Yeah, it's the air in them that floats, not the fuckin wood.

—Sho, but them all had freeboard. I built a plenty o' ships. This thing, its deck's gonna be level with the water, right?

—Only a little will show above the waterline, Theo said. —The less exposed, the less to catch a shell.

—Yeah, but that means when you push her down, ain't no more float left to her. Like a big piece of waterlogged wood. Just live enough to stay awash. Then you're gonna put this huge iron tower on it. . . . Besides they laid the damn keel on a Friday, and one of the molders had red mittens on.

The ironworkers looked to Theo, who couldn't remember if the keel had been laid on a Friday or not, but attempted to explain even a foot of freeboard extended over a huge area would give adequate reserve buoyancy. He didn't seem to be winning any converts. The whistle blew again. The circle broke, and the din began again, riveting and the steady thud of caulking mallets blending with the iron-clanging clamor that once again filled the cavernous, freezing shed.

He crossed the river on a two-cent ferry, then caught a stage across town to Clute & Brothers. Clute had built Ericsson's caloric engines, which ran most of the printing presses for the New York dailies. They were reporting problems on the gun carriages, which had to fit the very tight interior of a twenty-foot turret. He met with an Ordnance Bureau representative who made it clear his obligation ended at providing two sparking-new Dahlgrens; their further use in a privately designed death trap were of no concern to him.

Carrying the drawings back with pencilled questions from the pattern shop, he arrived at Franklin Street to find a gentleman ringing the bell. He was from the *Scientific American* and wished to interview the captain for an article. Theo offered to take him up. Busy as Ericsson was, he'd be keen to influence coverage by the premier scientific publication in the country. As they mounted the stairs he heard voices above. The captain's was one. The other was Barnes's, Griswold's fixer and a man of weight in the Consortium.

—But what about all these letters Commodore Smith is sending me? The old guard are doing their best to stifle this child in its cradle.

—Set your mind at ease, sir. Strong influence is being brought to bear on those officers.

—Twelve million for twenty ironclads. And they want to build the Bureau's design. Not mine.

—The Naval Committee is not about to give Welles another twelve million dollars after the way he's muffed things. Entrusting ship purchases to his brother-in-law! We'll build their twenty ironclads. For six million, not twelve—and a handsome profit besides.

—But the Department—this *dwarf* they set to check up on me—

—Sir, do not tax yourself. What the Navy wants or does not want is not germane. I have it from Representative Corning, Congress will fund no new ironclads until we have a chance to prove ourselves.

The reporter glanced at Theo. Hubbard cleared his throat and slammed his boots on the steps. *Dwarf.* He felt his face flaming. The disputants fell silent as he came into view. —Mister Supervisor, Barnes said smoothly, bowing. —And this gentleman? I believe we have met before. How nice to see you.

Obtaining alterations from the master's hand, Theo ran the drawings back to Clute. Then went on to the next notation in his personal book, a leather establishment on Canal.

After making clear the dimensions and specifications—butts of the hide, chrome-tanned, riveted joints—for the belts that would drive the auxiliary machinery, and that delivery by the first of February of three complete sets had been guaranteed for ten per centum below the catalog price, Theo gradually came to a stop. Like an engine that had worked off the last pressure in its boiler. Ericsson's dismissive, belittling tone rang in his ears. He stood alone on the brick pavement under a heavy wet snow, exhausted, footsore, vague. A whirring thunder filled his head. He glanced up; ten feet above spun the unguarded drive shaft of one of the engines that distributed their power up and down streets to job-printer's presses, shoemaker's establishments, and hat-making machinery. His left hand smarted where he'd inadvertently laid it on a blazing hot segment of freshly cast turret ring. He did not know where to go next.

Back to his boarding room? He shuddered. An iron bed, threadbare carpet, a Chatham-square mirror, and a closet he could only open by sitting on the bed and drawing his legs up. The sitting room was dark and smelled of must and boiled cabbage. The only good thing that could be said was that it was convenient to the Monitor Bureau offices. He simply could not return there, not yet. He wanted desperately to sleep but knew he wouldn't. His head was whirling with plans, details, deadlines. He needed to relax . . . needed a drink . . . a good meal.

Perhaps it was fate that at that moment a strolling tout thrust a handbill into his gloves for a well-known concert saloon. A low place, but it promised a show, music, a refreshing and invigorating draft. An hour's intermission before he found his bed.

He hiked up Broadway through the falling snow.

From each standard and shop front, light glowed. He passed Mitchell's Olympic Theatre, the Minerva Rooms, Wallack's Theatre. Despite the snow the sidewalks were thronged. He passed model-artist exhibitions, daguerreotype studios, auction houses. A woman called —Don't look so weary, darling. Lay your head on my shoulder. Another took his arm, chattering brightly and calling him Dear Harry. When he caught her hand at his watch chain, she fled, footsteps muffled by the drifts. A constable called from across the street, —Look alive there, sir. We should not like one of our naval men to come to grief.

He'd intended to go to Harry Hill's but was diverted by a large red and green lantern, the sort one saw on old ships, hanging between Henry Wood's Marble Hall and Taylor's Saloon. Its gas-fired rays streamed out to tint the falling snow emerald and scarlet. From a rambling frame structure came a raucous polka. A lanky black in top hat and frock coat, half red, half green, snapped his fingers and pointed in, grinning like a jack-o'-lantern.

Schweitzer's Dutch Garden was packed with so much segar smoke, piano noise, and tipsy humanity that he had trouble elbowing far enough past the door to be noticed. The steam heat felt like a boiler room at full power; the smell of bodies, and clothes unchanged from month to month, was overpowering. But once he cleared the lobby throng, he was surrounded by waiter girls in mock-Tyrolean blouses and short peasant skirts like a sugarplum by flies. In this struggle for existence a heavy blond won out. Her name was Miranda, and if there was anything he wanted, anything at all, he had only to ask. He asked for a table convenient to the show; and if any roast beef and fried potatoes were about, he would be glad to make their acquaintance.

At the table she showed him to, he applied himself to the schooner of the inky brew he'd formed a taste for here in the Western Berlin. Under brilliant limelight a bevy in flesh-colored tights rotated on a turntable, allowing the bald-pated front-rowers an ever-changing survey of their abundant charms. He wondered what made that turntable revolve. Ericsson's turret was driven by donkey engines bolted beneath the deck beams. A complex gearing fed power to a cast-iron spur wheel. Everything was so finely machined. If water or sand got down into the control and reversing rods . . .

He squeezed his eyes tight and submerged in sea-dark beer. Forget the fucking turret! Forget the impregnable steam battery, the Navy Department, the rebellion, the petulant and testy Scrooge for whom he Cratchited.

Miranda, bearing steak and potatoes. She leaned close, and he felt the squeeze of heavy breasts. —There's boxes upstairs friends can be alone.

—We'll see. Maybe.

—Have yourself a nice dinner and then you'll see everything. Ready for another schooner? A brilliant smile. She had not bad teeth. He applied himself to the fried beef with gusto.

A raucous cancan supplanted the tableau. As deshabillée girls flung their legs up, she brought more beer and a bowl of German cake with sweet sauce. Her musky scent and whispered enticement, and the well-turned limbs flashing on stage made his head swim, made his prick push up through the fly of his flannel drawers against the scratchy melton of his trowsers. He did not usually fancy heavy women, but if she carried it well, what objection could one have? He was spooning up the sweet when skirts rustled again. —Bring that with you, if you like. Ready to kick your heels up, sport? The gelt first . . . there we are. This way, lover.

He was weaving on the stairs, finishing the last licks in the bowl. Best not drink any more. Gaslight flickered on the landing above. A sudden pang of anger: remembering Barnes's cynical drawl, the pitying look the reporter had shot him. Pulling the girl to him, he tried to kiss her. She turned her face away. —No, no, not *me*. You don't want what I've got this week! She opened a door and ushered him in.

When the cabinet door closed behind him, a small form, no taller than his own, glided down out of the shadows into his lap. He couldn't see distinctly in what little light filtered past the curtains, but her hair was chopped off short. Her breastbone thrust out above the sagging top of her peasant blouse. Her long-lashed, slightly crossed brown eyes were both lewd and yet also somehow expressionless.

He was hastily undoing his fly, she her bodice, when recognition dawned. He choked, coughing cake and hard sauce onto the velvet hangings. She turned ashen beneath rouge. They stared at each other, frozen amid the noise and music.

—It's not . . . Eirlys? he managed at last.

—Theodorus, she whispered.

They'd met at a night class at the Mechanic's Institute. Had courted when he was the youngest master machinist in Hartford. He remembered a warm August night canoeing on the Connecticut. Young bodies pressed to each other, lying on the placid breast of the river. . . .

—You left town, she whispered. —They said you left on the train.

—What are you doing here? I mean, in New York?

She didn't answer, just stared, devouring his uniform, the gilt buttons, the cap shoved back on his head. —You look older. But still so determined.

—It's been . . . six years.

—I know, she murmured, looking now not at him but down through the slightly parted drapes. Some low farce was being staged involving a flop-shoed comic as a drunken Irishman, paired with a mock-English lord with monocle, top hat, and cane. The lord took a pratfall over the Irishman's back, and the crowd roared. In the box next door something thudded into the wall, accompanied by cries of sham passion.

—But what are you doing *here*?

—My parents wouldn't keep me. I lived with my aunt for a time. But she would not stop reproaching me for my folly and shame. Then I met a woman who was kind to me. She said I might find a position here in the great city.

He took her hand. It was cold as Maine ice. —Shame? What shame? Why did you leave Hartford?

—I was unfortunate.

A shadow moved over his heart. He said half angrily, —But *here*? Do you know what happens to women here?

She shrugged. —Perhaps I did. But what other choice had I?

—But you are not . . . you are not like these others.

Her glance dulled, and she looked away. Her hand went to her head. He remembered that gesture. Once it had been dear to him. But now she was a Phryne, an Aphrodite, a fair frail one.

—What happened to your hair?

She told him the sorry tale, how she'd met an elderly, respectable-looking woman in the street. When the conversation turned to clothes, the woman had offered to show her a nearby establishment where she could buy, at a cheap price, still-usable dresses left by those who'd ordered new and did not wish to wear the old away. The woman had led her into a basement in a low part of town where she was seized suddenly by brawny men. The ruffians had held her while the woman drew shears from her reticule.

—They sold it to a wig-maker, no doubt. She rubbed the lapel of his frock coat between thumb and forefinger. —So you are in the navy. Is that why you went to Washington?

—For the examination.

—And you're an officer?

—I rank with a lieutenant. He tried to shake off the fuzziness of beef, beer, and the sudden overwhelming sleepiness. He could not fall asleep here. He wasn't even sure he was not imagining this. It was so unlikely to encounter each other in the teem of the city. Could it be a sham? A sharp trick? This was unmistakably Eirlys Pinnell, six years older than his memories, a hardened, aged twenty-three. But was he being set up in some way with such a heart-wringing story? He tried to grasp the essential. —You said a child. That night in the canoe—

—You were the only one, Theo. She sat up and for just a moment he saw again the earnest open girl she'd been. —Her name's Lilibeth. She stays with my landlady when I'm at work. She doesn't know I sell drink in a concert saloon. I'd show you her picture, but you learn not to carry anything you don't want stolen.

—But my God, Eirlys, to work here, subject to the— He'd been about to say subject to the insults, then remembered how he'd been conducted up here after paying his dollars into Miranda's broad palm, and what they'd been about to do. He said more quietly, —I wish I'd known.

—I wrote you, Theo. The Mechanic's Fraternal Association said they forwarded the letter.

—At sea, letters often go astray.

Guilt gripped him through the alcohol haze. He had not loved her. After the night in the canoe, realizing he did not want to be tied to her, he had not called at her home again. He'd gotten her letter. Had read it and thrown it away. But she'd mentioned no child.

—Why did you not write again?

—If you didn't care enough to write back, I had determined not to annoy you.

His mind, accustomed to detect problems and set things right, perceived this as a problem that had to be set right. He could not contemplate a legitimate union. She had placed herself beyond the pale. But if the child really was his . . . He stood. —Earwig; by your soul—there *is* a child? And it is mine?

She looked up at him. Said with a turn of her mouth meant to be sardonic but that he found sublimely wistful, —By my *soul*? Have I yet one to swear by? If I do, then yes, Theo. It's not a panel game or bunco. It's the truth.

He began searching through his trowsers. He'd deposited the letter of credit Eaker had given him; had drawn against it now and then to move the work along more quickly. But most of the two thousand was still there. Moving to the edge of the box for light, he scratched with a stub of pencil. Held out the scrap. —Here.

—What is this?

—A bank draft. Enough so you need no longer work here.

—You don't have to do this.

—I can spare it. He felt a surge of pride, wanted to swagger. She'd known him as a precocious boy, a dirty-nailed mechanic with naught but dreams. —I have been entrusted with considerable responsibility by the Government. I have wealthy friends. Take it; it is yours. And more, should you need it.

Someone tapped at the cabinet door. She started up; the scrap vanished into the top of her corset. —Your time's up. Someone else wants me.

—You can leave now. You don't have to do this anymore.

—I'll finish out the night. She turned a stubborn scowl toward him; he noted her paleness, the prominence of her bones. Was she ill? Her lips came closer. He pushed her away, quickly, without thought, like something that might dirty his clothing.

—Take care of that draft, he said, to deny the hurt and shock on her face.

She recovered in a moment. Leaned close, to brush his ear with once-familiar breath. —Listen! They've marked you out to rob. They'll show you to a back egress. Pretend you left something at your table. Leave by the front door, quickly, and don't idle in the street.

He picked up his hat where it had fallen on the greasy, piss-sodden carpet. When he straightened, she was gone.

9

At Anchor off Newport News ♦ Rumors of an Infernal Machine ♦
A Tomahawking in the Berthing Area ♦ Unauthorized Absence ♦
The Christmas Party ♦ Hymns and Gingerbread ♦ Alone with Mrs. Mary
Peake ♦ Attempt at a Private Confession ♦ Waylaid in the Dark

L ATE that year *Cumberland* moved to a blocking position off the mouth of the James, anchoring under Newport News Point. In deep water, but only just. A hundred yards to northward ran a bar, rising and falling but too shallow for her to cross. She'd begun her life as a frigate and was still deeper than any purpose-built sloop. The boatswain had told Hanks this after a day spent sounding and marking the shallows with floating casks painted ochre, a color to see if you knew it was there, but that someone who didn't might miss.

They'd spent a lot of time in the boats. The rebels were building some infernal machine in Richmond. Richmond being at the head of the James, that pointed any such directly at *Cumberland*—or so the captain seemed to think as the orders filtered down through Mr. Morris, Mr. Selfridge, and Mr. Kennison. Guns charged to the muzzle with musket balls, depressed to sweep the water around. Boarding nettings of twenty-one-thread ratline stuff, boiled in pitch to a hardness a knife wouldn't dent. A circling boom of heavy logs. Nail boards along the bulwarks to puncture and snag boarders. Snot-nosed sailors shivering at the oars all night. None had caught anything in the months of watching, unless you counted a stiff-legged, crab-gnawed mule found in the nets one morning, or the skiffloads of contrabands that kept coming down. One had cracked into the boom at midnight and been fired on by a startled deck sentry. Fortunately he'd missed, and five terrified women had been directed onward to what they called the "freedom fort."

Cal had a full crew at the pivot now. Chubb Johnson was his second gun-captain; Lysander Henry his first loader; Calistra Tompkins his first sponger. Narcy Ewins was his second loader and Sundag Jock his second sponger. His levermen were Asberry Rollins and Sadrick Williams, and his compressormen were Ashduebal Smith and Mouskko Goran. Though he was thinking of moving Goran up to loader. The rest worked the tackle. They even had a powder boy, the ten-year-old who'd saved Cal's bacon in Slabtown. Puncie was an orphan; his family had died of the flux. Cal had exercised them at shifting, pointing, firing drill. But since winter had closed down, the captain had secured his practice of firing a gun a day, and now weeks went by without the smell of powder. Except when they were out in the boats, the men had a lot of time below. There was only so much junk to pick and bulkheads to scrape. Inevitably trouble started.

Mr. Kennison called him to task several times for cleanliness of his men's persons. Cal expected this. The whites thought black men were dirty. But the officers weren't the trouble. The master-at-arms wasn't either, though he always picked the colored to blacklist for spitting or skylarking. Cal had tried to figure how to get on the good side of the white boys. A lot of them didn't like having colored aboard. They'd knock their hats off going up and down the ladders. He'd thought if his men took over some of the rough jobs, they might at least show they weren't lazy. So he volunteered a hand every Friday to clean the galley smokestack, the dirtiest job aboard. Volunteered a working party to clean the bilges aft, and to scrape and paint the anchors when they shifted anchorages.

But it had the opposite effect. Pretty soon whenever a shitty job came up he heard, —Where's the niggers? That's their look-out. Their meat disappeared between cask and mess cloth, leaving nothing but gristle and fat. His men found soot smeared on their clothes when they took down drying on wash Mondays or happened on them torn down and kicked into the scuppers. Which meant they had to stand inspection in a dirty jumper or trowsers, which meant a rating from the first lieutenant. He stood up for them, but there wasn't much give to the exec.

But it was the business with the hammocks that really broke whatever half truce they'd had with the other hands.

During the day the berth deck was empty, bare, cold. The overhead was so low Cal had to walk head down to miss the deck beams. At night it was crammed with the warmth of so many crowded-together bodies it supplied the want of a stove. At reveille it was a scramble of seamen hastily rolling and lashing hammocks and clothing and other articles together to go topside. After several scuffles over swing space, the master-at-arms had painted a line across the deck. Forward of it was colored. Aft was white. This kept the peace a few more days, though it crowded his men elbow to jowl while the whites sprawled across the rest of the compartment.

It started the night before Christmas Eve. Hammocks were piped down, and skylarking, bullshitting, and cards reigned supreme until lights out at nine. That night one of the pivot crew had sentry duty. When he came back and in the dim gleams of the berth-deck reflector lamps tried to roll into his hammock, he found it was full of shit—so full it was plain a dozen men had joined in the fun. It was next to the paint line, so there wasn't any question who'd done it. The muffled laughter made it clear.

Unfortunately the boy they'd picked to shit on was Mouskko Goran, who came out of his befouled berth like lightning with a boarding tomahawk in his hand. The laughter gave way to shouts as he waded into the white section, hacking and bludgeoning with the hatchet, which he'd stolen during boarding drill and hidden in a crack in the overhead. —Mean as de tiger, mean as de tiger, he screamed as he swung, making an unholy melee in the crowded dark as some tried to escape and others to restrain the berserking Goran. Cal had to keep them from kicking him to death once they finally got him down.

—I had doubts from the first, said the first lieutenant the next morning. They were topside, on the quarterdeck, despite a raw northerly that came off the shore like off the pole. It whistled in the shrouds, through the gasketed sails that clung to their spars like the wrapped egg cases of insects, whipping the green Roads into a bleak chop. Cal, a battered Goran, and several bandaged white men stood at attention before him, along with the master-at-arms, Selfridge, and Kennison. —Having the Negro in close contact with the white. It seems events have proved me right.

Cal kept his eyes in the boat and his face blank. The master-at-arms described what had happened. There was no point in his trying to get a word in. He'd been to enough masts to know that. All Goran could do was take his punishment.

But now the exec was talking about how blacks needed to control themselves. Once again words formed themselves in his mind. He dismissed them. Nothing he said would make any difference.

—Hanks, these darkeys consider you their King Pinkster aboard. Anything to say for your boy here?

—He's a good hand on the pivot, sir. Got the fighting spirit.

—Battle is not a matter of swinging a tomahawk at defenseless sleeping men, the exec said.

—Sir, he done had provocation.

—You are referring to the soiling of his hammock while he was on sentry duty. The exec pressed his lips outward. —I daresay we have all been the butt of such pranks. Sent to fetch a fathom of shoreline, or to look for the mail buoy. No excuse for violence. Only that he had the weapon reversed, was striking—no doubt without knowing it—with the blunt end instead of the blade saved his shipmates from being severely injured or even killed.

—Yassah, Cal said after a moment. Morris wasn't looking at him, but no one else was answering up.

—You too have been put down by the master-at-arms several times for objecting to orders or insolent responses.

—Yassah.

—I am sorry to say this sort of melee exemplifies the turbulent behavior I have learned to expect from you people. I had hoped for a more fortunate result from this experiment, but I will have to recommend that we send you all ashore.

Cal blinked. He'd expected Goran to be punished, perhaps discharged. But not a blanket sentence on his whole gun crew.

Randall said unctuously, —Sir, if I may?

—Mister Randall?

—I recruited these men, sir, at the captain's request. One thing I've observed is that they differ in how they have adapted to freedom. We would not condemn all Germans for the misbehavior of one, or all Irish. And we so desperately need men, as the commodore's messages have made clear.

Morris pushed out his lips again. —Mister Selfridge?

—I must say I agree, sir. I have observed them at gun drill. They may perhaps be good material, with seasoning. It is too soon to make such a sweeping judgment.

—Well, well, the final decision will be the captain's. Morris glanced once more at Goran, who had so far not spoken. —Anything to say, Landsman? Though I do not imagine you will be rated as such after the captain's through with you.

—Any man shit on Mouskko Goran, he shits back.

—Sir, Hanks prompted. —Say "sir," Goran.

Goran glowered at the first lieutenant. He said nothing. Morris shook his head sadly and dismissed them.

Christmas Eve but no liberty. The only way he could go ashore was to take french leave, which would cost his rating if he got caught. He hated being ashore in Dixie anyway. Felt like he was walking not on soft earth, but on centuries of crusted blood. So when he handed over five dollars, half a month's pay, to the boatswain and stepped off the evening dispatch boat, he hurried quickly away from the windblown lantern flame at the end of the pier. Merging in his blues with the night as he headed for the sand spit that connected the fort's near island with the main.

The moon would not rise till later, but the stars glimmered above him like a thousand lanterns. There was the Gourd he'd followed north and the Digging Stars the old women in Georgia said meant it was time to plant. He could just see to direct his steps. He kept to the beach, away from the wagon road. Both because it was easier walking, away from the ruts ploughed deep by an army building for campaign, and to avoid late-night carousers. At its end, where a wooden bridge met the shore, a sentry stood beneath a lantern. Hanks approached him boldly, took off his hat, and told the truth: he was on his way to the Reverend Lockwood's cottage. He had his 'listment papers, case the gennulman wanted to see em. The sentry listened in silence, bored, no doubt chilled despite his heavy coat and the new pink knitted gloves someone must have sent as a gift from home. He waved the papers off and thumbed him across. Cal wished him a merry Christmas but got no reply.

Past the bridge he went back to the high-tide mark. The fewer who saw him, the better. Thin leaves of sea ice crackled beneath his boots. Scores of glimmering lanterns in Camp Hamilton, and singing and shouting on the icy wind. He skirted it, though a dog sensed him and set up a racket for a while.

He came up at last on the cottage, set back from the beach, and stood with all his senses searching, looking into the darkness beneath the trees. Then he swung open the gate, went up the walk, and knocked.

The children's faces, that was what stayed with him after as memory of that night. Maybe because when he stepped into the big white building and saw the tree, he felt like a child himself. But not such as he'd ever been. Maybe the child he might have been—that all children perhaps might be if the world were different from what men had made of it.

Candles and the scent of evergreen. Ribbons and mirrors dangled from the branches, glowing and tinkling to the tones of a harmonium played by a soldier not much older than the children who sat entranced in rows on the carpet as Mrs. Peake opened a hymnal and ran her finger down the crease. Took a careful breath, as if testing something within that trembling frame. Then lifted her chin.

> *Hark! The herald angels sing,*
> *Glory to the newborn King;*
> *Peace on earth, and mercy mild,*
> *God and sinners reconciled!*
> *Joyful, all ye nations rise,*
> *Join the triumph of the skies;*
> *With th'angelic host proclaim,*
> *Christ is born in Bethlehem!*

Lockwood beaming around, booming out the words with her. Other whites, teachers, pastors, soldiers joining in. The children watching them, then gradually trying the words themselves. And a sailor standing with hat twisted in callused hands, feeling tears sting his eyes.

> *Christ, by highest heav'n adored;*
> *Christ the everlasting Lord;*
> *Late in time, behold Him come,*
> *Offspring of a virgin's womb.*
> *Veiled in flesh the Godhead see;*
> *Hail th'incarnate Deity,*
> *Pleased with us in flesh to dwell,*
> *Jesus our Emmanuel!*

Children black as lamp soot and lighter than parchment, hair twisted in cornrows or springing free in dark aureoles; children in pinafores and jumpers some Ohio lady had pulled from a long-closed cedar chest or some mother in Wisconsin had folded with a tear for the dead. They rolled their eyes at him as he stood wordless, overcome. Lockwood's baritone beneath, Mrs. Peake's sweet voice soaring above them all.

—Brother Hanks, she said later, after the prayers and Chaplain Fuller's account of the Christ Child's birth. Taking his hand in hers. He could not believe how soft her skin was. In a different world he'd have been in love with her. Maybe he *was* in love with her. But not in the way up to now he'd thought such a thing could go. —I am so glad you could join us for Christmas Eve. Are not the little ones quite transformed?

—They're angels. And so are you one.

She smiled. —Most of them have never had Christmas before. And is not that blessed day the best gift in our power to give them?

Her daughter, Daisy, spoke a piece about Jesus and his love for little children. The spectacled boy he'd seen at the school recited "The Christmas Sheaf." Then Lockwood took the stage and welcomed all: the Third and Fourth Massachusetts Volunteers, the First Vermont, the Second

New York. He spoke of the contrast between the present and the past. How a year previous the only colored admitted to this building would have been maids dancing attendance on the belles of the plantation aristocracy. But now it was the Negro's child who swelled the choral song.

Recitations and speeches done, children and teachers adjourned to the cottage next door. The parlor where he'd sipped tea with General Wool was hung tonight with boughs and wreaths of evergreen, and the table was covered with dishes that made water spring to his mouth. Slave food, some would call it, but it was what he'd grown up with, and he heaped a plate hanging over with shoulder meat and sawmill gravy, poke sallat, baked peaches, polecat peas, rabbit pie with sassafras, sweet potato biscuits. It would gripe his belly after the ship food, but he did not care.

The children flew by, shrieking, —Merry Christmas! Merry Christmas t'all! Giggling like mad creatures. Longwood greeted him, but Cal's mouth was too full for any but incoherent sounds. The reverend pumped his free hand. The white man's face ran sweat like the melting candles on the tree and the melting candies on the side table, around which the children clustered like sweat-bees to molasses.

Still wolfing, Cal went through into the cottage's kitchen. But it was even hotter there. Flame glowed as a mammy in gingham unlatched the door of a black iron range, releasing a ginger smell and wood-smoke. Women looked up from whipping up icing, spreading it on cookies— brown shapes of men covered with white icing. They chaffed him and his size and his uniform, but their fingers never stopped flying. He went back out to refill his plate, and collided with Mrs. Peake.

—Mister Hanks, why didn't you bring any of our other sailor boys? I hear there are more than a few on the *Cumberland* and *Minnesota* now.

He remembered that morning's mast and Mr. Morris's threat. —All I could do to bring myself, ma'am.

You don't have to call her that. He took a breath, inhaled little pieces of sweet potato, coughed into his fist. Why did looking into her eyes make him feel like he was five years old again? —We there now, don't know how much longer we going to stay.

—I know you will do very well.

—Some think so; some don't.

—Well, despite what Mister Lockwood writes, we are not yet saints. But you must feel the stirring of the spirit. Around us, upcountry, all across the land. Like some great evil beast feeling the ground moving under it. Swinging its wary head. For the first time afraid. Don't you feel it?

—No, Cal said.

—You really don't?

—Marster'll never let us go, Miz Peake. Who else gone do they work? He shook his head. —They callin em contrabands, but these is still slave chillun. Ain't nothing changed but trade Ole Marster for the army.

—As you have traded him for the navy?

—I gots something to say to you. On the porch?

She glanced into the room. Perhaps at her husband, perhaps at Lockwood. —I could only stay a moment.

—That's all I wants.

Outside they looked across to where lights glimmered. The rush lights of Slabtown. He remembered the squalor, the degradation. A people uprooted. No, who'd uprooted themselves. Shaken the dust of Egypt from their sandals. What lay on the far side of this Sinai?

Her face turned up to his. She coughed, waving away the cold air. —What is it you wish to ask me, Mister Hanks?

—I kilt a man once, he said. Not bothering to put any varnish to it. Just telling her what he had to tell.

—Were you defending yourself?

—Had been. I kilt them too. That don't plague me. Slave catchers. The other, I kilt without needing to. Done it so he couldn't send more poor darkeys back to their marsters. He do plague me some.

—That's what you have to tell me?

—Well . . . not all of it. Man can live with killin.

—Then what?

—I seen the Devil. Near as you is to me.

He was watching her close in the light that came through the window, and she didn't blink an eye. —Where?

—Out of a fire.

—Did he speak?

—He did.

—And what did he tell you?

—No, wait. I gots to get this right.

He put a hand on his face, pulled cold sweat off it. He didn't even like to think about this, and talking about it was even more terrifying. Like *it* was watching, listening, warning him not to speak. But he had to, had to tell someone whose soul was clean, and this quiet sick woman was the best he'd seen so far. There was a word for what he hoped she could do for him, but he didn't remember it.

She coughed like something was tearing at her throat. He said, —We better go back in.

—No, Mister Hanks. If there is some demon in you, I know a Name that will cast it out. Tell me all of it. What you have to unburden yourself of.

Only his throat was closing up, as if something was squeezing it. Through a dry mouth he whispered, —Was de Mammy Griot tell me this. Said I didn't know who I was. Said I was de true emperor or something like dat. The one sent bringing the Jubilee.

He shut his eyes, and there it was. The shack in the backyard, the stink of rot and rum, the crackle of embers in a stick-and-mud fireplace. And the mad eyes of the old root woman. He squeezed his lids tighter and rasped out, —She said: I is the one sent bringin the fiery Jubilee. Descended of the kings of Ifé, royal blood of ancient time. The Hanged Man a-walkin, spat out de mouth of Death. No tellin which ogou I serve. Bacossou or Legba or Father Yahweh. The land will be devastated by fire, by water, by iron, and by lead. She seen all the sons and daughters of Africa layin dead in this land. She seen them singing with voices raised hosannah in freedom. Now, why she seen both two? Like there be two times ahead, two roads to Time, and confusion waverin between. And that's when I seen it, in de fire.

—The Devil?

—*Somethin* in there. Lookin out at me.

He shivered, fingering the juju pouch, the memory of that gaze hackling his spine. Mrs. Peake didn't say anything, looking off at the grease lamps, the bonfires of Slabtown. They too were making merry, the strains of stick rattling, fiddle music coming clearly across the creek. Then she turned her head, and following her gaze, Cal saw the far twinkle of anchor lights in the Roads. They bobbed and swayed, and he thought, Be a rough row back tonight. If I gets back at all.

—Two roads, she said, as if to herself. And for the first time he didn't hear a white voice out of her but a real one, her own. —The Devil, he know it. An' what the Devil know, why Jesus, he know it too. Sho, they kin kill us all. Lot of white folks, they ready to do that right now.

He didn't say anything, afraid he'd said too much already.

—You fated, Mister Hanks. But that don't mean it is the Devil. Could be God's work too. Might be a way to tell.

—How you fixin to tell that?

For answer he felt her hand on his brow. It trembled, and he felt the fever beneath the velvet. She said softly, —This man has sinned; but he has also been sinned against. He has murdered but asked forgiveness. In the name of Him who died for us on the cross, let his sins be forgiven. Say amen, Brother Hanks.

—Amen.

—As he has forgiven those who sinned against him and accepted You as his saviour, if there be a demon in him, Lord, let it be cast out now. I ask it in your name, Je—

His hand jerked, and she cried out. He heard the dry snap through his own bones as much as his ears. She cried out again, holding her wrist, staring at him in horror and disbelief in the light from the window.

He found himself at the foot of the steps, shaking with revulsion at what something within him had done. Some hate or haunt that had not forgiven those who'd torn him from those he loved. That had recoiled from the love that had shone from her eyes. And from all possibility of forgiveness, if it also meant forgiving *them.*

Weeping with horror, he stumbled back into the dark.

He came back to find himself slogging through the sand. Nearly to Camp Hamilton, he guessed. It wouldn't be easy, getting back before muster. Supposed to be a morning dispatch boat, but *Cumberland* didn't always run it; it went by rotation. *Saint Lawrence* next, he thought. Or Christmas, maybe there wouldn't be one? No, the officers would have to come back from ashore.

He was striding past the camp when a voice called peremptory —Halt! Who comes there?

He froze, hearing a musket hammer snap to cock. —Friend, he called. —On my way back to the fort. After a Christmas party.

—"On mah way back to de fo't." Black boy, eh?

—U.S. Navy.

—Navy, eh? Advance an' be reckanized.

He climbed slowly toward the clack of an unshuttered dark-lantern. A misshapen darkness loomed from a dune, tipped by starglint off metal. —Halt, it called again, and he did.

—What's going on then? said someone behind the sentry.

—Caught a black cat sneaking around. They got fuckin smokes in the Navy?

—I only know o' one. You, Sean—and a mutter he didn't catch.

He suddenly knew this voice. Took a step backward, intending flight. Not soon enough.

In the darkness he was seized from behind, an arm thrown round his throat. He didn't stop to think but roared and spun, catching someone behind him with the crook of his elbow.

—Quieten down, nigger!

He slammed a fist into a face, a kick into a leg. He'd had his share of fights, and he used his size and the dark. He still took a blow that staggered him, and a knee to the groin that all but put him on the ground. He sucked wind, bent, as fists hammered his back.

—Fucking sambo. All right, me lad, you want it rough.

Cal broke free and they circled. —Rough as you does, O'Leary, he said.

—Stick him, another voice said. —Use the sticker.

—He's a sailor, sarnt said.

—No he ain't. Just another thievin woolly head. Another flat-nosed, thick-lipped, know-nothing nigger.

O'Leary's voice. —White men's war, Topsy. Remember?

—I heard it said, Hanks panted, —paddies is only niggers turned inside out.

O'Leary bellowed and charged. Cal met them with instinctive fury, knocking one of the shadows to the sand. The other stumbled by, then turned. He heard a scrape and caught the glitter in the ray of the dark-lantern.

A bayonet. While he had nothing. Could not even draw his deck knife; did not wear it with blues, had left it with Chubb on the ship. He danced back from the lunge, in the sand, in the tufts of crackling grass, almost falling. If he went down, he'd rise up dead.

—Sergeant of the guard! Sergeant of the guard!

The sentry, shouting. Deciding probably whatever his sergeant was up to, it had gone far enough. But that wouldn't alter the next few seconds. Seconds in which he'd probably die.

O'Leary came in again. Cal tore off his heavy wool reefer coat and whipped it around where he figured the bayonet would be. Something snagged, ripped. He whipped the jacket to the side, hard as he could. Stepped in and battered his other fist into a body. Again. Again. With all his strength and terror and hate.

With a grunting cry O'Leary sank to the ground. Cal hit him again. Bone cracked. He drew back his boot to kick, but the heel caught on something behind him.

When he bent, it was driftwood or a drift timber, half buried; heavy, wet, icy. It sucked reluctantly out of the gritty sand. He hoisted it with a grunt. So heavy he could barely keep it aloft, his arms shaking.

Looked down, panting, arms quivering under the weight, at the squirming thing at his feet.

He should kill him.

O'Leary would do it.

He was struggling with it now. Someone else, inside him. He took another step forward, aiming the weight that was yearning to return to earth with crushing force.

Then closed his eyes and threw the timber from him. Contented himself with another kick, feeling ribs crack. A whine of pain. Someone was coming over the dunes. Shouts from the camp. His balls hurt. Something was torn in his arm.

The image of the pier, the dawn boat, came back, fixed as the North Star he'd followed out of Georgia.

He vised his hands over his ears. Groaned and waggled his head. His skull was coming apart. He was splitting down the middle, then realized with renewed horror that was exactly what Maman Griot had said. He could hear her cackling it.

Go on out of here, Lucas Caesar Calpurnius Augustus Hanks Verity. You got the legion of names, but you is the split twig. Y'all gone see it cut de feather, burn stronger'n red oak lye.

Whimpering, Cal Hanks broke into a limping run.

10

A Disappointing Servant ♦ Through the Even Yet Only Partially Ironed Hull
♦ A Literarily Inclined Workman ♦ Lieutenant Brooke, Mr. Porter, and
the Demon of Mutual Frustration ♦ A Most Delicate Labor ♦
Home of Mrs. Ker Custis Claiborne ♦ The Impulse to Revenge

MINTER woke to the creak and clatter of carts, the crow of a cock from a backyard. A distant thunder he dismissed after a moment; the Confederate batteries fronting the Roads often exercised their guns at dawn, and the Union squadron answered. And a loud, stertorous snore he recognized.

Throwing the bedclothes back, he thrust his legs into the silver-plated cold of a late January morning.

The old man lay huddled in a blanket outside his door. Lomax shook his shoulder, but he rolled away, smacking toothless gums. At last he left him in his sleep and set the pot to boil himself.

The servant rented for six dollars a month. Lomax had thought that rather a low rate at the time. He knew now it was five more than the antediluvian was worth. He could fix his own eggs, make his own tea. Still it was not done to brush one's own clothing, black one's own boots.

He resolved to find a boardinghouse and let the maid do it. A trim little maid, now. That had its appeal.

An hour later, shaved, breakfasted, and wrapped in greatcoat and scarf, he stood shuddering beside the eddying Elizabeth as a petty officer climbed the bank to report. Two long-barrelled, heavy-breeched guns aimed out over razor-thin sheets of the crackling-crisp ice formed in the creek mouths and dislodged by the tide. They pointed north, but at no enemy within sight. The foe lay miles downriver, where the narrow, twisting channel, passing forts and points and flats, opened at last into the broad open waters of Hampton Roads.

The guns were *Merrimack*'s, the new Brooke rifles cast for her in Richmond. Lomax had made the case to Commodore Forrest that such fine ordnance should not drowse in storage. He'd mounted them on Dahlgren carriages, scorched but refurbished to serviceability in the carpenter shop, and dug them in behind earthen ramparts where the ship houses had burned down. If the Yankees did stir themselves, they'd get a hot welcome.

In the month since his arrival, the yard commander had sent him first to Richmond. He'd witnessed guns being cast at Tredegar. Seen armor plate being punched in flurries of white-hot sparks. Had stopped at the Exchange, hoping to find Norris in; but his room was occupied by a hide dealer who'd never heard of him. He'd called at the Department, treated Quoddy to rum punch, but failed to find out who would be the new ironclad's captain. And called on Brooke for a conversation about rail lines and flatcars, turnouts and transportation orders.

After which he'd followed sixty tons of new-rolled iron from the Richmond & Petersburg depot on Byrd Street, all the way to Weldon, North Carolina, and back north again on the Seaboard & Roanoke. He'd rowed out to inspect the hulks and pilings that barred the river with General Huger's officers. Had helped set up a naval rendezvous in Norfolk to begin recruiting a crew. And in visit after visit, carrying orders and requisitions back and forth, had become intimate with the hulk that squatted in the cold embrace of New England granite, and with the feverish, clanging activity that went on from before dawn to long past dark, lit by lanterns and pine torches and a haughty winter moon.

The gunner completed his report. Satisfied they were alert and ready, Lomax paced along the seawall. Past jagged stumps where the pier face had caught fire from the torched vessels the year before. Past jury-rigged ordnance shears, *Germantown*'s masts lashed into an inverted W. In not too many weeks they'd sway carriages, guns, shells, and powder down into the casemate.

If all went well.

Which at this moment it did not seem inclined to do. The subject of today's meeting at the commandant's office? Why they had missed their launch date yet again and what was to be done about it.

Boarding the ironclad was like climbing an iron mountain. The gangplank angled steeply up from the stone lip of the dry dock. From atop the casemate he could see far down the river, past the tilted masts of the scuttled hulks to the spires of Norfolk.

Turning, he looked along the reborn *Merrimack*.

Porter called it the spar deck or the shield deck, but what he stood on was like no deck he'd paced before. Metal rang beneath his boots, a grid of two-inch-thick bars and below that beams of solid oak. A spindly rail ran along its edge. Forward rose the boiler chimney, a huge rolled-iron top hat painted mirror-black and well braced with chain. Just visible forward of the stack was a conical pilothouse. Porter had cast it of iron, in one piece. If a shell hit that, Lomax thought, he'd rather be somewhere else. It would probably shatter into a thousand fragments.

He reached the open well of the after hatch. Hesitated, peering into darkness, then twitched his sword aside and climbed down.

The interior resembled the attic of some gloomy European cathedral. It was lit only by the grated glow from above and the spaced rounded apertures of the gun ports. A long, cold, tenebrous, pinch-ceilinged space not yet filled with ordnance and crew but with wood scraps and bolts and boiler parts and the shadows of workmen trudging up and down the ladders. The casemate chamber stretched for a hundred and fifty feet, interrupted only by the black central column of the stack, the smaller columns of the ventilators, and a hoisting apparatus for hot shot. Heavy oaken knees, bolted at their bases between the original frames of the hull, bent in above his head. Eight-inch-thick rafters of yellow pine were bolted solid outboard of them, with eight more inches of oak planks over that.

He reached up to finger crudely threaded metal nuts, hastily daubed with coal tar. The inboard termination of the two-finger-thick bolts fastening her still incomplete coat of iron mail. He tried to envision a force that could penetrate four inches of solid iron and then twenty-four of oak and pine, and could not. The air smelled of resin and paint, pitch, tar, the corner pissing of the laborers, and the afterstench of heated iron from some work Williamson's engineers had been carrying on. Beneath these lay the damp dead whiff of river mud.

He paced forward, rounded the stack, intending to descend the forward ladder and inspect the crew's quarters and spirit room and powder magazine. Instead he came upon a workman perched on an overturned bucket, writing busily on a scrap of brown paper.

A white man whose hands were black as any Negro's. So ingrained with pitch they left inky stains on the screed Lomax snatched from his fingers. The laborer sprang to his feet, fists doubled. —What in the Hell d'you think you're at? Give me that.

—Who are you? Minter asked sharply. —And what is this I find you scribbling so secretly?

He said his name was Farnham Rutledge. He worked for the master carpenter on the pitching gang. He made to snatch the paper back, but Lomax turned away as he scanned it. Pencil on cheap brown stock such as one might use for wrapping nails. His eye caught one sentence.

The Thing certainly is approaching completion and reamains only after section of Iron to be prooff to Shot.

He bared his teeth in triumph. —What is *this*?

—Letter, sir. Just a letter to my brother—

—Rather to some Yankee spymaster. You will accompany me.

—Gentlemen?

He turned, clapping his hand to his sword.

Porter was letting himself down the ladder. Seeing them, his shoulders sagged under a stained black coat. With a weary voice he asked what was going on.

When he reached Quarters A, a servant was leading a roan toward the stables. The yard commander's residence was lofty and narrow, in rose-red brick. Twin iron-banistered flights curved up to the door. Lomax kicked yard mud violently from his boots, still furious at the confrontation with Porter. He threw coat and cap at a servant and stamped down the hall.

In the drawing room, officers and yard officials stood beneath a brilliantly glowing chandelier of intricately faceted glass. Minter counted Jones, Porter—how had he arrived first? He'd left the constructor back at the dry dock—then Meads, the master carpenter, Captain Lee, the yard's executive officer, and Lieutenant Brooke, who must have just arrived, accounting for the horse being led away.

Seeing him, Forrest's writer came bustling over. The flag officer had a delicate task for him, rather personal. Would he mind staying after the conference? Lomax had barely nodded before there was a stir. All came to attention as French Forrest entered.

The commodore was quite old, like every senior officer Lomax had encountered thus far in the Confederate Navy. He'd fought at the Battle of Lake Erie in 1812 and at Alvarado and Vera Cruz in the Mexican War. Forrest advanced with catlike tread, as if still ready to spring onto an enemy's deck. His pale-silver hair flowed over his shoulders, almost covering his epaulettes. His dark, weathered, high-cheekboned features made Minter wonder if back along the line he had Indian blood.

Forrest placed his knuckles on the table and leaned forward under the chandelier. —Gentlemen, we're here to discuss why our launch date has once again been postponed on the *Merrimack* battery. I will call first on Mister Porter as the one personally responsible for the work.

Porter said resignedly, —We are progressing as fast as the iron can arrive, sir. If the original design had been followed, without making necessary three and four repunchings of the same plates, we should have launched a month ago.

—Lieutenant Brooke?

The Confederacy's foremost ordnance designer had pale blue-white eyes, a receding hairline, and a coal-black beard to his chest. John Mercer Brooke wore it so thick his lips were hidden even when he spoke. Yet his voice was clear and perfectly serene. —I can only repeat what I've recounted in my letters, sir. Mr. Porter's original design was neither seaworthy nor efficient. Building so would have been a waste of iron and money. The rudder chain would have been exposed to fire. The plating, too thin.

And the center of gravity? I confess I still do not have the confidence in his reckonings I might have.

Porter flushed. —*You* are the one who increased the weight of iron on her, sir. The mathematics show clearly she will still float, however. If that is actually your question.

Brooke bowed with the courtesy of one finely bred speaking to a mere mechanic. —It *is* my question, sir. I believe you have erred in your calculations of buoyancy as well as in other portions of the work. If she does not actually turn turtle, at the very least she will not be stable enough to trust in anything rougher than a cat's-paw. If you had not cut her down so far, I would recommend adding more ballast. Unfortunately if we did so now, she'd go straight to the bottom.

Porter said angrily, —You may be an ordnance expert, Lieutenant, but now you are interfering in what you do not understand. You have not conducted the great and, if I may say so, skillful calculations of the weights and displacements involved in this piece of naval architecture. *You* have not had to struggle with the many and intricate arrangements for working this novel type of battery. I have.

—Your design was that of a trifler, not at all—

—The commodore has said I am responsible for her success. I am content with his confidence and that of Secretary Mallory. Frankly I neither require nor ask yours.

Forrest looked from one to the other. He started to speak, but then Jones stepped in, explaining some point Lomax could not quite catch, standing at the edge of the group.

The flag officer interrupted at last, steering the discussion back to the launch date. —All I am asking is how to get her in the water as soon as possible.

Porter said hotly, —The delay is not due to my workmen. They have exceeded expectations. No body of men could have done more.

—Despite that some are traitors? Lomax said.

The effect was electric. Every man turned to look his way; a path magically opened, and he stepped forward. The commodore said testily, —*Traitors?* What fol-de-rol is this, Minter?

Bowing first to Forrest and then to Brooke, Lomax explained what he'd found the workman doing. And, more to the point, how cavalierly Porter had dismissed it. Simply read the letter and handed it back to the pitcher, only advising him to rein in his epistolatory urge during shop hours. Jones looked grave, Brooke carefully noncommittal.

—Mister Porter, can you explain? Forrest turned to the constructor.

Who flashed Lomax a virulent glance. —The blacksmiths, machinists, bolt drivers, and finishers are working till eight o'clock each night without extra pay to finish the shielding. Under such circumstances are we to grudge one a moment to sit on a shit bucket and scribble a note to his brother? Mister Minter has the temerity to call this treason.

Lomax shouted, —You call me timorous? You'll answer for that. It's perfectly obvious to whom he was writing and who's shielding him.

Jones laid a quieting hand on his arm. Forrest looked displeased. Lomax mastered himself, but by very little. —You will pay for this insult, he told Porter.

—Withdraw that threat, Lieutenant, Forrest said in a tone that brooked no contradiction.

He hesitated, then murmured something about being carried away. Porter said the man was a steady worker and no more a Unionist than he was. Lomax was about to burst out that if he protected such men, he too was not above suspicion when Forrest raised his hand, like a white-maned Zeus rendering judgment.

—That will do, gentlemen. This is exactly what our enemy would most like to hear. The house divided, as Mister Lincoln has it. As you know the Union has so soothed the British lion over the *Trent* affair that an alliance no longer seems imminent. The outcome of this revolution thus depends on our own works. I believe, in a great degree, on what we are carrying forward here.

—In this great projection, we cannot do without either Mister Brooke or Mister Porter. I will also compliment Lieutenant Minter on his vigilance. However, the fact remains we are far past the date we promised delivery. I will ask Mister Brooke and Mister Porter to closet themselves and work out their differences on paper. He glared at each in turn. —After which they will present me with their proposals for hastening the work. We are not the only ones building an ironclad, but *we must be the first*. There will be no more *improvements* to the plan.

The meeting broke up with an uneasy stir. Lomax began to leave, then recalled the writer's remark. He followed the commodore down a corridor toward an inner office.

Forrest turned suddenly, fiercely. —What d'ye want now, sir? Have you not caused enough trouble? If we lose the workers, we lose all.

—I had understood—a personal matter—

—Oh, yes. Come in.

Forrest rooted through his desk. The note was from Richmond, on telegraph flimsy. The fluent penmanship of the operator scribed out the words.

Latest Boston papers carry information Captain Ker Claiborne of cruiser C.S.S. Maryland has been captured after sinking of that ship in battle with U.S. steamer Potomac. Claiborne confined at Fort Warren pending trial for piracy. Notify Mrs. Claiborne in Norfolk. Assure her the Department will make all efforts to secure his treatment as a prisoner of war.

It was signed by Franklin Buchanan.

Lomax came close to smiling openly. So Claiborne was captured. Not only that, doomed to hang. His glee at the traitor's fix warred with the indignant realization a moment later that if the Lincolnites *did* hang his enemy, he'd die so clothed in glory as to be impossible for any living man to match. What extant hero could compare with an immortal martyr?

—Have you finished reading, sir?

—Commodore, I have.

—You're acquainted with this Claiborne, if I am not mistaken.

—We have served together.

—I should like you to convey this news to his wife, if you would be so kind. Take my barge, if you like.

—Aye aye, sir. Lomax hesitated. —Shall they really hang him?

Forrest grimaced. —If Mister Seward has his way, he may be dangling by the neck this very moment.

Lomax thought bitterly that if he'd been able to sway the crew to his way of thinking in Boston, there'd have been no hesitation about hanging as many of them the nose-talking Puritan Pharisees could lay hands on. But this did not seem to be the time to bring it up. Forrest went on. —Convey to Mrs. Claiborne my regrets at this news. Reassure her we will bend every effort to clarify his status and to arrange, if it is at all possible, that he should be properly exchanged. Offer comfort as you can. You are dismissed, sir. And pray exercise less precipitousness than I have seen from you to date.

Lomax was hard put not to object to such an undeserved affront. But managing to hold his peace, he bowed and withdrew.

That evening he found himself in Norfolk, searching for Freemason Street. He had to inquire his way and push away two drunks who took him for a comrade and wanted to join him. But at last he stood before a two-story house. It had been painted in the not too distant past. An alley beside it led to a garden, trellises, a woodpile. A cow lowed from a grassy plot. He lifted the brass dolphin knocker and let it drop.

The maidservant showed him into the parlour. A coal fire scattered rosy light on waxed pine floors, hook rugs, framed ancestors in uncomfortable-looking stocks and pinch-waist dresses. A little rush-bottomed chair, very old, sat empty by the fireplace. A tad in knickers looked up from his toys. Minter felt the child's gaze climb from his boots to his greatcoat, to the cap he'd just taken off. Then fasten on the scabbard-drag of his sword, just showing under the tail of his coat.

—Lieutenant . . . Minter? I am Mrs. Claiborne.

Her accent was delightfully mild, transmuting her r's into an "ah" and lingering over each syllable. Her dark hair was gathered back. Her dress was dark green as the open sea, with black lace at throat and cuffs, and a little house jacket of the same material, piped in black. The attire of partial mourning. She was unhealthily pale, if such a thing were possible for a gentlewoman. As if all blood had gone, leaving only ivory. He bowed over her glove. —Delighted.

—Betsey tells me you bring a message.

She controlled herself well. Gesturing to an upholstered chair, she perched on a fainting couch. Lomax handed coat and hat to the servant, who disappeared. The boy crept closer to the sword, eyes shining like the coals on the hearth. —Rob, she said.

—Yes, Mamma?

—Leave Mother alone with the gentleman, if you please. She called to the servant, and a moment later the lad was whisked away. The girl came back once more to light a lamp, giving the room outline, depth; then went away again.

Lomax cleared his throat. Suddenly he wanted a segar, though of course it was impossible in a lady's presence. He found himself uncomfortable with this mission. Did she know he'd nearly fought a duel with her husband, not ten months gone? That her Ker, waverer, procrastinator, tardy patriot, had forestalled Minter's getting a command; euchred him as cleverly as any Jew skinning a farmer out of a dime, then stabbed him in the back with a poisoned letter. He couldn't tell what she knew or was thinking. She regarded him with a level gaze, ready, it seemed, for anything.

—For God's sake, delay no longer. Tell me what you have come to tell.

He cleared his throat. —I bring unpleasant news.

She closed her eyes. —He's dead?

—Not so bad as that. He's alive and, so far as we know, unwounded.

He drew out the message. She flattened it and read, giving him a moment to study the effect of the firelight on her hair, the curve of her neck. She was not as unhandsome as he'd first thought.

When she looked up, her cheeks held more color, her eyes more life. He said, —I was asked by Flag Officer Forrest to offer his sympathy and any more concrete assistance he might render. To which I might add my own best wishes if I may.

—This Fort Warren. It is in Massachusetts?

—Off the coast of Boston. It is being used by the Republican government for the confinement of those advocates of peace Secretary Seward wishes to deprive of liberty. As you know habeas corpus is a lost concept in the North.

She said steadily, —And the charge of piracy. Is there base to it?

Lomax teased her a bit. —Piracy is most definitely a capital crime. And as commander he should be the principal in any case.

—I see.

Disappointed at her lack of reaction, he went on. —However, the commodore assures me it has no basis here, and I agree. *Maryland* was a regularly commissioned ship in Confederate service.

—Which means he cannot actually be hung?

Of course he can, and I hope he will be. But aloud he said, —We doubt even Seward would go that far. Unless, of course, there is some substance or element to the charges we are not cognizant of.

—Something . . . dishonorable?

—As I say, ma'am, the details are sketchy at present. But the commodore did not wish you to learn of this from the newspapers, so had me present the message in person.

She smoothed out the flimsy, and he saw how firmly her lips pressed together.

—I must thank you then, Lieutenant . . . Minter, for bringing me this news.

As she gathered her skirts preparatory to rising, he realized he didn't want to leave. Not yet. He cleared his throat. —As you may know, Ker and I were shipmates.

This earned him a glance direct. —So you are actually a friend of his.

Oh, quite the opposite, he thought, but said smoothly, —We have been acquainted for some time. I was about to say: I am stationed at the navy yard, readying the new steam-battery for service.

She was watching him with what might have seemed like great attention. Her eyes, however, were focused not on Henry Lomax Minter but someone else far away. He cleared his throat again, wishing he could gain that attention for himself. —As I said, in the preparation of the armored ram for service. However, it is a mere step across the river. If you would extend me the privilege of calling on you . . . ?

She said rather distantly, —As you see, I am in mourning, and not receiving. I am very sorry.

—Forgive me for not thinking of it. Of course I had observed your bereaved state.

—For our daughter. She died suddenly, soon after she was born.

—Please accept my apologies. I should not have thought of intruding but for my orders. He bowed.

The maid brought his coat and hat. Behind her he glimpsed the bright eyes of the boy again. He raised his voice, said heartily, —This must be the little man Ker spoke of so often. Is it not?

—This is our Rob. Give the gentleman your hand, Robert.

Fitting on a smile, Lomax bent to take the extended small, trustful palm. —And shall you be a sailor too, like your father?

—I want to fight the Yankees, the boy burst out.

—Is that so? Well, I hope by then we'll have them licked for you. But here's a dime for being a true Southron. That is, if your mother says you may have it.

When he looked to her, a faint smile tinctured her pale lips. The lad talked on, half boasting, half imploring attention, his gaze fixed now on the shining silver. While Lomax listened gravely, nodding now and then.

He was already thinking how he could use him.

Outside he stood buttoning his greatcoat, listening to the thud of guns once more, far off, echoing from the houses around him. The artillery at Newport News or the Rip Raps, roaring out their challenge across the Roads. A gage of battle that could not much longer be denied. He would be there in that glorious day when the mailed knight ventured forth.

He found a segar, cupped a locofoco, then lifted his face to the first kiss of falling snow.

Suddenly a great burst of impending delectation filled his breast. His enemy, punished by Fate. Himself engaged in the initiative that would bring victory to the Confederacy, defeat to the scum of the North, and all the renown a man might desire. And more . . . Some further thought teased the edge of his consciousness.

Did he dare? Oh, *that* was not at issue. Lomax Minter turn from risk? The only question was, how would she respond?

At any rate it would help to pass the time.

11

Arrival in a Capital at War ♦ A Moment with Captain Claiborne ♦
Questioning by the Provost Guard ♦ The Members of the Army of Virginia ♦
Failure of an Attempt on Mr. Seward ♦ Conveyance of a Sleeping Powder ♦
A Story of Bull Run ♦ Eyes Like Polished Ice ♦
A Presentiment of Fearfulness

D R. Steele was still many miles out of Washington when he became conscious of the pickets. They stood along the right of way, a youth every hundred yards. Slouchers with slung Springfields and kepis pulled low against the rain. Beyond them sprawled fields of stump-clotted dirt. The hills had been shorn of trees and frosted with tents. And then, beyond them, more. At first he thought it was a camp. But as the train rolled on, hour after hour, and each surmounted hill brought more parks of artillery, more caissons, more lines of canvas-arched wagons, thousands of horses, and mountain ranges of fodder, firewood, coal, lumber, and shells, he realized he was seeing something akin to the migration of a people.

He'd left Fort Warren only days before, released on his written parole of honor as a medical officer and noncombatant. His friendship with Dr. Frothingham had probably helped, as had his consulting on Colonel Dimick's alvine flux. Frothingham had diagnosed serous diarrhoea. He suggested applying leeches to the anus to reduce the peccant humors.

Steele had advised less heroic treatment: calomel purgative, followed by strychnine for its antiparalytic action. Not long after, the fort's commander had called him into his office and proposed he take the oath of allegiance. If he did, his personal possessions would be returned and he would be released to go where he desired.

Steele had thanked him courteously, but declined. At which Dimick had pushed another form forward, which proved to be his parole.

The rail trip down had jostled him against a succession of seat companions. There were sallow, gimlet-eyed, fast-talking Yankees with schemes for getting government positions. Some clutched brown-paper-wrapped parcels that contained new weapons, which each swore would end the war in a fortnight if the army opened its eyes. Others, mostly older farmers and their wives, were coming to visit sons gone sick in camp or wounded at Ball's Bluff; they plied him with earnest questions about specifics for fever. He had a pleasant chat throughout a rattling night with a brawny young woman named Louisa May, of the Concord Alcotts; she was traveling to Washington to serve as a nurse.

He was arriving in the city penniless. Everything had gone during his stay at Fort Warren, bartered to the sutler for dinners and brandy. He didn't know where he was headed after this. Richmond, perhaps, to report himself released and await exchange.

But before then there was something he'd determined to do.

He had waked late the morning of his release, allowed to sleep by the other prisoners who must have tiptoed out for breakfast and then back in. They'd concocted a prank having to do with making him think he'd missed the boat to the mainland and must remain. Now they laughed as he rushed about in a blear, stuffing his clothes into a shoddy bag the sutler had demanded a dollar for. The guards were in on it too and guffawed as he shouted frantically for them to unlock the door.

He was in the open air when he suddenly remembered what he'd resolved to do before departing the island. He stopped so suddenly that Frothingham, who had come to see him off, collided with him from behind. —What is it? the younger physician said. —Did you forget something?

—To look in on my captain.

—He is in solitary confinement.

—I will not leave before assuring myself he is well.

—Colonel Dimick will not permit it.

—Then I shall remain here until he does.

Frothingham looked at their guard, one of the boys who'd brought in the lad who'd shot himself that first day Steele arrived. After a moment the lad shifted his rifle on his shoulder, gaze sliding away. —I got no objection, he murmured out of the side of his mouth. —Long as it's quick.

—A medical consultation, then, Frothingham said. —To get your opinion about the congestion of his lungs. Before we lose your services.

The eastern bastion seemed colder than their own. Perhaps it was only that he was unfamiliar with these somber, echoing granite passages. Finally a door was thrown open. He looked into a small, dim, stone-flagged cell sunk below the ground level. A handful of coal smoldered on a grate. A pale, bearded man glanced up in surprise from a worn Bible.

The next moment they were embracing, slapping each other on the back. —Like Luke, the beloved physician, Claiborne said into his shoulder. Steele stroked his shoulder, slightly overcome.

—I am being released, Captain. On grounds that I am a noncombatant.

—I am glad to hear it, very glad indeed.

—May I look you over before I go? Not that I doubt my esteemed colleague has your welfare well in hand.

The pulse was a bit fast, perhaps just due to the excitement of a visitor. A thickness in the chest, which he auscultated thoroughly but concluded was probably nothing more than grippe. And no wonder, in this dank, chill cell, subject to the hostile gaze of a guard at any hour of the day or night. Ears and eyes were clear. The captain seemed alert but subdued.

—He definitely has lost flesh, Steele said.

—He receives the same rations as you have.

—Doesn't eat them half the time, the guard put in from out in the corridor. They looked at him curiously. —Heard Cookie say so, he muttered.

—How is the state of your appetite? Steele asked him.

—Occasionally flagging.

—Bowel products?

—Firm. Regular.

—I wish I could say the same. And what of your—disposition?

The smile seemed forced now. —I confess to gloomy thoughts at times.

—An iron tonic would perhaps help.

—What would help is mail, and permission to receive visitors.

This last directed to Frothingham, who scuffed his boot toe and looked away. —It is not within his power, Steele explained for him. —Else he would be happy to grant any small indulgence he could.

Claiborne said he knew. Seemed eager to say more, but the guard cleared his throat. —I must go, Steele added apologetically. —The boat awaits.

—Time and tide wait for no man.

A handclasp, merging into one more embrace. As his mouth brushed his captain's ear, he muttered, —I shall not rest until I gain the ear of those who can help you.

Claiborne nodded but did not speak. A moisture glinted in his eye. His lips worked. They parted. He stood in the center of his cell, watching, as with many a backward glance and encouraging wave Steele moved off down the corridor. Till he was lost to view.

The railroad station was crowded with civilians, troops, colporteurs. Smoke and mud were everywhere. He swung himself down clutching the shoddy carpet-bag tight against thieves. He was wedging his way down the platform, wishing he had enough to purchase a dram of refreshment, when he was seized from behind and swung around.

Looking down he found a cocked Colt pointed at his belly. —What we caught ourselves now? a rough voice said.

—Gentlemen?

They were lean, bearded, good-looking boys in jaunty caps; he guessed regulars. Seeing gray hair they decocked the hammer but still held fast. —What sort o' uniform's this, Grandpa? said one, fingering his lapel.

—I'm a surgeon in the Confederate Navy. And you?

The taller soldier, a Westerner, by his accent, spat casually to the side, hitting a passing lady's boot. —Sawbones, eh? Didn't know the fuckin rebs had a navy. We're the provost guard. And I reckon you're fixin to tell us ezackly what'n Hades you're doin here.

Steele touched the watch pocket where he kept his documents. —If I may?

—Just take it slow.

They shoved his parole back. —So you're passin through, like, on your way back to Davisdom.

—Most like.

—Ye'll need a pass to get over the Potomac. And it'd help ye to get shed of that uniform.

—Where would I get such a pass?

—Provost marshal's office. The old Gwin mansion. Not open Sundays, but you can go by tomorrow.

—I may linger for a day or two anyway. I hope to find a way to put in a good word for my fellow prisoners back in Fort Warren. Some of whom are not in the best of health.

The short one grinned. —They won't have long to wait. Jeff better stand from under. Little George's going to go through his boys like a dose of salts though a goose. An' then he kin take the dictatorship and pack Old Abe back where he came from.

—So the army's advancing?

He ignored the question. —My advice: give up your rebel friends. Hang your shingle down in Swampoodle and cure the clap for six bits. You'll make yer damn fortune 'fore the summer's done.

They guffawed and strolled on, eyeing the passersby and occasionally raising a lazy hand to acknowledge an officer.

He stood astonished at the corner of North Capitol and C, the huge brick pile of the B&O station behind him. The first thing that struck him was the drooping festoons of telegraph wire on hundreds of tilting greenwood posts in the process of being sucked down into the mire. The old Cane Factory had become an intake station. Hordes of blue uniforms disgorging from the cars were being herded in that direction. The smoke and smells of cook-fires started the juices flowing in a neglected stomach. Beyond it lay an open plain murmurous with the voices of thousands; with bugle calls, the thunder of cavalry, the popple of musket practice. As if the same great camp that began south of Baltimore ended here, lapping at the foot of Capitol Hill.

The great white pile of which rose over him, lofting above its gray shawl of winter-stripped oaks like the rising moon. The last time he'd seen it, in the spring of '61, the iron dome had been just begun. Now it looked nearly ready for the statue of Armed Freedom that stood waiting in the park. A sublime and inspiring dream . . . but below it festered a city he no longer recognized.

Jostled, Steele galvanized aging, travel-weary limbs into motion. He stumbled over frozen mud, mortar composition, and sinking cobblestones across the ailanthus-lined expanse of Pennsylvania Avenue. Then turned east, drawn by cordial memories of the bar of the National Hotel. But that had been years before, with friends long dead. How in Heaven's name had he got himself into this? Him who'd only and ever wanted to be left alone with Cicero and a hooker of brandy, and not much to do in the way of cutting screaming men into disarticulated corpses.

Horsecars clattered by, packed with officers and well-dressed women. Teamsters maneuvered heavily laden wagons, cracking their whips over the wagging ears of bitter mules. There seemed no end to them, and judging by the way their rims sank into the muck, each was backbreakingly burdened. The dead horses lying with outthrust legs along the avenue testified to the urgency of their movement.

A boy asked him please for a penny, sir. He shook his head savagely. How was he to do what he'd set his mind to when he could not even afford a drink? His hands were shaking. The cold struck straight to his bones. He looked into pie stores and saloons, and searched passing faces for a semblance of charity. But each was cold as the frozen ground. At a corner a grim-looking dragoon eyed him from atop a handsome gray. Steele hurried past with gaze averted and was glad when no command to halt knelled the wintry air.

He was nearing the Center Market when he noticed a line of soldiers standing under a gas lamp on the southern, less inviting side of the street.

One or two were in gray, paroled like himself. All looked shamed and miserable. He thought at first it was a bagnio. Then he made out the sign amid the jumble of advertizements for stores, rooming houses, oyster cellars, and saloons.

Alphaeus Steele smiled to himself despite hunger and cold and his increasing need for a drink.

Perhaps it was not so bad an idea after all.

The name had looked familiar on the shingle, but Alphaeus could not for the life of him say why. The man who confronted him was no one he'd ever known.

Dr. Cornelius Boyle had a face like a thin blade, a District drawl, and a dignified imperial. Perhaps ten years younger than Steele, he received him with sleeves rolled and a dish of mercuric chloride solution at his elbow. The pasty private who was the subject of his attention was standing with trowsers dropped on his insteps, holding his member out between finger and thumb. —What may I do for you, Doctor? Boyle rapped out, jerking back the lad's foreskin.

—It is what I may possibly be able to do for you, sir.

—Sorry, don't need any patent gimcracks. Good day.

—No sir; no gimcracks. But by the looks of your queue you might very well do with an associate. At least until the tide retreats.

Boyle blinked rapidly and chewed at the corner of his mustache as he worked. Steele guessed him to be the kind of man who expressed his excess of nervous animation in all sorts of tics, motions, nail-biting, and the like. —Associate, eh? Any experience in the specialty?

—I have been in medical service in the navy for many years. I daresay I have seen my share of chancres, cordee, and condylomata. Steele put on his spectacles and approached the exposed penis. —But *this* does not bode well.

—What do you mean? The private, barely more than a boy, looked as if he was about to cry.

Steele told him gravely he ought not to have been placing the generative member in unwholesome locales. Had not his officers warned him about such? Had not his clergyman back home? He patted the boy's nether cheek lightly. The combined expertise of himself and Dr. Boyle could most likely heal him this time, given luck, rigid adherence to their prescriptions, and his youthful powers of self-reparation. But no guarantee could be given if he recontracted the malady of Venus.

—Sin not against your own body, my boy. No victory can be greater than that of the ardent man over his passions.

Boyle rolled his eyes. He limped jerkily to a sideboard, and Steele diagnosed a displacement of the hip, most likely congenital. Metal rattled. The private sucked in his breath, then screamed. Men muttered on the far side of a red baize curtain. Boyle waved for Steele to take over. He observed with folded arms as Alphaeus completed the treatment with fuming nitric acid.

When the patient left, his host pulled the curtain closed again. —Your terms?

—I should consider half my proceeds fair, as you are furnishing the office and the medicaments. Steele hesitated. —But I feel I should know you, sir. The name resounds in the mind's ear.

—You will recall the encounter of Senators Brooks and Sumner on the Senate floor some two or three years back.

—When Brooks beat Sumner with a cane. I was en route to Africa at the time but read of it some months later.

—I was called in to treat Senator Sumner's injury . . . and perhaps unfortunately, considering events since, was able to save his life. And you, sir; you are one of us, from your speech.

To Steele's delight Boyle opened a cupboard and tipped amber fluid into glasses. Over a fair medicinal liquor Steele acquainted him with his antecedents and the circumstances of his parole. Boyle nodded, adding that might be another reason he recognized the name. His father had been a clerk in the navy department for many years. Steele inquired about him, but Boyle said he'd died some time back. —I myself was active in the Jackson Democratic Association until the outbreak of war. Attempted to organize a militia group to join Beauregard but was forestalled. Since then I've had to be . . . chary about expressing my political principles. Like so many of our old families in a city that may have outright emancipation forced on it.

Steele blinked. —I had not heard of this.

—It has been moved in Congress. Emancipation for the District of Columbia! Won't that be Hell on earth for the white man. He seemed about to say more but diverted the conversation with a deft flip. —But are you not eager to return to the navy, sir? And to the bosom of your family?

—May I trouble you for just a fluidrachm more, sir? Indebted. I have no family; am a confirmed old bachelor, I fear. As to returning south, I have a grail to pursue in this town—the cause of my imprisoned ship-mates, especially of one who is doomed to be tried as a pirate.

The next morning Steele rose early. He helped himself to a beaker of tolu and codeine to steady his hand and soothe a scratchy throat, then shaved with a scalpel to the tap and hiss of rain on the back window.

Outside it was steaming cold. He bought a used top hat at a slop shop with two of the eighteen dollars he'd earned the night before. Some had come in the strange new "greenbacks." Boyle, seeing him examining them, had commented acidly on them as the final proof of Northern exhaustion. "They cannot back their armies with gold; it has disappeared into the hands of hoarders. The New York banks suspended payment on their notes. So Lincoln simply prints his own!"

"I had understood government paper money to be forbidden by the Constitution."

"Which it is! But does that stop the Dictator? Why, there is his own countenance adorning the thing—and note the sneer of contempt. He floods them out by the printing press, unbacked by gold or silver."

Steele too found the idea of government-issued banknotes ominous. Once the politicians controlled the money supply, what more to make tyranny complete? Musing over these thoughts, and stepping carefully in the rain-softening morass of mire and horse dung, he headed up the avenue to pay his first call.

The partners had worked into the night before the line tailed off. Boyle let him use a cot in a back room and lent him a morning coat in place of his uniform. Both were desperately tired, but they'd had time for a few minutes' chat before Boyle went home.

The younger physician had advised him he could have mornings free, since their patients were engaged in drill then. He could make his calls and return in the early afternoon. As a doctor, Boyle said, he was interested in the movements of the army whose members, both figuratively and literally, constituted the bulk of his practice. If Steele should happen to overhear anything of interest on his peregrinations, perhaps he could do him the favor of passing it along? Which of course he had readily agreed to do.

Past the Hay Market, bustling even this early despite the rain, and the Canterbury music hall. Past the *Evening Star* offices and the Kirkwood Hotel. Then came a mass of small frame houses that looked bedraggled in daylight. No doubt many of Boyle's clientele had picked up their afflictions here. Past Rum Row and the National Theatre, its gaudy flag dripping limp under the downpour. Down the side streets he noted dozens of Negroes milling about. Willard's, with a throng in top hats and raincoats in the brightly lighted lobby. Steele yearned toward the bar but kept himself manfully on course.

At the sandstone mass of the Treasury a gigantic wagon with a siege cannon fully thirty feet long lay hogged in the mud. A twenty-horse team waited in the rain, flirting their tails and adding to the muck. Women in drab pelerines or traveling capes and patent arctic gaiters were alighting from omnibuses. They dragged their skirts around the mired gun to trudge up granite steps between the bronze fascias that held the still glimmering gaslights. Steele grumbled at the sight and stopped to read a bulletin board of war news. Burnside was having difficulty getting his ships over the bar into Pamlico Sound. General Halleck was seizing the property of pro-secessionists in St. Louis. Federal gunboats were shelling Fort Henry on the Tennessee. A new steam battery was to be launched in New York.

Past the Treasury stood a two-story brick house. Its shutters were closed, but the door stood open. Steele mounted the steps and pressed one of the greenbacks into the palm of a son of Eire, who bowed double. —And it's who you'll be after seein', then, governor?

—Secretary Seward, if you please. On personal business.

Men looked back and guffawed. He saw now that the hallway was crowded. ——These gentlemen all have the appointments, sir, the usher said. —Perhap if ye'll tell me yer business.

—Some friends, unjustly imprisoned.

The men in the dry laughed again. Steele bared his teeth, but it only increased the merriment. The Irishman said wheedlingly, —Why then, sir, ye might profit by knowing no matter how long ye wait, Mister Seward will not see ye. But if I may ask, is your friends civilians or military?

—The latter.

—Then I will tell ye this, and for nothing. Mister Stanton, the new man over at War, why he devotes an hour to the public each and every morning. Not many knows that yit but 'tis so. And 'tis Mister Edwin Stanton who handles exchanges of military prisoners. 'Tis just too late today. But if tomorrow ye'll go along the street there, past the President's House, at eight o'clock, why, ye can get there just about in time.

That afternoon his hands grew weary and his head spun as an endless chain trooped through the dingy red curtains. Though his own patients displayed all the symptoms of venereal overindulgence, many of Boyle's looked perfectly healthy. Yet after auscultation, the Washingtonian pronounced them subject to fainting, palpitations, and stoppages of the heart due to ossification of that organ, and wrote out certificates attesting to their unfitness for service. In a moment between callers Steele remarked, —It is astonishing how prevalent the heart disease has become.

—It is indeed, Boyle said blandly. —One might even call it the "faint of heart" disease. It seems to have become quite universal in their army, has it not? From the very top on down.

As they worked on, he noticed too the other physician's casual inquiries as to his patients' camps, regiments, officers, and when they thought they might be ordered to move out.

At last Boyle pushed the curtain closed. He twitched, stretched, grimaced, and scratched as he lit a breva. The smoke cut the smells of copaiva and acid-escharred flesh, and Steele accepted one when presently it was offered.

—Your call upon the smiling Seward. Did all go well?

—I was unable to see him.

—Hear anything about army plans?

—I should have told you if I had.

Boyle looked abstracted, then flinched and finally seemed to make up his mind. —Doctor, I believe you are one of us. I had my doubts when you came to me. There are those who have tried to play the Judas among us.

—One of us, sir?

—I mean, faithful to the Union Democracy and to constitutional liberty. He drew a sealed packet from his coat. —Should you mind attending a female patient, Doctor? A cultivated lady of one of the finest families of the capital. It would be better for both parties if I did not wait on her in person. Convey to her this sleeping powder. Of course there is a gold piece in it for you.

Steele bowed. —No necessity, sir. Any favor I can do you and a lady, I will gladly do gratis.

The smoking brick-pile at the corner of First and Maryland was painted white to the second floor. In the winter gloom brassy light burned between battens nailed over the windows. Shabbily dressed Negroes huddled under the carriage entrance, collars turned against cold rain that poured as if it would never stop. A sentry in shako and belt eyed him as he presented his card. He was passed through after a brief search and a statement that upon his honor he was carrying no communications.

Steele remembered the Old Capitol as a seedy, easygoing boarding-house. Now the grimy hallways were busy with people passing back and forth between the rooms. Most, but not all, were men, and almost all in civilian dress. Some doors were locked; others stood open, showing families sitting within. A great many coloreds loitered about.

It slowly dawned that he was in the Republican Bastille.

The woman who did not rise to greet him had obviously once been handsome, with smoothly parted, graying hair. Now her face was lined with suffering. Her black silk mourning dress was fine enough, but the hem was stiff with filth. Black kid gloves held a shawl drawn close. The freezing room stank of chamber pots and sulphurated fumigant. In the hall women were quarreling in loud voices.

—And who might you be, sir?

Steele introduced himself, adding he'd recently had the honor of being taken into partnership with Dr. Boyle.

—I see. You are—taken into the partnership. That is very good! She laughed. —As you must know, I am Mrs. Greenhow. We are very sorry, but we cannot offer you much in the way of hospitality. How is my good and kind friend?

—Coining money hand over fist, so far as I can tell.

—Well, good for him. Little Rose, dear. Meet a new friend of Mamma's.

Steele bowed to the child, who presented her curtsey like a lady. Mrs. Greenhow invited him to sit. She asked him where he hailed from and seemed delighted to hear he was from her home state. She herself had been born in Montgomery County. Her voice was caressing, and she bent forward now and again to present glimpses down her dress.

—But you men! You have the resource of flinging yourselves across the border. Join the Confederate service and open a way to the redemption of your country. I am sure such has crossed your mind.

—Actually I am presently—

—You can meet our oppressors on the battlefield and wreak a righteous vengeance. But we frail ones have no such recourse. To see our country ruled by hordes and our haughty city cowering under the insolent sway of the coarsest of creatures!

Steele agreed politely. She went on, pressing a glove to her heaving bosom, about the tinkling of a little bell and the pollution of a Yankee prison. But after a time a frown puckered her brow. —You do not wish to examine us, then?

The child beside her regarded him with a cunning surveillance, a cynical and unsettling appraisal far beyond her years. Steele jerked his eyes from hers. —And how do I find you, madam?

Mrs. Greenhow smiled then, slowly, and sat back. —As well as can be expected of one kept close prisoner for five months. Shut away from air and exercise, the intercourse of society; denied all communication with family and friends.

—I am very sorry to hear it of one so charming.

The compliment amused her, but not much. She laughed sadly, tossing her head. —Patience is said to be a great virtue, and I have practiced it by now to my utmost endurance. But every cause must have its martyrs. Charlotte Corday had it: *C'est le crime qui fait la honte et non pas l'échafaud.*

—I fear my French has never been what it once was.

—It is the crime of which one must be ashamed, not the punishment. This crime is theirs. They have suspended every right pertaining to the citizen. Taught our people to condemn the supremacy of the law and to look to the military power. Even should the Southern states be coerced back into their iron-gated new Union—which I regard as impossible— they will need a military dictatorship to maintain their conquest.

Steele sat immobile till she asked him whether something she'd said had offended him. At which he shook himself. —It is nothing, madam. Only that my own feelings are not so clear.

—You cannot be in sympathy with our invaders.

—Not in sympathy. No. He bowed. —It is my shortcoming, madam. The sentimentality of an old man. But if I had my wish, it would be that some way might be found other than slaughter.

Mrs. Greenhow studied him. —Let us tell you a tale I heard after Bull Run, Doctor. The animosity is not ours alone.

—I never thought it was.

—Hear me out, sir. She leaned again, and the worn face shone like a transparency. —One of our friends who had been upon that field told us afterward, after the recoil of the beaten armies on this city, of something he had seen on the right flank of the battle. Two wounded men, a Federal and a Secessionist, were lying side by side. A stump separated them. Over that stump, as they lay wounded and bleeding unto death, they were each attempting to bayonet the other. Every few minutes, too weak for such an effort, they sank back exhausted and dying. But then sat up again and once more each strove to take his enemy's life.

Steele sat silent. No doubt it was true.

—You see, it *is* an "irrepressible conflict." No one and nothing can erase the enmity that lies between us now. No peace is possible ever again. There is no way back. We can only go forward, though it lead through oceans of blood.

He murmured that no doubt she was right. He was an old pettifogger and at any rate had come not to contradict or upset her, but merely to de- liver a sleeping powder. She excused herself while she opened it. He heard a crackle, a rustle.

He said to her turned back, —Perhaps there is something else, madam? I am not at present well endowed with the goods of this world, but if there is anything I can do—

—Visit us again, sir. It is so tiresome here alone. And bring me my mail if you can. You don't know how one's heart grows sick when there are no letters.

When he looked down again, the wrapping had been pressed back into his glove. —You will return this to dear Cornelius? For we are not permitted to retain writing paper nor any implements.

The child giggled as at a game, and once again he caught her cynical smirk. —Happy to, madam, Steele said gallantly.

—Assure him that we are as well here as can be expected and that the prayers of our friends are more valuable to us than fresh air and sunshine. And do visit us again, Doctor Steele. Your very speech brings back delightful memories.

The search as he left was perfunctory, a patting down outside of his clothes. It might have located a revolver, but never came near the crisp scrap inside his top hat.

In the upstairs reception room of the War Department a little, balding, pedantic man in a greasy frock coat leaned his arm on a writing desk as he waited irritably for each applicant to state his business. Steel-rimmed spectacles glittered beneath a hissing gasolier. His upper lip was freshly shaved, and his beard, which looked as if he had just glued it on, encircled the lower part of his mottled, rubbery face like the ruff of a lizard.

It was the morning after Steele's call at the Old Capitol, and this carpeted room of state smelled little better than those grimy cells. Through the windows the Ellipse slumped to the swamp behind the White House next door. A red-headed provost guard with a saber on his hip leaned against the doorjamb. No one spoke except whatever person the little man pointed at, listened to for five or ten seconds, then either approved or, most often, dismissed in a brusque murmur. The procedure went rapidly, and before he had gathered his wits, Steele found himself shoved up in front of the writing desk.

—Name, said Edwin Stanton in a low, soft voice, jotting something and handing the note to the guard.

—Doctor Alphaeus Steele, Confederate Navy. Formerly surgeon of C.S.S. *Maryland*.

After a moment when speech and stir in the room ceased, the Secretary of War said threateningly, —Well, I call this cheek. We do not generally hear applicants of the rebel persuasion here, Doctor. Especially those whom I had understood were still in our custody at Fort Warren.

—Sir, surgeons have always been regarded as noncombatants by civilized enemies. I doubt not this was the ground for my parole.

Blue-green eyes of polished ice, enlarged by spectacle lenses, peered at Steele with loathing. He felt damp seep down his scalp. After a moment the secretary said, —I am not certain I agree with that view. However, I will hear what you have to say. From the celebrated raider? Speak, sir.

—I am the only crew member who has been granted parole. The others are being held incommunicado. It is said they will be tried as pirates. I thought you might be brought to condemn such a miscarriage of justice.

The lawyer's spectacles glittered. —The prize master of the *Enchantress* was condemned to hang this October in Philadelphia.

Steele interposed, —If you mean that as a precedent, sir, with all respect, that case involved a privateer, not a commissioned man-o'-war.

—I will quote the president's proclamation of the blockade. "If any person, under the pretended authority of such states, shall molest a vessel of the United States, such person will be held amenable to the laws of the United States for the prevention and punishment of piracy." The "commission" you speak of is a robber's pretense, sir. Nor is your rebel rag a flag among nations.

Steele felt the animosity about him. He'd understood Stanton to be a Democrat, but it was obvious he'd stepped into a den of lions. He cleared his throat and tried again. —Sir, the men I speak of hold commissions from Richmond. Just as do the many army officers General McClellan has released. Surely it makes no difference whether they carry on their war by land or by sea. Perhaps they too can be—

But the mention of the general had turned the blue-green eyes savage. Stanton cut in, —As proof of my desire to serve General McClellan, sir, I should be willing to lie down naked in the gutter and let him stand upon my body for hours. But *I* am not General McClellan. Nor do I treat traitors and spies with forbearance. That is enough, sir! I cannot imagine how you were released, but let that pass. Your captain is a freebooter and pirate, and will be tried as such. Good day.

—I must ask you to consider—

—I said *good day*, Doctor. As for you, the provost marshal will be instructed in the matter of your overstaying your parole. Perhaps we shall be arranging a hanging right here in Washington. Shall we say, twenty-four hours from now?

Steele felt a hand on his arm, dragging him away; and the next man in line stepped up and began to state his business in a nervous stammer.

Alphaeus stood in front of the White House, buttoning his coat. The air was very keen. A generous hooker of mulled brandy, that was what he needed. He stared blankly at the pillars across the lawn. He'd thought to do something for his captain, for his shipmates. But the rot of tyranny was too far gone.

He shuddered in the wind. Not so cold as in Fort Warren, but mingled with the chill was a presentiment of fearfulness.

The zealots of both sides wanted to wade in blood. But had those who spoke of it so blithely ever *seen* "an ocean of blood"? Stood for hours in it, cutting away pieces of human flesh? Heard a boy scream as his life was pared away with saw and knife, his youth and beauty turned to palpitating, suppurating horror?

He had. And with all his soul, he didn't want to again.

12

Preparations for the Launching of U.S.S. *Monitor* ♦ A Frightened Child
at Play ♦ Proposal of Certain Changes in Design Rejected out of Hand
by Captain Ericsson, and His Reasoning Thereon ♦ Unpleasant Threats
by a Five Points Plug-Ugly ♦ Memories of a Connecticut
Toboggan Ride ♦ Theodorus Hubbard Stands Fast

A MISERABLE, drizzling, icy morning at the bitter end of January.
Theo, following Grandy as the superintendent made a circuit of
the shipway, shivered as his boots splashed through rain-slick
slush. No public announcement had been made, but the crowds had been
gathering since dawn, drawn by the sneers and doomsaying of the penny
press. Hawkers cried the *Herald,* the *Tribune,* the *Staats Zeitung,* the
World, the *Sun.* They preached hot coffee, hot chestnuts, hot rum. Two
steam tugs chuffed in the East River, a stiff northeasterly breeze ripping
dirty smoke off their funnels.

Two weeks behind schedule, but at last they were launching. Inside
the ship house all was bustle and activity, as it had been since he'd arrived
after spending a few hours with Eirlys and his presumptive child.

He'd moved them to a plain but clean boardinghouse rather far up-
town, but at least removed from her former haunts. Eirlys had bought
new curtains and a German cuckoo clock in dark carved oak. The night
before, he and the girl had played jacks as she prepared supper. Lili played
tentatively. She flinched, flighty as a dustbin kitten, whenever Theo made

a reach for the ball. He understood. He was still a stranger. But the child seemed frightened of her mother as well. After supper Theo had lain down (by himself) for two hours before dressing again at midnight and going out into the darkness and cold. To find Continental brightly lit, last-minute painting going on feverishly, and the night crew bolting large wooden caissons under the bow and stern overhangs.

—And what's the point of this, he'd asked Grandy quietly.

The foreman had said around the draggelty ends of his mustache, —Mister Rowland's orders. For extra buoyancy. Not to make a fuss over, all right? He'd just feel better with them there.

—*He* doesn't believe it'll float?

Grandy said reluctantly, —If Cap'n Ericsson says it'll float, it'll float. But I got my orders just like you got yours, all right?

Annoyed, he'd stalked away. Stoked his pipe and smoked furiously as he mulled over the trouble he was in. Gradually it bled from his mind, seduced away by the activity around him. He had not seen the mechanics of a ship-launching before and began asking questions.

The ground ways, which rested on piles driven deep into the marshy soil of Green Point, sloped from the house into the choppy lead of Bushwick Inlet. Workmen with trowels and buckets had coated them during the night with inches of heavy tallow. The sliding ways, a huge cradle to carry the machine into the water, bore the poised mass of the black-painted rivet-studded hull.

He peered up past the gigantic propeller at balks of timber that had been sledged into place between the sliding ways and the battery's bottom. Now, with heavy, echoing, strangely hollow-sounding blows, the workers were knocking out the keel blocks and shores that supported the still-turretless hull. That massive assembly would be installed when the ship was afloat. He inspected the fore-poppets. Climbed to the top of the way, inside the house, where four men sat smoking short pipes beside a pair of two-handed saws embedded halfway through thick pine beams. They explained how they'd make the last strokes in unison, shearing away the last inches simultaneously and freeing the whole immense weight to gravity.

—You think she'll float, though? one asked him. —I've got five dollars says she doesn't.

It was the last straw. He turned away, suddenly angry. Of course it would *float*. He'd checked Ericsson's calculations. His own guilt and doubt concerned what would happen after that.

Because he didn't believe the craft they were getting ready to launch should even put to sea.

The public criticism had nothing to do with it. The dailies were ignorant of any understanding of naval architecture. He'd checked Ericsson's calculations. This involved first determining the center of gravity, which took hundreds of extremely meticulous sums, specifying and then aggregating the center of mass for each major assembly on the craft. Finding the center of buoyancy was less difficult. But as the Swede had warned, finding the righting moment at various angles of heel required advanced mathematics.

Theo had to brush up on this, having lost his grip during years at sea. But he confirmed the inventor's figures for metacentric height and the righting lever. The hull form was unconventional but within acceptable bounds. Her rolling period would be about 12.2 seconds. But he'd gradually begun wondering about what even the shrillest yellow sheet pointed out: the vanishing-low freeboard, its lack of structure above the waterline. All the captain's calculations assumed calm water and zero ship motion. And he'd always said, it wasn't a "ship" but a mobile fighting machine intended for enclosed waters and rivers.

Theo knew that whatever the sea state, the average height on the hull would be the design waterline. This was only common sense; waves were preceded and followed by troughs. But his own experience at sea had finally gotten him to sit in front of the plan and consider what would happen should the "impregnable battery" encounter a storm.

The result of his analysis left him with clammy hands. Buoyancy wasn't the problem. And up to a certain extreme angle, the raftlike craft would be stable.

The difficulty was that a heavy enough sea could flood it in seconds.

The top of the raft wasn't a "weather deck" in the sense of a spar deck on a man-o'-war. In any sea above two feet it would be awash. But so long as the sea was sealed out, she'd plough through, mostly underwater but still perfectly seaworthy.

The problem was the turret.

This two-hundred-thousand-pound construction of laminated iron was twenty feet in diameter but only nine feet high. Theo found Maury's *Physical Geography of the Sea* in the Continental design office, and made sure of his figures. He closed it with hands shaking. A twenty-foot wave would sweep from stem to stern. It would dump tons of water down engine intakes, smoke pipes, pilothouse. The flooding would decrease the righting moment and increase the angle of heel. At some point she'd roll far enough to take the sea in through the top of the turret.

Anyone trying to get out would have to fight his way upward against tons of inrushing sea. There'd be no other way out save for the removable plate that roofed the forward pilothouse. And it would be beneath the surface by that time.

His calculations pointed to only one outcome: everyone aboard would die.

He'd sweated for hours over his solution. His drawing showed a low forecastle of thin plate extending back from the stem. Hollowed bows would turn back oncoming seas. He extended the engine room air intakes from six to twelve feet high, moved the wheel and captain's station from the bow to the turret, built a wooden pilothouse atop it, and designed a telescopic smoke-pipe that would prevent seawater from dousing the fires even in a whole gale. He'd checked it one last time and taken it in to Ericsson.

Who had handed him, the moment he entered, a letter from Secretary Welles attached to one of his own. Theo ran his eyes down them, distracted by the scene he'd shortly have to bring onto the stage. Welles had asked Ericsson for suggestions as to the new craft's name. Ericsson had proposed *Monitor,* both for its warning to the rebellious South and to European powers not to intrude themselves into a domestic war.

He took a breath and bit the bullet. —Sir, very interesting. A most apposite choice of name. May I say something on another subject? Relating to several very minor modifications you might wish to consider.

For once Ericsson listened, chin propped on his fingers as he studied the drawing, listening to Theo's explanation and his plea that in the interests of safety they be incorporated into the design.

The old man spun his chair to face the window. He mused over it for minutes that Hubbard found very long indeed.

At last he said, —We will make no changes. To do so would cause too much delay.

—Sir, I believe not. I've taken the liberty of consulting with Mister Rowland on riveting up a light forecastle structure and so forth. I understand the need for timeliness. But there is also—

—You do not, Hubbard. Delay will not only cost us our progress fees and possibly any follow-on contracts. It may cost the Union the war.

Theo fought to keep his voice neutral. As engineer superintending construction, he had to certify progress for Ericsson's fees to be paid. With any other man that would have earned him some measure of deference. But Ericsson believed his invention so necessary, and his Consortium so politically powerful, that anyone in uniform became just another obstacle. He had to keep this discussion on a rational basis. Given the inventor's insanely suspicious nature, seeing cabals and conspiracies everywhere, it was the only way he might carry his point. —Sir, if anything untoward occurs, this machine can no longer aid the Union in any way whatsoever. Certainly the Navy will not pay—

Ericsson stiffened. Too late, Theo remembered he knew how spiteful the Navy could be. When the Stockton gun had exploded on *Princeton,* killing the secretary of state, the secretary of the Navy, and five others, it had blamed Ericsson even though he'd had no hand in the gun's design. He spoke rapidly, sensing his chance slipping away. —I've spent years at sea. It's difficult for the landsman to believe, or the designer to quantify, the forces we encounter there—

—Pish! Don't pull this seaman's hocus-pocus, Hubbard. I understand what the sea can do. You forget I was on my *Ericsson* when she was blown on her beam ends and sank because some seamanlike *fool* forgot to secure the ports on the freight deck. Now—look.

He pulled down a scroll from a vast bin of them above his drafting table. Flattened the fine tracing cloth, and cast it out contemptuously in front of his viewer.

To Theo's bemusement the diagram, done with the same meticulous care as the one he'd seen the first time he came into this room, showed the guns aimed fore and aft within the turret rather than abreast. It also showed high telescoping ventilators and smoke-pipes, two more main-deck accesses, water drains around the base of the turret, and a pilothouse mounted atop it rather than on the main deck.

—But . . . why did you not stay with this design, sir?

—I assure you, I've thought this through. I have had thirty years to think it through. His voice turned sarcastic, the schoolmaster to the class dullard. —Why do *you* think I took these features out?

—To save time in construction?

—That is the wrong answer. It is because if I put them in, some brave and stupid naval imbecile would be sure to take it to sea.

—Sir, according to the need, they *will* take it to sea. That is what American seamen do. No matter what you have designed her for.

But Theo knew he'd lost because the inventor went on, —Seal it properly, and the—*Monitor*—will take a short tow in reasonable weather. Regardless of what you or Isherwood or your entire hidebound, pompous, totally *ignorant* service thinks. I know they're croaking in Washington about another Ericsson failure. Is that not what you're reporting, what you're telling these newspaper jackals behind my back?

Theo faced an inimical glare, a brow of iron. He tucked his hands behind him. —Sir, you are doing me an injustice. I have only your interests in mind. That, and the men who'll sail this new craft into battle—

—Pah. Enough. The inventor turned away, and his harsh breathing signaled his displeasure. —I have no further need of you, sir. I believe you know where to find the door.

He was making his way toward the ship house when his arm was seized. He spun impatiently, expecting another workman, another last-minute problem.

But this huge figure towered above him. By his lumpy red complexion and broken nose, a pugilist or brawler, some sort of tavern slugger. His long, thin mustache lent his face an Asiatic look. His coat was too tight, as if taken by force off some better man. His lifted cap revealed hair like black hog-bristle. Yet his address was respectful enough. —Chief Engineer Hubbard?

—Yes, Theodorus Hubbard.

—The handle's Hyer, Mister Hubbard. You might have heard a me.

Theo had, and who indeed had not? In 1849 the "Young American" Tom Hyer had destroyed "Yankee" Sullivan in sixteen rounds of bare-knuckle battering in a violent and illegal match that had scarcely stayed one step ahead of the police and militia of two states. Not a saloon in New York lacked a lithograph of that epoch-making battle. With more consideration he said, —Mr. Hyer. I have indeed.

—I have an acquaintance named Amos Eno. D'ye know Mister Eno?

—I do not.

—Mister Eno owns Schweitzer's Garden and a good many more properties about town besides.

Theo glanced toward the ship shed. —What exactly is this about, Mister Hyer?

—Call me Tom. It's about Miss Pinnell. You know her, if I ain't mistaken?

—Miss Pinnell? He turned back from the launching way, his attention engaged now. —What about her?

—Point is, a contract was made between her, when she come to New York looking for a situation, and Mister Eno's organization. Which I am here on behalf of.

Theo said, —I must set straight some misunderstanding here, Mister Hyer. I knew Miss Pinnell long before she came to this city. We were . . . close friends back in Hartford.

—True love ain't nothing to laugh at. Far too rare in this shitty world.

He dropped his hand when Theo didn't take it. —To business then. My message is, you're welcome to buy Miss Pinnell out of that forementioned contract I mentioned.

—I have no intention of paying anyone anything. Her activities for this "organization" you mention were criminal and illegal, and she's well out of it.

—Not arguing with you, little friend. But the point is, you got to furnish the rhino if you wishes to pop the jomer. Hyer looked toward the dignitaries on the platform. —I understands you give her quite a bit of chink. Wonder where'd it come from? Well, that ain't my business. But Elee Pinnell's safety is.

—She's safe where she is.

—Up on Sixty-first, you mean? For a thousand dollars she will be, Hyer said. —Otherwise, she and the girl—why, you might find 'em beat to death some fine day. Don't like it myself. But Mister Eno can't have folks welshing on their understandings.

Theo didn't believe anyone had advanced Eirlys a thousand dollars. But the sudden, naked threat riveted him.

—Mister Hubbard! Time to launch! Grandy, waving him toward the ground way.

—You're a busy man. I respects that. Escuse me; we'll talk later.

The shoulder-hitter tipped his plug hat again, turned, and was swallowed by the crowd, leaving Theo staring after him, fists doubled.

And now it was time for the machine to face its first test. Atop the wide down-tilted flatness of the raft, the roof beams of the ship house close above his head, he stood with chin raised and cap brim pulled down in the regulation manner. Outwardly self-possessed but inwardly a pudding of suet. The great doors framed the gray light outside and the cold-looking water that awaited. Rain poured down like a curtain. Under a canvas awning the band was crashing through the last slow notes of *The Star-Spangled Banner.*

Abreast of him in a loose rank stood those other few brave souls who'd ride her down the ways. Worden, the thin, womanish lieutenant, had just been released from hospital after seven months in a Confederate prison camp. For some impenetrable reason the Department had sent him, not home to rest and recover, but to command of the new battery. Mr. Greene, the exec, only twenty years old. Mr. MacCord. Mr. Barnes. Mr. Bushnell. Mr. Delamater. Mr. Rowland.

And, of course, John Ericsson. The old misanthrope stood in frock coat and top hat at their very head, near where tomorrow the turret would be swung aboard. It was barely possible they might meet their delivery date. Which would extricate Theo from a disagreeable hole, since at the Consortium's urging he'd approved as acceptable all the work done so far.

Was it conceivable Eirlys had actually signed some sort of agreement with this Eno? More likely it was simple extortion. Yet the threat was real. He could not protect her, nor the child, short of living with them. And that he could not do. It would put paid to any hope of ever making a respectable marriage.

For a moment he contemplated paying. A thousand dollars was just about what he had left of the letter of credit. Then he realized that if he did so, it would be only the first installment.

On the other hand, he couldn't afford not to. Lili was his. Her dreamy look, her already short stature, the loose curls testified to that. His very own face when he'd been small.

Shouts came from below. He heard Grandy's frenzied bellow, the nasal whine of saws driven by brawny arms.

A tremor buzzed through iron and wood. His knees felt watery. He bent them in case something should give way. They wouldn't have much chance if it did. But he'd inspected ship way and ground way, and gone over Grandy's calculations. They should hold.

When he looked up again, the walls were moving past. It did not seem as if they were sliding downward. Rather that the door was growing larger, the icy light brighter. The tremor became a rocking motion. The flags at bow and stern lifted.

Like riding a gigantic iron toboggan. Memories of childhood in Weatogue, the hill out back of the farm. The bent hickory staves beeswaxed. Curved snow falling away to the blue shadows of the woods. Being scared, and excited too. The crisp air pressing his cheeks.

A brush of rain, of cold wind. The opening sky. And a swelling, tumultuous hush as not a person in the whole immense crowd but held his breath. The river rushed toward them, faster and faster.

The curved prow, bearing the proudly fluttering Stars and Stripes, struck the water at full speed with a terrific splash. Parting breakers rolled out into the cove. Then the sea surged back, covering the still-descending stem. Theo's gaze riveted as it vanished, driven on and downward beneath the boiling surface by the unstoppable landslide of black iron and oak behind it.

Frame eight, frame ten, frame twelve followed it into the greasy-looking, gray, roiling river.

A gasp of horror susurrated through the multitude as the flag itself disappeared, sucked under in a tossing maelstrom. Beside him Rowland took a step back. Yet where could they go? In a moment they'd be swimming for their lives as the overweighted iron continued down to the muddy bottom of the East River.

Then the angle lessened beneath his boots. The stern dropped off the way with a booming crash and a blue cloud of grease smoke. The poppets crunched and splintered as she pivoted up off the last support.

With a tearing roar the huge iron drag chains began thundering out, braking her career toward the opposite shore. He felt a queer weightlessness; then pressed heavily down into his boots; then was light again. The wave of her acceptance rolled back from the shore and broke against the arc-pointed bow, which rose now from its baptismal immersion, shaking off the salt spume to lift staff and flag back up into the opal light. A transparent surge of water and fine ice a foot high rolled aft. It lost velocity as it came, though, and subsided at the caps of Ericsson's solidly planted, square-toed boots. Nor had the effeminate-looking Worden failed to stand fast.

The silence turned solid with cheering, the hoots of tugs and ferries, the renewed brassy banging of the band. The flag snapped off bursts of spray in the winter breeze. Caps lofted in the air, fell, were thrown up again in a turning fusillade. Theo stood sweating, shaken. Yet he had not taken a step back.

13

Two Days on the Cars ◆ A Struggle with Melancholy ◆ Wythe Hall in Winter
◆ An Ailing Father ◆ Visit to the Confederate Congress ◆ An Audience
with the Honorable Mr. Robert A. Toombs ◆ The Politics of Exchange ◆
Gold Above Honor ◆ The Broaching of Retaliation ◆
The Duty of a Wife and Mother

CATHERINE pulled her shawl about her and Robert as the cars
swayed and pitched. There was no coal in the stove. The vibrating
floor was covered with straw and tobacco spittle and segar ends.
The soldiers around them were respectful; they lifted their hats when they
looked in her direction. But they hooted and yelled over their card games,
smoked and spat every minute they were awake, and their muskets were
continually falling over with startling crashes from where they'd propped
them against the seat backs. She hoped none were loaded. Some great military movement must be going on. It had been difficult arguing her way
aboard even with her ticket, and the conveniences at the station stops
were so filthy she could barely bring herself to use them. In these days of
war fewer people took the cars, and now she knew why. If not for a truly
momentous errand, she would have preferred to stay at home too.

But having one's husband subject to being hung . . .

In the weeks since Minter had brought the news, she'd written to
everyone of influence she could think of. The responses had been meant
to soothe but had not had that effect. Wait, pray, leave matters to those in

charge—such had been their message. She'd tried, but without success. Taking care of Robert, the sewing circle, and the Saint Cecilia Guild seemed more and more like looking away from her plain duty to Ker.

She could wait no longer. Her father, the Judge, had retired years before but still had many acquaintances active in the new government. And if he could not, then perhaps what she carried beneath chemise and corset and corset cover and chemisette, a solid knot riding heavy above the void that still ached now and then within her, might sway the balance.

Across from her, Betsey snored. Catherine traced the familiar lineaments of her servant's face. The delicate nose, the high, Egyptian-looking cheekbones.

Betsey's mother and her mother's mother had been with the Bowens and then the Wythes from time out of mind. She was the light chocolate of many house servants. She was not so obedient as Catherine would have liked. But one put up with such failings as with any other member of the family. She didn't mess about with men, which was all to the good. When she'd started having her courses, she'd come to Catherine about it as a daughter would have, and gotten the same care and advice.

Really, she didn't see what those who ranted about how abused the colored folk were in the Southland had in mind. Afric and white had lived together for two hundred years in Virginia without trouble or envy—unless it was brought in from outside, as by that madman Brown. From what she'd read about their treatment up North, if she'd been born dusky, no question which side of the line she'd choose.

—Feeling better, Mamma?

She smiled down. —Is my little soldier awake?

—I tol' you, I'm not a soldier. I'm a sailor. Like Daddy an' 'Tenant Minter.

She smoothed his amber locks. The boy persisted. —It doesn't hurt now, does it?

—Not so badly as it did. No.

She lifted her head, determined not to slip back into the slough of despond. That valley of shadow from the depths of which she'd cursed God Himself and rejected the message of Christ's resurrection. She could not give way to it. Nor let Ker languish in durance vile. Not without bending all her efforts in any way she could.

—What is earth, sexton? the boy chanted, looking out at the passing fields. —A place to dig graves. What is earth, rich man? A place to work slaves.

It was a poem from an old copy of *Merry's Museum* she'd read to him. She said as gaily as she could manage, —What is earth, gray beard?

—A place to grow old.

—What is earth, miser?

—A place to dig gold.

—What is earth, soldier?

—A place for battle.

—What is earth, herdsman?

—A place to raise cattle.

He giggled and put his face down. She rubbed his cheek, so soft. Said into his ear, —What is earth, monarch?

—For my realm, 'tis given.

—What is earth, Christian?

The little boy murmured, cuddling into his mother's lap, —The gateway of Heaven.

At Church Hill old Tom's eyes lit when he opened the door. She kissed his grizzled cheek as he laughed, hugging the little boy. —Lorzy, Miz Cathery, he gets more bigger ever' time we sees him. Sure is good to see you back on your feet.

—I am feeling a bit more myself.

The house felt more welcoming now than when she'd lain here trying to understand where her little girl had gone. Once more it was the great warm home she'd grown up in. Once when she was Robert's age she'd asked her father if she could not stay forever. He'd said tolerantly that she'd want to leave one day, when she got married; but that for all of him, she could stay till the Trump of Judgment blew.

Her mother enfolded her and the boy, then held her to search her face. —You look more composed then when you left us. How are you feeling?

—Better, Mother.

—Are you sleeping all right? Taking your medicine?

She'd stopped taking the drug Dr. Lassiter had prescribed. It made her feel too attracted to death, and aside from that, quite stopped her up. She told her mother she no longer needed it, that she had too much to do at home to lie around. This seemed to be the right answer, and Mrs. Wythe went on, —Your father's been asking around about what we might do for Ker. He's not feeling well, though.

—Ker?

—Your father. He's upstairs. He wants to see you, but don't tire him. All right? Her mother kissed her again, then whisked Robert toward the kitchen-house to see if there was any angel's bread.

Judge Thomas Wythe lay with white hair frizzled out from beneath his bed cap. A cup of her mother's vanilla racahaut was on the bed table, with his glasses, the artificial teeth he had so much trouble with, and a tattered copy of Burns. She was backing out when he opened his eyes. Stretched out his hand. —Come in, daughter.

—I didn't mean to wake you, Father.

—I was awake. He turned his head away to fit the teeth, then added, more intelligibly, —And I've been active on your behalf.

He swung his legs out of the tall old bed, grunting, and she glimpsed withered calves under his nightshirt. She knew now not all families were as happy as hers had been. That wasn't all due to him, but much of it was. It wrung her heart to see him aging, and she waited in the hallway as his man dressed him, then accompanied him downstairs.

He craned around the library. —Did you bring Robert? Where's my favorite grandson?

—Azruiss has him in the kitchen-house. Mother said something about angel bread. Azruiss was Betsey's mother, a vast presence whose sausage croquettes and brunswick stew had fed the Wythes for almost forty years.

Wythe rumbled his throat clear and settled behind his rolltop. Rubbed his spectacles with a polishing cloth. Behind him hung his beloved Teniers, Dutch drinking scenes given him by a former governor. Also his diploma from the University of Virginia and various awards from the bar association. In the place of honor, the cavalry saber his grandfather had worn when he signed the Declaration of Independence. —Now. Ker. Have you heard from him?

—Not a word.

—I've made inquiry among my friends. Governor Wise, Mister Tyree, and others. I've also written to a gentleman in Boston I argued an intriguing case with once. An abolitionist, but not a bad fellow withal. I asked him to see if he could visit the fort and send a report to us by means of a fellow who raises gamecocks.

—What did he say, Father? Did he see him?

Wythe said unwillingly, —Well, I have nothing from him as yet. The man who raised the cocks may be in the army. Who knows. . . . Here's what I have so far. Army prisoners of war in recent battles have been exchanged on the field. Private arrangements, between the commanders. A private for a private. A major for a major. There's been talk of a more formal exchange. General Huger's attempting to open negotiations with General Wool. Unfortunately the venomous Lincoln fights every mention of parole.

—But why?

—Why? It grants us recognition as equals in war, child; and he's determined to continue his charade of treating this revolution as an insurrection and branding us as rebels and traitors.

Tom brought in a tea tray with hot scones. Wythe nodded to him and went on, —The Congress, in Washington I mean, takes a more reasonable view. But everything discussed so far pertains to the army. Naval matters are not so easily regulated.

Her father went on gravely and ponderously that he wished they knew more about the conditions of his imprisonment. —Are they healthy? Is he reasonably fed? Clothed? It *is* winter, in Massachusetts. If they were such as to threaten life, I hope he'd have the good sense to take the oath, resign his commission, and await the arrival of peace, either in New York or overseas.

Her father tipped his head to one side in a gesture she knew. Waiting for her reaction, perhaps her outrage. She preserved her demeanor and he went on, —A more honorable course would be his accepting release on parole. Giving his word not to fight again until he is fairly exchanged, one for one, with our own prisoners of war. Perhaps those General Winder is holding at the old Enders factory, what they're calling Libby Prison. He hesitated, looking away. —But he may not be granted that choice.

—Parole would be best, then. Can that be done?

—That is about where I had gotten before this damned liver attack. It put me down for a few days, I don't mind telling you.

She said she placed herself in his hands, but he was not to exert himself when he was ill. —If you'll tell me whom I should approach, I'll wait on them.

—You and scores of others, I daresay. Out of the question; I am not so sick I can't lay myself out for my loved ones.

—Mother would never forgive me.

—I imagine she will. I feel stronger today. And don't tell her this, but I can't stomach another bite of that damned racahaut she makes when we're sick. Are you ready, then?

He heaved himself up, reaching for a bell. When the old servant appeared, he rapped out, ——My cane, Tom, and order round the carriage.

The Senate was in its first session. Wythe could not help looking in; Catherine knew he still thought of the third seat on the left as his own. He'd arranged for them to call on the Honorable R.M.T. Hunter, the senator from Virginia. The ten minutes' interview was cordial though unenlightening, but Hunter gave them a note of introduction to Robert A. Toombs. The great Georgian, whose fiery speech as he quitted the United States Senate had been carried in every newspaper in the country, was secretary of state in the new government. Hunter said he was possibly one who could treat with Seward about prisoners of war on the basis of equality of office.

Toombs was in when they called, a muscular, fattish, rumpled gentleman with dissolute-looking eyes. His cravat was not properly tied. He was signing at a great rate documents that a secretary was putting before him. Wythe introduced himself and Catherine, and explained their business between Toombs's scrawlings of his signature. At last he spoke. His voice was low and forceful, almost a growl.

—Judge Wythe. I believe we last met at the president's funeral.

He meant old John Tyler, who'd died in the city two weeks before and been buried with great solemnity in Hollywood Cemetery, overlooking the James.

The secretary took himself off, and Toombs threw himself back with a sigh. —I am glad to see any friend of Senator Hunter's, Judge, and will be delighted to do you any service I can. But I shall not be here long, sir. I can render more valuable service on the battlefield.

Her father said, —That is certainly where men who value their liberty belong in these troubled times.

Toombs eyed him. —Those of us who still possess the vigor of youth, of course. It is men like you who should be in my seat, sir.

—You are too kind. It is for one of those who served in battle that we inquire.

Toombs forced loose lips into a thoughtful pout. —His wife was here inquiring about him earlier.

Catherine, startled, began to speak. Her father, frowning, beat her to it. —His wife, sir? My daughter here is his wife.

—Your pardon; a young lady from Petersburg. Or perhaps it was about someone else—clearly it was someone else. I see *so* many these days. Toombs hurried on. —And you, ma'am, you are not in want at present, I trust?

—I am receiving an allotment from his naval pay, thank you.

—We are capable of taking care of our own, Wythe said a little sharply.

—Of course you are, Judge. Nothing adverse was intended by my inquiry, Toombs said. —As to Lieutenant Claiborne's situation. This is a matter larger than one man, though— he bowed to Catherine —I comprehend your concern for *that* one man. I will try to be clear. If I fall into legal obscurity, perhaps the judge can assist me.

—I've explained to her about the exchanges the army has been doing. And she knows about parole and so forth.

—Very good. But the difficulty in Lieutenant Claiborne's case is that he does not seem to be in military custody.

—How is that? she asked.

—I suspect from what the Northern papers are saying that he is committed under what passes for the civil power now; confined under a *lettre de cachet* from Secretary Seward.

—This is not welcome news, Wythe said in a low voice.

—No sir, it is not.

She murmured, —It was Seward who branded him a pirate.

Toombs wouldn't meet her eyes. —That's the fly in the ointment, my dear. *Habeas corpus* is a thing of the past at the North. Seward and the Ape can commit whosoever they like to indefinite imprisonment, simply on suspicion of "disloyalty" —which is whatever they choose to define it as. If your husband is tangled in *that* web, it will be very difficult to extricate him. And, yes, he has expressed to several newspapermen the intent to try the *Maryland*'s crew for piracy.

Catherine said, —But he's in the navy.

Toombs nodded. —Operating as a raider, which up to now has been a legitimate means of war. That is our position. Yes.

Wythe said, —While theirs is that as we are no sovereign state but simply an assortment of insurgents, what we style a navy cannot be one, nor even a privateer organization.

—Exactly so, said Toombs. —Needless to say, if their view prevails, it would not have a good effect on our naval recruitment. But I don't think that makes this a matter for Mister Mallory. I will not play you off. Nor will I attempt to hide from you, ma'am, that your husband is in grave danger.

She said she knew that; told him about the lieutenant who had brought her the news, and what he'd said about the possibility of hanging. Toombs looked even more uncomfortable. —That is the traditional punishment. However, the little information reaching us is that the ultimate charge may or may not be piracy as such.

—That's good, isn't it? If it's something else?

—Not if that something else is murder or violation of the laws of war, the secretary said. —Or all three. Ker's raid on Boston knocked down a hornet's nest. They may do as they like in North Carolina and Florida, but the boot does not fit on the other leg, it seems.

She fished in her muff, and both men stirred. Expecting her to draw out a handkerchief and begin wailing, no doubt. Toombs said, —Be strong, Mrs. Claiborne. The difficulty is, as yet there *are* no charges. It's what the king used to do, imprison men without bringing specifications. And they accuse *us* of overthrowing the Constitution . . . To return to Ker. I have set matters in motion to elucidate the situation. If he's being held as a military prisoner, he'll be under the purview of Secretary Stanton. If he is under Seward's seal, the matter will be more difficult of penetration, as I said.

Catherine had taken the pouch out from her bosom at home, carried it in the carriage concealed in her muff. She now placed it on Toombs's desk. It jingled, a terse metallic ring. The secretary went tense. —And this is?

—Nearly a thousand dollars in gold. I have mortgaged my home and withdrawn what we have in the bank.

The men looked astonished, Toombs close to outrage. Her father said urgently, —I had no idea she intended this, sir—

—It is out of place—

—Catty, put your money away. This is most inappropriate. She is bereft, sir. Lost a child recently, under a doctor's care—

—I intended it to be used to help him—

At last they persuaded her to put it away. She persisted, though. —What then can we do? If you will not take my money.

Toombs rolled his great head like a wrestler. —First let us hope for peace. The recent news from the west is unsettling, true. But it is probable that other initiatives now in train will resolve hostilities in a manner favorable to us. And at no distant date. In which case, your husband's difficulty will resolve pleasantly as part of a general settlement.

—But if it doesn't?

—We have already attempted to win the release of these prisoners. There has been no response to our communication.

—You cannot intercede officially? A personal note to Seward?

Toombs told her, —I cannot imagine it would do any good, Mrs. Claiborne. Indeed, by showing we value your husband, it might so incite the vengeful spirit of the Black Republican cabal against him as to make any thought of parole impossible.

—Then I will go myself, Catherine said. —I have heard gold is rated above honor in the North. If that is true, perhaps my arguments will have more weight there.

They regarded her aghast. Her father spoke first. —That is quite impossible, Cathery.

—I am not proposing to undertake a bayonet charge, Father. Only a trip to Washington. She asked Toombs, —If that is not contrary to what I am permitted.

—I am unaware of any law human or divine forbidding a wife to beg clemency for her husband, Toombs said slowly. —Though you run the risk of falling into Seward's grasp yourself. Incredible though it sounds, he has jailed ladies. He spread his hands. —You are pressing me hard. We are as concerned for your husband as you are. What would you have me do? Tell me and I will comply.

She'd pondered her reply to this question since before she left Norfolk; had been considering it on the train; had thought of it anew when her father had explained the exchange policy to her. So that now she felt quite cool as she said, —We offer their men, whom we take prisoner, good treatment. Do we not?

Toombs thrust a tongue into his cheek, frowned, as if she'd spoken in Tonkin or Japanese. —I beg your pardon?

—We hold prisoners too. In the old Enders warehouse, my father says. And no doubt elsewhere.

—We do.

—Officers?

—We hold army officers at Libby, yes.

—Are they placed on trial? Subject to hanging?

—Of course not.

—Then I suggest you intimate to Secretary Seward that if my husband is hanged, one of theirs of equivalent rank will die. A major will do quite well. Someone related, perhaps, to one of the better families up North.

Toombs stared at her for some seconds. —You understand this strains the meaning of parole and exchange.

—It seems to me it is Mister Seward who is doing the straining.

—It is an uncivilized expedient. Even barbaric, Wythe put in.

—I call that an understatement, Judge. Hostages . . . reprisals . . . It puts us back to the . . . thirteenth century, perhaps. We are not Mongols, after all.

She said, —But if after we argue for fair exchange and fair treatment, we get nowhere . . . surely we cannot allow them to hang a man simply because he fought at sea rather than on land.

—True enough. Toombs weighed it, and her, for a few seconds before turning to her father. —They truly are more . . . *direct* than we, are they not, Judge? Heaven help us should they ever gain the reins of government.

Well, ma'am, I will ponder whether there may be anything in your suggestion. Repugnant as it may seem at first hearing.

—That is all I ask.

—I shall make you a bargain, the Georgian went on. —I shall think whether your proposal to . . . *dissuade* Mister Seward from executing our men by threatening his own has merit. However, you are not a man. Your calling is higher: that of wife and mother. Fulfill your home duties, as your husband is fulfilling his in the field, mine in the administration, and every one of us what appertains to his rank and station in this time of trial. Return home. Raise your son. And pray.

Her father put in anxiously, —He's right, Catty. You could be subject to insult. Even to outrage. It's no longer my place to forbid it. You're a grown woman. But I warn you, it would not be wise.

She sat with eyes downcast, knowing that was the proper way. Yet something in her breast, uncertain, as yet unincarnate, struggled against it. She felt again the stubborn anger that had cried out against an unfeeling Heaven. Yet she only sat waiting as Toombs went on with reassurances and words of hope and cheer. Till at last it was time to rise with a rustle of skirts, dignified in the knowledge of her privilege and birth and sex; and let him bow her out.

14

First Draft of a Prospective Crew ♦ A Menacing from the West ♦
The Ericsson Impending ♦ Precious Iron and Desperate Dreams ♦
C.S.S. *Virginia* and News of Her Commander ♦ The Night in Norfolk ♦
The Soft Earth of a Truck Garden ♦ A Profession of Friendship

THE troops shambled into a loose line, barking their pates on the beams of the old sailing frigate. The *Confederate States*, late the famous *United States*, was the only ship unburned when the general government abandoned Norfolk. Her new owners had anchored her rotting hulk a cable's length off the waterfront, run up the Stars and Bars, and pressed her into service as a guardo, store ship, and, most recently, berthing and training platform.

Lomax shouted, —Gun-captains, tell off your crews.

Old Ben Sheriff swore the men into their positions. A Baltimorean, he'd deserted from U.S.S. *Allegheny*. Sergeant Charlesworth, Confederate Marines, was holding forth at one of the other ports. These aside, hardly a one of the variously uniformed troops scratching their trowser seats around the old frigate's guns knew the breeching-thimble of a thirty-two-pounder from the dumb-trucks. They were volunteers from the militia regiments Minter had persuaded their colonels to release for service on the Experiment. From Virginia, North and South Carolina, Georgia, Alabama, Arkansas, Louisiana, Maryland, Texas, and his own Mississippi, they were a cross-section of the new nation.

Oh, he'd scraped up a few old man-o'-war's men here and there. They'd be invaluable leavening. Company C of the Marines, assigned to the navy yard since the spy scare in November, knew their way around a ship as well. But the massive new weapon would require over three hundred hands.

The answer was the army, and over the past weeks he'd played traveling revivalist around the Roads. The troops he scoured up were willing. He hoped that would suffice.

Sheriff touched his cap. They were ready to commence. Lomax decided he could manage, and dismissed him to continue the drill.

Climbing to the main deck, he looked to the yard on one hand, to Norfolk on the other.

This cold February morning all was leaden, the clouds, the river. It had rained and sleeted the day before. Puddles glinted gunmetal on the flats, and the wind's bite was deadening and sudden as a headsman's axe. He blew on his hands, lit a segar. Strolled, smoking, till he spotted the launch cutting toward him.

To his startle, a familiar figure welcomed him into the boat. It was Captain Norris, looking grim. The first words from the secret service officer's lips were, —Fort Donelson's fallen.

—Oh, no.

—News came in this morning. No details yet, but a thousand rumors.

—Floyd? Pillow?

—Got away somehow, but Buckner surrendered the fort and thousands of our troops to some drunk named Grant.

—Then Nashville's next.

As the oarsmen stroked toward shore, they agreed things had grown dark in the west since the new year. Crittenden defeated in Kentucky. The loss of Fort Henry had opened the upper Tennessee River to the Federals. Donelson's fall meant the Cumberland lay open, and the forts along the upper Mississippi were probably doomed too.

—It's a long road that has no turning, Lomax said. —Up till now we've done well for ourselves. And will do so again.

Norris agreed quietly but observed that Halleck's and Grant's success in the West would force McClellan to move in the east. He nodded toward the approaching yard, the rooflike casemate looming. —We most desperately require a victory here if he is not to take Richmond from behind. When will you be ready for service?

—We finished the plating some days ago, though we still have no port shutters. Porter will open the sea-gates today. Whether it floats is another matter.

—And put to sea when? Thursday perhaps?

—Not so fast. Two to three weeks to fit out.

—Two or three *weeks*?

Lomax said, annoyed, —It's been a damned hard haul to get this far. Between lack of iron and unskillfulness amounting to treachery. Unfortunately I can't lay the blame where it belongs.

—Blame for . . . sabotage? Delay?

—Delay amounting to sabotage.

—Let me know whom you suspect. I'll get that information to the authorities.

—Without my name attached?

Norris winked as he struggled to his feet. They were passing the massive gate that walled the dry dock from the river. The chuffing clang of a steam pump reached their ears. The captain shot a glance of mingled awe and doubt at the black upperworks towering above the stone. —What did you mean, "whether it floats"?

—I'm no naval constructor. Lomax shrugged. —But the workers say she'll never swim so heavily burdened. I cannot venture an opinion, but no one's to be aboard when the water's let in.

Norris steadied himself as the coxswain brought them alongside. A bow line flew up to a waiting marine. —It certainly looks top-heavy. And the officers? How do they impress you?

—Everybody with a dram of influence is here. We're going to have a lieutenant for every gun. Davidson, Minor, Ramsay, Catesby Jones, Littlepage, Taylor Wood.

What Lomax didn't say was how deeply such a roster satisfied him. With such men aboard, the finest blood and flower of the new Confederacy, no destination was possible but glory . . . or death.

Norris said grimly. —Well, you'd all best get this thing to sea as soon as you can. Our information is the Ericsson is ready to sail.

—Surely not so soon. It was only commenced—

—In December; that is correct. It seems too fast to credit, but our intimates in New York assure us they launched two weeks ago.

Despite himself, Lomax glanced downriver. The thing could be here any day. Might light on them loading guns and ammunition, even more helpless than they'd been a-building. All this occupied his mind as the special agent murmured, —So you see why it's essential that whoever her captain is to be, y'all must put to sea as soon as you can. Hazard all on a sortie.

—Has there been any word of our commander?

—That's the navy's lookout. You'll hear before I do.

The launch rocked as they climbed out, assisted by the strong arm of Captain Reuben Thom, commander of the marine detachment. Lomax was about to introduce Norris when he caught the latter's glance and did not, instead feigned difficulty with ash blowing off his segar into his eyes. —Damn . . . damn, that smarts. Reuben, are we about to—

—I have a squad aboard. With Corporal Aenchbacher.

When he looked next, Norris was hiking up the dry dock. The last workers at the bottom of the pit were queueing for the stone staircases. Hempen cables thick as a lady's waist sagged between the monster and the stone walls. More lines led down, to heavy pine balks that supported her now but would float free as she rose, buoyed by the water that already showed as a quicksilver pool far below.

Brawny black men braced to a great iron wheel. Far below, the trickle turned to a white-foamed torrent. Lomax paced a few feet out on the lock-gate, feeling it tremble beneath him. Then returned to the verge and lowered himself to a butt-chilling perch on a rusty bollard.

No bands, no ceremony, no officers even but himself and Thom. He noticed Porter standing outside his shack, hands deep in his coat pockets. The constructor looked crapulated, swaying, as if fresh off a three-day drunk.

A pair of boots shot through the after gunport, followed by the rest of the master carpenter. Meads skidded down the slanted casemate like a child on a greased board. He got up and dusted himself off, then made for terra firma.

—Who was that army fellow with you? Thom asked him.

—I don't believe that's any of your business, Lomax told him.

—It is my business. I'm in charge of the guard.

—A friend from Richmond.

—His name?

—If you wish to know more, you will have to ask him yourself.

More shouting, and suddenly more men burst from the iron shell. Scores of boilermakers and machinists who'd come in from the yards round about to help finish mobbed up onto the shield deck, crowded down the gangways, jostled and shoved their way across. Lomax smiled grimly. —A tenner says she'll show us her arse like a bitch in heat.

—No bet, the marine said.

Lomax saw who he was watching so closely: a scared boy in gray coat and white cross-belts standing rigid on top of the shield deck. After a moment he began edging toward the brow. Thom cursed and headed for the gangway to stop him.

A second gushing fountain appeared on the far face of the dock. The water was rising swiftly now. A pump thudded, thrusting black smoke skyward as it emptied the hollow dock-gate. Once the inner dock filled, the now-buoyant gate would rise from its seating, ready to float aside. Leaving no barrier between the colossus and the sea.

He slowly relit the segar, watching the human ant stream emptying the steam ram. From where he sat the stern was a gigantic wedge. A mammoth hand iron. A black armored tower raised against the gods. He could see every iron seam, every bolt head, every squeezing out of pitch. The upper blade of her massive screw. The huge vertical barn door of her rudder, plunging down to where the rising sea foamed and swirled. Bits of wood rose with it, trash, old newspapers. The frozen dried carcass of an opossum that as he watched tilted its nose downward, then slid from the sight of man.

He wondered if he was far enough away from this thing if it *should* turn turtle. But the question wasn't really what it would do in the shelter of the yard. It was what would it do in the river, the Roads, the Bay, when the wind blew up and the chop got heavy. Or when she fired a broadside on the up roll.

He felt sweat trickle under his arms. Watching the water mount. A pitch bucket bobbed, swirled, tipped suddenly, and followed the possum down.

He got up and paced forward. Ahead of him the naval constructor was checking the heavy hemp that led from the bow to the bollards ashore. Close to, Porter looked even more done up. He nodded coldly to Minter, who returned the acknowledgment with equal frost; then shaded his eyes to inspect the ram beak that had been bolted on several days before. Four feet long, of solid cast iron, it looked absurdly small compared to the bulk behind it. Lomax noticed that one of the spike eyes fastening it to the hull was cracked. Would the constructor notice it? He *had* to notice it.

But he said nothing. Simply straightened, as if all was in order, and sauntered on.

Suddenly he knew why the Yankees had never bothered to raid. They knew this doomed, burned, sunken wreck, this rusty junkyard jerked off a river bottom and overloaded with precious iron and desperate dreams, would never sail again. John L. Porter and his satellites had guaranteed that.

He grabbed his sword and broke into a jog. —Captain Thom!

The marine whirled. —Sir.

—Tell your boys to keep an eye skinned on Porter. If I'm right, he's going to slip away just before the launch.

Thom's eyes narrowed. He began to ask something, then seemed to think better of it. He hurried away. Lomax called after him, —And get your men off her. Before it's too late.

He walked swiftly toward Quarters A, expecting to meet Forrest coming down. Surely the yard commander would be on hand for the launching of his most essential enterprise. But not only did he see no Forrest, he did not see Jones or indeed any of the other officers.

The answer flashed on him: Porter had never notified them.

A groan echoed behind him. Frightened shouts broke from brawny throats. He whirled to see the upperworks surge into motion.

She inclined her head with an almost graceful bow. The whole tremendous mass of oak and iron stirred beneath its binding of hemp. Like a groggy, waking Gulliver beneath the threads of the Lilliputians.

A renewed shout. The men lining the dock surged back. A white flurry in the water. Out of it shot black masses of timber. At the gate a signal flag wagged back and forth. In the stream a tug shrieked, a long shrill scream of steam.

Lomax stood rooted as the whole enormous mass rolled slowly, heavily, sending a series of waves surging and clashing in the dock. It hesitated at the extreme of each list, as if deciding whether or not to continue on over.

Then slowly eased back upright. Continuing to nod back and forth, but gradually losing that sickening and, to a seaman's eye, truly frightening degree of roll.

Floated high out of the murky water, with only the faintest discernible heel to port.

A figure in somber black came strolling out of the agitated crowd. It carried a gray metal lunch pail. The constructor's hollow-eyed face showed neither triumph nor relief. He sauntered onward with a slow, mechanical stride, and disappeared at last in the direction of the main gate.

Over the next hour the yardbirds warped the newly launched ironclad out of the dock and alongside the ordnance wharf. Lomax reported to a tense-looking Jones that afternoon atop the shield deck. The exec returned his salute absently. —Good afternoon, Minter. What news on our people?

Jones listened without expression as Lomax reported on their training, that fifty hands remained lacking but that he hoped for more volunteers. Said as soon as he had done, —As you see, she floats.

—But damnably top-heavy, seems to me.

—I cannot disagree. She also displays far too much freeboard.

Minter raised his eyebrows. —I don't see that as a defect.

—Then you haven't observed how far down our armor belt extends. The ship is too light; or I should say, she is not sufficiently protected close to the water.

—What do you mean?

Leaning over the side, Jones pointed down. —The eaves of the casemate were promised to extend two feet below the surface. As you can observe, they are far above that, leaving us with only an inch of iron covering the waterline. Jones cleared his throat and straightened, locking his fingers behind him. —However, we should settle as we take on coal and ordnance. I must pass on two items of news. First, we are officially in commission.

Lomax blinked. —I must have missed the ceremony.

—There was none. Her name is no longer *Merrimack,* but *Virginia.*

—And our commander?

—That is the second item. The new commodore of the James River Squadron is Franklin Buchanan. We shall be his flagship. However, there will be no flag captain. He will function in command as well as flag.

Lomax's mood lifted. This was very much to his taste. The same ancient hawk who'd ordered him to Hampton Roads three months before, with the remark what the cause needed was fire. Buchanan was no youngster, but his thirst for action was famed throughout the fleet. He said with satisfaction, —Then we shall whip us some Yankee buttocks for sure.

Jones went on, —We'll move aboard this afternoon. Inform the men to bring bags, hammocks, and necessary personal gear, but no more. They may leave their sea chests aboard *Confederate States.* Prepare two muster lists. One for me. Forward the other to Quarters A. Put your spaces in order as quickly as you can. Once we are coaled and find the necessary powder, we will most likely be under way.

That afternoon Jones sent Lomax and Eugenius Jack, one of the engineers, across the river in search of gunpowder. They'd need eighteen thousand pounds before they sailed, as propelling charges and to fill the shells arriving from Tredegar. He called at Fort Norfolk but found its commander disinclined to part with his supply. Lomax argued forcefully and presented notes from both Forrest and Huger. At last he secured the promise of six thousand pounds. On the way back, as evening dimmed the western sky, he had himself landed at Cook's wharf.

He'd called at the house on Freemason twice since his visit to convey the news of her husband's capture. Mrs. Claiborne had been out both times. In Richmond, the servant said the first time; at her sewing circle, the second. The second time, though, the child, Robert, had come to the hallway to see who it was. Lomax had favored him with a few minutes' conversation and had at last taken the chimney off the lamp and shown him how to make smoke rings with the aid of a bit of paper and string. Both times he'd left his card and Portsmouth address, but had received no acknowledgment. He wondered as he turned up the walk why he persisted when he knew two houses on Bute Street where he could be satisfied in minutes for a dollar or two.

But it wasn't because he thought her attractive, though she was.

What had brought him back was another matter entirely. One he did not wholly like to look upon or consider in his breast.

He hesitated, looking at the single lit window, then cut across the lawn and around the house. Smelling in the dark behind it the cowshed, the woodpile. His boots crunched in straw, sank into the soft depression of what he guessed was a trench for the winter's truck. A glimmer in the dark. He stepped up and cupped his hands to the glass of a rear window.

She was in her chemise, making up her hair in front of her mirror. He watched for some seconds, admiring her bare arms as she combed her long hair, then made it up with firm, quick gestures into a chignon.

Her hands stopped. She half-turned her head, as if sensing him. He ducked back, then continued on his circumambulation, to the front piazza.

The servant looked confused to see him. He had to step past her into the hall. When he asked if her mistress was at home, she glanced nervously over her shoulder. —Really, suh.

—Well, is she or not? If she's not—

—Don't rightly know if she is or ain't, suh.

—Lieutenant Minter. I have called several times before. Tell her . . . He hesitated. —Tell her I have news.

—I'll ask her, suh.

—News? He has news? The soft urgent voice called from back in the house. —Ask him if he will wait.

She wore a dark canezou and a plain full skirt in the same sullen color. Hard to tell in the dim lamplight, but it seemed to be a dark maroon. She seemed even thinner than before. Her face was puffy. He could see she'd been crying. That explained the servant's hesitancy. Her eyes were wide and very bright, almost frightening.

He bowed over her hand, feeling its warmth through the thin knitted cotton of her glove, and scenting a faint perfume. —Miz Claiborne. I hope I do not find you distressed.

Her laugh was bitter. —Distressed? What could make you imagine that? No . . . I should not have said that. Forgive me.

—There's nothing to forgive. It is always the innocent who suffer most, is it not?

—Will you sit down? she said with false brightness. —Betsey, another chunk of wood for the fire. Will you have a cup of tea, Lieutenant?

He accepted; he was chilled through. The servant left. She swept her skirt up, giving him the toe of a kid shoe, and they sat. He became aware of the steady tick of a clock, the slap-bang of a back door as the servant went out.

Her pale eyes rose to his. —Now, sir, your news.

He cleared his throat. —I'm afraid I have no actual intelligence, Miz Claiborne. I said that to make you see me. You see, I admit that.

—Not the act of a gentleman, Mister Minter.

—I have always believed true gentility consists in putting the good of others before one's own.

She watched his face carefully and did not speak, so he had to plunge on. —No actual information from Boston. That, I would have forwarded immediately by post. But from what I hear *via* the naval grapevine, I am afraid things look rather dark. The longer we go without word, the worse his chances look in the hands of the vengeful partisans in charge of the Northern government. They are blatant, bullying cowards. Thank God we're independent of them now.

A handkerchief twisted in her fingers. He went on, looking about, —I do not see Robert. Is he this early to bed?

—I must thank you for playing with him when you called. He seems to have quite taken to you.

—He is a delightful little lad, Lomax said. He added, perceiving what might be an opportunity, —I might perhaps stop by for him one day and take you both to see our new Leviathan.

But instead of agreeing she dropped her eyes. —I am considering sending him to his grandparents in Richmond. It may be safer, considering the possibility of invasion here.

—It is worth considering, ma'am. But what about you? Why did you not stay in the capital? If I may make bold to ask.

—I preferred to be at my own home. Do you not have a home, Lieutenant?

—I did once. As a child.

—Have you no family? No dear ones?

—There Ker has the advantage of me.

Her eyes were on the handkerchief again. —And why did you wish to see me? So importunately as to shade the truth?

He said, perhaps too boldly, —I am not without flaws, ma'am. Few men are. I admit, as I said, I merely wished to see you. To offer what comfort I can.

She didn't respond, and he bent forward, fashioned his voice toward earnestness. —I was Ker's shipmate. I've offered my services before. If you require anything . . . intervention with the naval authorities . . . perhaps financial help.

—If I should, I have my father to apply to.

—Well, well; you might recommend the Virginia stock to him. They are at ninety now and will fall on the news from the west. But with God's help we shall get off soon with our new ironclad, and you will hear such tidings as will strike our enemies quite blind. He stopped, wondering how in hell he'd gotten onto the subject of investments. —Forgive me. Such matters must be far from your mind. I wish you'd call me Lomax. And consider me your friend.

She still did not raise her eyes. —*Are* you our friend, Mister Minter?

He dared it: reached for her glove. Her hand lay unresponsive in his. —It is my dearest wish to be considered so.

She was silent, and he feared he'd gone too far. He'd made love to widows before, and this attractive, well-born woman was not far from being one. If things went as he hoped . . . and even if they didn't, his visits would be noticed. Neighbor, pastor, some nosy biddy from the sewing circle the servant had mentioned. Perhaps *he* would even hear about his wife's visitor.

At last she removed her hand. Yet she did not ask him to leave. He brushed his hair back and relaxed.

The servant came in. Mrs. Claiborne looked away from him, then reached out. Took the pot from the tray. In a strangely muted voice she said, —Cream, Mister Minter . . . I mean to say . . . Lomax?

He said that would be perfectly fine.

15

Touring of the New York Customs Collector ♦ Erection of the Turret ♦
A Disappointing Test Cruise ♦ Evening Interview with Lieutenant-
Commanding Worden ♦ Reports on the Armor of the Putative Opponent ♦
Prudent Admonition by the Superintending Engineer

MIND your step on the ladder, ma'am. It is polished wrought iron and inclined to be treacherous.

—My, my, perhaps you ought to put a handrail here. Someone could take quite a tumble.

Theo glared at a workman lingering under the ladder, hoping for a glimpse of stocking. —Step through here, he said, holding out a palm for her gloved hand.

The woman said, smiling at him, —And what do you call this room? How nicely it is furnished, to be sure.

—This is our wardroom. As you see it is illuminated by skylights. They are set flush in the deck above and will be covered with iron scuttles during battle.

They were now a month beyond the hundred-day deadline. The turret had been hoisted on board the day after launch, but it didn't fit. Continental had consumed several days draw-filing the bottom of the inner-most layer of plate, the one that seated in the train ring, to make it meet flush all around when keyed down.

Meanwhile, everyone of note and many of none had to see the elephant. The mayors of New York and Brooklyn, councilmen, aldermen, businessmen, a notorious abortionist known as the Wickedest Woman in New York, cranks, abolitionists, Southern sympathizers, madmen, and everyone else who had the pull to get invited or two bits to tip the watchman at the gate. Usually they fobbed the duty off on Bill Keeler, the purser, but this morning Keeler was out buying stores, and Hubbard had gotten stuck as tour guide. In the current party were several ladies with a bearded gentleman who'd introduced himself as the collector of customs for the Port of New York, a Melson or Marvell, something starting with M that had evaporated instantly from Theo's memory. He said he had served in the Navy once himself, aboard the old *United States*. One lady was young, and he allowed himself a fantasy as her golden hair swung this way and that, as she glanced into the officers' staterooms. The little bunks would be just big enough for two if one was on top of the other.

—Above your head you will see Captain Ericsson's patent anchor-hoister. The anchor well is five feet in diameter to fit Captain Ericsson's patent four-bladed anchor. If you will follow me aft, please, and mind your hats as you duck through this hatch into the engine compartment.

Since the launching he'd been so busy fitting out he'd had little time for Eirlys and little Lilibeth. Eirlys had told him she'd signed no "contract," though she'd heard of Mr. Eno. But the day after he told her about his encounter with Hyer, she'd removed to another boardinghouse, in Brooklyn, and bought herself a wicked big Bowie.

—You are now looking at Captain Ericsson's patent turret operating mechanism. The turret revolves on the cast-iron spindle before you. Atop the stanchion is a wedge-shaped key operated by this large screw. When the screw is fully tightened, the spindle is keyed up two and three-quarter inches, freeing it to rotate under the drive of the turret engines you see bolted beneath the beams of the main deck. No, miss, I'll show you the controls when we reach the turret. Step this way.

The guns had been installed on February fifth: two big Dahlgrens, great bottle-shaped masses of varnished cast iron, borrowed from U.S.S. *Dacotah*. The twenty tons of guns and carriage made the iron beams of the turret deck sag. Ericsson had designed vee braces to compensate, but on taking up the slack Theo found they were too long. They had to be dismounted and hurried back to the West Side for remachining. On the tenth he lit fires for the first time, turned the engine over, and ran the blowers to test the ventilation.

Mr. Former Man-o'-War's Man asked why there was a groove in the bilge. Theo told him the keel plates were dished out to provide a bilge limber the length of the hull. —We will now step aft to observe the Martin fire-tube boilers. Mind your hat on the waste steam line, ma'am. Each boiler contains three hundred and forty-six copper tubes for the rapid raising of steam. To your left and right are coal bunkers arranged to protect the engine should a plunging shot penetrate the armored deck. Aft of this observe the vibrating-lever engine, patented by Captain Ericsson, which provides four hundred horsepower from a relatively small prime mover.

By the eighteenth the braces had been reinstalled. He'd keyed up the turret for the first time and applied steam to the turret engines. The pistons fit too tightly, making them run slow, but the contractor assured him they'd wear in with use.

In the turret the ladies exclaimed over polished brass and copper and wrought iron, and the paucity of standing room available to crowd their skirts into. Theo told them that at a steam pressure of twenty-five pounds it would make two and a half complete revolutions per minute, controlled by a crank handle in front of the turret officer's sighting slit. The ladies fanned themselves and confessed with a laugh they should be rendered quite dizzy. Miller, or whatever his name was, smiled patronizingly at him, one seaman to another. Hubbard sighed and looked aloft at the rail iron that roofed the turret, the charcoal sky that showed through drilled holes in the sheet metal above that. —These eleven-inch Dahlgren shell guns weigh fifteen thousand seven hundred pounds apiece. Cast in Mr. Robert Parrott's West Point Foundry in Cold Spring, New York. They fire either eleven-inch shells weighing a hundred and thirty-six pounds or specially designed cast-iron shot, at a hundred and seventy pounds, for use against other ironclads or fortifications.

The battery had been turned over to Worden on February nineteenth, though legally the Consortium still owned it, the Navy having made no move toward acceptance or final payment. This afternoon, with Delameter artificers manning the engines, the captain planned to leave Green

Point. At Brooklyn Navy Yard, two miles downriver, they'd take on ammunition and crew. Theo hastened the remainder of his explanation, showed the guests back down into the hull and out the berth-deck hatch. On the afterdeck Mr. Millville, which apparently was his name, pressed a copy of a book he'd written about whale hunting on Theo, who explained he was honored but had little time these days for reading. As soon as they were off the deck, he slid down the ladder and resumed getting things organized for lighting off.

It turned out a fiasco. The valve gears didn't work right, and Theo couldn't get more than forty revolutions per minute out of the engines. Then one of the blower engines blew a valve, spraying steam into the engine room. It scalded a worker and sent the others scuttling. Since the tide was flood, they sat chuffing helplessly in the river, making three and a half knots but holding steady relative to the shore, until Theo realized the cutoffs had been set for backing, not for forward motion. Delamater must have assumed the propeller would rotate in the opposite direction in which it actually did. With that corrected they began to creep ahead, but still didn't reach the yard till after dark.

When all was finally secured and the fires banked, one of the workers brought word that Captain Worden sent his respects and requested the honor of his presence. Theo looked down at the wreck of his clothes. He and the machinists had taken turns stoking. He twisted grease off his hands with a rag and smeared coal dust around his face. He thought of changing his shirt but had no spare aboard. Worden would have to take him as he was.

The commander's quarters were all the way forward, reversing the usual practice, where the senior officer inhabited the aftermost quarters and the crew berthed "before the mast." Theo thought with grim satisfaction that this little craft would upset quite a few of the braiders' cherished perquisites. No quarterdeck to strut. No flag officer's cabin. Nor any of their cherished sails, although the contract had specified a full set. Ericsson had simply ignored that requirement. No doubt, if they failed, it would be another pretext for the government's not paying him.

He did not like to contemplate how much his sympathy for the inventor was due to what he now realized had been nothing more nor less than a discreetly camouflaged *douceur*, to place him on the side of the interests who had invested in her.

The first thing Worden asked about was a sea trial. Pointing to a chair in the luxuriously appointed stateroom, he asked courteously if the Chief Engineer would take a dram. Theo wiped his mouth with a sweaty sleeve. It was cooler up here, even with one of the ventilating engines out. The Swede's inventive knack channeled fresh air from topside beneath their feet, where it came up through brass registers.

—Sea trial, sir? We have much to see to before then. The compass must be regulated. I should like to have Captain Ericsson look at the windlass. We'll need several more days of engine trials. Then there is the little matter of a crew.

The new captain crossed his legs. His expression was wistful. His long locks and long brown beard were carefully curled. A perfume of lavender oil pervaded the cabin, only partially diluted by coal-smoke and the smells of new wood, paint, wool carpeting, and Emery's Naval Varnish.

A tap at the door, and the barrel chest of a darkly handsome and very young man pushed in. His hair was rumpled, and his enormous handle-bar mustache sagged off to chewed-ragged ends. —Sir. I took the liberty of taking *Sabine*'s boat out, since it didn't look like you were coming in to the pier.

—Come in, Sam. To Theo he said, —Let me introduce my exec, Mister Samuel Dana Greene. Naval Academy, class of '59. Plank owner on *Hartford*. Has spent most of his service in the Far East. Sam, this is Theo Hubbard, our supervising engineer. Mister Greene has been ashore, attempting to pull together a crew for us. How did it go?

—Better than I expected. I had a talk with the execs on *Sabine* and *North Carolina*. They were willing to let us ask for volunteers, as they'll be in the yard for some time.

—Commodore Paulding?

—Gave his permission to raid them.

—And the result?

—Actually, we got more than we shall need. I'll interview them tomorrow with the bo's'n and make our selection.

—The gun crews?

Greene consulted a wheel-book. —I allowed fifteen men and a quarter-gunner for the two guns; eleven men in the powder division; one for the wheel. That will leave twelve, including those in the engineer's department, to supply deficiencies at the guns, casualties, and so forth.

—That will give us how many in the turret proper? The captain pronounced it "tuwwet."

—Seventeen men and two officers, sir.

—How for master's mates?

—We might take one more. We're at the limit for accommodations, though. Only hammock room for half the crew at a time as it is.

—Then let us hold off on the additional master for the time being. Mister Hubbard: I should like you to look over an item or two which the assistant secretary, Mr. Gustavus Fox, has been so good as to forward me.

Theo read the crackling flimsies, barely legible letterpress copies of other copies. One was from a master's mate from Massachusetts who'd been imprisoned in Richmond and then Norfolk before being exchanged. At one point he'd shared a cell with a carpenter of Union sentiments who'd been employed on *Merrimack*. Theo furrowed his brow. —Twenty guns. Rudders at both ends. Angled sides, to throw off shot. She seems to be fitting out as a ram.

—All accounts agree on the sloping sides. Note the mention of throwing jets of hot water.

—She'd need to get very close to do that. Theo read on, then marked a passage with a finger. Glanced up.

—The thickness of the iron plates he observed going by on the railroad cars, Worden said, leaning back in the upholstered armchair. —A vewwy nice piece of observation, one might say? Given his being a prisoner at the time.

—Two to two and a half inches.

—One layer of which we might penetrate. Two layers, we most probably could not—at least with standard charges. Beyond doubt, by this point she is out of dry dock and ready to make her move.

Theo kneaded his lower lip. —Our iron shot? Would they not penetrate four inches of iron?

—They are experimental, Mister Hubbard. Very heavy. And Captain

Dahlgren seems from the tone of his telegrams not to trust overmuch in the soundness of his guns. He has limited me as to the powder charges we may employ.

—Which may not suffice, Greene said.

—Nevertheless those are my orders, and you will take note of them. Do you understand? Greene nodded. —He's preparing a Greek fire shell as well, but doubts it will reach us before we sail. Worden shifted his position, coughed into a linen handkerchief. Closed his eyes a moment, then went on. —What I should like to know from you are two points. These continual *deways* are alarming the Department.

—All concerned are working hard as humanly possible, sir. These mechanisms are all novel, have not even been broken in—

—No weproach intended, but nonetheless anxiety seems high concerning our near term availability. How close are we to being able to . . . I suppose one may not say "to sail" in such a craft . . . to get under way for service? The hitch with the engine today, for instance.

—I am happy to say we have gotten the cutoffs nearly to the proper setting. I shall want to make steam pierside for some final adjustments. But on the whole we are doing well first crack out of the box.

Worden nodded. —Then we shall be able to cast off in a few days— say, by Friday? I must wespond to a telegram from Secretary Welles. He is becoming peremptory about us footing it down to Hampton Roads.

—I sincerely hope so, sir, Theo said through gritted teeth. All the braiders were like that. Demanding assurances, as if he was a spirit rapper who could ask the demon Asmodeus when something would crack or slip or shear. —And your *second* question, Captain?

—Whether you'll remain aboard with us, Mister Hubbard. Worden exchanged an unreadable glance with Greene. —I am sowwy, I cannot offer you a stateroom. You will have to sling your hammock on the berth deck. But you have supervised her construction. You understand this radical new craft. And I observed you today coping with the difficulties in the engine woom. Of course we have Mr. Newton. But I should very much like to have you along as well should we encounter anything unforeseen—as no doubt we will, this being the first cwuise of such "fighting machines," as I have heard Captain Ericsson styles them.

Theo debated. The implied slur in his berthing arrangements was no more than he expected from line officers. He still believed in the craft, despite her teething problems. But as a coastal battery, not as a sea boat. —I am still in doubt as to her safety in heavy weather, he said.

—Then I should be even more eager to have you with us on the tow down. Weally, Mister Hubbard, when *Mewwimack* comes out of her den, we must be there to meet her.

It occurred to Theo that the moment *Monitor* left New York, Bushnell and Barnes would expect him to approve all payments due against the contract. And he was not sure he could, considering her lack of seaworthiness.

On the other hand he'd accepted two thousand dollars from that same Consortium. Pledging him to use his influence in their behalf. Otherwise they had every right to demand their "expense account" be returned. Unfortunately he'd spent it all—on new boots, priority telegrams, and train tickets; and by far the largest single item, on the housing, clothing, and support of his unexpected and clandestine family.

But neither could he let men go to sea in a craft he himself would not venture out in. That would mean he'd sold others into danger for his own selfish gain.

The only correct solution to this equation, it seemed to him, was for him to go along. And bowing to this Theo said, —If you deem my presence desirable, sir, I shall of course make myself available to accompany you on the tow. After that, I must wepowt—I mean, *report*—back to the Bureau of Steam Engineering for my next assignment.

—Fine, fine. Worden nodded. —That will be all, then, and please draw the fires, if you would. We shall need steam in the morning but not before eight. And now I believe I will seek the arms of Morpheus, if you will pardon me—

—Let me ask a favor, sir, Theo said. He was on his feet, but one thing remained to be said. A very important thing.

Worden inclined his head courteously, though he looked very tired. —What you will, Mister Hubbard. We are all in your debt, I am sure.

—Do not commit this vessel to sea in anything resembling heavy weather. I must earnestly make this representation. It would be most dangerous, in my professional opinion.

—I will bear your warning in mind, Chief Engineer, Worden said, coughing into his handkerchief again. —Make a note of that, Exec, if you please. But we *must* get under way soon. The crew. The mechanical arrangements. The ammunition. Then we *must* be off. Are we all quite ag-weed, then?

With something less than peace in his breast, Theo agreed.

Part III

THAT ANVIL WHEREIN
IS HAMMERED OUR SOULS.

January 1862–March 7, 1862.

16

Dawn in March ♦ Fast by the Royal Standard ♦ Those Who Abide ♦
A Reprimand from the Commodore ♦ Passing Colley Farm ♦ As Slowly as
the Tide ♦ Scalpels in the Mess ♦ The Union Squadron ♦
For How Can Man Die Better

MISTER Minter, I will ask you to step aside, if you please.
—At once, sir. He stood away as Franklin Buchanan, resplendent in full dress, sword, and epaulettes, trailed by Catesby Jones in the same splendid uniform, proceeded toward the ladder. The crew straightened from the guns as he passed, gazing on the spare old man, nearly bald, angular as a mason's square, his expression that of a vindictive eagle.

Below their feet a grating rumble began. Its pace gradually increased. Until the wheeze and slam of the engines vibrated the shadowy length of the long, narrow nave in which two hundred men stood waiting, hoping, dreading.

> Fast by the royal standard,
> O'erlooking all the war,
> Lars Porsena of Clusium
> Sat in his ivory car.
> By the right wheel rode Mamilius,
> Prince of the Latian name;

And by the left false Sextus,
That wrought the deed of shame.

At the Brooke rifle next forward, Hunter Davidson was entertaining his boys with a recitation of Thomas Babington Macaulay. They listened avidly, eyes shining in the dark.

A little after ten o'clock, Saturday, March eighth, 1862. By rights they should have been under way the day before, and anchored overnight under the batteries at Sewell's Point. But cold rain had so reduced visibility, and made the pilots so nervous at the idea of navigating such a deeply laden craft in the dark, that Buchanan had postponed their trial trip till this morning. That was all this offing was, officially. But there was speculation their fiery commander would thrust them into the limelight. Certainly they were very late on that stage.

The ship and the wharf alongside had been a boil of activity all the night through. He'd lain in his wet bunk, but hadn't slept a moment for the din and shouting of mechanics and fitters rushing to finish jobs that in Minter's opinion should have been done weeks ago. Chief Engineer Ramsay had fired the boilers at midnight. This turned his cabin from icy to sweltering. At first light two score yard workers arrived with cartloads of tallow. They swarmed the sides till the sloping iron was coated an inch thick with the greasy yellow stickum. Jones thought it would make the projectiles glance off, though from what Lomax understood, Brooke's tests on Jamestown Island had shown no such advantage. At any rate, her dipping of pork fat would make it hard for any boarders to scramble their way up to the shield deck.

He'd stayed by number four since a breakfast of fried ham, redeye gravy, and a cup of good black tea. For some reason he'd ended up with all Georgia boys. Most were from the Third and Fourth Infantry, some from Cobb's Legion. One wore the short jacket of a cavalryman, another the work smock the soldiers called "battle shirts"; still others green, blue, or buff in a haphazard motley. His gun captain, Tharpe, was short in stature, but a quick study; he'd been a schoolteacher in Marion when the war started. They'd never actually fired the big Dahlgren. It was a much newer and heavier weapon, on a different carriage, from the thirty-twos he'd drilled them on aboard the receiving ship. They'd never handled hot shot before either.

No help for that. No time, as there'd been none for so much else, including fitting the protective shutters. With the gun inboard he could look out onto the river as through a large window. If a shell came through it, or one of the fourteen other openings spaced along the deck, the oak and iron of her shield would only tamp the explosion.

> *On Astur's throat Horatius*
> *Right firmly pressed his heel,*
> *And thrice and four times tugged amain,*
> *Ere he wrenched out the steel.*
> *"And see," he cried, "the welcome,*
> *Fair guests, that waits you here!*
> *What noble Lucumo comes next*
> *To taste our Roman cheer?"*

Along the shadowy deck grizzled troopers and callow youths yipped encouragement as to an actual combat. It needed no great imagination to see the Yankees as Porsena's invading Etruscans, themselves as the noble warriors of the ancient Republic. Lomax grew envious as Davidson unrolled stanza after stanza. He tried to remember something he could recite, but all he came up with was "The Wrath of Peleus' Son, the direful Spring / Of all the Grecian Woes, O Goddess, sing!" Which might entertain them but not for long.

Sweat trickled down his neck. Finally he told Tharpe to let the men strip off their jackets, and detail a boy to run them below. For himself, he'd be stepping topside. Adjusting his sword, he ran lightly up the central ladder.

Into a late morning created for battle. Clear blue between shining clouds. Warmer than one expected for early March, and only the merest zephyr. He lowered his eyes from arch of sky to the circle of horizon, and then to the twenty-foot width of vibrating gridwork beneath his feet. Through which, looking down, he could dimly see the alternate black tubes of the guns, the tensely waiting forms of *Merrimack's*—no, *Virginia's*—people.

She moved with ponderous massiveness and a slow hunting yaw. Beyond the flamelike flutter of the commodore's broad pendant, the two tugs that would accompany them out into the Roads threshed toward Hospital Point. With only a pivot gun apiece, they were along mainly for assistance should the ironclad touch ground.

Looking over the rail he saw the sloped iron drop away into the almost glassy water. Like the tumblehome of a ship of the line. But the quivering thud of massive pistons and the inky boil of coal-smoke above the towering stack served notice this was no seventy-four like those Nelson had led at Trafalgar. He remembered how the mudsill engineer on the old *Owanee* used to hold forth about the Age of the Machine. How the others had laughed, predicting sail and oakum would last till the end of time.

Perhaps the dirty little mechanician with his wild talk of electricity and missing links had sketched after all the face of the Future.

Jones came aft, asking whether the howitzers were loaded; relaying the question from the commodore, most likely. Buchanan stood aft of the iron pilothouse, surrounded by pilots, officers, quartermasters. Lomax caught a gray uniform amid the navy blue—Norris, who'd somehow managed to put himself on the ship's list as master-at-arms.

He strolled aft to check, skirting the hatches, which had been propped open to snare whatever fresh air could be coaxed below. His gaze dwelt on the indolent stir of the Stars and Bars. The new cloth shone with spotless color. The two short-barreled weapons topside were charged with case. The marines would blast any boarders or small boats that came within range. The Dahlgrens and Brookeses would deal with heavier prey. Prey . . . which today all that floated would be to this armored Behemoth that pitched gradually now beneath their feet, picking up a faint swell off the open Roads.

As long as her abused, misaligned engines continued to revolve. And no poisoned dart found one of her many Achilles' heels.

His nape prickled as he recalled the most glaring one. He leaned to stare down again at where the river burbled green along the edge of the shield.

The *only just submerged* edge of the shield. Even loaded with coal, crew, guns, armor, and two hundred tons of pig-iron kentledge straining the keel timbers, *Virginia* still floated too high. A shot at her waterline would crash through into the berthing deck, the engine room, followed by an explosion of white water, the fatal bursting of the impatient sea into the overloaded hull. Jones had cautioned the officers not to tell the ship's people. They'd go into action believing themselves invulnerable.

Porter had erred after all. Some reckoned he'd forgotten to subtract the weight of the old steam frigate's missing spars. Others, that he'd just blown his arithmetic. The charitable allowed as how he might have just missed his guess on a nearly insoluble problem; the less trusting, that he'd erred from a darker design. Lomax was past caring why. The question that obsessed him was, Did the enemy know? Had the spy Norris still suspected passed that information? Or had their vigilance yet preserved that fearful secret?

Behind him Taylor Wood said, —Well, one thing's clear. The former Academy seamanship professor commanded the after pivot rifle.

—And what is that?

—She won't beat a turtle in a downhill race.

More and more of those who could were climbing topside to look out on the passing grounds of the naval hospital to port and the wharves to starboard as they steamed slowly past Colley's Farm. Guides in rowboats flagged the path through the obstructions. Small craft were assembling, skiffs, cutters, pungies, dinghies full of towheaded boys. As the ram slipped through they fell in with her, accompanying her progress with shaken handkerchiefs and the occasional whoop, though most were reverentially silent.

A few hundred yards on, Wood lifted his cap to a crowd packing a wharf. It was only a few rods from Freemason. Lomax wondered if *she* might be watching. But no cheer, no huzza came from those who were looking on, he suddenly realized, from each facing hill, each sloping lawn. Save one thin cry of —Go along with your old iron coffin! She'll never amount to anything else!

—Inspiring, drawled a midshipman, joining them. Hardin Littlepage was a soft-spoken but vacant-looking young blood commanding the other hot-shot Dahlgren. Lomax thought he was a Virginian but wasn't certain. He offered segars around; they bent their heads to get a light off his locofoco, which popped and sputtered from the damp belowdecks.

—Yet we seem to be moving, he told Wood.

—That is the tide. The log gives us not over five knots.

About the speed of a trotting horse. Wood glanced forward, then aft. His lips bent downward. —It'll take an inland sea to turn around in. And we draw twenty-two feet. We must be gingerly of light water. If the tide kicks us out of the channel, we'll be as dangerous as a beached whale.

Littlepage said eagerly, —But we've got us a captain.

—There I agree, my boy. If they'll stand and fight, he'll make this a day the world won't soon forget.

—But *will* they fight? Or just skedaddle?

They looked at Littlepage, at his boyish fading grin. But none had an answer to his question.

She churned along so logily and turned so very reluctantly as the channel angled around Lambert's Point that at last Buchanan signaled one of the tugs to pass a towline. Presently Jones passed the order "Load." Lomax went below to supervise. He showed them again how to select a shell and check it, and how to cut the fuze. He reminded his boys that strict silence and careful attention to each motion were called for if they weren't to get in each other's way. Also to stand clear of the port when the shooting started, as balls and fragments from exploding shells would most likely be abroad.

The ululating shrill of "mess call." He trooped down to the mildew-smelling wardroom, where a Norfolk caterer had provided a picnic luncheon. He felt less like eating than vomiting, but to maintain dignity took a slice of tongue and a biscuit and accepted a glass of wine from the steward.

The surgeon came in, a mahogany box under his arm. He was muttering to the assistant surgeon beside him. Alphaeus Steele was new to *Merrimack,* but not to Lomax; they'd served together on the Africa station. Steele had joined their complement only a week before. His odyssey had led from captivity at Fort Warren to Richmond; then had followed a long wait until his official exchange arrived. Lomax lifted his glass. —Doctor Steele. Doctor Garnett.

—Mister Minter. The old man bowed. His cheeks were flushed, and Lomax caught the fruity bouquet of brandy. —I trust I find you well and that this evening discovers us both the same.

—Our cause is just, Doctor. Liberty, glory, and revenge!

—Revenge, sir? Is that the sentiment I heard?

—For Fort Donelson, Hatteras, their invasion of Carolina. Our armor is strong, and we are in the right.

—Then you are as brave as we expect of youth, Steele said.

While he was thinking this remark over, the old man centered the box on the table and flicked the catch. The lid sprang open, revealing a glittering of cutlery. Knives. Saws. Probes. Clamps. Lomax threw the tongue on the sideboard, drank the wine off, and went topside again.

The steam tug churned and smoked ahead, the hawser dipping, then drawing taut. Surely the velvety volumes pouring up above them could not be overlooked. The Confederate flag stirred above the ramparts on Craney Island. Its guns would protect them for yet a mile and a half, after which they'd be on their own.

Looking beyond it, his neck prickled again.

The Union squadron. Yet many miles distant across the expanse, but there, visible to him as they must be to the enemy.

He pushed suddenly watery legs into motion and strolled forward with as much insouciance as he could muster. Tapped Wood's shoulder and borrowed his glass. Distant iotas leaped across sun-flashing flatness. *Cumberland* and *Congress,* still in their anchorage off Newport News. He moved the flat disc of sight to reveal the rest of the fleet coming gradually into view around Sewell's Point. *Minnesota. Roanoke. St. Lawrence.* Behind them the prickly mass of anchored transports and storeships. The sinew and might of Union occupation, the gathered resources of McClellan's convocating army.

—Nothing indicates they see us, Wood remarked after some time.

Lomax passed the glass back. —They must know we're coming out.

—Then tell me why they've got their laundry hung.

They glanced at each other with wild surmise. So far, at least, the black ships ahead lay like sleeping swans.

Then a smudge pushed up. Smoke, bursting from *Minnesota's* stack.

Another blot materialized above U.S.S. *Roanoke*. Far distant over the blue, but already nearer since they'd first glimpsed them.

Suddenly he remembered it. At least part of it. Not enough to declaim. But his lips moved silently.

> *And how can man die better*
> *Than facing fearful odds,*
> *For the ashes of his fathers,*
> *And the temples of his Gods?*

The gentlemen lingered still, looking toward their enemy. Then, as the order came aft, ducked beneath the hatch covers, leaving the bright day for the hot and noisy darkness below.

17

In the Belly of the Beast ♦ Collision with a Fuel Dock ♦ Delays of an
Uncertain Nature ♦ To Sea for the Land of Secessia ♦ Symposium on the
Nature and Possibility of Glory in the Modern Age ♦ Spectacle of a Storm,
Viewed from Atop the Turret, with Inaudible Remarks by Captain Worden
Anent the Rage of the Elements ♦ Ingress of the Sea ♦ Leather Belting and
Rivets ♦ Combat with an Imperceptible Adversary

PRESSURE, Mr. Newton?

—Twenty-seven and holding, Mr. Hubbard.

Clank-clink-*whump,* went the engine over and over again. Clank-clink-*whump,* clank-clink-*whump.*

Dawn on the seventh of March, or presumably something like dawn topside; for down here nothing altered from day to night, and the repetitive deafening din encased the mind like a crust that walled out even the thought of an existence unenveloped by iron, undriven by steam. Theo mopped his brow with his sleeve and looked the length of the gloomy, slanting, rolling space he'd inhabited, sleepless and even without sitting, only squatting on the deck plates occasionally, for the last forty-eight hours. It was so hot he found it hard to breathe; but not as hot as other such spaces he'd worked in, in the Service and out. In fact, in shirtsleeves, trowsers, and a dirty bandanna around his neck, with leather coal-heavers' gloves and heavy work boots, Theo Hubbard was actually comfortable.

To any but one accustomed to marine engine rooms, however, the noise and heat and unending motion would have been daunting. The ten-foot-high space was solid with hot, fast-moving, unshielded machinery, uninsulated steam pipes, two boilers, four roaring furnaces, a dozen men, and so much noise they could not communicate without cupping their hands and yelling from inches away. A steady dripping fell, as in a lime-stone cavern. The March sea overhead leaked through poorly fitting scut-tles and ran along the underside of the deck beams before pouring on their heads with each roll. One might think the baking heat and the wet cold might balance out. Unfortunately it didn't work that way.

—What I'm worried about is the blowers, the man opposite shouted.

—What?

—The blowers. We keep taking water down the intakes.

Theo nodded. —We've just got to keep them running.

His interlocutor was Isaac Newton, a good name for *Monitor*'s chief engineer. Theo was senior to him, but since he wasn't officially crew, they were uncertain where that left them. Fortunately they agreed on most pre-cautions, and so far they'd worked together as conditions had steadily got-ten worse.

Monitor's crew struck him as very young. There were forty-two all told, al-most all foreigners, Germans, Italians, Hungarians, with a sprinkling of blacks, mostly rated as boys or coal heavers. Two dozen were assigned aft of the main bulkhead: firemen and coal heavers, with not a single experi-enced mechanic among them. Some had come from men-o'-war in Brooklyn for repairs. Others, like Fireman Geer, were fresh enlistees with no more naval experience than a week on the recruit hulk. He and New-ton organized them into port and starboard watches, posted each at his station, and explained his duties to him. For the coal heavers this was easy, but with the others, considering the language difficulties, they were re-duced to charades with the oil can. His feeling of doom grew. But when he told Worden he needed more experienced hands, the captain cut him off. He and Newton, and Greene in the turret, would have to shake down in what time they had.

Which turned out to be days only. They'd taken the last of the ammu-nition aboard on the twenty-sixth of February and tried to get under way for a sea trial on the twenty-seventh. They'd cast off in a snowstorm and headed for the Narrows, intending to exercise the guns for the first time. Almost at once the steering gear failed and they slammed into a pier. Ericsson had been aboard within the hour, anathematizing Theo and Worden when they proposed drydocking to replace the rudder. He'd fixed it without docking her, working the yardbirds around the clock for two days to re-rig the steering gear.

On March third they tried again. This time the heavens opened with so fierce a deluge Worden put back in. The engines worked, though, and the steering was better. Theo would have liked a full sea trial, but Worden announced they'd get under way the next day. But that morning dawned windy and rough, so they delayed again.

They'd cast off at last the day before, into what at first had been fair weather. Westerly winds, smooth sea, and a sky that looked unthreatening, although partially overcast, the last time he'd examined it as they passed Sandy Hook. Not a steam whistle, not a cheer warmed their departure, and the gloomy handshakes and somber valedictions of the contractors as they went ashore seemed better suited to a funeral than a maiden voyage. A hawser connected them to the tug. Two gunboats rode a quarter mile off to either side, escorts against Confederate cruisers. *Maryland* had been swept off the board, but *Nashville* was rumored this side of the Atlantic. Then a warning sea had come across the deck, wetting the onlookers to their boot tops. Theo had looked back then, toward land, with some longing, then climbed to the top of the turret. The other hatches had already been sealed, and he slid down to his chthonian realm.

Some hours had passed with nothing untoward. The engine settled into its throb. The big horizontal piston shafts plunged in and out on opposite sides of the engine. The iron lever arms, longer than a man, transferred the motion to the shaft that rotated steadily beneath their feet. The fire crew sang lusty ballads as their shovels fed a stream of Pennsylvania's finest into the big Martins. A fine dust hung like powdered night. Blowers clanked and hummed; the air pump for the condenser wheezed and thumped.

By midnight conditions had begun to sour. Even down here Theo noted the change in the ship's motion. From time to time they could hear the wind through the iron above them. In the wardroom, breaking for a sandwich and coffee, Keeler told him it was near hurricane strength. The seas were coming over the bow with such force they'd knocked the helmsman back from the wheel in the little enclosed pilothouse forward. Theo thought bitterly of how he'd begged Ericsson to move it.

At noon, as the seas continued to increase, he made his way forward. When he undogged the door to the berth deck, he was instantly soaked by icy spray blasting down from above his head. Groans came from the off watch, hanging like bats in their hammocks, curled like dying tadpoles in corners. The smells of wet wool, bilge water, and sea puke made him gag. The doors of the storerooms clapped closed and then open again as they pitched. Looking up the hatch that led into the turret he saw someone standing on the ladder, pinpoints of gray light above. A thrumming whistle and faint shouts came down with the leaden light. He ducked and grabbed a coaming as the deck took a steep upward lean. He let go as it nosed over, pushed, and was able to float through the air until he fetched up against the bulkhead dividing the berth deck from officers' country. It was slightly drier forward of it, but the smell was the same.

The purser, the surgeon, and a couple of the others sat at the folding table, on which a single candle flickered. The heads around it nodded in a ghastly simulacrum of confraternal orison each time the bow crashed down. The deafening boom was preceded each time by a long-drawn-out, spine-chilling groan.

—What in blazes is that?

—Mr. Ericsson's patent anchor-well harmonium, one of the ensigns said. He sat with fingers digging into the wood and lips jerking. He wore a new mackintosh jet black with wet.

—Crackers, Mistah Hubbard? A grinning steward slid a plate toward him. —Gots plenty, those who care to partake.

—Thank you. Theo put one in his back pocket. A dose of steam served to soften them up. —Anyone seen the captain?

—I put him on top of the tower, Surgeon Logue said. He too looked close to giving up the struggle. —He's suffering from a violent species of . . . *nausea marina,* exacerbated by his deprivations in secesh prisons. How are . . . how are matters in the nether regions?

—We're keeping up steam.

The ensign said, swallowing and digging his fingers deeper, —How about these damned leaks?

—Worse than I expected, but the pumps are keeping pace. He didn't mention his worry about the doses of water down the stacks and the air intakes. If the fires doused, he'd lose steam. They didn't absolutely need the engine—the battery could wallow along on the end of the towline, though their forward progress would slow—but they did need the pumps and blowers. So far, though, the auxiliaries were holding.

—The topic of conversation, said the ensign heavily, and now Theo noted that he was not only seasick but inebriated —is whether men can truly be brave behind iron walls.

—And why should they not?

—Anyone can fight from behind armor, said Keeler. —But it takes true courage to fight on an open deck. Let us suppose our walls truly are impregnable. What glory can we win from behind them?

—Were not knights of old encased in armor? said the surgeon.

Theo couldn't believe his ears. It was a typical braider conversation: fanciful, supercilious, revolving around their own dignity and perquisites, and fuddled with wine. Yet those around the table were almost all volunteers; a few months ago they'd been civilians. He tried to keep his voice neutral. —Don't you think glory rather an outmoded expectation? In the nineteenth century?

—Outmoded or not, it's what I'm here for, bawled the ensign. He waved his glass, and a boy came forward from the shadows. —I know you mechanicals 'd like to take all that out of it. Make it machines fighting machines. Maybe we'll come to that, but not yet. Let's drink to your engines.

Theo said at present he was on watch and would decline the honor. As for glory, he'd prefer to concentrate on getting them safely to Hampton Roads. —But you might show me one favor, sir.

—Name it, Mister Mechanic.

Theo borrowed his mackintosh. He stepped into the little separate cubicle provided for Ericsson's patent pressurized toilet and set the levers. Pumped the bowl clear of the slurried awful mess the last user had left. Did his duty, pumped clear again, and headed for the turret. The ladder treads up were desperately slick, and he clung hard as the ship rolled.

When he poked his head up, he was facing Worden. The captain was lying at full length on the perforated metal turret top. His eyes were closed, and his face was the hue of crème de menthe. The others had their backs to him either out of delicacy or to duck the spray that howled past in sheets.

Theo got to his feet and swayed, trying to get the rhythm of the iron steed that galloped beneath his boots. Above his head a large new flag cracked in the steady wind. Its stripes glowed like heated iron against the colorless sky. He clutched the iron handrail that edged the tower.

He stared out over a waste of waters. Nothing but gray sea, gray sea, gray sea. Then from a welter of foam surfaced a black pointed wedge. It took a moment before his bewildered sight understood this was their prow. They climbed on the back of a great gray comber. The tower tilted back, till it seemed it must topple. The wind shrieked and snatched at his clothing. It was burning cold, and the iron under his digging fingernails sucked life from his flesh. Then they avalanched forward, the prow disappeared, and the green solid sea came up hissing, white-streaked, like limeade eked out with cream.

It flooded with frightening speed over the lashed-down forward lifeboat. It obliterated the iron steering house, tided up over hatches, deadlights, and intakes. The turbulent, seething surface rose till he started back, convinced she was taking her last dive. He blinked at the froth hissing halfway up the tower, the entire forward half of the battery submerged many feet deep. A few seconds passed. Then suddenly the prow surged up again, like a shark lunging up out of the deep. The broad, perfectly flat expanse of deck emerged after it, uncanny, startling, the sea roaring off, its evenly spaced plates like a wet-shining, slate-paved boulevard precipitously rushing up from under the deep.

Looking back he saw an even more chilling sight. As the seas passed over the afterdeck, their crests came within inches of the tops of the vertical stub stacks. The two nearest him, squared-off, riveted iron boxes belching volumes of inky coal-smoke, were the stacks. The after pair, only four feet high, were the blower intakes, or "air conduits," as Ericsson called them.

Worden was making a come-hither gesture. Theo bent over the recumbent form. Heard faintly, over the howl and whine and crashing, —Matters all right below, Chief?

—As well as can be expected.

—Can your pumps keep up with the leakage?

—So far they're doing so, sir.

—At least we have company.

The captain's finger flicked to starboard. Blinking salt spray from his eyes Theo saw after peering seconds a tossing speck. It took another look before he recognized it as one of their escorts, all sail set and smoke streaming from her stack. She was rolling to her gunports. He looked to port and made out the other. *Sachem,* if he had them right.

—They seem rather far off, he yelled. —In case of trouble.

The captain's lips moved, but Theo couldn't make out words. He might have been saying he had the utmost confidence; might have been cursing him for incompetence. —What?

Worden repeated himself, but with the crash of sea and the whine of the wind Theo at last gave up. He threw a worried look around. Then groped his way to the ladder and slid once more below.

The motion grew more violent. One of the firemen staggered into a hot steam pipe and screamed with pain. Newton sent him forward to the surgeon. The engines clanked and gasped steadily. By now Theo wanted nothing more than to find a place to lie down. But the whole after space was packed, and in the berthing compartment the water kept pouring down, apparently from under the bottom of the turret. The off watch sat about miserably on sodden hammock rolls, heads down, in a funk of vomit and seawater and coal dust and mildew. The glow through the portlights was wavery. Looking up he saw many feet of water covering them. But he finally found a place to wedge into in the engineering storeroom, his back on a bale of rags, boots up on a crate. And gradually sank into exhausted semiconsciousness, jerked back to waking with each laboring in the engine's rhythm.

A black-smeared face broke through uneasy dreams. One of the firemen, Garrety, shaking him. —Mister Hubbard. We're havin' trouble.

As he shoved his way through the hatch, a shrieking, undulating hum was audible even above the cries of iron scantlings as they flexed, the scrape of coal shovels, the clink-clank-*whump* of the engine, the steady suck and gasp and thud of condenser pumps and bilge pumps.

Newton and Park and Hands were standing under a veritable cataract of white water, struggling with the starboard blower. As he came in, Newton pulled one of the younger men back. Howled into his ear, —Don't get your hand in there, or you'll be wearing a hook.

—What's the problem?

—The fucking belts are slipping.

—Shit, Theo muttered, seeing the ductwork quiver as another slug of solid sea bolted down the intake and slammed into the blower blades. Not only was it braking the fan blades, but it cascaded down on the leather drive belts. Making them slip and squeal, unable to get a grip on the wet iron hubs. Newton and the others were trying to take up the slack with the tension pulley. There wasn't room to help, so he grabbed a handhold and clung, trying to figure out not why they were taking so much water, but what they could do about it. Because if they couldn't keep the blowers going, *Monitor* was destined to decorate the seabottom.

The blowers were driven by one-cylinder auxiliary engines, fed by steam through copper piping that had been polished bright but that heat and fumes had turned coffee brown. They were bolted to the forward side of the engine bulkhead, one to port, one to starboard. Rotary motion was conserved by a four-foot iron flywheel, and transmitted to the forty-inch blower fan by a ten-inch flat belt and flanged pulley. The drive was simple in concept and easy to access, at least by the cramped standards of the battery's arrangements. There was no clutch on the belt, nor any jackshafts or loose pulleys; Ericsson intended to control the blowers by steam pressure alone.

Which had looked straightforward on paper. Unfortunately, as Theo knew from his days in the cotton mills, short-center pulley drives were bitches to keep in adjustment. The belt tension had to be constantly re-tuned as the leather stretched. If the belts got loose, or anything slick got on the pulleys, slippage went up and power transmission went down, and he'd seen vibration tear belts apart.

In this case there was very little arc of contact on the driven pulley, which meant that as soon as water hit it, the belt started to skid. You could put more tension on it, which was what Newton and his boys were trying to do, but friction generated heat, and he could already smell roasting leather. Every time the deck fell away under their feet, he could wait three seconds and hear the water coming. When it hit the blades, the whole drive went into a seizure, the hub slowing, the belt whipping and bucking, a cloud of saltwater bursting off the shrieking leather, stinging eyes and faces, blinding men already working too close to the big fast-rotating flywheels. He'd seen mill workers after their arms or legs had been caught in the spokes.

Newton reeled back, teeth bared in a grimy face. —That's better, but sooner or later this son of a bitch is gonna go.

—As long as one blower's running we're all right.

—But we're taking water down both of em. The chief engineer looked anxiously forward to where the coal heavers crossed and recrossed from the open doors of the bunkers. With rags wrapped around his hands, one man flung the furnace doors open. Outlined by the white glare of anthracite flame the other flung in coal, leaning from the terrific rays of heat that streamed out. But the sea was coming down the stack extensions too. Feeling its way through every aperture. The battery bottomed out, like a wagon on a heavy road, and the stokers staggered back as water hit the beds of coals, bursting instantly into steam and hot gas. —Think we should slow 'em down? The fans? Newton howled.

—If we do, the fires'll blow back when that seawater hits them. We've got to maintain positive pressure.

—I'll get the slack out of the port one if you can keep an eye on this one—

The deck plunged. He threw his hand up to protect his head should he simply float up off the deck plates like a soap bubble. The screw shuddered, transmitting its frisson the length of the shaft, and with a yielding groan a solid charge of water plunged down through the conduit.

The belt parted with a crack louder than a musket shot. The whirring spokes instantly tore it to shreds, blasting scraps and rivets across the engine room. Theo got to the steam valve and cranked it closed. It scorched his ungloved hands, but he had to shut it down before the engine scoured bearings, broke valves, and blew apart into mangling fragments. He heard the blades running down to a halt. Felt the icy blast of air from above falter and cease. Through the vertical access came now only the terrible organ moan of the storm wind. Christ! Why hadn't he insisted on taller intakes? Ericsson might be a genius, but Theo had a thousand times his sea experience.

He remembered then, with a surge of guilt, that if he hadn't taken the Consortium's money, he'd have been free to do exactly that. And maybe he and fifty-seven other men wouldn't be in imminent danger of drowning in a leaking iron box that even at its best was already halfway to the bottom.

—You, Joyce, forward. Get one of the spare belts. Port-side compartment, hanging on the aft bulkhead. Mister Watters! Take a man and clear away that busted leather.

They scrambled into action, and he got the wrench out of his back pocket and started on the tensioner bolts. To get the new belt on they'd have to take the pulley off. Only his head was directly under the intake now, and every sea drenched him in icy water. Watters yelled that the flywheel was free. Theo worked on, squinting burning eyes, till the bolts came loose and Hand stepped in with a sledge and with ringing clangs drove the staggeringly heavy wheel off the shaft into his waiting hands.

He was just barely holding it, feeling the strain in his guts, when another report and a chorus of screams burst from the far side of the engine space. He sucked in his breath, unwilling to believe *both* belts had failed simultaneously. Full fires in the furnaces, no air draft, and taking water fast. If they lost steam, they'd lose the pumps. But he couldn't make steam without the blowers.

The battery avalanched down into the sea, and he grew first heavy and then, even cradling two hundred pounds of cast-iron pulley wheel on his thighs, light as an ascending angel. —Don't open the fire doors, he screamed.

But it was too late.

A fireman knocked the latch off, a casual flick with an iron bar, and the heaver started his swing. But before the coal could leave the shovel, an ethereal-looking tongue of pure indigo fire breathed out. Ten feet long, its end vibrating in a soundlessly massive roar, it passed over him, wilting him like a flower held over a fire.

Theo stopped breathing. That dragon's exhalation was superheated steam and hydrogen and carbonic acid gas and oxides of nitrogen. The same process used to make illuminating gas: spraying water on beds of incandescent coke in the absence of sufficient oxygen for combustion. The delicate blue was burning hydrogen. The other gases were invisible. None would support life. Without sufficient air, doused with water, the furnaces would produce more and more, and instead of going up the stacks it would back up into the hull.

Snuffing out all life within it, like bugs in a killing jar.

Shouts and screams and flickering light, the lambent writhe of flame, fully a yard across, that played like a blowtorch across the boiler flat, from which men recoiled and danced like the imps of Hell. Hubbard screamed to close the furnace doors. Instead the ash doors blew open on the other boiler, and a second bar of flame streamed into the depleting atmosphere.

Oilers and firemen were running forward, deserting their posts. The engine was still going, though its pounding was lessening, fading away. Or was he going deaf? As well as blind? For around him the space was darkening as the gas first flared up, then doused one after the other of the kerosene lamps. A tightness began in his chest. He panted. But there was no relief in breath nor any escape from darkness.

Dying at her heart, U.S.S. *Monitor* wallowed helplessly in the gale.

18

Wash Day in Hampton Roads ♦ The Bugaboo at Last ♦ Beating to Quarters ♦ A Gathering of Wings ♦ Anxiety Among the Pivot Crew ♦ Beating Retreat for Dinner ♦ Exchange of Compliments Between *Merrimack* and *Congress* ♦ Hauling Round on the Springs ♦ A First Receiving of Fire

THE whistle rose and held and then trailed away, and the bellow of the boatswain chased it through the decks. Cal considered his emptied seabag. Everything needed washing. It smelled of mold and worse. He wished he had some buttermilk for the mildew, but he didn't. Finally he rolled everything in his dress jumper and took it topside.

Saturday was wash day. And a beautiful morning it was. Hardly a ripple disturbed the water. The sun as warm as summer. He and his boys had their own washing place on deck, away from the white hands. They stripped to the waist and got everything, socks and trowsers and skivvies and hammocks, scrubbed out in the buckets and rinsed in fresh water and lashed in the rigging with junk rope ends, whites to port, blues to starboard. With the wind so light the first luff had loosed the sails to dry as well. *Congress* lay anchored not far away, the same festoons mounting into her rigging. The old frigate was a lovely sight with her long yards and great masts, every line taut and spar squared. A band was playing ashore, from the army batteries on the point, practicing out this tune and that. They didn't sound too certain of any of them.

The sun climbed. The topmen clewed up the first set of sails, unbent them, sent them below, and began bending on the second suit to air.

Twelve bells sounded. Noon. The lookouts passed the call aloft, alow. Cal's stomach rumbled. He couldn't decide if it was hunger or his bowels.

—Move your slops aft, a voice said.

—Eh, Boats?

—Move your negritians' slops aft, Hanks. The men don't like them mixed in wi' their own.

Despite the exec's threats, his boys were still aboard, no doubt due to the man shortage. The ship was so short-crewed they could man only one broadside at a time. Not a season to discharge a gun team, black or any other color. But they'd been shifted aft and below, to Mr. Stuyvesant's division; the crew of one of the after nine-inchers replaced them at the pivot. Their punishment for Mouskko Goran's lashing out, apparently. That landsman himself had been demoted to third-class boy, fined three months' pay, and double-ironed below for two months on hardtack and water six days out of seven. He'd emerged quieter, thinner, with the hate in his eyes banked to a fiery glow. He walked silently now, and neither sang nor did the breakdown; but Cal had the feeling more than one cannon might break loose aboard *Cumberland* should the weather turn heavy.

He passed the boatswain's order on and went forward to the heads.

He was waiting patiently to get his ease when a smoke caught his eye. It was far down the river, but it was black, like from a coal-fire. He watched it for some time before a flat detonation sounded. A lazy cloud pushed out from *Roanoke*'s side, the flagship, miles away, toward the fort.

Followed a few minutes later by the rattle of the clackers and the call to man up the starboard guns. He pulled his trowsers to and jogged down the spar deck, colliding off the other running hands. Passed Mr. Morris and Mr. Selfridge on the quarterdeck, touching his head as he jogged past. They took no note of him; their faces were turned, etched with anticipation, toward the distant veil of slowly sifting smoke, like charcoal powder trickling upward into the bright March sky. Selfridge had a glass to his eye.

—Three of them. Something strange in the center.

—The Great Bugaboo? At last?

—It may be.

On the low-roofed gun deck, his men were standing to. Braced at attention, Johnson reported all present and held out the gun-captain's waistbelt. Hanks buckled it on, a worn leather apron with pockets. —Man up, he snapped. Henry, Tompkins, Ewins, Jock, Rollins, Williams, Smith, Goran, and the others ranged around the black shining barrel, the heavy oak truck-carriage. The gear was freshly blacked, sanded, and polished in preparation for tomorrow's inspection. The powder came up, and the orphan lad, Puncie, set the bucket down a few paces off.

Hanks watched Mr. Stuyvesant, who paced back and forth at the companionway where he could pass word from topside. The minutes stretched. Down here he could no longer see the smoke, could see actually nothing at all with the port lids closed. Just the line of guns, the men, waiting in tense expectancy. But only half those they needed; only one broadside manned.

Stuyvesant cupped his ear upward. Then shouted, —Starboard side: cast loose and provide.

The line of men and iron broke into noise and motion. Tackle squealed as it reeved through blocks. The port lids lifted like opening eyes. Their own came up, revealing suddenly, as in some bright-lighted theater, the Roads, the sky. One far-distant jib sail, some oyster dredger headed for Pig Point. And far away, whatever was coming. He could make out now three separate smokes and a shadow beneath the central one.

—Seen the cap'n when you was topside? Chubb Johnson said out of the side of his mouth.

—Ashore, Cal muttered. Then shouted, —Get those breechings cleared. Clear away those housing chocks. He checked the side-tackle, then pulled the lock cover off and handed it to one of the train tacklemen. Primers came up, and he counted them out and stowed them in his waistbelt, along with the priming wire, boring bit, and thumbstall. He tucked one carefully between first and second finger, the sensitive fulminate head fisted in his palm. Like a thick but strangely light copper bolt.

—Captain's ashore? Goran said.

—First lieutenant in charge den, someone said. —Mister Morris.

—Pipe down, Cal told them. He shaded his eyes, looking out toward the smoke.

—You sees it? asked Goran.

—Can't see much yet.

—Like de roof off de barn. Smokin away there in de middle.

The bargeman had sharp eyes. —Move that water bucket away from the carriage, Hanks told him. —Pay tention to your fuckin duties, Goran, not to nothing else. An I told y'all to pipe down.

—I hears ye, Marster Driver.

Cal popped him on the back of the head. Goran's skull snapped forward, and he went quiet, though his hands gripped and regripped the loading staff. —Anybody else just got to run his lip? Hanks asked them all.

Nobody did.

They loaded with solid shot and ran out; trained left, pointing at the oncoming smoke. Stood for minutes and then more, nerves drawing like wound-up banjo strings. Cal wasn't the only one to rub a juju, cross himself, or hop on one foot. At last the word came, passed from crew to crew. —It's going back in.

They muttered. Some whispered curses. Cal waggled his head angrily. Going back in? After months of waiting? What were the Marsters thinking on? But then after a time came word she was standing on again. Whatever, he thought, she was coming very damned slow.

Mr. Selfridge came halfway down the companionway. He said in a loud voice that in a moment he'd beat retreat for dinner. He wanted all hands to eat before the action. All gear, implements, powder, and shells would remain on station. The smoking lamp would stay out. Cal sent Puncie down for their fletch of meat and pot of beans. They ate sitting around the gun, looking out over the rippled surface that glowed with the lofted sun. The mist was gone now, and the Roads stretched like a silver field before them to the low purple, miles distant, of Sewell's Point. Goran sang and hollered out the port. The white crews shouted for Cal to shut him up, he was making too much noise. Cal ignored them.

The distant vessels drew onward. Two were much smaller, he judged, than *Cumberland*. The thing they escorted was like no craft he'd ever seen. Not like a ship at all, more like a three-quarters-submerged barn with only a slate roof showing. Later he made out gunports and a bump that might be a pilothouse. The single stack was pouring out smoke at a gigantic rate, staining the eastern sky like an oncoming storm. The detonation of a gun tolled lazy and small across the water. The monster did not respond.

Puncie came up with water, set the bucket aside against need. Then stood watching, head cocked like a curious puppy. Even Goran was quiet now, watching the oncoming juggernaut. Its slowness was daunting, like the creep of some huge black alligator intent on its prey. For a time it had looked as if it was headed downriver, toward the shipping anchored off the fort. But then it had turned, veered this way and that, as if testing its steering. And finally steadied, right for them.

Cal's belly congealed around the overcooked beans, the fatty pork. The tugs were lagging back, angling for the center of the roadstead. Behind them more black columns were building into the heavens. The other sloops and frigates of the federal squadron, he guessed. Coming to their aid, he hoped. Whatever this thing was, the more guns trained on it, the better. He took the priming wire from his belt and twisted it in his fingers.

It was here, the time they'd dreaded and anticipated for months: There weren't enough men, but they were well drilled. The guns were ready.

Half a mile short of them the thing drew abreast of *Congress*. The older frigate—unengined and deep-keeled, like the ship he stood on, and thus all but unmaneuverable in light airs like today's—lay anchored off east of the point, *Cumberland* to the west. The enemy was a couple of hundred yards to seaward of her when the frigate's side turned into white smoke and lightning.

A second later the rippling thuds of a twenty-five-gun broadside reached them. They were followed by a strange discordant clanging, like a flatcar full of rails turned over and dumped on stone. He shaded his eyes. White foam burst around the newcomer, but he didn't see any overshoots.

He caught his breath. His gaze had tracked a black speck upward, to the zenith, where it burst suddenly into a cotton boll. Caught other specks bounding backward, like India-rubber balls.

The monster kept approaching. Not until it had almost reached the motionless frigate did it curve away, presenting its own broadside.

Flashes, thuds from the Leviathan. His heart bounded into his throat. Heavy guns, all right. Heavy as their own, though it didn't sound to be as many. He could hear the crumps as shells went off inside the frigate. Could hear the thin distant screams of men being torn apart.

Around him his boys stirred uneasily. Someone was saying —Mah Lord Jesus, mah Lord Jesus, over and over.

—Stand to, came Selfridge's shout, passed on instantly by Stuyvesant. Then, a moment later, —Starboard side: prime!

Cal jumped up on the carriage, directly behind the great black bell of the breech, and leaned over it to check the vent. Clear. He jammed the stiff wire downward. Felt the resistance of the woolen charge-cloth, then the yielding as the wire pierced it and grated into the corned grains. Jerked it out, pushed a primer in with his other hand, and pressed the wafer down firmly on the vent field.

—Point!

As the train tacklemen took a strain, the handspikemen levering the carriage around, Cal bent to peer out. He judged the range at eight hundred yards. He decided against ricochet firing. He wanted their blow to strike hard as possible. He loosed the screw and set the brass staff of the breech sight. Threw back the hammer and jumped back out of the way. —Train left, full left, he shouted to the train tacklemen. Chubb spun the handle on the elevating screw to bring the barrel down to match the sight angle. The roller handspikemen levered the rear of the carriage up, and the great black bottle glided around, the starboard-side tacklemen giving way. Till he shouted them to a halt and bent to peer again.

The oncoming pyramid had grown. He could see rails now, and davits, and the guys of the stack. A ripple, as at the base of a shark's fin, as the sea parted a few yards ahead of the visible iron.

Feathers of foam leaping up. The shore batteries were opening, but not accurately. The monster was still advancing. The broadside from *Congress* hadn't stopped it. In fact he didn't see it had slowed or even damaged it, while smoke was burning off the frigate. He told Chubb to come down a trifle, and stood poised on the balls of his feet, lockstring taut. He wouldn't have to wait for the roll. Not with this calm a sea. He didn't like the way the frigate's projectiles had *bounced* off the thing. But the older ship had only eight-inchers. He was standing behind a nine-incher, firing a shell twenty pounds heavier, ahead of twice the charge of powder; Mr.

Selfridge had increased the normal cartridge charge to thirteen pounds and made them double the breechings to take the increased recoil. Their forward pivot was even heavier, a ten-inch smoothbore, and their stern gun a seventy-pound rifle. Guns like these would slam through four feet of oak, punch through one side of a ship of the line and out the other.

But as he watched, the thing sidled out of their view, out of their arc of fire, too far on their bow to bear on. —Man the port guns, Stuyvesant called. —Shift.

—Ports down, Cal shouted. —Haul taut the train tackles.

With an almighty scramble two hundred men left the guns to starboard, raced to the port side, and began frantically repeating every action and movement they'd just completed. But when the port lids swung up, Cal saw blinking out in the sudden light that they couldn't bear from this side either. The monster must be dead ahead. The shout came down to shift again, and back they raced, panting, slipping on the sanded decks.

Apparently the forward guns could bear, because the slam of firing came down the companionway. Smoke began to seep along the overhead. A deeper boom made the Avengers look at each other. It was their old bow pivot. Cracks and explosions from topside made them flinch. But they still stood waiting, Cal cursing and trying to lever the carriage around to bear. Till finally she did, and he raised his hand to Stuyvesant.

—Starboard battery . . . ready . . . fire.

A massive slam and recoil. The world turned white as molted cotton and bitter as quinine. He didn't see where his shot went. The sponger and then the loaders stepped up to work furiously.

When he looked out again, the angle was changing. *Cumberland* was swinging ponderously around. Coming in on the spring line, hauling her stern around to present her broadside to the enemy. Along the deck echoed the scrape and squeal of carriages slewing, the knockety rattle of loading staffs, hoarse shouts of gun-captains. He caught another glimpse of the monster, in grape-distance now and still coming on, as he stepped up to prime and cock. Goran yelling, —Yah, yah, Marster, take dat licking. Come suck my arse. Cal bending to aim. Sealing behind his eyes to keep forever the black slanting sides, glistening in the sunlight; gun muzzles protruding from open ports; that broad-banded flag, stirring in the light wind. Tripping the lockstring in a fury of flying fire, unburned powder grains sizzling around like scorching fireflies. He batted a spark off his blouse sleeve, but it left a smoking hole. Another two dollars gone. He felt annoyed before he reflected there was a good chance he'd never have to pay it.

Because when the smoke rose again in a misty curtain, he whispered, —Gor a mighty.

The iron mass was still coming on, not even touched by the shot he was certain must have hit. *Had* to have hit. He couldn't have missed at this range.

If it could endure that, if its sides could take a solid shot flung hard as that—

—Fire, Stuyvesant called again, and he realized they'd loaded while his mind was someplace else. His sights were filled with iron now, so close he could see rivet heads. Then the flash and fire of an enemy salvo, the shock blast hitting their faces across the water, and simultaneously great tearing crashes around him, the quiver of shells ripping into oak and pine.

A tranquility came over him. Face to face. Gun to gun. What happened now wasn't up to him. It was simple now.

He set his feet and pulled the lockstring again.

19

The Confederacy Expects Every Man to Do His Duty ♦ Close Passage
of U.S.S. *Congress* ♦ Ramming of U.S.S. *Cumberland* ♦ Loss of C.S.S.
Virginia Only Averted by Shoddy Workmanship ♦ A Close Fire Heartily
Returned ♦ How to Make a Dog Civil ♦ A Tack-Country Reel
Before the Slaughter Resumes

COMMODORE Franklin Buchanan, C.S.N., stood foursquare in the center of the casemate, telescope under his arm. The flushed, windburned old man was finishing what Minter thought was the most inspiring harangue he'd ever heard. Or perhaps he and the others huzzaing themselves husky had never been so ready to be inspired. The phrases rumbled like an oncoming thunderhead. Devotion to our cause . . . strike for your country and your homes . . . the eyes of the world are upon you . . . the Confederacy expects every man to do his duty.

He ended with the command to beat to quarters, and as the pulse-quickening tattoo began, Henry Lomax Minter roared with his boys until his throat rasped and tears blurred his eyes.

Outside, a single report quieted the din. He shouted for silence and pushed his men back into their positions. Slipped past to the port and craned out.

But could see nothing. Their starboard faced Sewell's Point, not the Foe toward which they steamed. Troops waved from atop the fortifications. He caught the flash of a spyglass lens, but saw nothing of their enemy.

Assistant Engineer White, in charge of the signal bell on the gun deck, stepped back from a forward port. —That was *Raleigh* signaling. She and the other tug are falling back. The Federals are steaming to intercept.

The air seemed hotter, the engines to be vibrating faster. The massive structure around them had picked up a long, disturbing pitch that angled the deck gradually up, then very gradually down. The bright oval of the port framed a distant cloud in the shape of a horse and rider. Or so it appeared to Lomax for a time, but gradually altered till it lost any semblance and became merely cloud again.

—Run out, came a shrill voice. The flag lieutenant, perched on the forward ladder where he could hear the commodore and relay commands.

Lomax turned to his Georgians. They wiped their hands on their trowsers. —Start her cautiously, now. Tharpe, heave up on the handspike. Volentine, Dunlop, pull out those truck quoins and tend the breeching.

Since the slanting overhead restricted the space so severely, the ports had been placed alternately and not opposite one another. When run in, the carriage butts of each gun overlapped the next. With a grating rumble that shook the planking a central aisle now magically opened down the casemate.

—Prime.

Lomax reprimanded a man talking to his comrade. He checked that the quill went in correctly and made sure Tharpe and the second captain were ready for the elevation order. In the bright circle that seemed unreal, like a screen on which some magic lantern casts a slowly moving scene, the beaches of the point were giving way to open water. They were turning. A massive wheel to port that went on for many minutes. It brought the battlements of the Rip Raps into view. Lomax caught the scarlet lick of the enemy's flag. Past it, sail were standing out. Many sail, luffing in what looked like a stronger breeze over there, possibly from the Chesapeake. Puffs of whipped cream burst from Sewell's Point. The detonations reached them seconds later as distant bumps, like iron tubs being flipped over on soft ground.

—The transports are getting under way, murmured Lieutenant Butt. Gun number six, to his right.

—Too bad we couldn't have gotten among them.

But it might not be too late. There were transports in the James as well, upriver of *Congress* and *Cumberland*, which seemed to be Buchanan's initial targets. Perhaps they could take them as prizes after disposing of the warships.

During this time he'd heard in the back of his thoughts the occasional closer thud of a gun of moderate size. He couldn't see who was firing, though. As the wheel continued, the warships steaming in from the Chesapeake came into view. Only one was under way of its own power. The others were being drawn by gunboats or shouldered by thrashing tugs lashed alongside. The smoke of their laborious advance stained the bright sky like an oncoming squall. Thinking of the heavy guns they carried, hundreds to their own meager ten, Lomax was hard put to keep his knees from quivering. A wooden ship took her time going down, but this iron carapace would plummet like a sounding lead. With two hundred men, a hundred more below, all trying to get topside up narrow ladders . . . He locked his hands behind his back and put on a careless expression. —What time have you there, Mister Butt?

The other drawled as unconcernedly it lacked a few minutes of two.

Virginia veered toward the oncoming Federals, then swung back to port. He looked out over the gun at the low coast. White wings dotted the blue curving expanse of Hampton Flats. Small craft, fleeing for the shelter of Hampton Creek.

Behind that low beach lay McClellan's hordes. Despoilers of Southern soil. The scum of crowded cities, inflamed against a free people with promise of loot and rapine. If he elevated for full range, he could plant shell in their encampments from here.

But no order came. The engines labored unevenly, faltering, wheezing, like some massive invalid. He shifted his feet and wiped sweat from his brow. The men, jackets off, were in colorful shirts or the upper garments of their long underwear. He must retain his, and in the heat coming up from the furnaces, the heavy wool was like a Turkish sweatbox.

My God, he thought desperately. Let us get to this business.

—Bow gun: *Cumberland* dead ahead. One thousand yards.

Lomax watched Charlie Simms at the bow pivot bend to look along his sights. An instant later a terrific crack, different from the bellow of a smoothbore, lashed through the casemate. A whiff of smoke followed it, filling their nostrils with burnt powder.

—Stand fast, he told his boys. —We'll have our chance presently. Southall! Stand away from that port. If you need something to do, clear the chains on that shot hoist.

A tremendous *clang* walloped the forward shield. Wood dust and chips jumped off it, fogging the air. The bow pivot fired again.

Now his lads were openly restive. Tharpe was shouting them into silence like unruly schoolboys when suddenly a savage onslaught of heavy, wrecking impacts marched down the whole side, one hitting, as far as he could tell, directly above the port of number four. The noise was terrifying. Faces went pallid, looked about anxiously. Someone screamed, far up the interior, and was instantly silenced. The noise ebbed away, ringing in his ears. He saw men reaching up to touch the interior of the shield, to knock on the heavy oak. Like bettors rubbing a good-luck piece. He reached up a furtive hand himself.

They were turning. Peering over the barrel, Lomax saw a ship swim slowly into view. Smoke walked toward them across the calm water in a shining bank. *Congress*, moored fore and aft, but men aloft setting jib and topsails. Most likely it was her broadside they'd received.

—*Cumberland*. Starboard battery. Three hundred yards.

Tharpe glanced at him, questioning his cue. Lomax nodded. He stepped in when the private was done, checking the sight. —Signal with your hand to raise or lower, Lomax told him. —When the band begins to play in earnest, you'll not be able to hear a thing. You need to point farther left to bring your line of aim on your target.

—*Fire*. The division officer's yell triggered a succession of deafening blasts as one after the other the starboard guns flung themselves inboard and snapped to a halt at the end of their tackles. The flashes lit the crew's faces. Tharpe jerked the lanyard, and number four crashed back, blotting out everything outside the trapped world with a white-yellow, seething, sulphurous gloom over which slanting rays played through the overhead. They could see nothing of the target, but as they finished reloading and the air cleared slightly, Lomax saw it was passing rapidly astern and out of their field of fire.

Beneath their feet the engines were raging. He'd understood Jones to say they were at full speed back in the river, but obviously the engineers had been holding something back. The racket increased. Smoke poured from where the shot hoist led down to the furnaces. The interior was so gloomed now from firing and fumes he could not see the far end of it. Glancing up he saw blue-trowsered legs on the ladder. Leaning and twisting he saw they belonged to Buchanan. The commodore was standing in the hatchway, chest and head exposed. The minutes dragged by. Occasionally a tap would sound on the outside of the shield. Like a raindrop. Then they'd all stagger as tons of iron crashed into them. The most savage blows seemed to be falling on the forward casemate. The iron was weaker up there. Built-up one-inch plates instead of the two-inch layers farther aft. If a shot came through, it would sweep the length of the deck, wreck the guns, and turn the interior into an abattoir.

Meanwhile he'd been watching smoke puff out from the batteries ashore, so near he could sometimes see the troops working the guns. The order came down at last for the starboard battery to take them under fire. Here was employment, and he set his lads to firing with shell, cutting the fuzes to five seconds.

The din and smoke became overwhelming, sight and understanding limited to a few feet. The blast of their guns mingled with the clangor of projectiles colliding with iron inches above their heads. He screamed at the men to keep away from the ports, not to give targets to sharpshooters. At one point he heard Buchanan shout something and caught White's thin voice repeating engine orders. The bell jangled. The engines slowed their beat, slowed further; for a few seconds stopped. A cyclops whaled mightily on the shield with a brazen maul. Then the racket below started up again, but the rhythm was different. Perhaps they were running in reverse.

They labored, stopped, labored again. Shouts echoed below, through the hoist hatch. Then the legs changed their position on the step. The beat increased its tempo, became a resounding clangor like a junkyard tearing itself apart.

—Stand fast. We're going to run into her.

He shouted to his men to cease fire and brace themselves, and grabbed a stanchion.

The impact was a thrumming crunch, a push forward. Perhaps a rending sound, but it wasn't very loud. All this time the forward pivot had been firing, and number two and three when they could bear.

But now began a tremendous battering. Broadside after broadside crashed into them along with a continuous rain-rattle of bullets. Through the port Lomax saw pieces flying off the casemate, whether shell fragments or chunks of armor he did not know, and splashing into the sea. They could hear top-hamper carrying away, clanging and scraping down the slide-slant of greased iron. Smoke seethed, walling man from man.

He was looking at a pool of piss on the deck when he realized it was running forward. Yes, the bow was tending downward. The engines were pounding away. Something must have come loose, as a clatter was added to each stroke.

A massive explosion blasted their eardrums from directly above. Fragments pelted down through the grating, pinged off the hot breeches.

To his horror, he saw water pouring in the forward gunports. Their victim still had hold of them. Was dragging them down into the depths with her as she went.

By now Tharpe and the boys had the rhythm, still awkward, but they had their movements down, and he was able to step back. From the next gun Davidson's glance crossed his. The lieutenant put his face close and yelled, —The James squadron's joining. Past the batteries and on their way to help.

This was good news. Anything to distract some of this fire. The shore batteries were throwing light shell, but even a six-pounder could spread havoc if it found one of their open ports. Which he could not believe none of them yet had.

A tremendous crack, right outside. Iron blanged around. He threw his arm up. When the smoke cleared, the boys pointed and cried out. The tapered barrel ended in a jaggedness, like a cracked-off tooth.

He pushed his way through to inspect. A full foot of the muzzle was sheared off short. A clean break, though. He couldn't see any cracks that might expand under further firing. A shell or ball must have hit it square. They were lucky it hadn't ricocheted inboard. He glanced out at a lowering mist. Powder-smoke and coal-smoke hugged rocking, jostling waves. A bullet spanged by, and he turtled back hastily.

—Cease firing, sir? Tharpe bawled.

—No. Keep firing, he shouted. —But stand clear of the muzzle.

When they lanyarded her next, the ravening blast of flame out of the cropped tube set the wood framing of the gunport on fire. As the men shouted and threw sand and beat at it with their jackets, he panted, bent, hands planted on his thighs. Fighting a red tide of rage that nearly overwhelmed his rational faculty.

When he looked forward again, the inflooding water had stopped. It seemed they'd regained an even keel. Her motion was different, too. Still logy, but freer. The impacts on their shield continued, though more raggedly now—a sporadic drumfire rather than the battering of broadsides.

The smoke cleared slightly, drifting up through the grating. The charred wood around the gunport still smoked, but the flames were out. Through it he glimpsed a wharf with a steamer alongside. He pointed it out to Tharpe and Davidson. After two broadsides the steamer was on fire, and so was their port, again. He saw one shot, perhaps not his own, plough down the pier, throwing boards into the air before it exploded.

When the flames were under control again, he shifted his attention to a shore battery that seemed to have found their range. They dueled until it drifted beyond their traverse. And gradually the battering fell away. Their own firing slackened. Wood, in command of the stern pivot, found a target and sent three rounds on their way. Then he too ceased. Panting troops stepped back from their weapons, bent, gasping the impure fumy air, or plunged their hands into fire buckets to splash water over the visages of coal miners.

An uncertain quiet drifted like powder-smoke down the hollow chamber of iron and oak, underscored by the dragging thud of the engines. Till the flag-lieutenant came running down the aisle, waving his cap. —We've sunk her! We've sunk the *Cumberland*!

As the casemate rang out in cheers, Jones came down the ladder. The exec's face was filthy. He was rubbing his hands like a rag dealer ready to haggle. —Boys! Listen up. A little breathing space. Boatswain! Organize something to restore our strength.

A ragged second huzza, broken by coughing. Jones held up a palm for attention. —*Cumberland* has gone down. Never was such a gallant fight. She never struck. Not to the last. But we ran a hole into her big enough to drive a cart through. He took a breath. —We've taken over a hundred hits. We're past the point and beginning a turn back to the east. It'll take a while to get our head round. We must be cautious. The Middle Ground's close, and the tide's starting to ebb. The commodore's trying to wind her. Our keel's dragging in the mud, but we're still moving.

The huzzaing sounded faint after the clamor of the guns. But the hands thronging to the ports called that it was all true. Lomax caught a glimpse of their late foe's mast slowly inclining. Caught another, minutes later, of a large paddle wheeler, he guessed *Patrick Henry,* heading down the river, smoke drifting ahead and splashes leaping up around as the federal artillery banged away from the shore.

Jones resumed pitching his hoarsened voice toward the overhead as the purser served out rum. The rest of the Government fleet had either run themselves aground or turned tail. *Congress* was beached and helpless. *Minnesota* was aground too, as was *St. Lawrence. Roanoke* was retreating toward Fort Monroe. After finishing with *Congress,* they'd take on the others. Clear out the whole nest.

—The only way to make a dog civil is to whip him, he shouted. —That's what we're doing, boys, and I expect Old *Ape* to be more polite the next time he tries to deprive a Southron of his rights. Liberty! Or death!

Lomax found a handkerchief and mopped his face. It came away black. His eyeballs felt scorched. The rum cask got to his position. He let the boys drink first, then tossed back the tin cup, rim greasy from many hands and lips. The raw spirit smoldered his gullet like lava.

Safe behind an iron bulwark. Invulnerable to the heaviest charges the enemy could throw. The greatest naval victory of all time. Wooden ships, history. Sails, history. The blockade, history.

He gagged rum fumes and smoke. Grinned as his boys pounded him on the back, as they danced wild tack-country jig-reels elbow in elbow.

He could hardly believe it. But this day's work might end the war.

20

Butting Heads with the Leviathan ♦ Forward, and What Was Found There ♦
A Hail to Surrender ♦ Blood in the Scuppers ♦ The Advance of the Sea ♦
Every Man for Himself ♦ A Parting Fire ♦ Turning from the Shore ♦
Belowdecks in the Sinking Sloop of War *Cumberland* ♦ The Dying
and the Drowned ♦ A Committal to the Sea

THE shell burst with a flash, but it wasn't its bursting that killed
the crew at the next gun. It was the jagged oak splinters ripped
from the side as it went through. Some went down without a
word. Others rolled and kicked, spewing blood in whirling jets.

When Cal looked back, Goran was down too, grunting as he tried to
cup the small of his back. His fingers traced an oaken dagger big as an axe
handle, driven in so solid that when Hanks braced his boot against the
bargeman's back, it wouldn't budge. Goran said he couldn't feel his legs.

—You git on below, get fixed up, Cal told him. —We'll finish this up.

—Serve it out to the marsters, Cal. You fuckin big dumb Georgia
nigger.

The lazarette mates hustled the wounded below. The dead, and those
portions of the living the shells had torn from them, they dragged to the
disengaged side and left in the scuppers. Cal kept firing, until the monster
filled his sights, then passed from vision beneath the muzzle.

The thing lurched into them with a grating shock that slopped water
from buckets, shattered lanterns, and knocked every spare staff and chain

pendant and selvagee wad and every other piece of racked gear down out of the overhead. *Cumberland* groaned. An iron clatter ran aloft and along, rattling her blocks and spars as she reeled hard over. Timbers snapped with echoing cracks, like bones being crunched by a bear. Chubb stepped back. The gun was loaded again. But Cal, kicking loose gear out of the way of the carriage trucks, couldn't depress the barrel enough to bear.

He couldn't even see the monster that was chewing into his ship's vitals like a raccoon into a hog carcass. Only a glimpse through smoke of a black slanting, smeared, it looked like, with tallow, and down below the rebel's guns flashing in the murk. Of the placid green of the Roads, gored into a creamy boil by shot and shell. He rammed the carriage against the sweep piece and jammed the side of the barrel hard against the port sill. A yank of the lockstring sent a solid shot crashing through the stack that volcanoed out black clouds which mixed with yellowish powder-murk in a swirling, choking gloom that closed off the sun.

The deck rolled back, bringing his sights back down, and the Avengers loaded and fired as fast as seamen probably ever had. Sparks flew as a shot ran along the casemate and glanced off into the water. The black hide of the thing smoked, glowed with yellow grease flame where his ball had flinted off it. He aimed at a protruding muzzle. A prolonged, many-voiced bellow shook the sloop. All the guns were firing. Shells tore up through the hull and burst, reaping men down. A screaming cheer rose from forward. Cal didn't know why, but he too howled his pipes raw, voicing his own feeble defiance into the mighty din of huge guns, explosions, the shrieks of the dying, and the laboring stroke of what he realized was the engine of the monster, close alongside.

—Hanks. Hanks! Shift your boys forward to number one.

Hanks stared at a Stuyvesant barely recognizable in blackface. His collar was torn open, he was hatless, and dark blood soaked a shoulder. —Sah? He struggled to understand. —Forward?

The division officer repeated himself as a shot glanced down the gun deck, bowling men down till it came to rest, spinning wildly, under the companionway. Whether it had come from the thing alongside or from the howitzers banging away ashore was impossible to know. Cal screamed himself deaf, getting the Avengers' attention. Then shouted, —Follow me.

At quick time, up the disengaged side. Past recoiling guns, still being fired though the crews had to shoulder the mass of tube and carriage up-hill now against the list. Then up the companionway, into daylight turned yellow as piss by overarching smoke.

He blinked, so completely had the world changed. Above his head the masts tolled off a pendulum knell. Sand grated under his boot soles, and grains of powder sodden with blood. The galley had been blown apart by a direct hit. Bricks and pots lay everywhere. The scuppers were clogged with powder boxes, broken rammers, and bodies in every twisted abandonment of posture. They lay in that curious relaxed limpness he'd seen before in the dead, as if all trouble and strife had passed. And of course blood, drooling overboard from the scuppers. Shells howled in the murk. Fragments whacked through the smoke haze, the darkness of twilight in the midst of day. The pops of muskets sounded muffled, as if they were going off inside hogsheads. Here and there the small-arms men stepped to the bulwark, aimed down carbines to burst out more smoke and fire. Forward, past the mainmast, insane shrieks burst from an armless hulk being half-carried, half-beaten below. Cal recognized Kirker, the coxswain. Past Lieutenant Morris, standing stiffly erect, kid gloves locked behind him. Morris nodded as he passed, and Cal touched his cap.

Past the foremast his steps slowed.

The entire pivot crew had been wiped out by the same shell. It had come up through the gunwale and main-deck planking before exploding. Not just killed, but butchered, blown apart into gory morsels that lay draped across the still-glossy gun-lacquer like red meaty ribbons, flayed yellow strips of human fatback. A pale white hand, still in a blue blouse sleeve, gripped the compressor, attached to nothing. He pressed his palm between his jaws and bit down. The smell was just like hog-killing, the same stink of blood, shit, chitterlings, and smoke.

Chubb stepped past and shouted the boys into position. After a second Cal gripped himself and joined them, kicking the hand over the side. The roar of gunnery went on and on, but the pounding of engines had lessened. He noted with a detached calm that the monster that had fucked itself into them like some randy bull attacking a tethered heifer was no longer alongside. It had backed off but was still pouring in fire from no farther away than he could have thrown a line to.

—Will you surrender, sir?

The shout carried faint across the monstrous anger of the guns. Lifting his head, Cal saw a slim figure in blue across the water. Exposed from the waist up, he was shading his eyes toward them. He heard the question but not the reply. It must have been in the negative, for the midships battery boomed out, and when he could see again, the rebel was gone.

Chubb ran the loading staff free and stepped aside, holding it up with his hand gripped at the red loading mark. Cal checked the priming. The cap was in place but unfired. The ball must just have been rammed home when the crew killer went off. When he grasped the lockstring, it was sodden with blood. Cal didn't know if she had shell or shot in her, but it didn't matter. He tried to get the sight on where the casemate armor bent around the corner of the barn roof. There was no vertical at all in the ram, nowhere his projectile would meet anything but slanting iron. He could see daylight through her stack, which was leaking great gouts of smoke, and the davit dangled along her side, shot free of its moorings. Perhaps the submerged body, which he could faintly see at times forward of the casemate. It wasn't much of a target, but he aimed for it and let drive.

When he looked back toward the waist, he saw dimly through the murk that the sloop's stern was rising. She was settling by the bows.

He turned back to see Chubb peering into the smoke. Then suddenly he had no head. The copper New England visage, the dark smooth hair, gone. Vanished. Simultaneously came the rush of something gigantic passing just over his own crown. A terrific bang succeeded. The trunk staggered back, pumping blood, hands opening and closing. Its heel caught on the pivot rail, and it went full length. The train tacklemen grabbed it by the arms and hauled it to the disengaged side.

Gesturing woodenly, Cal motioned Narcy Ewins up to the loader position. Another crack and flash, and something fast as light scooped the meat off the length of Asberry Rollins's right arm. The shamefaced regretful look Rollins turned to him was the same with which he'd confessed not taking a hint about calling himself a freeman, back in the Grand Camp. One of the new men went down too, gurgling, clawing at his throat. Perhaps a rebel musket ball.

The Ethiopian Cannoneers were being winnowed. The timbers beneath them shook and rang as something heavy burrowed through the chain locker. A shell burst just beyond the dropped bulwark, showering them with cold water, and looking down he saw that murky surface closer than it should have been.

The ship lay over like a tired thing wanting to rest. Someone shouted to aim at the ram's gunports. But Cal couldn't see it anymore. The firing was slackening. He couldn't see the stern; the smoke was too heavy now. The choking coal-smoke from the monster's colandered stack, and its powder-smoke, and their own. He couldn't see what he was aiming at, but when Ewins pulled back the staff, he leapt up to push home the primer, carefully because the slide was blood-slick and he didn't want to fall. He aimed at a flash in the fog and let drive again.

Something cold washed over his feet. He looked down to see the bowsprit lying its length down. Green water gushed and bubbled up through the bridle ports like some miraculous spring.

A supernaturally hollow voice aft jerked him from his reverie. Mr. Morris had a speaking trumpet to his lips. —Every man for himself. Abandon ship. Boats are standing off astern.

—Get the hell back to your place, Cal snapped at one of the younger train tacklemen. Who hesitated, then took his position again. To their credit, not one of the boys at the gun itself had moved a muscle. Just looked to him for orders as the sea rippled toward their brogans.

—One last round for Chubb an' Goran. Yeah, and Loftis too. Solid shot and a double charge.

They didn't hesitate, though they knew it meant the gun might burst. His whole being was concentrated on the unnatural thing that tormented them from within the seething cloud. The sponge, in and out. One red-woolen cylinder of powder, rammed home. A second, and two boys strained to hoist the shot. Seventy pounds of solid wrought iron. It had to be as hard as whatever covered the monster. With a long shove the loaders drove it home.

He stood in a foot of water now. It was rolling aft as the sloop began burrowing her nose under the shell-torn, splinter-flecked surface. She lurched sluggishly as if deciding which way to capsize. He clung to the breech, squinting for a glimpse. It was still out there. The thud of its guns told him that. But he couldn't see it.

The boys were leaving now, slipping off. He couldn't blame them. He was going too. Directly he got off this last pop. The deck shuddered, and in the screams and crying from aft he heard something give way below. Another shell exploded in the fore-rigging, spearing iron-tipped spirals of smoke down into the struggling sailors, two and three deep, who lined the shoreward bulwark. Morris had mentioned boats, but Cal didn't see any. Men were clambering over the bulwarks, sliding down dangling braces. The smoke-covered sea was dotted with bobbing black heads like those of seals.

It was time to leave her. He couldn't train now nor elevate, his men were either dead or wounded below or gone aft, so he simply judged the roll as best he could and stepped aside, cringing away in case it burst, and triggered the last round off.

The sound was enormous. The gun blew backward, sheared off the compressors, and slammed into the opposite bulwark, dismounted and useless. A clang came back, a tolling from the fog that might or might not be a bolt colliding with an iron wall.

He dropped the useless lockstring and waded aft.

Uphill against and through a shoving, elbowing, howling melee. All discipline gone. Officer and man fought for safety without distinction. He thought about his seabag, his hammock. His bag was below, and his hammock was still lashed in the nets. The most important thing, his gold, was around his waist, thank God, strapped secure in the canvas money belt. He stepped up onto a horse block and looked down. The water was almost calm except for the disturbances of bursting shells. Small wavelets jostled the men who swam and struggled there. A party of white men was struggling to push a fallen spar over the side. It toppled onto a warrant officer struggling to swim with only one arm. He did not rise again.

Cal grabbed a bucket, then discarded it. He could see already that the two boats aft weren't going to hold all those who clamored and pushed along the sinking deck. But the bucket was all there was, and since it was wood, he picked it up again and climbed up on the bulwark and stood there, clinging to a shroud.

He hesitated, not looking forward to the shock of that water. He guessed it as four, five hundred yards to the surf-line, maybe more. He gathered himself to jump.

Trembled there, then stepped back from the brink.

He had one thing more to see to.

Water shimmered at the bottom of the companionway. He pushed through men who cursed him, struck at him as they fought their way up from below. Many were wounded, bleeding, limping, crying. Where was the surgeon? The surgeon's mates?

The berthing deck was a cavern with light streaming in smoky beams through jagged holes. He couldn't see where the thing had run into them, but it must have ripped her open, judging by how fast she was going. Splinters, shoring timbers, tarpaulin-caps, broken fire buckets, paper, shot-wads, the detritus of defeat circled on the swiftly rising water. The boatswain gazed emptily up from beneath its surface, blond hair waving, a gaping wound at his throat. Hanks hissed through his teeth.

He waded toward a howling darkness of wailing and pleas.

Most of those who'd gone below wounded were dead now. They lay with arms crossed, as the surgeon's mates had left them or as they'd composed themselves when the knowledge of death came. Those who weren't he turned his gaze from. Bowels torn open. The wheezing gasp of holed chests. To drown would cost them nothing. They knew this, and most lay without fuss in the rising water, though a few begged for help as he passed. He raised his hand but didn't answer. He was looking for his own. But the only one he found, Rollins, didn't open his eyes when Cal touched his shoulder above where his arm had been.

—Ovah heah.

Mouskko Goran had dragged himself up on another body whose face was in the water. The runaway's cheeks were gray, a hue Cal had seen on bad seasick darkeys. —They pull that splinter out of you? Cal asked him.

—Doctor man cut me. Then put me aside to die. You gone get me out of here?

—Sling your arm over my neck. This gone hurt now.

—Just get Moussko out of here, honey.

His arms gripped like a crab, but his legs dangled as if they'd already died. Cal waded and staggered toward the companionway. A few of the badly wounded and abandoned were still trying to crawl up it. The ladder was almost vertical now as the stern kept rising. Burbling screams rose as a flood tide rolled forward. —You hold on now, he muttered. —An' don't grab me round the throat like that. You like to stranglin me.

—Tote me up that ladder, nigger, an' don't waste your breath flappin your tongue.

But getting up the companionway with that dead weight on his back was the hardest thing he'd ever done. Halfway up he realized he wasn't going to make it. His arms were tearing off. Everything was going red.

Then he looked down and saw the water was keeping up with him. Rising as fast as he climbed. Timbers cracked deep in the hull. She was going down, and if he didn't get up to that square of light, they'd both go down with her, because he could tell Goran wasn't going to let go of him. He panted and kicked off desperate hands and with a blinding, despairing effort far beyond what he'd ever known was his strength hauled them sodden and wheezing over the hatch coaming out into the clearing light.

The monster wasn't firing at them anymore. The concussions had stopped, at least close to; he could still hear shooting from shoreward. When he tottered up on shaky pins, Goran still clamped to his back like the Old Man of the Sea, he saw the black thing a mile off and headed upriver. Smoke burst from its sides as it replied to the batteries on the point. Heading for Richmond, most like. Looking in the other direction, he saw the rest of the squadron bows on, although they didn't seem to be making much speed. So the battle wasn't over. But it was done with *Cumberland,* and it was time and past time to think about saving his own skin and Goran's if he could.

Which didn't look as if it was going to be easy, to keep from drowning. The sea was up to his knees even midships, flooding in through the freeing ports. He waded to the side and looked for a boat. But they were on their way to the beach, oars dipping and rising. A dotted string of bobbing heads trailed behind them, clinging to beams and casks as they kicked their way landward. He watched them, not feeling good about his chances.

At his ear a weak voice muttered, —You swim, nigger?

—Not a lick.

—It be nine o'clock bell for us, den.

—What you mean, darkey? Is you all right?

—Oh, I is jist fine, Goran said. —I done stood on my own bottom. Now lemme go and save yo'self.

—You go to Hell, Cal said. —We goin together, thass all.

He stood for a time more to see would any better idea come to him. None did. The water waited, sparkling and restless. He searched it with a terrible fear. He didn't see any sharks, but he knew they lurked down there. The man on his back silent too, yet gripping tight, Cal Hanks hesitated at the brink.

He turned his head and spat. Then, like a judged and doomed murderer from the gallows, he stepped grimly off onto the unbearing air.

21

Recuperation atop the Turret ♦ Ruddy Cheeks Against a Gray Sea ♦
Leaks and Hot Gas ♦ Evacuation of the Engine Room ♦ The Necessity
of a Lee ♦ One by One into the Breach ♦ Hand to Hand with
the Starboard Blower ♦ Four Hours with Morpheus, Succeeded by
a Struggle with the Tiller Ropes

THEO Hubbard came to with the wind streaming back his hair
and wailing in his ears. For a moment he didn't know where he
was. Then he felt the heave of iron beneath his recumbent body,
the sting of icy spray.

He heaved up on an elbow, glanced out across black sea, and was suddenly wrung by nausea like a hawser under strain. He vomited till his eyeballs started from their sockets. Then sagged back, so weak he couldn't
hold his head up any longer.

Around him on the turret top lay others, faces an unnatural cherry red.
They were gasping, stirring, vomiting. A nightmare scene illuminated by
the jerky gleams of a lantern whanging back and forth on a pennant-staff
atop the tower. He passed a hand over his face. It came off slick with a
greasy amalgam of seawater and vomitus and blood and coal dust.

The blowers, yes, the broken belts . . . the backflash from the furnaces . . . and the terrible choking as his lungs filled with poison gas. But
knowing he couldn't flee. If the engine room crew abandoned their posts,
the battery was doomed and all in her.

Then a shadow, staggering burdened out of the darkness, caroming into him.

To his astonishment it had been Joyce, and his fardel, looped over his neck like a soldier's blanket roll, the spare in its paper wrapping. Ten inches wide and half an inch thick, the leather drive belt was so heavy they both had to struggle to fit it onto the drive wheel. Then wrestle again to get it around the flanged pulley. And finally hoist the assemblage of the two, enormously awkward and backbreaking, into position to key into the shaft.

First Hand, then Joyce had dropped, suddenly sagged to the deck plates, eyeballs rolling white. Joyce going into a fit, back arched, heels drumming on the hollow iron, splashing in the icy sea still pouring down from above.

Hubbard had jammed his face as close to the blower housing as he could. Sucking in its frosty ice-breath, the cold pure air that wouldn't last; as the interior filled with toxic gas it would begin flowing out here too. But he got enough that his head cleared, though the shocking headache stayed. Through near blindness and in the dark he grabbed Hand and Joyce and dragged them by main force across the boiler flat, through the bulkhead hatch, and into the berthing space.

When the hatch sucked closed behind him, he could see again. The air wasn't solid smoke. He could breathe without that agonizing constriction, as if hot rollers were ironing out the lobes of his lungs. As if he'd smoked a dozen segars, one after the other, without bothering to breathe out.

But here too was confusion, crowding, torrents of numbing-cold water. The purser, who was helping pass unconscious men up the ladder, shouted that the turret was leaking. The plaited hempen gasket work the captain had insisted on putting between it and the base ring wasn't holding. Keeler looked past Theo at the others fighting their way out of the hole, smoke pouring out after them. He asked anxiously whether the pumps would keep working if no one was back there to attend to them.

Hubbard couldn't answer. He was bent over, coughing as if his kidneys were about to come up his throat. Strings of drool hung off his chin, black with soot. An iron spike had been hammered straight between his eyes. Keeler clapped at his back, and he whooped and finally got enough air to speak. —They'll run . . . for a time.

—Then what?

He didn't bother to answer. Even a land-green bean counter could figure out what would happen to an iron ship whose pumps stopped.

Newton staggered back. —I've told the captain what's happening. Asked him to find us a lee or we are lost.

—Can any be near?

—I don't think so. I heard Greene order the boats to be prepared.

Hubbard didn't like the sound of this any more than anything else that had happened in the last hours. The sea had been sweeping over the lifeboats, lashed down on the intermittently submerged deck. —What about our escorts? Can they take us off?

—Visibility's getting worse. And I don't think they've got any way to call them in or signal to them.

—It'll be full night soon, Keeler said. His pince-nez quivered, and he rubbed his little beard.

Newton said, —We've got to put the fires out. That's the only way we can get back in there. There's a fitting to wet them down, put them out—

—The fires are already wet. That's our fucking problem, Hubbard told him. —If you put them out, we'll lose steam pressure, lose the pumps, founder before we get them going again. Going cold iron's not the answer.

—What *is* the answer?

—If there is one, it's the blowers. That'll put everything right, if we can get those blades turning, get air coming in again. He looked at the hatch. —I'm going back. Who's with me?

A couple of the firemen said they'd go, but they didn't sound enthusiastic. He couldn't blame them. He pulled them in close and explained what they had to do. —First we must close up the furnaces. All right, you . . . you are—

—Feeny, sor. Coal heaver.

—The very man. You go in first. Bandanna over your mouth. Wet it, that's right. Take a deep breath, open the door. We'll dog it behind you. Close the ash pan doors and the furnace doors. Dog them tight. Then come back. Understand? Don't do anything more. Don't stay another second. We must have you back before the next can go.

Feeny came back reeling, wheezing, but with the report the furnace and ash pit doors were sealed and latched. —You then, Hubbard told the next man. —Deep breaths now. You will go all the way aft to the starboard blower. The damper. Latch it up; then find the belt. It should be lying on the deck, and drape it over the blower hub. Then come back. Mr. Watters?

—On the turret, sir. Passed out up there, I b'lieve.

—Then you, Mister Stodder. You and I will go next. We must get the belt properly fitted on the drive wheel, in position for the next team to mount the pulley.

With a hatch-clang and a gush of water, like a birthing infant, Greene dropped down the ladder from the tower. The exec's mustaches ran sea, he was soaking. His collar was ripped open, buttons missing. —Any chance of saving her?

Theo told him there was, but only if they could get at least one blower restarted. It was their failure that had started this chain of disaster. The exec looked little reassured. —What's your chances of doing that? Since the smoke drove you out.

—It's not so much smoke as the gas in there, Lieutenant. It is invisible and odorless and very deadly indeed.

While Greene chewed his mustache tags over this, Hubbard asked him whether it might be possible for the tug to get them into shelter. The exec said flatly that was impossible. The military situation precluded any thought of return to New York.

—I didn't mean New York, sir. I only asked if there might be a harbor along here, or an island we could duck behind for a few hours. If we could get into calmer water, we could desmoke through the deck hatches.

Greene said they might try to run under Cape May or up into the Delaware. Unfortunately, as the wind was from the northwest, that would require steaming into it; and since the tug was making very little headway as it was, head to wind they'd make none at all. —Can't you keep just the pumps running? With perhaps a skeleton crew?

—That's all you'll have in there come morning, sir. Skeletons.

—We all have to accept some risk, Mister Hubbard. Even engineers.

Theo ignored that. —What I meant was, they wouldn't live long enough to keep steam up. Nor can we achieve a full draft with these stubs of stacks. The only solution's to restart the blowers.

—How long will that take?

—I'm trying it now, Lieutenant. If you would be so kind as to go back up into the turret and try to get us into shelter, I will do my job down here.

Greene glared as only a large man of superior social status can at one much smaller, turned, and fitted himself back through the hatch again. Theo looked to the third assistant. —All right, Mr. Stodder? Then after you, sir.

The abandoned space was dark, the water swirling inches above the deck plates and rising. He pushed the terror back and plodded after Stodder's shadow. Already his heart was pounding. He needed a breath, despite dog-panting his lungs full before slamming open the door. He wanted to gasp in the dark atmosphere, but dared not. This vaporous brew that swirled about him, through which they struggled from stanchion to bulk-head, was deadliness personified.

Around him he sensed the flagging pulse of the elaborate machine the human ants had pitted against the sea's fury. That had enclosed them, pro-tected them, but had now become their trap and perhaps their coffin. Gleams glinted off sliding water. Sight-glasses flickered a ruddy glow, like gas lamps in fog. With each crashing hiss from above they crackled like spit on a waffle iron. Ahead in the darkness the engine was still clinking and whooshing, the shafts and levers of bilge pumps and condenser pumps; but its beat was retarded, reluctant, like the expiring cadence of some great heart.

Which lapsed with a last grinding *whump* as they reached where he and Hand and Joyce had struggled together and failed. Its wonted thun-der was succeeded by an expiring hiss, a dropping whistle of exhausted steam. There was no longer enough pressure to turn the engine over. It might already be too late.

As much by feel as by sight, he got his hands on the pulley wheel. Some essence of desperation must have got into him, because this time when he lifted, it came up as if made of papier-mâché rather than cast iron. He felt Stodder's arms around him, trying to work the stiff new leather, sodden heavy, over the flange while he held it up. It was impossible; his arm was in the way, and he had to bend and set it down, all two hundred pounds of it, and help push the belt into position and then pick it up again.

Midway through this he had to take a breath. The air was hot, and he knew as soon as it was past his teeth it was not what his body craved but the dense and scorching atmosphere of Hell itself. His gullet spasmed closed. He struggled hopelessly to force the suddenly incredibly heavy wheel onto its shaft. But it wouldn't go. Some corner of his failing mind understood the belt was too tight. The spacing was set wrong. He should have slacked the tension before trying to fit it. But it was too late for that now. A burning scarlet like a bed of coals flamed across his vision. Beside him, Stodder's fingers clutched at his shoulder, dragged down his side. He staggered. Screamed soundlessly, teeth bared, trying with all his might to force iron upon iron, weight upon weight.

Suddenly it gave way beneath his raging fists and slid into place. He wrenched desperately at the key. Thrust it in, not all the way but maybe enough to hold. Reached up and with the last remnants of purpose hung on the stop-valve, cranking it around to full open. Then gave way and weaved blindly downhill as the stern rose, slewing in a sickening lean.

Only as it sank into blackness did his maddened mind recall he'd left Stodder behind.

Blindness, incredible cold, incredible pain. He came to atop the tower again. Sprawled like some antediluvian creature on hands and knees. Freezing and wet and barking up what felt in his mouth like panfried morsels of his lungs. Now it was dark, the motion was doubly terrifying, his blurred vision doubly frightening. He seemed to be peering over a cliff. The seas that seethed below, that broke and surged, would sweep anyone on deck away to struggle and perish in the freezing waters astern. Apparently they were being towed across the wind. A faint light ahead, eclipsed by passing waves, must be *Seth Low*. Others moaned and tossed around him; as his vision cleared he saw the whole iron circle was carpeted with blackened, tattered husks, weeping, hacking, vomiting, convulsing. The surgeon was moving among them. Theo hawked and spat. He accepted a cup from someone who pressed it into his hands, assuming it was water. Then coughed in new paroxysms as the raw spirit burst into living flame in his throat.

But it put strength into him. As soon as he regained some gagging semblance of breath, he crawled to the ladder and tried to match shaking legs to rungs. To be received by shouts and upstretched arms as he sagged and fell, nearly braining himself on the cross brace.

One of those who caught him was Watters. —Where's Stodder? Theo gasped out, clinging to the assistant engineer's shoulder.

—His case is doubtful, Mister Logue says.

Theo closed his eyes. —Newton?

—Up on the tower; passed out on the berth deck. Geer and Driscoll found him in there and brought him up. The rest of our boys are in the space, trying to keep things running.

—The blower? They mustn't go back there unless—

Watters told him to calm himself. The starboard blower had been running for some hours now. The belts were still slipping, as they were still taking water down the air conduits, but by taking up the tension screws to the end and running at reduced speed both blowers were now on line, providing combustion air to the fires. The atmosphere was close but breathable. The deck and turret were still leaking, but the pumps were keeping up with it. —We're about to start the engine again. Fortunately the sea seems to be moderating.

If it was, he couldn't tell. —How long have we been without motive power?

—About four hours now. I must go. Sit here. Rest. Don't come aft until you feel well.

He sank to the slide rail of one of the Dahlgrens. Slumped his cheek against the wet shellac-smelling iron, feeling cold grease on his hands, his trowsers, but not caring. Something hard under his rump. He felt around, withdrew the remains of a hard cracker. He was suddenly ravenous and gnawed at it. And in a little while, when the renewed shouting brought word the tiller ropes were slipping, the blowers failing again, the pumps falling behind, he only stirred a little, grunting in an exhausted and hunted sleep.

22

⬥

A Combat with the Sea ♦ A Life Paid for in Gold ♦ Goran Triumphant ♦
Whiskey and Blankets ♦ Search for the Paymaster ♦ A Barefoot
Beach Stroll ♦ Musketry and White Flags ♦ A Single Bullet,
into the Gathering Night

CAL Hanks came near to drowning in that first despairing plunge.
His staring eyes opened to sun-shot, shifting depths. A coppered,
slimy wall an arm's distance away. Above him, the searching
beams of the sun; below, in a green murk, swaying blotches below his
kicking brogans that in a horrified recognition his eye identified as
drowned men, kneeling on the bottom.

To join which, he was rapidly heading, though Goran's arm was so
tight around his neck he might suffocate first. With a frenzied clawing he
fought his way back up. Sucked air, strangling, fighting the man on his
back, who seemed to be trying to push his head under. They submerged
again, Cal dragged under helplessly. Why was he so damned heavy? Then
he knew. Not just boots, wool clothes, a soaked pea jacket. Not even the
rigging knife a sailor used like another hand. It was the dense metal
around his waist, hidden from view but still dragging him down.

A frantic instinctive struggle, and he rose once more, seeing the sun
through a bleeding mist of air-need and sea-terror that made his heart labor and his arms plunge about. Till his taloned fingers snagged and pulled
in something round, covered with lines.

He threw his arms around what proved to be one of the marines' snare drums, gaily painted, taut-covered. Goran grapneled a hand in its webbing as well. They clung to it, sobbing and retching. Only after some minutes had passed and they realized the current was carrying them away from the sinking ship into the open Roads did they strike out with their free arms.

The dull concussions of heavy ordnance traveled over their heads. Sheets of smoke hung above the near shore, through which lanced jets of fire. But these barely registered on the mind of a man struggling for shore through icy water, a man who could not swim and whose only support was steadily riding lower. Unnoticed when they'd latched on to it, the drum was stove in on one side. It leaked air with a bacon sizzling as they sculled onward. Goran went under with each stroke. He wasn't getting any kicking from his useless legs. But he kept paddling, spitting water like a roused cobra. Cal kept reaching and pulling the sea toward him, blinking through salt-sting toward a beach, smoke, tiny running figures. But the shore didn't seem to be coming any closer. Not until he looked back did he see they'd made any progress. The sloop's rigging was black with a heavy fruit. When he dashed sea from his eyes, he saw it was men, climbing into the tops as *Cumberland* settled beneath them.

With a zip and a smack bullets skipped across the water. A distant popping told him the soldiers ashore were firing.

—Goddamn . . . iggerant buckras. Musket can't shoot dat far. Even I knows dat.

—Save your breath, Cal bubbled. He jackknifed in the water, trying to pry his brogans off. A cord wrapped his hand, a lanyard, and with a savage tug he snapped it, and the rigging knife sank away, turning and twinkling in clear green sun-shot space. Snot-water slid down his throat. In a choking panic he thrashed his way back onto the drum.

But it was going fast now, the crack in the side opening up. Across it he caught Goran's rolling eye, like a spooked horse's. When the drum went under, the bargeman would grab for the nearest object, which was him, as he'd grab for his shipmate. Each fighting to climb on top of the other, they'd go down together.

He coughed out the sea and doubled again; succeeded in freeing himself of boots, at least. But he was still battling just to stay afloat.

It was the gold. He could feel it dragging him down, the belt looped and dangling at his belly. When the drum went, his precious hoard would kill him. He stroked desperately, trying to get a few yards farther before it happened. They passed a body in an officer's coat, floating facedown. As they kicked past, it rolled over, releasing a bubble from its clothing, and slipped beneath the greasy surface.

—Yah! Yah!

Another sailor, wet hair plastered over a skull streaked with blood. He didn't seem to be calling to them or asking for anything, just jerking out this abrupt meaningless ejaculation over and over as he pounded the water into foam. Again Cal thought: *sharks*. His stones drew up into his belly with the dread of something dark, moving, intent, to which he was nothing more than food. His terror was sharpened by the steadily sinking drum to which he clung, the weight dragging him down, and a violent explosion not far away.

Something punched him in the chest. He folded, grunting, and went under. He struggled up again, panicking, coughing, splashing, reaching toward the shore as if he could drag it nearer with clawed fingers. Beside him Goran was struggling too, hatchet face sharpened with a grim, abstracted look.

Cal's fingers went to the belt. Hesitated on the knot. It was a fortune. Enough to buy his family out, if he could get to them.

But he couldn't buy anybody out if he was dead. The gold wouldn't do him a damn bit of good wrapped around his drowned body. And not just his; if he went down, Goran would too.

Two lives, for two thousand dollars?

He felt the weight fall away, glimpsed something fluttering below them.

It was gone.

Goran bubbled in agony, face jerking under the foam. Cal hauled him up bodily, paying for it with a mouthful of water, but he could feel the difference; he could float now. He stripped off the sodden pea jacket for good measure. Grunted, —Keep a-swimmin, you. Ain't much farder.

For answer he got a rapid blinking of reddened eyes, a straining of lips off yellow teeth like an enraged dog. A maddened beating at the slight waves that rocked past them, sparkling gaily, untouched by madness and suffering and the steady dropping away, one by solitary one, of those who bobbed among them.

Cal felt himself losing strength, losing heat itself to the congealing sea. Despite the flashing sun it was cold as ice water from the bottom of an oyster barrel. Finger-numbing the first moment he plunged through its roof, the Roads were chilling his legs into the same uselessness as Goran's.

Despite having jettisoned all he could, he sank again.

This time he caught something black moving below him, and beat his way upward with weakening terror. But this time he didn't rise, even without the gold. He seemed heavier than before, made of iron, of lead. He thrashed frenziedly, losing all control over his panicking body.

At that moment the drum gave a last bubbling wheeze and sank. It was instantly thrust below by both men's simultaneous attempt to climb on top of it, then each other. He felt Goran's fingers, surprisingly strong, around his throat, and struck back in sudden explosive rage, the last outraged protest of a dying animal. But his fists seemed to have lost all power, robbed of it as if in a dream by cold, by exhaustion.

Lassitude succeeded rage. He blinked through inches of water at the sun. Watched it turn watery and distant as he dropped, no longer struggling, raging but too weak to fight anymore, away from the surface toward which he still longingly gazed.

His toes dug into sand.

When he thrust against it with one last effort, his face came above the water. He could stand, albeit with head tilted back, while the waves tried playfully to leap into his mouth. He groped beneath the surface, caught rough melton. Hauled Goran up by the neck flap of his jumper. Then waded toward shore, first on tiptoe, then with a more confident stride.

He trudged up out of the surf, out of gentle waves lapping the sand, with Goran's feet dragging ruts behind them. Seagulls whirled on a raucous carousel above coughing, glaze-eyed men stretched on the weed-dotted strand. He dropped the seaman and crashed facefirst into the sand. Clutched gritty grains as a man grips a mother long lost and at last restored. Nothing else in the world seemed worth the least grain of it, the sweetness of air and light.

A creaking, a bray made him look up at last. A rickety-looking mule cart, accompanied by Zouaves in bright madder pants and sashes, was moving along the beach. The soldiers threw each survivor a blanket. They spilled doses of whiskey into cups and handed them to men shaking with cold. When they came to Cal and Goran, their faces closed. He had to stagger to the cart and drag two blankets off himself.

—A Zouave laid a hand on his arm. —Only one per each, boy.

—My mate needs one too.

—No blankets for the dead.

He dropped to his knees beside the body. It lay stiff, tongue protruding. Cal struck Goran on the back, turned him over. Water ran from his mouth.

—Let me, said a white sailor who'd been watching. He rolled the bargeman to a log and draped him across it. Began lifting and lowering his arms. He worked for some time before dropping Goran's hands and shrugging. He got up and walked off toward a driftwood fire that was now crackling a few yards up the beach. Gradually being walled off by gray-blanketed, shuddering forms who crowded so close around the flames they were enveloped in rising steam.

Hanks cursed and punched the flaccid flesh. Gradually the eyes drew closed, sucked under, as if the eyeballs were sinking away. The head lolled. He ceased troubling it and got up and walked a few paces away. He threw back his head, closed his eyes, undid his buttons, and pissed on a clump of beach wrack long and long.

He remembered then, dully, he'd lost all his money. He'd never be able to buy his family out now. He lurched back and forth across the beach. The shipwrecked squatted around fires or sat looking out across the smoky Roads with eyes that gazed at eternity.

Cal cursed and slammed his fist into his palm. He went back to where the bargee lay. He put the log on top of him and began rolling it back and forth over his belly. A little more water ran out of Goran's mouth, but his eyes stayed closed.

—He's gone, darkey, a passing marine said. —Gi' me that blanket. He don't need it no more.

Cal ignored him, leaning on the log as it ironed out Goran's gut. —Goddamn you, he told the stiff corpse, whose face had turned dark blue. —I paid good gold for you, nigger. By the devil. You better fucking breathe.

He leaned again, and again, till his arms no longer obeyed. Was staggering to his feet, yielding at last, when a tremor ran through the stiffened body.

He fell to his knees and blew air into the Richmonder's mouth. The marine, who'd stopped to watch, snorted in disgust. Cal ignored him. He let the air come out, then breathed it in again, like blowing up a hog bladder.

With a mewling cry Goran turned his face and disgorged a stream of water and blood. It sank instantly into the sand, leaving only a stain.

—Son of a bitch. You done that good, the marine observed. —I took him fer drowndt fer sure.

Cal didn't answer or look at him. —We best get him on the wagon with the others that's hurt, the marine said. —Come on. I'll give ye a hand.

When he came back down to the beach, barely able by now to drag one bare foot after the other, Mr. Selfridge was standing there. The gunnery officer was looking out at the slanted topmast, at the flag that still dangled, smut-stained, at its peak. —If we could have made way, we could have rammed her, he muttered as if to himself. —Or at least kept away from her. It wasn't iron that defeated us. It was not having steam.

—Sir? Cal asked him. —What do we do now?

—We didn't even bring off the log, the lieutenant said, not looking at him. —Or the muster roll or the captain's letter book.

Cal sank slowly back to his knees. Gradually, slumping like a sack of sand, he lay full length, again, on the muddy tracked beach.

Some interminable time later he woke to a racket of musketry. He dragged wet sand off his face, puzzled by his sodden clothes, the soreness in his bones. Then recalled everything.

Gritting his teeth, he propped himself up.

The sun was sagging like a glob of melted glass. Only a few of the sailors remained on the beach. The fires were dying to embers. He sat up, stretched, and gazed around.

A moment later he was on his bare feet, staring down the beach.

The monster had returned. It stood off a distance down the strand, shelling *Congress*, which lay bow toward shore, grounded and aflame.

He stared, clenching his fists as he saw reenacted the same scenes he'd just lived through. In the afternoon glow the rising smoke was gold and lilac. The ram was raking the helpless, stranded frigate, which Cal saw could not return fire save from her stern battery, which was outclassed by the heavy rifles of her enemy.

Then he saw her flag coming down. The white flag going up.

Shambling on wooden feet, he began running down the beach.

The fire did not slacken as he ran, slowed to a walk, ran again. As he neared he made out figures leaping from the stricken frigate, stroking toward the beach. Others floated facedown. The frigate was no longer firing back. The flag of surrender floated plain at the mizzen. But still the Leviathan's guns lashed out, still shells exploded.

A squad of troops was kneeling, firing volleys from the dunes. He ducked and kept running. Came up at last so near a shell passed over him and whumped into a dune, tossing a cloud of sand as it burrowed in. He tensed for the explosion, but none came.

More soldiers lay in hastily scraped rifle pits above the tide mark. They were loading and firing, muskets jumping and barking. A sergeant with a sword eyed him through the smoke-fog. Cal recognized him too late to turn back. O'Leary, who'd chased him through the camp and nearly killed him Christmas night. They circled like hostile dogs.

—An' what're ye after doin' here, Mingo?

For answer he pointed seaward, where *Cumberland*'s flag still flew atop the canted topmast. The Irishman's shaggy-browed gaze followed it, then returned to him. Examined his sodden clothing. Dropped to his splayed toes.

—Off that ship out there?

—Aye.

—The one fought till she sank? Ye were on her?

—Pivot gunner.

—Lost men ye knew?

—Aye, I did.

—And ye'd like yer revenge, I'm thinkin'. Leastways a white man would.

Cal looked seaward. To where the monster was still firing. Someone stood atop it now. Standing in full view.

—Gi' the nigger your musket, Brady. Let 'im pay his respects to 'is old master. That's it. Go on. It's loaded.

Cal accepted the weight of a long Enfield. He checked the cap, then the rear sight. It was graduated to a thousand yards. He gave the sea a look, and set it at eight hundred. Thumbed the hammer back to cock.

Above the sight the figure swayed. It seemed first very distant, then so near he could almost make out his expression. A lean old man in a blue coat. A glint of gold from his sleeves as he raised an arm—no, it was a rifle he raised.

Cal squinted, puzzled. A rifle when he had heavy guns at his service? But it seemed to be so, the distant rebel was aiming it at the troops. About Cal on the beach, above him on the dunes the musketry tat-tatted away. A howitzer boomed out from time to time. But the figure made no move toward shelter. Simply discharged his weapon shoreward, then handed it down to someone below.

Cal felt something strange touch him then. A sense of some dark presence behind him. Almost the same, no, the exact same as he'd felt with the sharks. He twisted, but there was nothing there.

When he turned back, his sights had drifted off the target. The fire crackled out on the frigate, then caught in the furled sails and began to roar. He began to lower the rifle, then raised it again.

Yes. He wanted revenge. For more than O'Leary could know or even imagine. For it was not just for this day he asked repayment, but for all that had been taken from him and withheld from him and torn from him, and from so many down the echoing centuries since the first bewildered African they'd led to the block in Jamestown.

He tucked his chin against the stock and sighted again.

A rifle bullet flew the same arcing course as a cannon shell. Lofting, then swiftly dropping. Even more if you were firing against the wind like this. Which meant probably most of the soldiers around him were firing short, throwing lead away to no use. He lifted the barrel up and up, until a line drawn from it would pass far above the standing officer's head. And squeezed off.

The rifle thumped his shoulder, and a sulphurous cloud blew back into his face.

—Cor, said O'Leary, and the soldier whose musket it was muttered too. —See 'im drop down?

—He was goin' below before 'e fired. Besides, he shot too high.

—No, no, 'e dropped 'is rifle. Our shiny-faced boy 'ere 'it 'im.

Could he have touched him? Cal doubted it. The odds were against. He handed the rifle back and stood watching the now fiercely burning frigate. Her crew was straggling ashore, just as *Cumberland*'s had, and like the sloop she was surrounded by drifting dead. As he watched, the mizzen began to topple, drawing a sweep of fire through the glooming sky. A keening chorus of screams quivered on the wind. When it crashed in a shower of sparks, the keening stopped, cut off suddenly as a snipped thread.

He grated his palm over his scalp, trying to grasp all this. Death. Iron. Firing on a white flag. Two of the most powerful ships in the navy sunk and wrecked in an afternoon. Hundreds burned, torn apart, crushed, drowned.

A fresh gush of black from the ram's stack signaled she was getting way on again. And gradually she moved off. Cal couldn't tell her intention, whether to go after the other blockaders or to head back into her lair. But the sun was sinking fast, melting a path across the Roads. Surely the monster could not maneuver, could not fight by night.

Behind him on the beach men were calling out. He was about to go back to his mates when O'Leary grabbed his arm. The sergeant looked shaken. As if his thoughts traveled the same road as Cal's, he muttered, —Navy can't stop this iron divvil, then.

—We tried, sarnt.

—I seen that. I seen that. But ye couldn't stand agin her.

—No.

—It's brave ye were, but that weren't enough. An' tomorrow she'll be back to sink the rest. The archangel Michael himself, could he stop this thing?

—I don't know.

—She'll shell us out of here, an' burn up all Little Mac's supplies. Bring in the fucking English against us. This war's lost, nigger. Lost right here today with us watchin'.

Cal Hanks looked out over the glowing sheet of the Roads, at the darkness stealing out of the east. At the flames climbing the frigate's rigging, consuming the white flag, turning it to a flame-hearted cinder fabric ballooning on the wind. At the smoke of the parting monster, far beyond. His heart felt ironed in manacles and molded in lead and sunk to depths where there was no light at all, just eternal night and everlasting cold.

—It look so, sarnt, he said slowly. —It surely look so to me.

23

Taking Station for the Coup de Grâce ♦ A White Flag at the Gaff ♦
Buchanan Merciful ♦ A Heavy Fire from Shore ♦ Buchanan Vindictive ♦
Sustaining Close Musket Practice in a Small Boat ♦ A Fateful Shot
from Shore ♦ Onslaught Against U.S.S. *Minnesota* ♦ Evening, and a
Deliberate Retirement ♦ Farewell to Captain Norris

T HE respite didn't last. Fortified by the spirits, Lomax's men were again ready for action. It began very soon. Though this time, as the steam ram was now heading back east, it was primarily the port-side battery that was engaged.

At a little after four by Davidson's watch they opened again on *Congress*. The glimpses Minter caught showed the sailing frigate aground and smoking heavily from the previous hits. Her stern faced her returned enemy. Safe from ramming in the shallows she'd sought, but not from ordnance. Three or four raking broadsides brought flames and explosions. A gun or two fired back, then fell dumb as *Virginia*'s shells ripped through her length.

At last the Stars and Stripes fluttered down. A scrap of white climbed her gaff. Another floated out half-masted at her main.

The word came down to cease firing. The engines slackened, and the great ironclad rode sluggishly hove to. Looking out his port, Lomax saw one of the James Fleet gunboats approaching. A speaking trumpet blared, and it wheeled and made for the frigate.

Jones passed the word to stand easy. Sunlight flooded down, and looking up Lomax saw the hatch covers were open. The fresh air set him coughing. He hadn't realized how bad the murk was they'd been breathing. He told his boys to stay out of the water buckets; drinking water in hot conditions was debilitating. Unable to stay below, he all but ran up the ladder.

All hostile demonstrations seemed to have ceased. Buchanan, Jones, and the quartermasters and pilots were gathered forward of the stack.

Which looked as if it had been gnawed by some immense beast. Smoke streamed out of dozens of rents and blew away to southward. Davits, deck railings, and guy wires lay smashed or strewn or bent. Not a scrap was left of the howitzers or their mountings. The flagstaff had been shot away, and someone had lashed the flag to a protruding piece of the twisted stack. One of the cutters had taken a cannonball through its bottom, smashing it into what would serve very well for kindling.

He bent to inspect the side armor. It too was furrowed and dented. Whole courses of plate were crushed in where the heaviest blows had fallen. A black patch showed where his cropped-off barrel had set fire to the tallow on the shield. The smell of crisped pork was strong.

He lifted his gaze to a declining sun. A pall hung over the whole open bowl of the Roads. A gunboat was chuffing away in the direction of Sewell's Point. Other craft, flying the Stars and Bars, were standing off between the immobile armorclad and a gaggle of shipping huddled under Old Point Comfort. A shrieking hurricane of gulls wheeled above where the t'gallant-mast of *Cumberland* stuck up. Lomax did not like to think what had attracted their interest. *Beaufort* was standing by the burning and surrendered *Congress,* apparently offloading the wounded. Another tug was making up to her other side.

He turned to find Buchanan pacing toward him. His hand went to his cap. —My congratulations, Commodore. It is victory. Without question.

—I shall only be satisfied if I can bring relief to the brave men suffering over there. Buchanan frowned. —My brother, McKean, is aboard that ship as paymaster. I wish this terrible war were over. But perhaps this will suffice, and they will let us depart in peace.

The commodore seemed about to speak again when a crackle broke out ashore. It quickly grew louder as blue-clad figures poured onto the beach.

Buchanan called, —What are those troops doing, Mister Jones?

Telescope leveled, the exec said, —I see two light guns setting up, sir. Field guns.

—They had best not open fire. If they do, they condemn their own wounded.

—Well, sir, that is the army over there. They may feel it is the ship which has surrendered and not they.

—Even militia know not to fire on a white flag. That signal terminates all hostile activity on the battlefield, from whatever quarter.

Lomax wondered how Parker Trezevant, his old commanding officer and a law wrangler of the first water, would have responded to that assertion. Whatever the niceties, the pop of musketry was still building. —A dose of grape might discourage them from interfering, sir.

Jones lifted an eyebrow. —There are wounded on that beach. Nor can we fire on a surrendered enemy.

But Buchanan was growing visibly angry. As he cleared his throat Lomax saw the junior officers exchange glances. —They had best cease this. Have we a signal book? Where is my flag-lieutenant?

—Sir, we do not hold army signal books. We might hoist in international code, but they would most probably not understand it.

A puff of smoke, a report. One of the field guns had come into action. The small-arms fire was still growing. Lomax could see the pockle of it on the waves. Some had to be hitting the frigate as well, endangering the wounded being carried off.

As they watched, the tugs cast off lines. They backed water, and the splashes around them grew as blue appeared between them and the grounded frigate. They cleared, wheeled slowly, then steamed past the ironclad, out into the Roads.

Buchanan's face turned to flame. —*Where* is that fool Parker going? I told you he was unfit to command. Has he taken the officers prisoner? Has he set that damned ship on fire? Or not?

Jones said soothingly, —He'll execute your orders, sir. He most likely has set combustibles. Let's wait and see if they take effect.

But no more smoke was rising from the doomed ship. In fact it seemed to be lessening. Buchanan's temperature, though, was rising fast. He shot out a finger at Jones. —Parker's let us down again. That ship must be burned, sir.

Lomax stepped forward before he knew he was going to. —I'll burn her, sir.

Buchanan did not even look at him. He snapped, —Very well, sir. Take the cutter and go. Have *Teaser* cover you. Board her. Set her afire.

—The wounded, sir? Jones put in.

Buchanan screamed, shaking his fist. —*Damn* the wounded. I granted quarter. They rejected it. I want that fucking ship *burned,* do you hear?

Before he could catch up with what he'd let himself in for, he was in the remaining boat. Launched by skidding it down the casemate from the spar deck, the men sliding down after to take their positions at the oars. Bullets skipped the waves like flying fish. But so far none had come close. He had his sword, but no pistol. Nor were any of the cuttermen armed with anything but cutlasses. Little *Teaser* moved in as they oared away. He cupped his hands and explained what was to be done. A fat man nodded and went into the pilothouse. Lomax turned to the coxswain. Navy, thank God, a swarthy salt in baggy blues and black neckerchief. This would take seamanship. —We're to set her afire. Steer for her stern and try to keep the tug between us and the shore.

—Aye, sir. If that field piece don't get us first.

As the men bent, Lomax arranged himself. Sitting erect, one hand braced on the gunwale. The hum and whack of balls grew as they advanced. A crack of shattering iron some yards off: the field gun was feeling for their range. At just the point where he was appreciating the tug's lee, it sheered off. Her men swung their caps in a scrappy huzza. He'd have preferred their company to their acclamation, but if he could burn her and make it back alive . . . A ball struck a man in the bow; he clapped his hand to his shoulder, then laughed, holding it up for all to see. It hadn't even pierced his jacket.

A tremendous blast and howl overhead; *Virginia,* firing shoreward. Covering him. He shouted to the men to put their backs to it. They bent with gritted teeth, cracking sinews, grunts of effort. The distance narrowed.

But even as it shrank, the tracks of foam multiplied. Like swarming cicadas the troops poured out of the tree line, to drop to their knees and steady their muskets. An army of them. Literally . . . a line of smoke burst out nearly simultaneous with a crash of fire. They were firing by volleys now.

A leaden hail swept the surface like a flurry of hailstones falling strangely from the bright afternoon sky. One of the oarsmen pitched forward. The same who'd laughed at a spent slug a moment before. This time he didn't get up, and a stain spread across the back of his jacket.

Lomax forced himself to his feet. Buchanan, Jones, others were watching. He drew his sword and faced the enemy. Bullets cracked into the wood, drilled through a thwart. The blade of an oar, flashing in the sunlight, burst into splinters, sending its wielder toppling as the jagged end whipped through the foam.

He waved his sword, yelling them on. Another eighty yards . . . but the blasting smack of musket balls into the strakes and the scream of shrapnel told clear they'd never make it. Another oarsman screamed and went down. He splashed into water Lomax hadn't noticed before. It was welling above the floorboards. The cannonade must have started her planks. A shell whipcracked, and something struck his breast, so hard and hot and numbing he sat down willy-nilly. His fingers came away glued with blood.

—You're hit, sir, the coxswain shouted.

—So I see.

The cutter was slowing, slewing as the mismated thrust of missing oars twisted her. The coxswain struggled with the rudder. —We're not going to make it, sir, he shouted.

Another salvo from *Virginia* roared over their heads. It sounded like the angel of death flying over. Glory, he thought, or extinction? There was no choice. Not for him. He pointed ahead, seeing as he did so waiting men along *Congress*'s rail. Leveling pistols in their direction. The Yankee officers who'd run up the white flag, then decided to change their minds.

—Steady as she goes, cox'n, he shouted.

He struggled to his feet again. Lifting his uninjured arm, the blade glittering. Seeing in his mind's eye an image of himself shot through, pierced, but with sword aloft. A heroic engraving generations of schoolboys would trace, hidden in their geometry books.

Fifty yards.

One of the rowers was shouting. Pointing behind him. He cupped his ear to hear over the burst of another shell, the screams from the frigate that loomed over them, so near, yet so far away.

—The recall, sir.

Twisting, he saw the quartermaster swinging the Blue Peter back and forth.

Tasting the bitterness of glory denied, he nodded at last. —Come about, cox'n. Take us back.

The ironclad's full broadside roared out over his head again as they oared the last few yards, the water rising fast around their feet. He scrambled out onto the fantail, waded along the submerged afterdeck, shouting for help for his wounded. Guns crashed with the racket of doom, blotting out shore and sky with a saffron eclipse. The glowing bases of the shells were perfectly visible. There was no arc to them as they came out of the muzzles, flew low over the flat sea, shedding sparks and wadding, and crashed into the helpless frigate. Buchanan's visage was iron. Scarlet-faced, he was screaming to lay under her stern, rake her gun decks, rake her quarterdeck.

He turned his head as Lomax came up. —You're wounded, Mr. Minter.

He went to raise his cap and found it was no longer there. —I would have pressed on, despite the fire. But we saw your recall and intuited you intended to resume firing.

—A most gallant venture, still. I am glad you returned from placing your head in the lion's mouth. While such as you abound, our new nation will never lack for examples.

The others touched his unwounded arm, murmuring congratulations, as he made his way toward the ladder. The pain seemed so little next to their envious glances.

The surgeon bandaged him, fortified him with a cheering glass, and told him he was fortunate. If the fragment had struck edgewise rather than flat on, it would have pierced his heart. Lomax refused to stay in sick bay. Said he'd return to duty if there was no objection. None being offered, he resumed his jacket, complete with rip and blood, and made his way back to the gun deck.

Back into thunder and murk. At number four Private Tharpe was carrying on a vigorous cannonade. He'd nailed wet burlap around the port sill to stop the muzzle flare from setting it on fire again. Lomax saw they'd approached the burning frigate so closely there could be no missing. It was point-blank fire and horribly cruel. Screams rang from the burning ship, corpses bobbed around it.

—Hot shot, coming up!

The chain-hoist grated, and the iron spheroid, toasted to white heat, came rattling up through the deck scuttle in its iron cage. It glowed and smoked; he felt the caloric ten feet away. Two boys tipped it into an iron trivet. Powder canister. Rammer. Dry wad. Rammer. Wet wad. Rammer. And shot. Tharpe stepped back, aimed, tripped the lanyard. For men who'd never fired a naval gun before today, the sons of Georgia were doing very well.

Then a shout jerked his head around.

Jones, the flag-lieutenant, and two of the pilots were coming down the ladder. They supported a sagging form that for a thunderstruck moment he could not believe was Buchanan's. Blood pumped out onto the deck as they lowered him. The flag officer's eyes were clenched. His hands closed and opened.

—What happened?

—He caught a bullet, Jones said grimly.

—He wasn't under cover? We are in quite close range.

The flag-lieutenant said tersely that the old man had become so enraged at the sniping from shoreward he'd demanded a carbine. When one of the marines handed it to him, he'd let it off at the infantry whose bullets whizzed around him, then handed it back to be reloaded. —We kept trying to get him into the pilothouse. At least, take cover between shots. He wouldn't listen.

Lomax knelt by the commodore. The old eagle had been the soul of their attack. With him in command, no one had doubted they'd conquer or die. But now the firing was falling off as the men discovered the scene behind them. The officers bending close above their fallen commander reminded him of the painting of Nelson at Trafalgar. Buchanan was gripping Jones's hand. The old man's face was pale as bleached bone. —You must carry on, Catesby.

—Yes sir.

—Don't leave till she's well afire. My brother . . . no matter. Hot shot. Incendiary shell! Make them pay for this perfidy.

—I shall, sir.

Buchanan lifted a blood-smeared hand. Stared at it, then around at the hovering scared faces. —Hear me, lads. Take *Minnesota*. Goldsborough's flagship. She's aground. Helpless. She must be sunk before dark comes. Fight as long as a hand can stand to the guns. Seal the victory, boy.

—I shall, sir. Recover and return to us. Jones stood. —Now take him below, to his quarters, and notify the surgeon to attend.

Jones's first order, once the commodore was carried below, was to cease fire. Next, four bells for full speed. The engines began to rumble again. The shore fell slowly back.

They were headed for *Minnesota*.

Poking his head above the coaming, Lomax made her out forward of the iron pilothouse no one had yet used the entire day. Beyond her the twin bastions of Monroe and islanded Fort Calhoun guarded the exit to the Bay. To starboard, the Confederate batteries on Sewell's Point. The remaining heavy units of the federal squadron lay in a rough line between them and the fort, pointed northwestward, their heading when they struck the flats. Tugs chuffed around the far two. Her attendants had abandoned *Minnesota,* though. Tucked close to their armored flagship, *Jamestown* and *Patrick Henry* were lobbing shells in her direction already. The great steam-frigate, *Merrimack*'s sister ship, lay with sails furled and guns run out, awaiting her attackers.

Lomax suddenly realized why Buchanan was so insistent on capturing her. Secured with engines intact, she could be converted much more quickly than *Merrimack* had been. With two such ironclads operating together, no force could hope to stop a run to Baltimore or even Washington.

The frigate's side lit up with flashes. He ducked and slid down the ladder as the broadside hit, rocking and clanging the shield, knocking up dust in a way that was by now familiar. Still deafening. Still making his heart leap. But now he was convinced their iron would hold, no longer frightening.

The engines were slowing, however. Jones stood on the ladder, only the lower part of his body visible from within. He was shouting down to the pilots, asking how much closer he could go. They yelled back that it shoaled rapidly here. The tide was ebbing. He must find a safe anchorage, or dark would find them aground.

Another salvo whanged and roared about their ears. Lomax began to sweat again. How much higher did they float after burning coal for seven hours? How much more of their vulnerable waterline was exposed? Just one of the shells ricocheting past could still sink them. Granted, they'd just settle on the bottom here. They needn't fret about drowning. But if that shell happened to crash through into the magazine . . .

And maybe Jones was thinking along those lines too because after trading several broadsides he brought the head round to the south.

Backing and filling, dragging her stern in the mud, the great ironclad slowly pointed herself back whence she had come.

But not back to Norfolk. Jones moored to a buoy south of Sewell's Point. The hands reeled away from the guns, dropping to stare up in speechless trance at the stars now visible through the gridwork. Lomax shouted them up again to scrub out the bore, sweep down, and reload with canister against any attempt by small boats. Then dismissed them to evening mess. —Try to get what sleep you can, he told them. —No doubt we shall be under way again at first light, to finish the affair.

He went below, tried to lie down, but could not. His legs kept jumping on the bunk. Scenes passed in front of his eyes. His chest and shoulder ached abominably.

At last he got up and went topside. Most of the others were there already, probably for the same reason. Along with visitors from the rest of the squadron. The wounded were being lowered into boats. He lit a segar—strange, he'd not missed smoking all that day—and paced back and forth, looking out on the nightlit Roads.

Far off, the stricken *Congress* was still aflame. At intervals a gun or shell cooked off, sending sparks whirling upward. Lights moved out toward the Chesapeake, no doubt trying to work the stranded warships free. If they were still there at dawn, he hoped they yielded without a fight. Shelling those powerless to resist was not his idea of triumph. One might even call it murder. No, that was too strong. The Northern tyrant wanted to dominate free men? This was his just desert. Buchanan had shown no reluctance to fire on his own brother. There was a hero to emulate.

And Buchanan had called him *gallant.* . . .

—Mister Minter?

It was Norris. —Have you seen a boat from the *Beaufort?*

—That may be it making its way toward us.

The light from the burning frigate was so bright he could see the signal officer's pointing finger. —I am leaving, by Mister Jones's orders. To escort the prisoners we took to Norfolk. You have done well today, sir. A most noble exploit.

Lomax decided a becoming modesty was called for. —In my view we all rose to the occasion. Have you seen the commodore?

—Briefly. He is suffering, and in low spirits about his brother. You know he was on *Congress.*

Lomax said he'd heard that. Norris said tomorrow would wrap up the victory with the destruction or surrender of the rest of the Federals, and making prizes of remaining transports.

—And our spy? You think him still aboard?

—It is hard to believe so, Norris said. —I rather suspect someone back at the yard. But despite him, you have covered yourselves in glory.

—Will you mention my name in Richmond?

—Most assuredly. The signals captain saluted from the boat, down to which he'd scrambled during their exchange. —Farewell, and good luck.

Lomax paced for hours, unable to find quietus. From time to time he smiled and struck his hand against a bent section of rail. Absolute victory! Total triumph! The blockade was played out. McClellan could make nothing of his great offensive now. The war, as good as won. No ship afloat could stop them, nor all the Yankee fleet together. And he part and parcel of it. From now henceforth, when men remembered the epic cruise of the *Virginia,* they'd read of Henry Lomax Minter.

The moon was in its second quarter and quite bright. At one point, by its shimmering illumination, he thought he saw a shadow slide past one of the lights out in the Roads. Then shook his head. Only a tug or picket-boat. He ought really to lie down. Find something to gnaw on. A swallow of wine. He wasn't hungry, nor sleepy.

But tomorrow was another day.

24

―――――――

Preparing for Battle ♦ Doubts of One's Skill ♦ The First Wounded ♦
Interlude of Suspense ♦ A Second Interchange of Fire ♦ Red Hair upon
India Rubber ♦ A Wounded Commander ♦ Hunter's Procedure for
Ligation of the Femoral Artery ♦ The Commodore Must Go Ashore ♦
Return of *Virginia*'s Wardroom to Its Accustomed State

D R. Alphaeus Steele entered the wardroom that day with considerable trepidation, though he tried not to show it. He'd had to for-
tify himself. Had barely gotten his shaking hands to his mouth,
spilling whiskey over his coat. Only gradually had the tremor eased, the
familiar surcease of perturbation risen to his brain.

Was he the only one who understood what horror impended? Or was
it that being young, those around him could not conceive of their mortality? Youth, beauty, courage glowed around the mess table like a gemlike
flame. It wasn't his death that frightened him, but the prospect of theirs.
And the worse dooms than simple eradication iron and lead could pro-
nounce upon the human frame.

He'd seen them more times than he cared to remember.

—*Isan d' es te ton olbion, ton te kheirona dok' ekhein, oinou terpsin
aloupon,* he muttered, half to himself, half to the younger associate beside
him. Doctor Algernon Garnett did not rise to the bait, though. Or perhaps knew his Euripides so well he didn't feel the need to comment.

They were eating, joking, laughing raucously. Obviously they'd been up for hours already, making their preparations. The keen-faced lieutenant raised his glass as they came in. Flaming hair tumbled to his shoulders. —Doctor Steele. Doctor Garnett. Welcome to our somewhat noisy company.

—Mister Minter. Steele bowed before jade-green eyes that struck him to the quick, and tried not to stagger as the deck rolled. He could not tell if it was the sea or too much *spiritus frumenti,* but maintained his *sangfroid* as best he could. —I trust I find you well. And that the evening of this fateful epoch finds us both the same. For I fear we may suffer casualties today.

—Our cause is just, Doctor. Liberty, glory, and—revenge!

—Revenge, sir? Is that the word I heard?

—For Donelson, Cape Hatteras, their invasion of Carolina. Our armor is strong, and we are in the right.

—Then you are as brave as we expect of youth, Steele said while thinking: It is such lovely fiery fools as this who'll slay each other today. And perhaps us all as well. He felt his stomach sinking. Perhaps another dram . . . No. Too liberal an indulgence just now might be misinterpreted.

He centered the box on the table and flicked the catch. The lid popped open to a hidden spring. It revealed a full set of Shepard & Dudley instruments. Saws. Tenaculums. Various sizes and types of scalpels. The others noted the shining implements and fell silent. Steele flicked a finger at the tablecloth and lifted the case. The wardroom attendant whisked the linen away, and the green baize beneath. Albright, a paymaster's clerk who helped the surgeons during general quarters, began setting up. First he laid down a heavy black india-rubber cloth to protect the tabletop. Bandages, lint, sealing wax, emplastrums, muslin, and surgeons' silk followed. Steele ran an eye over the loaded sideboard, set this morning not with tasty dishes but with persulphate of iron, oil, whiskey, opium, chloroform, sponges, ligatures, adhesive plaster, and a big demijohn of good fresh water.

Then an interminable wait. It would be a long trip down to the Roads. The only danger before then was a torpedo or some such infernal machine. Below the waterline as they were, with the mass of iron above, he had no doubt as to his fate if they ran upon one. Which was both unpleasant to contemplate and impossible to avoid, so he and Garnett finally resorted to that universal anodyne: piquet.

They played for an hour. The principal assistant had taken his medical degree in Philadelphia and had been aboard *Wyandotte* at the outbreak of war. He was married to a Scott of Richmond and pleasant enough company, though young, Steele could not help thinking, for a surgeon. But except for Buchanan, Steele was the eldest aboard. The assistant surgeon lost most of the tricks. The air grew hot and close with smoke and gas. They coughed incessantly, but there was no source of fresh atmosphere and nowhere else to go.

Garnett kept glancing at the clock. Finally he said, —We had best head up if we expect to see anything before the action begins.

Alphaeus said he believed he'd stay where he was. But as soon as the other had gone, he went forward to his little damp cabin. Groping in complete darkness—all lights had to be extinguished on sounding the tattoo—he found smooth hollow glass and uncorked it.

He was back in the wardroom imperturbably setting out a hand of solitaire when the younger man returned. —Any torpedoes? Steele asked him.

—Torpedoes?

—I had heard a rumor that they had perhaps laid something in the channel for us in case we should come out.

—They don't seem too disturbed by our appearance, Garnett said. —You think that might be why?

Steele didn't answer. He laid out the cards for another partie.

The first shot rattled the dishes in the sideboard. The loblolly-boys flinched and murmured. Steele barely noticed. He was close to a repique and trying to keep the points straight. So far he'd won six dollars and twenty-five cents. He had a premonition he'd die in this battle. But then, he'd had the same premonition before every action of the Mexican war, in China, in Africa. It might still be true, but he'd learned to masquerade as if it was not.

They played with heads close through the next hour. The hull shuddered as the ship collided with something; with what, the surgeons did not know. The engines shook the bulkheads. The deck took on a slant. Sweat streamed down Garnett's cheeks. Steele's fingertips were white as he pressed the cards down. The assistant surgeon had come back, and Steele was now down nearly a dollar.

Garnett cleared his throat. —At what point, I wonder, would we hear, down below, if the battle were not going well.

—I am certain they will notify us if there is a necessity to abandon ship. Steele had meant to be reassuring, but it didn't come out that way. And in fact in the rush of a sinking, the surgeons and the wounded they tended were not exactly at the forefront of the commander's attention; they were often left to save themselves as best they could.

However, they did not come to that test then. He won that partie, and shortly thereafter the increasing tilt gave way to a surge upward, a nausea-inducing reel as they floated free again.

The guns had been going off above them all this time. Separated from them by only beams and deck planks, they heard clearly the shouts of command, the grating of gun trucks on sand, and again and again the deafening slam. A sulphurous fog filtered down. Steele thought grimly this must be how a cockroach felt, trapped and ineffectual and slowly being choked with fumes from sulphur pots. He kept checking his new watch. He'd not been able to replace the English one, but this was New England made and seemed to keep good time.

When the first litter came down, the case was beyond help. The skull was a bloody ruin, the bone crushed in. The bearers said a shell had exploded as he stuck his head out a port. Steele reflected how one often sought one's own death. He ordered the corpse taken back to the berth deck. As the bearers maneuvered in the passageway, more appeared at the top of the ladder. With a sigh he got to his feet, restored the low cards, shuffled the deck one last time, and slipped it out of sight.

Their first case slid onto the table. The boy's face was white and shocked. His fingers wriggled like white worms. —Shell splinter, said a bearer. —Hit the bow port just as it exploded. Two more coming after this one.

—Lay them in the passageway. We'll attend to them directly. To the lad on the table he said more gently, as he lifted his boot and stropped a scalpel on the sole, —Where are you hit, my boy? How were you standing when it struck you? And what is your name?

—John Capps, sir. Company E, Forty-first Regiment. In the back, I think. I was turned round, reaching for the shell—

—That's all right, don't talk now. Turn that lamp up, Doctor Garnett, if you please.

They were allowed a single lamp above the operating table. By its buttered light he found an entry wound in the boy's shirt but no exit rent.

Steele had always felt a naval surgeon operated under some considerable advantages over those in the field. For one, he was often able to treat his patients minutes after their injury. He'd found examination and treatment more easily accomplished when the body's initial disbelief at its own injury had not yet given way to the nervous depression that followed. He'd learned his trade when whiskey, opium, and loss of blood were the only anesthetics, and he did not feel obligated to employ chloroform in every case. Pain had a tonic effect, after all. Stripping the shirt off, he exposed a pale shoulder blade, a massive bruise, and an elongated wound.

—Are you doing all right, John?

—Yes sir; it is not too bad, really it isn't.

More litters were laid down as Steele examined the entrance wound. When he got his finger in past the scapula, carefully pressing along it with his free hand as he advanced his index, he felt the outlines not of a shell fragment but of a dense object that felt more like lead than iron. Dissecting forceps got it, though it took a deal of force to pull the thing out from the bed it had made for itself.

A massively deformed minié ball gleamed dull silver in the smoky lamplight.

—Ricocheted off something before it hit him, Garnett ventured.

—I should tend to agree. Can you sit up, John? You came off lightly today. Trim those edges off and bandage him, if you please. Such a clean penetration may perhaps heal at first intention. The next, place him up here. That's right.

Alphaeus at first thought this injury involved the head, but when the sailor took his hand away, found he was looking at a ruined eye. He dug out the remnants with a finger as Garnett held the patient's head and Albright the arms. He flicked a scalpel through the optic nerve and flushed the cavity with water and then persulphate. That stopped the bleeding, and he packed the cavity with lint and stepped back. —Bandage, he told the operating assistant, and pointed at the next, who was shrieking and sobbing on the litter. —And what is the matter here?

—Gut wound, sir.

Steele's own stomach turned hearing it. There was usually little one could do in such cases, and lifting the blood-soaked cloth, his worst anticipations were realized.

The boy's midriff had been torn apart. One learned to judge such wounds by the nose. This smelled of excretory products, but not bile nor urine. Neither liver damage nor bladder rupture, then. The wound was very bloody, but as yet it probably did not hurt much. The boy's screeching was due to terror, not pain. Yet his death was on him. No surgeon living could do other than prolong his agony. Steele questioned him gently, holding his hand. His name was Louis Waldeck. He was from Charleston. He was young and dark-haired, barely into his twenties.

—Opium? Garnett glanced sidewise.

—In the form of laudanum, if you please, to hasten absorption before reaching the lower digestive tract. Set him in the passageway for now, Steele told the bearers. —I will look in on him later.

They slid the litter off despite the boy's pleading, then his hopeless bursting scream as he realized his doom. Steele set his teeth and looked away. This was what glory meant. These broken bodies, these smells. These soul-tearing shrieks, and spattered blood on the overhead.

—What is wrong with this next? Garnett asked when Steele couldn't speak.

—Stunned, sir. Was standing by the shield when a shell hit it. He's bleedin' from the ears and can't talk.

—Hoist him up, and we'll have a look.

The lamp swayed as the deck heeled, sending shadows surging through the smoky air. But neither surgeon noticed it, only shifted to follow the reeling light as they probed, snipped, and administered lavage. Smoke rolled forward in clouds, seeping through the bulkheads from the engine room and roiling in inverted billows just above their heads. At times the operating lamp was obscured, and they had to grope for instruments by feel. Now Alphaeus Steele did not think of his own fear, or of his misgivings for the boys. His hands moved without tremor, without hesitation, pausing only now and then to mop at his streaming face.

Surrounded by shadows, he labored without cease.

That first wave of wounded was followed by a hiatus, during which he strolled to his cabin once more. His head felt woolly and his bloodstained hands numb. The influence of the noxious atmosphere they were all sucking in, no doubt.

He sat on his bunk until at four p.m. the renewed clamor of guns, like the slamming of enormous iron doors, brought him starting to his feet again. Really, what was he doing here? A man of his age should be at home. Should *have* a home . . . But he had nowhere to go, no people to go to . . . A few years and he'd be helpless. Perhaps if all ended now it would be for the better.

He staggered back into the passageway.

The table lay empty, its rubber surface gleaming with a grisly dew of blood, excreta, and condensation. Astringent whetted the murky air. From forward came the moans of the early wounded. Coming out of shock into pain. The stomach wound was still shrieking steady, ear-piercing keens, though weaker than he'd voiced at first. Young Waldeck would be quiet soon, but not soon enough. Neither for him nor for those who had to hear him die.

Steele placed a hand on the lad's cheek. A dark cowlick stuck up. Sweating, eyes starting from his head, the boy seemed to look past him into some approaching other world. Steele hoped, but had never been able to say he believed, that one existed. So young, so brave, yet already the process of dissolution was upon him. He could not bear to look upon it, yet remained kneeling beside him.

Holding the spasmodically gripping hand, Alphaeus Steele thought how easy it would be to ease his departure. A few grains of the proper drug, and young Louis's suffering would end. But no physician could long think along those lines, and he wrenched his mind back to those he could still help. He made sure they had liberal alcoholic stimuli and that the passageways were kept as clear as possible. If they had to abandon, it would be his responsibility to get them topside and into the boats.

He was engaged in this when a renewed burst of shouting atop the ladder warned him to stand clear.

Several more injured came down. He and Garnett bent over them. As they worked, another appeared at the doorway. A straggle of red hair drew Steele's reluctant eye.

Minter, holding a patch of blood on his breast. Steele quickly finished with the case on the table and wiped his hands. He bit his lips, suddenly for some reason nervous as a girl. —Lieutenant. Can we serve you in some way?

Minter climbed up onto the table, shaking off the helping hands. He swallowed greedily at the fortifying glass Garnett offered. When he lay back, his shining hair spread over the black. Steele wanted to touch it. With an effort he turned his attention to the creamy skin, the cinnamon dusting of chest hair and freckles that shortly lay revealed beneath the glaring betty lamp.

The wound was ragged, and he saw to his relief the fragment had not penetrated deeply. There was no need for anesthesia. —You're a lucky fellow today, Steele told him. —Turn toward the lamp, if you please. What have we here? Rather a pinking than a puncture.

—Most likely a Napoleon shell.

—How do things look topside? We have been rather busy, though the toll of mortality is less than I had been prepared for.

The lieutenant winced as Steele thrust his finger into the laceration. —We've sunk *Cumberland*.

—I had heard that.

—And *Congress* is afire. Is that the engine I hear? We are most likely moving on *Minnesota* now. The enemy flagship. She is aground a mile or two ahead. He turned his head to look down the passageway. —How are our casualties?

Steele said, —We have actually lost only Dunbar so far, though young Waldeck will not live much longer. Mr. Marmaduke is lightly wounded, and some few others. A concussion or two from leaning against the shield. The men who came back with you, of course.

—Burns, said Garnett.

—And a burn or two. For being in action for so long now that is a short butcher's bill . . . and there we are.

Steele extracted a piece of iron. Held it aloft for them all to admire, then wiped it on his apron and offered it. —I daresay you'll be happier with this on your watch fob than in your *pectoralis major.* If it had met your breast with this point foremost, rather than its flat surface, it would have pierced your heart. I'll patch you up and then put you to bed.

But the lieutenant reached for his shirt. He'd rather return to duty, he said. Steele looked after him, then was recalled to his own task as another shattered body was carried in.

He was back in the passageway, yearning at the foot of the ladder for breathable air, when more shouts came from above. He swung away, then back as he saw who was being half-supported, half-carried down.

Franklin Buchanan's aquiline countenance was contorted. He said nothing, but sweat was starting on his forehead. A stain ran down his leg, blackening the blue cloth. Someone shouted to attend him in the flag officer's cabin. Steele said firmly he would not. His instruments and specifics were all in the wardroom; they could bring him in directly. His table was free.

—And what is wrong here? Steele asked more or less by rote, though it was perfectly obvious.

Catesby Jones said, —He's taken a ball in the thigh. Was shooting back at the troops ashore. Lucky he didn't break his neck coming down on us.

—Lay him out, if you please, swiftly.

Stripped of trowsers, the old fighter's legs writhed like white eels against the black india rubber. He waved away Garnett's proffer of whiskey, spluttering, —They have no honor. There's no such thing anymore. Firing on a white flag! My God! Even among savages. Sew me up and get me back up there.

—You'll be going nowhere, Steele told him, turning the thigh out to examine the wound. Not liking the flood seeping from a bruised tear, running down the rubber sheet. A man of this age could not bear excessive exsanguination. —I should advise you to turn your command over, Flag Officer. We will now roll you over and look for the exit. Ready, Doctor? Now.

The ball, probably a standard Yankee minié, had passed through the fleshy portion of the inner thigh, bruising and smashing tissue on its way. This was not the source of the blood, however, which was welling through the exit wound as well. Two or three inches higher, and Buchanan would have been emasculated. An inch to the left would have smashed the *os femoris*. Which would have required disarticulation at the hip; time-consuming, delicate, and in all probability terminating in death anyway. Steele was glad; he hated amputations. But that did not mean the situation was not crucial. The steady pulse of blood from the ragged lips implicated the femoral artery. One of the largest in the body, it would bleed a man out in minutes. Direct compression could not stop such a hemorrhage. He nodded to Garnett. —We'll have chloroform for this case. *Oleum olivae* on his nostrils and lips, if you please.

—I will not have it. Take it away, I will stay in command.

—You're not capable of exercising it, sir.

—Then plug hot shot into her and don't leave her until she's afire. Do you hear me? Destroy the *Minnesota*. Swear you will obey.

His lieutenants standing around him, the old man ranted out vengeance even as the chloroform cone came down. They swore again and again they'd press the attack, not put back in until *Virginia* was mistress of the Roads. Buchanan's words became muffled, then disjointed. At last they ceased.

—You may attend to the enemy, Steele told them calmly, tying his apron more firmly in back. —The flag officer is in my hands now.

To them he might have looked self-possessed, but within he was terrified as any soldier ordered to charge a fortress. He was not at all sure they could stop this bursting forth of the springs of life. When the large arteries were injured, patients died so rapidly most of the resources of the surgeon were of little avail. They fell rapidly into nervous depression, syncope, and death. He checked the pulse at the ankle point and found it nonexistent compared to that of the right. Somewhere along its length the artery was either cut or torn.

By now the patient had ceased struggling, had entered the chloroform trance, snoring loudly. Garnett stood ready to assist. Steele had him flex the limb and rest it on its outer side, and roll the trunk toward him.

Spreading the lips of the wound with his left hand, he took his bearings with the other.

The wound felt smashed and messy. It was not long before his fingertip searched out the slipperiness of the weakly pulsing artery and vein. They were attached here, running side by side and protected by fat and connective tissue. They felt flexible, which was good. Some men Buchanan's age had arteries that crunched when touched, as if filled with little chunks of mortar. Also, it wasn't retracted, which meant it wasn't wholly severed. But still blood was spurting around his probing digit, splattering both surgeons. Digging more deeply, his being concentrated in the tip of his finger, he glided it along the slick tube until he found the welling-out jet pressing rhythmically against his skin.

A ticklish situation. With the heart's pressure behind it, such a large vessel, half an inch in diameter at this point, would empty the body in minutes. He had to stop it, or nothing else would be of use. But he couldn't reach far enough above it yet to use the best method: pressure on the artery itself.

—Doctor Garnett, will you be the Dutch boy, please.

Garnett, face as pale as his own must be, wiped his little finger on his apron, then inserted it into the wound. Steele adjusted it over the torn area. —Can you feel it? Press the tip directly into the tube itself. Your finger in the dike while we consider what to do next. A bit more pressure. Very good. Maintain.

The spurting stopped abruptly, though generalized bleeding continued. Steele pulled the sponge out of his apron pocket. It was still bloody from the previous wounded, and he squeezed it out and mopped the hole till he could see.

The bullet had ripped the sheath open along an inch of its length. Between swipes of the sponge he could just make out the artery within. Even with Garnett's fingertip plugging it, blood was still welling up. Most likely coming up the artery. He instructed the assistant surgeon to press below the tear with his other hand. That helped. The vein, bundled with the artery in the femoral sheath, seemed undamaged. He could not make out the saphenus, the accompanying nerve. The structures were difficult to separate even with skillful dissection. He was less concerned with these, however, than with the artery.

Risking a glance at his patient, he saw the signs of deep blood loss. Blue shadows around the eyes. The pulse, nearly gone. He could think of only one way to stop the flag officer's dying on his table. Ligate, or tie, the artery off both above and below the tear. But to do that he had to be able to reach an undamaged section.

—Scalpel, if you please. Albright, assist Doctor Garnett. Pull back on the lips of the wound. I will extend in the direction of the trunk.

The scalpel parted skin, then the superficial fascia. He found the great saphena vein and carried it carefully inward away from the incision. A mahogany-colored layer of muscle tissue came into view. He used a bistoury, a blunt-pointed scalpel, to deepen the cut, just touching the soft tissue to divide it.

The sheath and artery of the femoral canal lay below this, but he approached as warily as he could consistent with the necessity to hurry. He was close to the great division of the femoral. An accidental nick would force him to repatulate and ligate even higher, in a vastly more complicated anatomy of ligaments, muscles, and nerves, most likely dooming Buchanan to loss of the leg and probably death not long following, if not during the amputation itself. He shook perspiration from his eyes; beads of mingled sweat and blood dripped into the wound. —Can you see? Can you see? Garnett kept asking. —Just keep your fingers where they are and shut up, Steele snarled.

The upper part of the sheath came into view but was immediately obscured by blood leaking from the smashed tissue all around. Coagulation should have started by now, but it was still oozing. Steele's hands were shaking. His nerves shrieked for another nip, but he could not go back to his stateroom. Buchanan's sleeping face was taking on the waxen look of blood loss, shock, approaching death.

Steele crossed to the sideboard and under pretense of looking over his instruments found an opportunity to inspect the medicinal whiskey as well. Allowing himself a mouthful only, he returned to the table and briefly discussed Larrey's, Hunter's, and Scarpa's different points of approach with Garnett.

He wished his hands would stop trembling. He couldn't do this. It was beyond him. He wanted to be somewhere else, where a slip of his fingers wouldn't kill. Where the imperative of life or death could be evaded, passed on, handed to someone with more authority.

But it was those in authority who'd dictated this suffering that surrounded him, who'd carpeted these decks with bleeding flesh. God! Wasn't there enough death, enough pain, that men had to manufacture it by the cannon's mouth? He tried to discipline his thoughts. Exorcise this terror and weakness. If Garnett could control the bleeding for a few more minutes, and if Alphaeus could do a very skillful dissection around his encumbering hands, the patient might make it.

Garnett looked wary but didn't disagree. Steele squeezed the sponge out and mopped his brow with it. He laid the threaded curved needle on the unconscious man's bare stomach, ready to hand. He sponged the wound again, blinking and squinting as the lamp swayed and shadows shifted in the wound. Then pinched up the sheath with the forceps and denuded the artery with a sweep of the grooved director.

Albright sponged and coughed, working around the surgeons in a twisting dance of intertwined limbs above the central wound. The smoke was bothering Steele too, but he could not cough or flinch at this point. Instead he swallowed the tickle in his throat and very delicately passed the director under the vessel.

Both he and Garnett were dripping sweat into the wound now. His nightmare at this moment was that the damaged artery would part. It did not. But unfortunately his thread got the vein along with the artery. He was tempted horribly to let it go, just get the damn thing ligated, but this was a sure recipe for phlebitis given Buchanan's age. He still hadn't ever made out the nerve in the bloody, confused topography of macerated flesh, but it was too late to worry about that; he assumed the bullet had carried it off. The second time he snagged the artery alone, and from there things proceeded straightforwardly. He tied it off, released it, and Garnett gingerly pulled his finger out.

The ligature held. Steele took a relieved breath and stepped back. He took Garnett's place applying pressure below the wound, and let the younger surgeon handle the lower ligature. This would stop backbleeding.

Now he felt blithe, bubbly with relief. He came back to place a drainage tube, then drew together and roughly sutured the fascia around it. He left the ends of the ligatures hanging out and secured them to the upper thigh with an adhesive plaster. He crammed the rest of the wound with picked lint and bandaged it. The assistant lifted the anesthesia cone, and the loblolly-boys slid the old man off the table.

—Not badly done, said Garnett. Steele nodded, acknowledging the compliment. The younger doctor added, —You'd better sit down, though. You look at the end of your string.

—It's not so easy, once one passes fifty or thereabouts.

He rested in a chair for some minutes, then forced himself up. —I shall check on our cabin patient. He should be coming out of his twilight about now.

Which Buchanan was, vomiting weakly into a basin held by his manservant. Steele checked his pulse, elevated his limb on the pillows. Then had to dissuade the flag officer from trying to go back on deck. —If you tear that ligature free, sir, you shall die within minutes. Not from loss of blood, though.

—No? What then?

—From me throttling you, sir. Do we understand one another, you and I?

The old man grumpily subsided back onto his cot. Still Steele did not dare leave him until Jones came down to report.

Sealed below, they did not hear they were falling back under the guns of Sewell's Point until they were nearly there. As soon as he heard this, Alphaeus started preparing the wounded for departure. He went in to give Buchanan the news. The old man was astonished and enraged to hear they were leaving the field. He refused to haul down his flag. He insisted he would be carried up on a litter and direct tomorrow's attack from the top of the casemate. However, he fainted in the midst of his diatribe.

When he got back to the wardroom, Garnett was packing up the last of the instruments from the sideboard. As he did so, the stewards replaced them with serving dishes. Others were wiping down where men had so lately thrashed and bled. They covered it with green baize and then laundered linen. Steele slumped in a chair, chin propped on his hand. The screams still lingered in his ears. Then he realized they were real. The wounded were recovering from shock into pain. Not Waldeck, though. The Charlestonian, mercifully unconscious at last, had died not long before.

He wasn't saying there hadn't been enough, but there had not been so many. Not for a daylong battle, two ships destroyed, others damaged. God knew what the butcher's bill had been on the other side. The officers reeled as they came in. They were powder-stained and exhausted, but save for Minter and Marmaduke they were unwounded.

Jones, square before his chair. —Will the flag officer live?

—He has every chance of doing so.

—Will he lose the leg?

Steele assumed the gravity proper to a prognosis. —Difficult to say for one of his age; but it is possible he may not. A deeper artery feeds the limb during the healing period. With time, alternate circulation should develop. He may even walk again if he survives the normal suppurative process.

—He wishes to fight again tomorrow.

—*He* cannot possibly fight, Lieutenant. He must stay altogether quiet, free from excitement and at perfect rest. It is obvious this means he cannot remain aboard. Therefore you must persuade him to let himself be put ashore.

Jones looked as if he didn't relish that duty. —Surely as the surgeon in charge—

—I am quite outranked here, sir. We medical men are only staff officers, after all. Surely he and the rest of you all have done today everything anyone could require. Have you not?

—The enemy flagship remains unvanquished. Tomorrow we must finish the job.

Steele thought of asking how many more lives the dip of a flag was worth; decided at last such sentiments were best left unexpressed. He was exhausted and his head was splitting, no doubt from breathing bad air all day. The babble around him was rising. A wineglass was pressed into his hand. —The blockade, history, someone was saying. —Tomorrow we shall pass Monroe and clear the last of them out.

—That French corvette saw it all. Even shifted position to see better.

—A thorough enema for the Yankees. Eh, surgeon? With an iron clyster! Ha, ha!

He lifted his glass when toasted, but a crushing weariness stole on him. Their hubris terrified him. Could it end like this? In conquest? Triumph? Final victory? With all prisoners released, forgiveness, and peace at last between the warring sections?

With all his heart he hoped so. But still remained that germ of doubt. That ominous foresense of inimical Fate.

The Greeks, so wise in all their ways, had called it Nemesis.

25

---

16 Freemason Street
Norfolk, Virginia
March 8, 1862

Dearest Ker,

I take my seat tonight to write as I so often have since we parted. Is it indeed now almost a year? So much has happened in that time. The war—your command—our loss of our tiny darling—your captivity, and the weary months since not even knowing as I set pen to paper whether he to whom these words are addressed yet draws breath. Surely our enemies would not take their vengeance on the <u>celebrated pirate Claiborne</u> without boasting to the world of it. Yet was that not the practice of the old regime in France? It is so sad to see those once compatriots in liberty betraying and outraging our common heritage.

We are all well here and so much to tell you!—It has been a memorable day in the annals of our Country. Pistol-shots and horns are sounding outside. Perhaps you already know of which I write long before this letter reaches you across rivers and hostile lines. But perhaps they do not allow you the newspapers—or will not print the truth as it is in no wise advantageous to the North. Still it gladdens my heart to think of your eye scanning these lines one day.

I rose early today, as I long anticipated reasonable weather to get out in the garden. I have to root out all Mother's lovely flowers, and put the plot in vegetables. The less we have to purchase this coming year the better it may be for us. I still receive your allotment but that sum does not change while the rise in prices has become alarming. Some of the older ladies tell of when the English burned the city during the first Revolution. They fear the Yankees will starve and burn us out. They may do the latter, but with enough potatoes and carrots they shall not do the former.

I had asked Betsey to tell Gager to come by today. I do not know if you recall Gager—he is a free colored boy whom Mrs. Mears had recommended to us as a steady man. I was out contemplating what to have him do when I was accosted by a man passing in front of the house. I did not respond, but looking over the fence noted people streaming toward the waterfront. Curious, I called to a passing lady and was told the "Merrimac" was coming! I immediately called Betsey, got Robert out of bed and dressed, threw on an old bibi and my green coat and dragged all down to the drawbridge across Colley Creek to see what the fuss was about.

Of course we had all long known an iron-clad ship was being built, and read of it in the journals. But from one thing and another had not expected much of it. Some said it was prone to sinking. Others, that the armor was not proof against cannon-fire. Reverend Crandall had gone to see the work but had been turned back, they were no longer admitting the public, even the respectable.

I find the bridge down and the whole occupied by a perfect crowd. The toll booth closed and boys looking on from atop its roof. And the most utter silence. Then, as we watched, a great black Presence glided out. It lingered for a time, sending up more smoke than a score of locomotives. Then slowly turned about and came down the river.

At first it looked like nothing more than a long barge of coal on fire. But as it passed the ice company wharf we could examine it at our leisure. It was eerie to see something so huge passing without the aid of a scrap of sail. I helped Robert to a perch and pinched him so that he should remember. But I think he will anyway, he was as excited as anyone there at the <u>big black boat.</u> The crew waved their caps as they drove past. We heard cheers from the town point but there was none from us, no not a one. I confess my heart was in my mouth. An old gentleman was saying angrily we'd never see the brave boys again. The whole thing would turn over as soon as it got out of the river. But it did not, and our Flag made a brave show as very slowly and majestically it steamed off.

I was thinking of returning home, though dreadfull curious as to the outcome of the impending contest, when who should come rowing down but old Captain Johnson, the one Mr. Wise introduced us to when we visited at "Rolleston" on the Eastern Branch back in '60. He was in his old felucca with his wife and sister. His Coolies were at the oars—the six he brought back from the Indies as apprentices. I fluttered my handkerchief and he lifted his hat and called up that he had wished for a little lad to see this day with him and here he was, meaning our own bright-faced boy.

Here perhaps I assented to something I ought not to have done. But Robert hearing this was frantic to go. I confess I too was eager to see the issue when such a novel construction faced those who barred us from intercourse with the world. That is, I gathered my skirts about me and very carefully stepped from the open side of the toll-bridge down into the boat. I held up my arms and Robert hurled himself down almost knocking me over onto the old captain. He is growing quite fast, our boy, and it will not be long before picking him up will be beyond me.

The Coolies up close did not smell so bad as one might expect. In fact they seemed more cleanly in their persons than old Captain Johnson. Robert ran from one end to the other until the old skipper, who looked quite grand in his marine rig, told him a true salt stayed in his seat so as not to rock the boat. He then gave him the tiller and we were off upon our adventure.

Slowly as the Leviathan progressed, we were able nearly to catch up with it under the vigorous plying of the Coolies. Other pleasure-boats moved along in a grand flotilla. All was like a regatta, most pleasant in the sunny weather, but withal underlaying an anxiety for the brave men whom we could see moving about atop a platform. Captain Johnson, being a bluff old seaman of great experience, stayed behind it and did not play about under its bows as the other boats did. He explaining that such a machine had been proposed years before by his friend Captain Barron, who called it a <u>marina catapulta</u>. Also that a Mr. Stephens, of the North, had proposed another such. But this being the first time such an one had thrown down the gage of battle to an enemy.

As we breasted Seawell's Point the beaches were lined with our lads in gray cheering themselves hoarse. Captain Johnson seeing the Yankee squadron in the distance thought it best to stop a little ways off and observe. Upon a word from him in their language the coolies at once put up their oars and proceeded to rig up an awning of scarlet canvas that gave the ladies protection from the sun, which by now was growing quite warm. Presently Mrs. Johnson produced a hamper ram-jam with the most curious things: a spicy chutneep, balls of sticky rice, pickled martinas, meat croquettes which tasted of currie, and other exotic delicacies. It was quite a change from Dilla's cooking.

As we ate the "Merrimac" had been heading up as if going toward Old Point and the Hygeia Hotel. But then turning it made for two ships anchored far out across the water. One of the gunboats went out in advance and opened the fire. Then she fell back and the "Virginia"—a man on a boat nearby advised us that was the noble vessel's new name, and so glorious and right it was—advanced to the fray. We saw the "Cumberland" fall on her side and sink. We saw the battery and the Yankee frigates sending their death messengers at each other. For a time all the ships and all the land guns were engaged, and O the sight was sublime, the smoke rising in a grand shining curtain pink and yellow in the sun. Robert will always remember this day and the great success of our arms. I reminded him not all was show, that men were being slain. He shouted out in his childish voice that then the bad Yankees should not have come down here to fight us, and he was glad they were getting "licked."

As for myself I could never see how it is the Lincolnites can imagine they could impose a union on us by force. If we do not wish it "<u>They can't do it, nor any man.</u>" We are free Citizens, not

Subjects. One Section can be Conquered but it could never be kept. If it is really the colored at stake they have always been well treated in my family. But that is only their pretext for riveting on us chains that would last for ever.

As evening drew on the great and now forever famous Southern Ironsides came back quietly to anchor. We sailed past and examined her honorable wounds, which consisted only of a few plates bent & pipes shot off her top. A man on deck said they had only a few wounded & one who stuck his head out and was killed. But that brave Buchanan was gravely hurt and might not live out the night. We also saw some captured Yankees aboard the "Patrick Henry." They looked quite miserable. Captain Johnson landed us at Mrs. Cook's pier and we walked home, tired from the day but with our hearts uplifted in joy at its result, telling everyone we met of the Victory.

As I write you now I am weeping. Not with happiness, for I will not be happy until I clasp you in my arms again. But with relief, for after these weary months of fear and misgiving we have seen our deliverance. I had almost forgotten this past year how merciful God is. But now "the sun at last shines." I pray a most earnest Prayer to the Almighty and to his Son Jesus Christ our Lord that this will be the last battle and our Country saved; that this cruel war may end and you and all prisoners be returned to the bosom of their families.

I shall close. May this letter reach you in good health and regular digestion. May it find you making preparations to return to us! The thought makes me weak. I would lie down but for the dyspepsia the strange food brought on. I find chutneep and tandoor do not agree with me. Robert wants corn bread and milk before bed. Betsey is nowhere to be found.

I will write again as soon as there is more news.

Truly Thine,
C.W.C.

PART IV

THE CLANGOR OF THAT
BLACKSMITH'S FRAY.

March 8–9, 1862.

26

Thunder in March ♦ Arrival in Hampton Roads ♦ Aboard U.S.S. *Roanoke* ♦
Depredations of the Confederate Monster ♦ Dismissal of the Nondescript's
Effectiveness ♦ Keying Up, with Doubts as to the Sufficiency of Armor ♦
Alongside the Steam Frigate U.S.S. *Minnesota* ♦ Conversation with
a Tug Captain ♦ Death-Pyre of a Ship ♦ Nothing Left but Waiting

TOWARD dawn the sea became not as rough; whether because the
wind had died or they were creeping under shelter, Theo wasn't
sure. He moved in a fog of fatigue. He'd slept about an hour, all
told, in the last four days. He was also suffering, along with most of the
engine-room gang, from a peculiar nauseated lassitude unlike any he'd ever
felt. He suspected it was from the toxic gases they'd inhaled the night before.

They raised Cape Charles a little after noon. Newton reported from
the tower that the seas had dropped, it was pleasant and sunny and the
water smoothing. Their escorts had closed in as if to protect them as they
neared Secessia.

At eight bells, four in the afternoon, word came down Cape Henry
was in the offing. The pilot-sloop was standing out. He considered going
up, but decided to check the bunkers instead. As he'd feared, the coal had
shifted, shoaling up against the outer hull. He started to tell Geer to put
the stokers to shifting it back, then decided it was well enough where it
was. The pressure was holding steady, the blowers were running normally,
the men looked tired but were keeping up.

He stumbled into the wardroom, rubbing what felt like sleep-grit from his eyes, to find almost the same persons in almost the same positions as the night before. The air was thick with segar smoke and excited talk. Worden was nowhere in sight, nor was Greene. The junior officers spoke in loud voices of hearing guns in the distance. One said it was mere thunder. The others scoffed; who ever heard of thunder in March! Keeler, who'd just come down, said he could see clouds of smoke beyond Fisherman Island and, through the glass, little black spots occasionally springing up into the air. They remained stationary a moment, he said, then expanded into a white cloud. —I have no idea what they can be.

—Those are shells, Frederickson grunted. One of the acting ensigns, a former quartermaster who'd come up from the ranks in a mail steamer.

The word wilted the purser, who pushed his beans around nervously. —Shells?

Frederickson grinned. —Aye. So those as wonder if they're brave enough, you'll soon get your chance to glimpse the groundhog.

The door opened on Lieutenant Greene and a stranger in civilian clothes. The mess quieted. The civilian glanced at the wineglasses and segars, the whiteware with *Monitor* in gilt Old English lettering, the carpets, the Negro mess boys with waiter caps and napkins over their arms. He said in a New Englandish accent, —The captain sent me down to see, as I did not believe. But it's true, you don't live so bad down here under the water.

—This gentleman has news, Greene said. —Best lock up the wine, Lawrence. We may need our wits about us.

The pilot, for that was what he was, said *Merrimack* had come out that day a little after noon, accompanied by two secesh gunboats, and had in the course of an afternoon used up every ship it could get at. —The traitors rammed *Cumberland* and sent her to the bottom. *Congress* ran ashore to escape, but the monster shelled her till she caught fire. Hundreds killed and wounded. They're saying on the telegraph she'll be out again tomorrow to finish the job.

—Aye, that's well; but she'll have us to contend with then, Frederickson said.

The pilot smiled and started to speak; looked up at the sunlight shining through the deadlights. Then bowed and said he wished them good luck; that he had best get back topside and make sure they were clear for the channel.

Dusk again. He and Greene were lounging against the rope that encircled the crown of the tower. The freshness of the air was shocking, the space around one vertiginous. After a curt nod the exec had nothing to say to him. Greene and Mr. Flye, the only other lieutenant aboard, were discussing whether they should shift the deck watch to the pilothouse or keep to the turret top as they'd been forced to by the storm. Shading his eyes, Theo looked ahead anxiously.

The Chesapeake opened at their right hand, broad and markless, and to port the sandy vellum of the Lynnhaven shore. An occasional wave washed across the flat iron deck. Ahead *Seth Low* smoked and plodded with unvarying stolidity. Far ahead the moon was rising; either that or something large was on fire. All around, though, dipped and wove the running lights of vessels, making either for the open sea or farther up the Bay.

A stir at the hatchway, and Worden climbed into view. The captain was in frock coat and service cap, and wore cotton gloves only slightly soiled. Greene lifted his cap. —Good evening, sir. Cape Charles on our starboard quarter; Lynnhaven to port. Fort Monroe and Old Point Comfort more or less dead ahead.

—Very well, Mister Greene. Have you made out the flagship? We shall want to report in directly we arrive.

—Not yet, sir.

Worden flicked a handkerchief over his uniform, then shaded his eyes ahead. —Is the hawser holding?

—I have the bo's'n checking it on the half hour. It is thoroughly frapped against further chafing. I have seen to the anchor and cast loose the gig and cutter, in case you should need them. Greene nodded to where their boats towed along astern, rocking in what sea swell remained.

Worden studied the flat expanse of iron below with a trace of disdain. —Is that rust I see aft of the pilothouse? We shall have to weblacken this entire deck, Mister Greene. Have you given any thought as to black varnish against gun-blacking?

—I have considered the question, sir. Either would tot up to such a sum I doubt the Department would accept our account.

The captain turned, clasping his gloves stiffly behind him. —Engineer Hubbard. I trust you are well this evening?

—Yes sir. Theo remembered, too late, to lift his cap. Worden's look conveyed he'd noted the hesitation.

—Let me sound you on the matter. What would you suggest for such a quantity of iron exposed to the salt air?

Theo suggested coal tar mixed with saltwater, warmed in buckets with steam and laid on as thin as possible with paintbrushes. They could eke it out with lamp oil if the forty gallons aboard were not enough.

Worden's look grew more sour. —I should *very* much dislike to use *coal tar*, Hubbard. Daresay that may do in the engine room, but should anyone track it belowdecks, it would play vewwy *hob* with the carpeting. Paint oil, litharge, and lampblack. Two or three coats of some such mixture will see us through with the least cost and messiness below. It would look well if it should have some *gloss*. Perhaps gum shellac?

The tug smoked and thrashed, the engine thudded and clanked. The steady though achingly slow shifting of trees along the distant beach told him they were still moving, albeit at a snail's pace. Probably the tide was still going out.

He lingered for some hours as they crept with that agonizing deliberation across the mouth of the Bay. It was well after dark when they hoisted the signal light that would allow them to pass under the guns of the fort. The shadowed battlements of its water battery and the ramparts behind them were unrelieved by the light that the chart showed should be burning to mark its southernmost point. The lack was supplied by an immense pyre that burned to the northwest. It was so bright it illuminated the curving shore and the silhouette of a frigate, motionless and lightless, that stood a little way out from it. To port, another low mass. He guessed it was the fortification on the Rip Raps that together with Monroe closed the gate of Hampton Roads. More shapes rode close against the fortress. Their masts flickered against the sky. Dim blue lights burned to mark each's stern.

Worden's languid voice, close in the dark. —Mister Hubbard? I shall be going aboard the flagship. I would be grateful if you would accompany me to answer any questions the commodore may have welative to our machinery.

Climbing the boat-ladder up the immense sides of the steam frigate *Roanoke,* which shone like polished coal. Past the gun deck, where flickering lanterns within open ports silhouetted the hulking projections of run-out Dahlgrens, tompions clear and muzzles agape at the hostile night. Despite the late hour Theo did not see a single hammock rigged. Frantic screams ebbed to a sobbing wail. Some poor devil was under the knife. Anxious faces glanced down through the spar-deck ports but did not watch long. Then the spar deck itself, with more guns in close ranks, men moving about with drawn faces lit by the distant firelight. At the opposite boat-stage wounded were being lifted aboard with whip-tackle. Some made no sound, sagging in their litters. Others shrieked piteously as they revolved in the dark air.

Captain John Marston received them in his cabin. Ten candles illuminated it. The flames pointed straight up. A steward was bundling books and letters into wooden sea chests. The stern windows stood half open, but with no breeze whatsoever the cabin felt close despite the coolness. Through them and below Theo could see the *Monitor*'s stern deck as a pointed absence of the firelight that sparkled on the water's surface.

—Sir, Lieutenant-commanding John Lorimer Worden, seeking Commodore Goldsborough to report the arrival from New York of the Ericsson battery.

Marston acknowledged Worden's bow. —Commodore Goldsborough is in the sounds of North Carolina, sir. I command in his absence.

—Very well, sir. Then I beg the honor to weport U.S.S. *Monitor* to you. We are manned and armed and prepared for a fight.

This, Theo thought, was no longer the languid fellow their captain had seemed thus far. Worden stood straight, hat tucked under his arm, at attention. He still lisped, but the unenergetic voice now conveyed a certain cool determination.

Marston did not seem impressed. —Very good, but I am surprised to find you here. I had understood your battery to be headed for Washington.

Worden looked puzzled. —I have received no such orders, sir.

—Perhaps they reached New York after your sailing. At any rate I cannot employ you here.

—I beg your pardon, sir?

Marston gestured toward the firelit night. —I will be plain with you. We have today suffered the Navy's greatest defeat since *Philadelphia* was captured in Tripoli. Perhaps greater in terms of loss of men. We cannot hold Hampton Roads against this devilish *thing*. It is anchored this night under Craney Island, six miles distant. In the morning it will return to finish its work.

—Surely they will not come on a Sunday.

—Sunday or no, the army is evacuating Newport News as we speak. What is worse, two more of our frigates lie grounded out there, and my own engines have been out of service for some time. We are helpless when she comes again.

Worden bowed sympathetically. —Unpleasant news, sir.

—And all under the eyes of the French and British.

—Very unfortunate, sir. But it need not mean—

Marston splayed his fingers to forestall interruption. —You may not fully understand, Lieutenant. I have served forty years war and peace but will henceforth be remembered only as presiding over the greatest rout in the annals of the United States Navy. But regardless of my reputation, I cannot let the Confederates capture additional warships, and father more of these miscreations on their frames. We have tugs standing by. As soon as *Minnesota* and *St. Lawrence* float off, I am taking the squadron north to a defensive position off the mouth of the Potomac.

Worden pointed out politely that to abandon the Roads would leave the rebel craft a free cruiser. She might go to sea and attack New York; run up the bay to Baltimore, which was half Confederate anyway; or down to Charleston, stopping at Hatteras on the way to disperse the invading fleet.

Marston said, voice hard, —That is neither here nor there. As I said: I have my orders regarding you, sir. You are to go up the Potomac.

Worden passed a hand across his brow. —To *Washington,* sir? Are you certain?

—That order is direct from Secretary Welles by telegraph. Both to Commodore Paulding in New York and to myself, should they not reach you in time. Which apparently they have not.

—Sir, that cannot stand. Surely in the light of developments . . . the secretary cannot mean . . . I submit we must stay and fight. To simply flee could be subject to the most unfortunate interpretation abroad.

Marsden took a turn around the cabin, hands locked behind his back. Peered out the window. Down, Theo assumed, at their little craft. —How many guns does your . . . armored battery mount?

—Two guns, sir.

—*Two*, Mister Worden? Only two?

—They are eleven-inch Dahlgrens.

—And fine guns we thought them up to today.

—What do you mean, sir?

—I mean *Cumberland* mounted twenty-two of them; nine-inchers, to be sure, but still she fired broadside after broadside to no more effect than throwing a handful of dried peas. This terrible engine is completely invulnerable. We are like the naked hosts of the Inca confronting Pizarro's mailed conquistadors.

They were interrupted by a tap on the door, a petty officer. Marston scanned the message with glooming brows. —Van Brunt cannot budge from where he has taken the ground.

—Sir, let me stand by her.

The senior laughed bitterly, and Theo saw how the pain and responsibility of the day weighed. —You would, eh? Well, sir, you may have faith in your little nondescript, but I have been to sea a good many years longer than you have. I well recall how many good men Mister Ericsson's previous *novelties* have cost us. He is at his most inventive at scheming to obtain money from the government, it seems to me.

Worden waited politely. At last Marston added, —What precisely do you suggest, sir?

—That we stand fast and meet her when she returns. No human construction can be completely impenetrable.

Marston looked troubled. —You do not know what you will be confronting. Even here under the fort, perhaps even within the fort, it will not be safe come morning.

—Sir, let me stand by *Minnesota*. I can protect her till she can be floated off. Or fired if there is no other resort—though we have burned enough of our own ships in this war, it seems to me. The commander lowered his voice. —At worse, she'll crush us as well. But we are an ex-pewwiment. The government need not even pay should we not be proof against enemy shot. At best we may retrieve the honor of the Service . . . perhaps wipe out the disgrace that weighs so grievously on you.

Theo stood silent, admiring. Worden was offering a wager. His men's lives and his own against a possible retrieving of Marston's career. But he was phrasing it in terms of the Service, in terms of honor. Was it a kind of braider code language? Or did he believe his flag-waving?

The acting commodore cocked his head like an old gray squirrel con-sidering a hard acorn. At last he waved his hand. —Well, if that is your wish, I will defer to it. You are an ironclad, I grant you that. Set a thief, eh? But I must leave the responsibility for such a windmill tilt upon your head.

—I accept that charge, sir.

—Also, I will relieve you of your tug. If you have motive power in your steam battery, that is. Do you? I really do not know.

Worden glanced at Theo, who cleared his throat. —We are mobile, sir. Discommoded in heavy weather, but capable of navigating around an en-closed body of water.

—A pilot?

—We had one coming in but discharged him.

—I will assign you Acting Master Howard from Rhode Island. He has made himself familiar with the harbor. Your draft?

—Eleven feet at present load.

—Coal?

—We have sufficient for two more days' steaming.

Marsden unbent so far as to offer them a glass of wine, but with a tone Theo did not like: that of sending brave fellows off on a forlorn hope. Worden declined politely, pleading the necessity of seeing to duty. Min-utes later they were descending the boat-ladder again. Theo cast a regret-ful glance at the spacious decks, the rows of heavy guns. He understood Marston's misgivings. Beside this massive hull their new machine looked negligible indeed.

Worden ordered him to key up the turret. He did not believe their adversary would sortie by night, but did not wish to be taken unawares. Theo passed the order to Newton, then went aft. The engine-room gang had settled back into routine: stoke, steam, expand, condense. It was even relatively cool, no more than ninety degrees at the boiler-front thanks to the volumes of night air sucked down by the blowers. They were running tight and fast with their third set of belts. He hoped no more broke. He had no more spares.

As he climbed back up through the engine-room hatch, fear suddenly gripped him, a bone-deep article that made him want to run. He wasn't part of this crew. He could go ashore and make his way back to New York without violating any order, incurring any censure.

Except his own. He vacillated on the iron deck, fingering his collar. Watching the pyre toward which they advanced, clink-clank-*whump,* clink-clank-*whump,* slowly and steadily over the flat water.

He'd never faced enemy fire, not in eight years in naval service. Apparently the enemy construction had torn through two of the heaviest first-rates without damage. Resisting whole broadsides of the most powerful guns afloat. Four inches of iron, the spy reports had said. Slanted, which would increase its resistance to shot. *Monitor* had only two inches on her flat deck, five on the side armor, none slanted; the full eight inches only on the turret itself. If Ericsson was wrong, they'd be laid out in short order.

The same thoughts must be going through other minds. The men who moved about with lips set and eyes calibrated beyond what they were looking at.

What would Theo Hubbard leave behind if the worst happened? All he could point to with any sense to it was the little girl. All, if Mr. Darwin was right, that he *need* leave behind. Survive and reproduce . . . But Lili had been afraid of him. He'd only hugged her once. The little girl had fought like a cat to get away. Then gone tense, quivering, like a small animal caught and waiting to be devoured.

But he could never acknowledge her as his daughter. Not and have any hope of an advantageous marriage to a woman of good character.

Clink-clank-*whump*. Clink-clank-*whump*. Iron pulsed beneath his feet like a living creature.

Yard by rod by mile they walked toward the fire ahead.

The loom of the grounded frigate was surrounded by smaller masses, some lit, others not, that resolved as they neared into oar boats, tugboats, and things bobbing low in the water that at first Theo could make no sense of. Half a mile beyond lay the burning wreck they'd seen from bayward. Smaller fires sparkled along the shore. As they closed further, the amorphous mass resolved into jetsam: spars, beef casks, bales of slop goods. They bumped along the hull as the engine slowed, gave one last thump, and stopped. He visualized what was going on below: steam valve cut off, the hand crank spinning, the eccentric rotating counterclockwise. Then the first reverse stroke. Then the next, faster and faster.

The screw throbbed, braking their progress. Thudded as debris kicked through it, then quieted again. Apprehensive visages drifted close above them, smeared with powder and mud. Theo remarked the turbulence along her waterline, though the great ship remained stationary. *Minnesota* had been one of the *Merrimack*-class steam frigates, so heavily armed and threatening the British had built a new class to counter them. Now she was a mass of immobile wood, hard aground on an oyster bank. The chuckling noise was the tide still going out. They'd not be moving her soon, no matter what they threw overboard.

—What boat?

—United States Armored Battery *Monitor,* Greene's voice sang out.

Silence. Then, —Say again?

—The Ericsson battery *Monitor*. Permission for the first officer to come aboard, to consult with Captain Van Brunt.

The voice granted permission dubiously. Greene strode past, shouting to the gig crew. Theo walked aft with him, expecting to be asked to accompany him, as Worden had, but the exec took no notice and pulled away.

A churning, a chuffing in the semidarkness, and a black shape appeared around the stem of the stranded warship. It came on rapidly, paddles thrashing. Theo was edging toward the tower from his exposed position on deck when the wheels slowed. The craft sheered off and drifted. —Ahoy there, said a gruff voice.

No one answered from the tower, so Theo went up to the ridge rope. —Ahoy yourself, he called.

—Damn near run ye down. That the *Reindeer*?

—No. The *Monitor*.

—Water tank, are ye?

—The Ericsson invention. Freshly arrived from New York.

—What, this little barge? The voice turned scornful. —The *Merrimack*'ll sink ye with one broadside. Best go back to carrying water. Unless ye can help us tow her off.

—We are not equipped for towing.

—What good are ye, then? This was apparently a rhetorical question, for the tug captain didn't wait for a reply. —I say, don't be nippent. Show your heels, that engine of destruction comes out again. She give pure hell to the best you got.

Theo was opening his mouth to reply when the night parted with a mighty flash. Iron shuddered. He cowered on the solid plate, fingers scrabbling before he realized there was no way within. The roar arrived then, tremendous as the descent of an avalanche in a snowy range. But it did not subside. It went on and on, each showering of sparks bursting higher in the astonished night. The shore flickered, lit, unlit, brilliantly lit, dark again. Ruddy sublightnings glimmered within a boiling mass. Comets soared, then plunged, detonating in heavy crumps. The crashes rolled across the night-draped Roads like the finale of a Fourth of July fireworks display.

—She's gone up at last. And a many good souls with her, said the gruff voice when the last rumblings died, when only a drifting glint showed where a ship had lived. —Clear out, whatever you are. It's the devil in an iron box, and bigger than a Pennsylvania barn.

Theo didn't answer, and after a moment the paddles started thrashing again, the tug moved on. Hands thrust into his pockets, he looked after it. Past it. Into the south, from whence the Behemoth would come.

27

The Second Dawn Afloat ♦ The Necessity of Victory ♦ Under Way as
a Squadron ♦ Speculation on a New Arrival ♦ The Opening Salvo ♦
A Ludicrous Notion

LOMAX was awakened by pipe, whistle, and drum at five. Early, but
not as early as he'd expected. The cooks must have been up all night.
Corn bread, fried ham, and hot black coffee laced with whiskey relieved his headache somewhat. His chest was sore but not exceedingly
painful. At table someone said Buchanan was going ashore. The surgeon
had insisted he be moved to the naval hospital. Lomax flexed his arm,
touched his breast. He decided he could do without renewing his dressings.

At six he was on the spar deck, relieving Wood so the latter could eat.
In the early light the upperworks and stack looked even more battered.
Cumberland's gunners had not let them off unscathed. The boatswain was
supervising the erection of a new flagstaff. Fog lay over the water. A single
report off to the northeast he guessed was Fort Monroe's morning gun.
He examined the fog with the officer of the deck's telescope as he listened
to the litany of watch relief. Wind light from the west. *Minnesota* in sight,
not moved from her previous evening's position aground on the Hampton Flats.

He expected at any moment to be ordered to get under way, but instead an hour went by. Boats came alongside from *Patrick Henry*. It was a
difficult evolution to get the wounded down into them, given the iron-

clad's sloping sides. Buchanan came up last, attended by Jones and Steele, Garnett and Norris; a waxen-faced old man strapped tightly into a litter. He said nothing as he was being swayed down into the ironclad's single serviceable boat. Lomax heard only one harsh intake of breath, when a clumsy hand knocked against him as he was being lowered. Dr. Garnett got into the cutter with him. Minter nodded to the boatswain. With a blast of the whistle Buchanan's pennant came down hand over hand. Catesby Jones was *Virginia*'s commander now.

The old surgeon stood watching the boat draw away, hands clasped behind his portly figure. He caught sight of Lomax and bowed. —Lieutenant Minter.

—Doctor Steele. Lomax lifted his cap. —The flag officer. Will he live?

—Provided his leg does not mortify.

—Will he walk again?

—That is out of my hands, young sir. Only time will answer that question. Steele began pressing above and below his dressing. —Your breast; how does it feel this morning? Any shortness of breath, fever, weakness, pain?

—I feel capital, Doctor. You are a wizard, and no mistake. He smiled, tried to look healthy. He didn't want to join those being rowed ashore. Not on the morn of the deciding event of the war.

—I daresay it is youth healing you and no skill of mine. Steele patted his sleeve. His eyes were watery; he had not shaved. Lomax smelled spirits on his breath. He felt repelled and took the opportunity to move away on pretext of shouting down at the anchor party. When he turned back, the surgeon was letting himself heavily down the forward ladder.

Catesby Jones returned Lomax's lifted cap. Perfectly groomed despite the early hour, he took a look round the horizon, then borrowed the deck glass to study the distant frigate. —Have you logged the Commodore's departure?

—Yes sir.

—It is for us to complete his work. We must destroy all men-o'-war remaining in the Roads. There is no half victory here.

—All we require is the resolution to do so, Lomax said.

He and Jones measured each other before the exec said coldly, —As soon as you have tested the engines, you may weigh anchor.

Lomax rang down for one bell. His pull was promptly answered, but it took ages for the massive ironclad to surge against her chain. He debated trying a backing bell as well, but Ramsay had mentioned something about his reversing linkage being about played out. So he just went to all stop, then sent word forward to hoist.

Jones stood observing. Finally he said, —As I have inherited the mantle of command, Lieutenant, I have decided Mister Simms will move up to the position of exec.

Lomax reflected bitterly that Simms had very little seniority on him, but of course he was a Virginian, like the new commander. But aloud he only said, —Aye aye, sir.

—I should like you to take his place at the head of first division. If you feel up to it, considering your injuries.

Lomax said they were minor and that he'd take over first division and the bow gun directly. Jones waited, as if for some other reaction. Not getting it, he bowed curtly and went below.

They were off a little after seven. The rest of the squadron, the paddle wheelers from up the James, fell in astern. Their massed smoke blackened the sky once more. Various sailing-craft and row barges had put out from the shore. Gaily waving Virginia and Confederate flags, they cheered the flotilla as it steamed ponderously northward. Lomax shouted at one yachtsman who cut too close. He could not maneuver to avoid; shoal water lay close on either hand.

The fog was burning away. The Roads opened before them. Lomax put his glass on the fort. *Roanoke* lay close under Old Point. They must have gotten her off during the night. *St. Lawrence* and *Minnesota* still lay aground. The action should be over before noon, the Roads clear, the way to the sea open. Never again to be closed on a proud and warlike nation.

He swung his glass back to examine the black object alongside the stranded frigate. —What in blazes is that?

Other glasses lifted. Jones, who'd come back up as they got under way, took Lomax's back and studied it.

Hunter Davidson said gleefully, —They're abandoning! It's a raft. Their crew's leaving her on it.

Simms said, —I think it's a water tank.

—It's one of their boilers. They're floating it ashore for repairs.

—There are men walking on it. Whatever it is.

Midshipman Littlepage ventured that it might be one of the iron craft the Yankees were supposed to be building. This was dismissed; it was much too small to be anything of the sort. A gaggle of tugs and small boats milled around the grounded frigate. Lomax thought it most likely a raft brought alongside to hoist out the guns. Though that still didn't explain the cylindrical object. He studied it again. Maybe it was some optical trick, lending the illusion of depth in the morning light.

Catesby Jones was telling the pilots he wanted to go in within half a mile. As they passed the point, the pleasure-fleet gradually lagged aft. *Teaser, Jamestown, Patrick Henry* dropped back too. Lomax knew why. The enemy flagship carried almost as heavy a battery as *Cumberland* had.

Presently Jones relieved him of the deck. But he lingered to see at least the opening of the battle. After the cannonading of the day before the Roads seemed eerily quiet. Jones did not make directly for their target. Instead he carried his head east toward the Rip Raps for a long time, making sure he was well clear of the Middle Ground before putting his rudder over for the turn back.

Pressing the bandages over his heart, Lomax surveyed the Roads with a proprietor's pride. As if he himself held in fee simple everything within this vast circuit of still water and lowlying land warming under the spring sun. A stain of smoke still rose from the *Congress* wreck, shoreward of where their next victim waited. The tugs had come back when Jones turned away, like flies returning to bad meat. Now they were scattering again. Perhaps they'd hoped their tormentor was heading out, into the Chesapeake.

And perhaps soon it would. . . .

Yes, their victory opened a range of possibilities. Like gems found in the sand, his magnifying fancy picked them up, examined, and then discarded one after the other as not glittering enough. Richmond was safe now. No invasion fleet could pass up the James. But why keep content with that? If the heaviest shipboard guns could not penetrate their armor, the vaunted columbiads of Monroe could be no more potent. From the Chesapeake Bay, *Virginia* could impose a blockade of her own on the whole federal position on the Peninsula. The fort was dependent on supplies carried down by sea. Cut off, it must inevitably fall. Of course they'd have to beware the weather. Find a sheltered bay in the York or Mobjack if the wind rose. But they had it in their grasp to end the war. Today. This morning.

—Gentlemen, if you'll go to your guns, Jones called. —We shall be within range in not too long.

Tharpe and his Georgia boys looked ready for anything. They welcomed him with jokes and inquiries as to whether the Yankee iron in him meant he had to stay away from magnets. He chaffed back as he checked the tackles. Muzzle shattered, the nine-incher would have less range and power today. But the rifles would probably take the brunt of this engagement.

—Sir, the commodore going to be all right?

—They'll take care of him ashore.

—Mr. Jones is in command?

—He'll lay us alongside, never fear. Though inwardly he didn't think the exec was the fighter the old man was. But all they had to do today was stand off and shell helpless ships into submission. If their crews didn't abandon first. —But we officers are being shifted round. Midshipman Littlepage will take this gun. I shall be up forward, in charge of first division.

The Brooke looked much the same as a large Dahlgren except for the heavy iron ring shrunk around the breech. The sights were Richmond products like the gun itself. Crude but functional. Lomax checked the shell hoist and powder scuttle, then ducked to peer through the port.

—Mr. Simms used the lookout up there, the gun-captain said helpfully. His name was Eli Johnson. Solid and deep-chested, he looked a steady man. Minter knew he'd been a butcher until the war started. Glancing up, he saw where the galley smokepipe had passed from the deck below through the casemate, and out through a piercing in the upper deck. Someone had had the bright idea of dismantling it, since galley fires were doused when they beat to quarters. Stepping on a water barrel and poking his head up through the hole, he found himself with an excellent view.

Minnesota lay ahead. Stranded and immobile, she was surrounded by a swiftly widening ring of small craft. They were three thousand yards away when Jones sent word to open the ball. The projectile went out with a teeth-rattling crack, much faster than the shells from the smoothbores. From this angle he could track it with his eye. It went out nearly flat and struck close to the waterline on the frigate's counter.

Seconds later, as the gun crew toiled to reload, the frigate's side blossomed. Lomax began to duck, then steeled himself as iron plunged from the sky. It caromed with massive sledge blows off the forward plating. The enemy gunners were making excellent practice, but *Virginia's* armor was proof.

He bobbed down to pass that their shot had hit squarely, to aim a bit lower and to the left, intending to ricochet the next shell into the midships area. When he popped his head up again, he saw the low barge thing had pushed away.

—Hold fire, he shouted.

—Sir?

—They're abandoning ship. On a barge, it looks like.

But even as he said it, he saw that wasn't what it was. It was leaving the grounded frigate. But not drifting. Moving with purpose, under power. Turning, as if under command. It was advancing over the flats, so it couldn't draw much water. There seemed to be a fire on its deck. And that cylindrical construction sitting on it . . . seemed to be . . . *rotating*? To his astonishment two black markings came into view.

When he realized they must be gunports, he jumped down from the barrel. —It's the Ericsson. Let's give her some hot work.

The gun-captain aimed, then stepped back for Lomax to sight as well. He nodded, and with a crash and recoil another high-velocity shell was on its way.

He jumped back up on the barrel in time to receive a full and flawlessly aimed broadside from the frigate, which apparently was going to fight it out. The shield shivered and rattled under the pounding. He wondered how many such onslaughts it could stand. Surely there was a limit.

When the smoke cleared, he saw the little raft-battery again, now clear of the lofty length of the man-o'-war. Insignificant compared to it, but bow on now. A scrap of cream at its stem. Trailing a wake. Behind it, licking out, the enemy colors. Smoke boiling off the afterdeck. How did it manage without a stack? He could see now the black ovals held the open muzzles of guns.

But only two. Really, it was a ludicrous contraption. Some Yankee crackpot's gimcrack notion. He picked out the juncture of cylinder and deck where a rifled shell would blow it off into the water. Or they could run it down, trample it as they had *Cumberland*.

He had to admire their pluck, though. Preposterous as it was, it was headed directly for them.

28

Corrosion and Jamming of the Turret Mechanism ♦ A Tense Breakfast ♦
Dawn and the Flag ♦ First View of the Enemy ♦ Short Exchange with
Captain Van Brunt ♦ A Shot Overhead ♦ The Struggle for Existence

CAP'N'S orders, everybody t' eat breakfast, the messboy said. —That hackum's a-comin'. Eat a good breakfast, get some hot coffee.

Theo straightened. Blinked. Then, like an automaton, reached a ragscrap out of his back pocket. Scraped stinking tallow from his fingers, leaving nearly as much. His brain still engaged in clutches and spur wheels, control-rods and reverse gearing.

—Cap'n's orders, the boy said again, and went aft. He said the same sentences to each man he passed.

Newton, face as blackened and eyes blighted as his own, said he could go first. He and Watters would keep at it. Theo threw the rag into a bin and went forward.

The lookouts had reported the enemy armorclad. A grime of smoke on the dawn horizon, accompanied by two other vessels. But it was still miles off and had to pick its way around the shoals between it and *Minnesota*. He felt nauseated, knowing that in an hour or two they'd be in battle. Especially as the turret controls weren't working, which would leave them close to helpless before their adversary's guns.

But no smells of fried eggs met him on the berth deck. The galley was still out of action. He got two pieces of hardtack, but a tin cup of steaming hot brew accompanied them. Suddenly his stomach flipped from queasy to ravenous. He plumped down cross-legged on the still-soaking ceiling planks with the ratings and dipped the bread and gnawed it down. Spoons clinked. Cups clattered. The men behind him were speaking German, others what sounded like Hungarian or Russian.

Since *Congress* had exploded, he'd been working with Newton and the third assistant on the rotating mechanism. They hadn't noticed anything wrong on the cruise down because you couldn't rotate the tower unless it was keyed up, jacked up from its base ring by a brawny seaman wielding a wrench of Samsonian dimensions. This was in his view the only weakness of the Ericsson turret, that it had to be elevated to rotate. Which meant it couldn't fight in a seaway, since jacking it up would admit tons of water through the gap.

The difficulty this morning was that three days of saltwater baths had rusted the splines running down through the spindle that controlled the speed and direction of the turret engines. Rusted them solid, in fact. The engineers had worked all night through, interrupted every hour or so by reports the *Merrimack* was coming back. Each proved false but made any thought of sleep impossible for the whole crew, no matter how exhausted. Many had not slept since leaving Brooklyn.

They'd broken the control rods loose at last, but they still didn't work as they had in New York. Even after chisels, sledges, Kerosene, brute force, and axle grease. The turret engines had gotten soaked too, and the gears ground as they meshed.

The rattle of a drum. Plates hit the planks. Theo stepped over broken crockery. He didn't have a place on the battle bill, so he could go where he wanted. He went forward now through the wardroom and the captain's quarters, the doors standing open, and checked on the anchor party. Everything seemed to be in order; they were seesawing hard on their handles, so after a moment's hesitation he went up the forward ladder.

A slow breeze cooled his sweaty hair in the rose dawn. The cold air made him cough. A light mist wrapped the southern shore in old gauze. Then what lay beneath jumped forward into his sight.

It did look like a barn roof, but one that sent up huge volumes of inky smoke. He read its hue as that of a soft bituminous and through his astonished dread wondered where they got their coal.

Through the gritty, greasy-feeling iron pulsed the first halting revolution of the engine, and his mind recurred from their enemy to the fabric around him. Both the ventilator intakes and the stack extensions had been struck below during the night. The turret canvas and stanchions had followed. Nothing extended above the flat but the little pilothouse forward, the cylindrical, bolted mass of the tower, and, all the way aft, the flag. Its folds shifted uneasily. The wind had not yet decided which way it would blow this day.

His legs wanted to go somewhere. He paced to the edge, looking down at the seam where the thin upper plates met the laminated side armor. The water was so lime-clear he could see individual oysters on the reef below.

Worden came up. He shaded his gaze up the lofty sides of the frigate. Lifted his service cap. After a moment an older officer lifted his own in acknowledgment.

—What do you intend to do, sir? Worden shouted.

—If I cannot lighten off before she gets here, I shall destroy her. My matches are laid.

—I will stand by you to the last, if I can help you, Worden called up.

The other officer, Van Brunt, Theo guessed, shook his head glumly. —No sir, you cannot help me, he called. Then aimed a glass toward the oncoming enemy.

—Ahead one bell. Worden bent to call through the narrow slot in the heavy iron billets of the pilothouse. —Starboard your helm. Come left to south by southwest.

The surgeon and the purser stood near the turret. Theo nodded to them, and the three stood watching as they steamed slowly out from beneath the shadow of the man-o'-war.

The fog was gradually rising, revealing an empty Roads. Not a sail on it save for those clewed and gasketed on the helplessly waiting warships. To his left hand the dissipating land-mist disclosed the low tree line of Hampton. The flag still fluttered from the slanting topmast of the sunken *Cumberland,* and farther along, closer inshore, he could make out jutting timbers, still smoking. To port of *Monitor*'s now slowly advancing prow was the white wedding cake of the Hygeia Hotel, and beyond it the dark mountain of Monroe. A gap gave a glimpse of the Bay. Then the fortifications on the Rip Raps; the dune scrub of Sewell's Point, rebel territory. He couldn't make out their batteries, but they were there.

And between him and them, turning with tremendous ponderous elephantine inescapability, the smoking pyramid that even as he watched was obscured by the bursting-out of a woolly cloud.

He watched a red-glowing speck that grew swiftly closer. Before he could react, the shell howled over, only yards above the turret, and crashed into the ship behind them.

Worden called, in a harder voice than Theo had heard from him yet, —Gentlemen, that is a rifled shell from the *Mewwimack*. You had better go below. And ushering them ahead with a bow, he was the last to leave the deck, carefully lowering the hatch behind him.

The interior was dim indeed. On going to quarters, most of the lamps had been extinguished and iron plates bolted over the deadlights. The engine was pounding away deliberately, bearings still getting warmed up, and Theo went back to check on it. Everything seemed in order at slow speed, and he trotted forward again. He felt tightly strung, and moving about helped. Worden was giving Greene instructions at the foot of the ladder that led up into the little bow pilot shed. Peering up, Theo caught the helmsman's downward glance and the trowser legs of another, he guessed the pilot.

The captain asked him, —Are the turret controls working now, Mister Hubbard?

—Sir, they are, though the linkage is still rather stiff.

Worden nodded, set his boots on the ladder, and began pulling himself upward. —Where will you be? Greene asked Theo brusquely.

—I believe I can best serve by moving about, Lieutenant. Wherever my services seem to be needed.

—I want you in the turret. To make sure the fucking thing works.

Theo touched his cap, then was angry he'd done so. They were of equivalent rank. But Greene was gone, headed aft. The sound of the engines grew. The doors were being opened to let the powered ventilation operate. This was probably reasonable, unless they were rammed. In which case the battery would go down like the iron burial case it was. Sweat broke anew under his woolens, which had been soaked for a long time now, ever since the storm.

He couldn't shake off his view of the approaching monster. Its sloping sides, black and somehow slippery-looking. The somehow blacker apertures that spaced it. Its sheer size, the impression it gave of massive invulnerability, of reptilian malevolence.

The struggle was at hand, beyond which was nothing: no Heaven, no afterlife, no pipedream in the sky. No benevolent God directed events. Every moment of existence had to be won anew. Those who were strong would survive. Those who were weak would die.

He swallowed, trying to steady his legs. And began walking again, not meeting the eyes of those he passed, as their gazes too avoided his.

29

Face-off with a Bantamweight ♦ Rapid Closure to a Negligible Range ♦
Speculation and Rage ♦ A Deadly Spiral ♦ Report to the Commander ♦
Misgivings as to Available Projectiles ♦ Aground ♦ Disabled, My
Propeller Is ♦ A Proposal for Boarding ♦ Helpless Before the Lilliputian

LOMAX kept his fire on the frigate as the raft drew closer. Every
now and again salvos from their stranded enemy landed, tight bar-
rages that hammered on her shield like a giant wanting in. *Minnesota* carried over forty guns, and they were making remorseless practice.
One shell crashed into the lip of the bow port. As it broke up, a fragment
mowed down a man at the train tackle. Six inches higher and it would
have raked down the crowded smoky casemate. The wounded soldier,
eyes shocked vacant, stumbled toward the surgeons. Each of the others
moved up one position, faces locked against whatever they were feeling,
fear, rage, regret, requital.

Meanwhile the range was closing. A mile short he felt the quiver of the
keel kissing soft ground. Passing over the lumpy mudbanks that presaged
the shoal on which her prey and sister had come to grief. Immediately the
engines slowed. Their beat, already irregular, became knockety as she
groped her way ahead.

The thing, still coming on, had opened fire. Minter missed its first
salvo; his head had been ducked below, listening to Simms passing orders

from Jones. The commander thought it was the Ericsson machine. Lomax was to concentrate the forward gun's fire on it. Once they disposed of it, they'd go back to the frigate.

When he popped his head up again, it was only a couple of hundred yards away and still coming, positioning itself in front of *Virginia*'s original quarry. Which was still firing, its rounds flying directly over its diminutive watchdog. As he blinked, one struck it, glancing off into the water.

Now he saw rivets in what seemed to be a movable turret. Streaks of rust ran down black paint. With a flash the starboard gun fired. Then the other, not long behind it. He jerked his watch out of his trowsers, almost falling off the barrel, and marked the position of the hands.

Jones was sheering off, putting his rudder to starboard. Bringing their broadside to bear. As her head came around, the pivot gunners shouted, hauling hard with the train tackles, and let off another round. Lomax watched it sail over the turret. —Too high, he shouted down. —Drop your sights to fifty yards.

As their head came round, the other steamer, if steam was what drove it, altered course as well. It was circling to starboard. As they passed, it let off another salvo, both shots of which missed. Lomax made it seven minutes by his watch. It reloaded even more slowly, then, than his own scratch crews.

He shouted down, —I want a dead hit on the center of that turret. Pierce that, and we'll kill everyone inside. He thrust his head up again, wincing as a ball from *Minnesota* roared overhead, and concentrated on the machine passing down their side, close enough that he could have shied a stone down onto her flat raft-deck.

The gun-captain shouted, —*Fire* and tripped the lanyard. The carriage leaped back.

Lomax goggled in disbelief as a seventy-pound Brooke rifle shell disintegrated like a mud clod hitting a brick wall. At the same moment something akin to an eyelid lifted behind the port. A muzzle emerged. It erupted into flame and smoke, and something battered against their side so fiercely, shouts erupted inside the casemate.

The balls, if they were balls, shot over his head and away, carrying what sounded like pieces of cable with them. He ducked within and glanced along the interior, expecting to see broken wood, toppled guns. They were still whole, but John Eggleston was pointing halfway up the shield.

Now the enemy was in reach of the broadside guns, and they lashed out. Jones was shouting at the helmsman, ramming the rudder hard over. Dragging herself over the lumpy bottom, the great ironclad began to yaw back to port. The stern rifle cracked, then the starboard battery crashed out. There was so much smoke, Lomax couldn't see anything anymore.

When it cleared, more savage blows fell on their side. Their *starboard* side. He realized that while they were turning, the gun-raft had circled them.

Lomax had the men train around so they were ready when she came back into their field of fire. He couldn't see where the shell went. The turret was so small and so low that it was hard to hit. If you did strike it, but not dead center, the projectile would carom like one billiard ball off another. The flat on which it rested was level with the sea; even a square hit on that landed only a glancing blow. The thing was cleverer than it looked. Still all they need do was jam the turret or the rudder. He sent his next couple of shots along the waterline, but they had no more effect than the others. He tried for the little henhouse on the bow but missed it both times as the craft churned past, too fast to follow at this close a range.

At one point a jolt told him they were in contact. Unfortunately the sponge staff had just snapped off, and they were waiting for the powderboy to fetch a new one. He roared, —Grab those rifles, boys, and shoot the first man you see.

The troops snatched muskets off the racks that lined the inner shield. When the smoke parted, they were looking directly into the muzzle of one of the Ericsson's guns. It was huge, Lomax thought, staring into it as into some immortal eye. It had to be twelve inches across.

The riflemen recoiled as it went off. Burning powder, fiery wadding, and solid smoke extended in a pillar of seething flame. But by some miracle the ball impacted just far enough below the port to glance upward past it.

—I niver saw no man to shoot at, a trooper bawled.

Minter brushed burning fragments off his clothes. This can't go on, he thought blankly.

But it did. They kept firing. The murk got heavier instead of lighter. Bells rang, men shouted, rifles cracked.

And every few minutes came the double smiting of those turreted twins. Slamming at their port quarter, their side, their bow. When they hit, splinters flew off the wood lining. A man on the next gun jerked them from porcupined cheeks. Looking along the casemate, Lomax could make out the sides gradually denting in. Blackened with powder, sweating in the terrific heat, the men crouched alongside their guns, staring at each other as they waited for the next blow.

Like a safecracker tapping along the outside of a vault. Knocking here, knocking there.

Searching for the weak point that would let him in.

Much later he ducked inside and went to the narrow ladder that led up to where Jones was peering out the slits in the pilothouse. He turned his head as Minter thrust his up. It was dark inside this iron nut-case, except for bars of light that crossed the commander's face.

The port battery let go with a shattering roar. —I don't believe we are making any damage on her, Jones shouted.

Minter yelled through a cracked dry throat, —Nor is she hurting us, at least not to notice.

—Until she hurls one of those balls through a port. Or decides to probe our waterline. Jones applied his face to a sight-slit. —We must put a shell through her first. The gunports is what I am thinking. Notice she does not seem eager to hug us too close.

Lomax reflected this was not so simple as the Virginian made out. Whoever was controlling the foe-machine had evolved a new trick: revolving the turret so its solid back faced their opponent as they loaded. Then spinning around and letting fly just as the guns faced front. The ports were only visible for seconds before circling out of sight again. He said, —If we had solid bolts, I feel sure I could pierce them with the rifle.

Jones nodded with an expression that said he too wished they had the wrought-iron bolts Brooke had mentioned. —But no one expected to have to fight an ironclad.

—Don't we have round shot?

—Only a few, cast with extra windage, for hot shot. All for the Dahlgrens, not for the rifles. As I said . . . all this is unanticipated. Captain Buchanan expected to face only wooden ships.

While Lomax was thinking furiously *someone* should have thought there just might *be something* to all the rumors about Yankee ironclads, Davidson shoved his way up the ladder too. He warned that the impacts of the heavy balls were pushing in the wooden backing. If several charges struck at the same point, they might batter their way through the shield. Jones waved that away, but Lomax pressed, —We can't just keep going round and round like this.

—Are you continuing to fire on *Minnesota*?

Lomax said he was doing so as opportunity presented. The frigate was still fighting back, too, though he'd seen several of her shells hitting their own ironclad.

Jones said he'd try to ram, but the shallows were presenting problems. They'd just have to keep fighting. He dismissed them with a wave, but his eyes had the look of a man with fever. Lomax thought contemptuously that it was not fever at all, but rather something more akin to fear.

The casemate was opaque with seething smoke. The shortened guns blasted it out each time they fired, and more was coming up from the furnaces. When the Ericsson was upwind, its exhaust too came through the ports and added itself to a murk that made drawing breath like sucking on some sulphurous hellish factory chimney. Lomax told the gun-captain, —We've got to punch harder. If we can blow one shell through her plate, we'll destroy that thing.

—A double charge?

—I was thinking of it.

The single-banded seven-inch Brooke took twelve pounds of powder. Increasing the charge would increase the hitting power. But it might shatter the gun too. In fact the chances of that were good.

But something had to be done. The troops didn't object. They rammed first one bag home, then the other. They cut the fuze for two seconds. They put their shoulders to the gun, ran it forward. He motioned them aft. Then, when they didn't move, cursed them back toward the ladderway. They retreated unwillingly. Alone, he shook the lanyard out, waited till he saw the black can crossing ahead. The gunports were coming around. He waited till they were pointing at him and pulled.

The gun recoiled with savage force and knocked him down. It was like being kicked by a horse. He scrambled up again, feeling his shins. Bruised but not broken. But when he pushed his head through his peephole, all he saw was another dent. Perhaps a bit deeper this time, that was all.

Around eleven the raft-battery began to draw away. At last it turned tail and went off into shallow water.

The men were too drained to cheer. Jones levered the bow slowly around—the behemoth was becoming inexorably more sluggish—and edged back toward *Minnesota*. They'd only traded a few salvos though before the little thing came steaming back. Once more it interposed itself directly between them. Jones's cursing was audible down on the gun deck.

Just at that moment *Virginia* ran aground.

It wasn't a dramatic event. They simply ceased to move. They'd been flirting with the mucky bottom all morning. But losing the ability to maneuver placed them in the devil of a situation. Lomax told his boys to keep firing, either on *Minnesota* or their smaller opponent, whichever was in view, and went aft to see if he could help.

He found Jones berating the pilots, who were giving as good as they got. As Minter came up, he swung to White, the assistant engineer. —I don't *care* if you burst the boilers. We must get off.

—We've tried full aback. You saw the results.

—Then make more steam.

—These are old, patched, rusty boilers.

—Lash down the safety. I don't need to tell you what to do. But we must get off.

White swung away, lips pinched, and vanished below as the commander told the signal officer, —Make signal to *Jamestown.* "We are aground and need assistance."

Sinclair worked the signal book. —Nothing here about being grounded. You'd think there would be . . . How about "disabled, my propeller is."

—Hoist it.

Lomax protested. Bringing the wooden ships in just meant they'd be sunk. The Ericsson would fire a round through their boilers, and they'd explode. Jones waved him off. —Make the signal as directed, Mister Sinclair.

A resounding crash shook the frames around them as another heavy ball slammed into the quarter. The thing seemed tireless. Perhaps there were no men within it at all. Perhaps all worked by steam, governed by telegraph. Even face-to-face with the muzzle in that horrifying instant he hadn't seen a human form within.

A crashing thud from aft. Captain Thom loomed out of the murk. —It's right alongside, he reported. —Between number nine and the aft pivot.

The marine officer looked as relaxed as if he'd just come up from dinner. But his news wasn't good. As *Virginia* had burned coal and fired ammunition, she'd risen in the water. Combined with the low silhouette of their opponent, he could no longer depress his guns enough to hit it. —But I can board. My men are ready. It's worth a try.

Another violent concussion and more cries from aft. A runner sent by Wood brought word the Ericsson was firing repeatedly at the same place. The oak lining was crushing inward. The exterior plate must already be shivered.

Men were banging away with muskets, aiming down at the enemy machine. Lomax didn't think that was going to do much good. Not if a double charge from a seven-inch cannon did nothing worse than dent it. The thing was shotproof, bulletproof, and was running rings around them. It had heavier guns and solid shot. A whiff of canister would blow Thom and his men off the spar deck as soon as they showed themselves. Even if the marines got aboard, then what? "Charge bayonets" was no good against this apparition.

If he *only* had steel-tipped bolts . . . He pounded his fist into the shield. Who had so mismanaged everything? What chance did a country have with such incompetence? They were led by julep drinkers, imbeciles, indolent fools. If only Buchanan were still here!

The crash came again, and more splinters whicked across the casemate. A signal quartermaster stared down at one protruding from his stomach. The heavy timbers were bulging in. It was mauling its way through to them. The deck shook as the engines rose to a frenzied pounding, the screw thrashing at full astern. But she did not move. She did not move.

Coughing, sweating, they stared at their failing defense and waited for the next detonation.

30

Morning Thunder ♦ The Prodigal Servant ♦ A Painful Renunciation of
Heirloom Lilacs ♦ Plans for a Spring Garden ♦ Depopulation of a Town ♦
An Unpleasant Rumor ♦ The Sowing and the Planting ♦
News of Renewed Victory

WHEN Catherine woke to the panes rattling against the muntins, she lay for several minutes listening to what she first thought was morning thunder. Until attention told her it was not. The renewal, no doubt, of the climactic battle of the day before.

Then she remembered that Betsey still hadn't come home when she'd finished her letter to Ker the night before. Aunt Dilla swore she didn't know where the child had gone.

She threw back the covers, shivering in the fireless cold, and went into the upstairs hallway barefoot. She looked in on Robert. He snuffled as he breathed. She hoped he hadn't picked up a chill out on the water. So much excitement. But such good news.

She rose on her bare toes and clasped her hands thinking of it. The shadow arrived a moment after. She'd never forget her departed darling. But there were others who needed her—Rob, Ker, her father.

Her country. Though there was little enough she could do for it.

When she peered into the narrow room at the servant girl's cot, she was sprawled out, stick arms sagging off the counterpane, snoring.

Catherine shook her awake, furious. —Where on earth have you been? Dilla and I were worried sick.

—No'm I was just . . . getting those onion sets you wanted. Put em back in the kitchen, keep em warm.

—Miserable girl. Onion sets! How long does it take to walk to Mrs. Tankard's and back? She almost slapped her, but restrained herself. She went back to the kitchen shack, a lean-to against the back of the house.

It was rich with the aroma of frying bacon, of beaten biscuits. Aunt Dilla was already up. The old woman hardly seemed to sleep. —When did Betsey get back in last night? Catherine asked point-blank.

—Lord, Miz Claiborne. When did she get in? Ain't no clock back here.

—It was nine when you brought my tea. How long after that?

—Don't rightly know, Miz Catherine. But that girl is sure going to get herself in a peck of trouble. Staying out all night like that.

—I want you to speak to her. Let me know if she's mixed up with some man.

The old woman heaved herself up at once. Catherine heard joints snapping as she came off the stool. She put her hand on the stooped shoulder, feeling worn bones under worn cotton. —I didn't mean right this minute, Dilla. Sometime today will be fine.

—Gon' be a bloody day, Miz Claiborne.

She froze. —What did you say?

—Seen that red mist around the sun when it broke dawn. Hear them guns out there now. O yes, gone to be a bloody day. But all gone turn out for de best. Massa Ker's friends in the navy gone chase them Yankees away, keep us all safe.

She said quietly that she hoped it would be so.

She sent Betsey out to milk. Ate a piece of bacon and a biscuit alone in the dining room. Then when the girl came back in, had her help her into her dark gray day dress. She was still in half mourning. She kept glancing out the back window, wondering if Gager would show today. Mrs. Mears had said she'd send him over . . . The lane beyond was filled with people, horses, carriages. More so even than the day before. She debated joining them but finally decided not to. Without her personal supervision nothing much got done around the place. And Robert needed to rest. All this excitement couldn't be good for him. When she saw Gager saunter in, she threw her pelisse around her shoulders and went out to greet him.

A distant bumping crackled and rumbled from the horizon. The light outside was the sallow tint of spoiled cream. A great bank of saffronish smoke blew slowly through the town. It stank of saltpeter, of the acrid pungency of battle. The houses looked washed out, paler violet as they grew more distant, like a range of hills as they receded from the eye. A shiver ran up her back, to think she was breathing the very battle that would decide the fate of her country.

Gager looked like something dried on a stick. He didn't ever say much. His master had freed him many years ago, before the law changed so you couldn't. He kept a little house back of Ghent and knew about as much about gardening as Mr. Jefferson at his great house in Monticello ever had. She'd kissed Katty Mears when she'd agreed to lend him to her. He bowed silently on his walking staff, and she began sketching out what she wanted to do.

—Not your mamma's peonies, he objected mildly.

—Yes, Gager. They must all come out. We will miss them, but they just take up too much space.

—That's a beautiful lavender bush.

—Yes, it is. She bent stiffly in her stays and buried her face in it. Crumbled a leaf between gloved fingertips. The smell brought back her mother's sachets, the scents of her childhood.

The German irises, the peonies, the lavender, lilac, and lily of the valley were all pass-me-downs from her mother's garden. —They must come out, she said again, straightening. —Spade it all up. Leave the herbs, the rosemary, the chives, and the mint patch. Dig in the straw and manure. That part should be easy to turn. Then spade up the grass where I've marked out with the string. I'll send Betsey out with the hoe.

The dead, heavy rumbling that had underlain their words, that seemed to underline everything they said with significance this buttercup morning, grew louder. They stopped to listen. When it trailed away again into an ominous mutter, the old man said, clearing his throat and spitting carefully clear of her skirts, —Yes'm, sure a beautiful lavender just to dig up and throw away and burn.

She stood irresolute, not because she didn't understand he was asking for it but because she honestly couldn't decide what to do. Two futures warred in her mind. In one, they'd be grateful next winter for the vegetables the additional rod's length of tillage would produce. She had to feed the servants as well, four mouths, not two. In the other, the war would be over, Ker would be home again, and she'd berate herself for having torn out all these lovely heirloom plantings. In the end she said offhandedly, as if it didn't matter one way or the other, —You may have it, Gager. We can replant when this unpleasantness is done. If you would like any of the other flowers, you may take them as well. Now, do you think you can finish with all that today? Because I want to put in my peas this afternoon.

He said with a measuring look over the yard, bounded by the cowshed, the kitchen-house, and the picket fence on either side, —That'll be a day's work. I probably can git it done though. If'n it don't rain. Don't look like it; but they says cannons makes it rain.

In the house she measured out a dram of Ker's whiskey from the decanter. The cook took it out to the garden. Catherine looked down from the second-floor window as she got her sleepy boy dressed. Listened to the intimate music of Negro voices. The old man received the glass with a dignified inclination of his head, a toss back, a slow savoring. Then handed it back, and the chunk, chunk of the spade floated on the morning.

When everything was set going, Gager spading, Betsey scowling but hoeing, Dilla and Robert taking out the last of the winter cabbages, she set off into town for the rest of the things she'd need. Also, she did not care to be around when that remorseless spade reached the peonies. She and the cook had sketched out what would go where. Spring peas, lettuce, potatoes, onions, spinach, carrots, and collards. It was too early yet for corn; they could still get a frost. Too early for squash too, and Mrs. Mapp, two houses down, raised lovely cymlins and was generous with them. She might not put them in at all. Fortunately she had almost all the seeds she needed, traded with friends and neighbors or sent from Charlottesville or

Richmond. When the soil warmed, she'd do beans, corn, perhaps melons, though they were not good for a body in the heat of summer. Beets, if she could find muslin to protect the leaves from the birds. There was nothing nicer than beet leaves for greens. And Mrs. Tankard had volunteered the start of an asparagus row.

But when she got downtown, the stores and banks were shuttered. The streets were deserted. Since Davis had declared martial law in the town, all white men had been pressed into a militia, and most supplies confiscated by the military. She found Sodger's open though and purchased the last of his lettuce and beet seeds. Looked longingly at a pair of English gardening gloves, but did not buy. She passed the hotel and wished she could buy a newspaper and read it on the piazza. But no unaccompanied lady could sit alone in a public place. Even marketing alone, walking about with parasol and bonnet and her basket on her arm, she felt daring. In Richmond no lady would ever do such things. Here in the hinterland things were a little more free and easy.

The continuous thumping, like kettle drums far off, began to fill her with dread. After seeing how quickly the ironclad had disposed of two towering ships, she could not imagine what had prolonged this engagement into afternoon. Yet the cannonade continued. To the north a huge wall of smoke barricaded the sky.

On her way back she stopped at the Tankards' for the asparagus. Joie was in and said breathlessly, —Have you heard about the other ironclad?

—Another?

—A Northern one, just arrived. The two are fighting it out.

They discussed it over mint tea. Catherine gave her opinion: that the great beast she had seen shouldering its way down the river could not be vanquished by anything the Yankees brought down. Especially by something as diminutive as described by the fragmentary reports, hardly enough to be called gossip, filtering out from telegraph offices and word of mouth.

When she got back, the garden was half turned over. The cow had come out of her shed and stood munching on the shattered remains of blossoms. She shooed her away, afraid it would affect her milk, and put cabbage leaves in front of her instead. Gager was working like some rusty but dependable machine. A familiar smell of sweat and whiskey and tobacco came off him like a vapor, the smell of labor under the sun. Betsey was not exerting herself. She stopped every few chops to lean on her hoe and stare toward where the thunder had continued all day, now louder, now fallen away nearly to nothing.

Catherine had a cutlet for lunch, made sure the servants were fed, then had Betsey carry a chair outside. She put Robert at the side of the house with his toys, then settled herself with her darning in her lap. She unfolded her drawing and went over it, with the blacks hovering over her shoulder as she pointed out where each vegetable would go. Then decided they weren't going to get this done with only three hands. Gager had not even started on breaking the new ground. She set the darning aside and went in again for an apron and an old ripped pair of dress gloves.

She and Betsey began putting the seeds in. They knelt together along the rows. The smells of turned earth, of old manure returning to soil, came up from the warming ground. The girl giggled, her good nature returning. Old Gager made a joke about getting the cow to help. She stared placidly at them, a cabbage leaf wagging as her jaw worked. Robert shrieked, tossing his ball in the air. It fell outside the fence, and a passing gentleman tossed it back in.

—Heard the news? he called.

—What news is that?

—The *Virginia's* licking the Hades out of that Yankee toy.

She wiped a sleeve across her forehead. Hope and fear struggled in her heart. She took a handful of small black seeds like pepper grains from the paper poke. Raked the warm earth over them and reached for the watering can. The other backs bent around her. She was surrounded by their breath, their murmurs, the scrape and clunk of tools. The entranced murmurous self-conversation of a child at play, intent on a hole he'd scraped. Putting his toys in it, covering them up with dirt. And for a time, those small sounds aside, all was silence.

Then, bursting out all across the horizon, thrilling her heart within her breast with a fear unlike any she had ever felt, the distant guns broke out again in renewed and inhuman clamor.

31

In the *Monitor* Turret ♦ Adumbrations of a Mechanical Future ♦
Sick Monkeys in a Sour Apple Tree ♦ Doubt and Faith ♦ Boxing the Compass
♦ Suggestion as to the Powder Charge and a Brusque Rebuff ♦ Two Stunned
Men ♦ The Telescope of Centuries ♦ Coming on to Ram

T HEY couldn't have lanterns because of the powder. The turret was
lit only by shafts of diced light from the pierced iron overhead.
Since it was early, the sun low, they didn't penetrate far. Leaving
Hubbard, Greene, Stodder, and eighteen brawny seamen, all in full uniform and caps, standing in near darkness as they waited for whatever
came next.

The space within the circumambient iron was less than twenty feet
across and perfectly compacted with stanchions, braces, gun-slides, fire
buckets, handwheels, side tackle, gun carriages, ladders, and the swelling
black dolphin shapes of the Dahlgrens. Curved racks on the white-
painted interior held shot and powder-charges in their red wool bags. The
men were not so much surrounded by machinery as inserted among it like
twisting vines. Flesh and metal intertwined. As if, Theo thought, he was
vouchsafed a glimpse of some horrible future where machines had en-
gulfed their makers, the two intergrown into some monstrous hybrid.
The young seaman closest to him was biting his lips, and sweat was trickling down his neck. Others were crossing themselves. The air *was* very
hot. With the hatches closed, the pressurized, heated atmosphere below

had only one exit, upward through the tower. He found himself breathing fast and shallow, and tried to slow his respiration.

From outside distant bumps occasionally penetrated. It might be the Confederate continuing her fire as she closed; might be *Minnesota* firing back as she found the range. He could not tell. Could not see daylight except for the pocked sky. Only the turret officer, crouching at a slit, could see outside at all. Theo realized he wouldn't know how the battle was going unless one of the enemy's shot came through the laminated iron. In which case no one in this crowded, explosive-crammed space would survive.

He put a hand on that curving circumambience. The smooth painted coldness felt like cast ice. Eight layers of inch-thick wrought iron, overlapped and bolted. Of course he was not feeling the shield itself but the inner guard Ericsson had added to prevent sheared-off nuts from wounding the occupants. The Swede had been pondering his design for years. But for all those years guns had been improving too, their power steadily increasing. The reports agreed this enemy was armed with the new rifled guns. Higher velocity, greater penetrating power than the smoothbores *Monitor* carried.

He hoped the inventor had estimated the resisting power of metal better than he'd calculated the reach of the raging sea.

A sepulchral spirit-messenger voice reverberated in the speaking-tube that connected them with the pilothouse. Unfortunately once the turret began to turn, they'd lose even this tenuous communication with Worden. The commander would maneuver the ship and the turret officer fight the battery with almost no communication between them.

Greene exchanged his ear for his mouth. —Aye aye, sir. We'll do so at once.

—Captain's heading us for it, the exec said to them all. Simultaneously Theo heard the clank and thud aft speeding up. —Test your turret engines, Mister Hubbard. Make sure we have steam and that everything works.

Theo took a deep breath, hating Greene and all his pompous tribe, and stepped carefully around the slide. A momentary nightmare-dream unfolded in his sleep-cheated mind as he did so. He saw his ankle wedged, the gigantic guns recoiling over him. The gun crew stepped back to let him pass. He ran his gaze along the linkage.

Two four-inch-diameter iron stanchions set between the guns supported the roof of the turret. A bolted-in bracket halfway down stiffened them. The control rods, of once-polished, now rusty wrought iron, ran down between them. The control handle faced in the same direction as the guns, more or less in line with the trunnions. He put his hand on the vertical brass handle. It felt cold and slick, sucking the life from his flesh.

—Brace yourselves, he said and wrenched it to the right.

It took all his strength to force it over. He heard the rods grind and a moment later the *pocketa pocketa* gnashing of gear teeth as the turret engine engaged below.

The tower juddered into rotation. Clockwise first. He let it go for twenty degrees, watching the white marks they'd painted on the main deck to orient by. Greene, watching him over his shoulder, nodded. Theo braced himself again and threw the handle to stop, letting the eccentrics engage on the donkey engines, then to full left. The interior quivered. Something rattled below their feet. Then, with a slightly higher-pitched grinding, the whole massive construction reversed itself and drove back toward the paint mark.

He released the control and it jerked to a stop, sending one of the gunners stumbling. In Brooklyn he'd been able to govern the travel to inches, point the guns exactly where he wanted them by nudging the handle this way or that. But despite all their hammering and greasing the night before, the splines were still binding. That fine regulation was gone. It was either stop, full left, or full right. All he could hope was that it wouldn't seize up entirely. If it did, they'd be curled up like sick monkeys in a sour apple tree; simply have to fight with the guns aimed wherever the turret happened to play out.

—Trice up to starboard, Greene said. He didn't speak loudly. It wasn't necessary. No man stood more than three paces from any other. Stocking, the boatswain's mate, and Lochrane, the other gun-captain, redeployed their men. For some minutes they strained at the hoisting tackle. The heavy iron stopper, hung like a pendulum, gradually rose. Staring directly eastward, the piercing shone like the open door of a furnace, an ellipse of pure sunlight so igniting bright in the obscurity he had to raise his sleeve to safeguard his blinking eyes.

—Run out!

With a scrape and the rattle of blocks, one immense black tube rolled slowly forward on its greased iron rails. Both guns were loaded, of course. Had been since the night before when the burning *Congress* pushed over the horizon. But the port stoppers swung inboard, and there was only room to swing one in at a time. Theo reflected grimly that not only did Ericsson's invulnerable steam battery mount only two guns; only one could be fired at a time.

—Compressors! Men bent, twirled the handwheels on the compressor brakes.

—Prime!

Lochrane checked the vent and pricked the charge. Inserted the primer and turned the patent Hidden & Sawyer hammer down on it. The crew rearranged themselves clumsily, bumping into one another and into braces and stanchions. Not only were they all green, some fresh off the farm, but everything in the turret was novel, untested, unprecedented in experience even for the petty officers. The gun carriages were also newfangled Ericsson concoctions of forged iron, quite unlike the Marsilly carriages they were used to. It was too much to ask, to send such men into battle. Too much to ask of all of them.

Yet here they were.

Greene crouched at the sight-slit as Theo, still standing at the control post and present here in the turret with every particle of his being, noted with yet another part of his mind that the main engine was slowing. Its beat dropped down the register, then hissed to silence.

Free of the propeller's impulse, the battery floated onward. Save for the hum and thump of the auxiliary machinery, the fizz of steam from the turret engine couplings, all was hushed. Another thud came down the gratings, louder than before. The men stood waiting. The rasp and suck of their breathing filled the circular space like one of the whispering domes he'd read about, where a whisper could be heard at any point as if the interlocutor's lips were at one's ear.

Keeler's goatlike beard twitched below, visible through the deck gratings which, when the turret was pointing ahead, lined up with the floor hatches in the main deck. His glasses flashed. Theo gazed down at him curiously.

—Captain says commence firing, the paymaster shouted up.

—Aim, Greene shouted. The gun-captains threw back the hammers. They spun the elevating screws, sighting along the barrels. Then looked up, frowning. Nothing was visible through the ports but gray-green water.

—Set elevating screws at zero degrees. Starboard, starboard, Hubbard, goddamn it! Greene shouted, staring out the sight-slit. Theo hauled hard on the handle. *Pocketa pocketa*. The turret shuddered, tracked right.

—More. More. Stop! Greene stepped back, gestured for the lockstring of the starboard gun. He half-turned and bent to aim along it, throwing one of the side tacklemen against the inside of the shield with his hip. Hesitated, then jerked the lanyard.

Theo had barely time to flinch out of the way as the recoiling mass plunged back. Smoke filled the interior but cleared within seconds, blown upward by the artificial breeze from below. His ears were ringing, but with the muzzle outside the gunport, the blast had not been as bad as he'd feared.

Greene was scrambling over the slide, to the port side, as the men hauled desperately at that shutter. He grabbed the other lockstring. The hammer snapped down, and a jet of pure white fire blazed from the touch-hole. An instant later the gun bellowed, kicking backward so fast it would smash anyone in its way to a bloody jelly. Theo's heart sank. It was too crowded. Someone was going to get mangled. He coughed in the swirling pungent fumes, tried to listen through singing ears to what Greene was shouting. But it wasn't to him, it was to the crews. It was a hit, they'd hit the thing, and to reload at once, why were they standing around.

He had not been in the turret during the only previous firing, and observed with astonishment the contortions necessary to sponge and load. There was so little room the staffs of the sponge-rod and rammer had to be fitted through a hole bored in the port pendulum. He'd wondered what that hole had been for on the drawings. Imagined what it must look like outside, with the staff ends poking out, frantically jerking, then hastily withdrawn.

At that moment something jarred into them, raising a clang that set his head buzzing and made several of the men cry out. Dust and dried salt and loose paint sprang from every surface, and above their heads the clamped-in rail iron jangled with a heavy dull gonging. The sounds of other impacts came from outside.

—Don't stand against the shield, Greene shouted. —Test the rotation, Hubbard. Left, then right.

He threw his weight against the control handle. More balky? Less? About the same. The engines perked and shuddered them this way and that. He brought them back to what he guessed was the bearing they'd fired on. —Turret controls respond.

—Sounded like a broadside, boys. They touched us, but we're still in the fight.

They fired another salvo, then a third. Greene set off each gun himself, though Theo had understood this to be the gun-captain's task. It took every ounce of strength he owned to keep the handle over and the turret rotating, and every ounce of judgment to stop it where the turret officer wanted it. Greene yelled at him when he overshot and had to reverse. But it was difficult to manipulate the thing at all, much less get the turret to stop exactly when the exec, bent to the sight-slit, suddenly clenched his fist.

Crouching, as Greene aimed the next round, Hubbard managed to look along the gun and out the drilled-out semicircle above the outthrust muzzle. It was a tiny gap, not meant to look through. Still he peered, and was rewarded with a partial and momentary glimpse of their antagonist, bow on, huge, and no more than a quarter mile away.

Greene tripped the lock. Theo flinched back. Eight tons of iron blasted past like a gigantic piston. The turret officer pushed by and fired the port gun. They both pressed against the curved interior as the men went forward again.

—This isn't working, Greene shouted. Theo shook his head, pointed at his ears. The lieutenant's voice came from far away and was overlaid by a note like the top pitch of a violin. He leaned closer. —Takes too long to work those stoppers.

The heat and smoke and fear were making his throat so dry he could barely speak. —If we leave them open, a shell can come in among us.

—I know that. But I don't see any port covers at all on this other fellow.

—Can you aim for them?

—What in the hell do you think I've been doing?

Theo didn't have an answer to this. Greene yelled, —What if we rotate away to load, then back to fire? Then we won't have to keep tricing up these goddamned stoppers.

—I can try. But remember, the armor's not as thick on the back side.

Indeed it was not. Once Ericsson had decided to face both guns in the same direction, he'd added another inch of plate to the front of the turret. But the stopper arrangement wasn't working. It took the whole gun crew to hoist the huge diamond-shaped castings, brought them close to exhaustion, and during that whole period the guns sat idle.

They fired. Instantly, a blow more violent than any before rocked the tower in reply. A boyish sailor shrilled and spun, holding his ears. An older man shook him by the shoulders, shoved him staggering back to his position. Theo squeezed his own throat shut, trying to hold back the terror. It centered on his privates, as if whatever was hammering at them out there, if it broke through, was aimed with malevolent precision directly at his lower belly. He couldn't decide which frightened him more: having someone outside sledging at the shell that protected them, or being locked inside. Outside this circle of iron was only death. But inside could be death as well, from powder ignition, gun explosion, smothering, capsizing, sinking. It was as much a trap as it was a shield. Men coughed, spat, spewed into the fire buckets. Dust and salt powder seethed in the powder-smoke, and the hot air blowing up milled it into an acrid brume that grew thicker with each salvo.

Greene stabbed his finger furiously at the control. Theo slammed it over. The turret powered around till he judged, squinting at the paint marks, that they pointed away from the enemy. Although it was getting difficult to tell. As the burnt powder and grit accumulated, the marks grew less distinct. But when he released the handle, it stayed over, and he had to haul again, with all his strength grunting, till it suddenly popped back to the stop position. Around him the crews worked like madmen, loading faster now that they didn't have to contend with the stoppers. He dragged sweat off his face with his sleeve, hoping a shell didn't come through the iron behind him and wipe them all out with their backs to the enemy.

—Rotate back.

The juddering groan as it lurched into motion, the irregular clatter of the turret engines as they powered it around. He was almost to the point he wanted when the whole tower lurched under a savage, cracking blow. Impacting, as far as he could tell, directly above and between the gun-ports. He stared at the nut-shield, expecting to see a fissure starting.

—They're not penetrating, one of the gun-captains yelled. —They can't get to us.

—Is the control responding? Greene asked him.

He slammed it over again and rotated the last few degrees to where he guessed their enemy bore. —Yeah. Still working.

The men looked more confident. Three hits so far, and they were still alive. Theo was impressed. That last shot had sounded bang-on, dead center, and very heavy indeed. He was by no means sanguine, though. That they'd resisted three shots meant little. Simply because they saw no effect within did not mean the enemy was not battering his way in, layer by layer. Peeling off laminations like an onion. The guns recoiled, squealing to a halt as the compressors braked them. If a seaman set the compressor wheel wrong, the massive tubes would recoil off their rails, crushing equipment and men. The burnt-urine stench of powder filled the enclosed space. He wished he could see what the exterior plating looked like. But to step outside in this storm would mean death.

Greene's face was pressed to the sight-slit. Alone of them he could see. But he was gesturing impatiently: first right, right, then left, left. Hubbard put his weight to the control. The turret shimmied to a double clang that rocked them. Yet the engines still clattered, and the tower still drove around, straining against his locked hands like a panicked horse against the bit. Greene gestured impatiently, then leapt back from the slit, dropped to the floor grating, and shouted down into the hull as the moving aperture went by: —Run forward, quickly. Ask the captain how does the *Merrimack* bear. At once.

—Can you see it? Theo yelled. —Point where you think it is.

—We're in a turn. I lost it. Are you loaded? Yes, what? Where? Port quarter. Port quarter, Hubbard, d'ye hear?

The turret shook, quivering, skating around. He could no longer tell which was forward, aft. Had no idea where the port quarter was. So he just kept going around until the turret officer yelled. They fired, and he slammed the control over in the opposite direction as the gun crews leapt to reload. He heard the main engine laboring at full speed, felt the deck tilt in a turn. No, he *could* tell which way was aft. The engine sound came from there. Worden seemed to be boxing the compass. Looking for advantage, perhaps. Seeking any chink in their opponent's defense.

Just as that adversary was no doubt doing to them.

A distorted, mustached face, flaming eyes. —Goddamn it, can't you stop where I tell you? Forget it. Forget stopping! Next time, just keep going. We're only about a hundred yards away. I'll try shooting on the fly.

—Don't hit our pilothouse.

—Thanks for the warning, Hubbard. I wouldn't have thought of that.

Theo ignored the sarcasm. —What's the effect on the *Merrimack*?

—We keep hitting her. But I don't see much result. Greene bent, resting his palms on his knees. He spat black drool. His face was raccoonish, burnt black around the eyes. —*Minnesota's* firing too. Right over our heads. I hope they don't hit us with one of their ten-inchers.

—Any damage to her armor?

Greene didn't answer.

—You've got to use a heavier charge, Theo said. If we cannot drive this thing back to its den—

—You just work that control when I tell you, Mister Engineer.

The gun-captains straightened, gave the "loaded" signal. This time as they tracked around, the exec crouched behind the starboard gun, sighting down it. As a black side came into view, streaming smoke, horribly close, he stepped to his left, between the gun rails, and made a graceful quarter turn, stiffening, presenting his right shoulder, like a duelist facing fire.

He pulled the lockstring. The thunder was deafening even to deafened men. Theo could not believe it. Though the center line of Greene's body had been screened by the vertical support stanchions, the rest was not. The trunnions and cap squares of the huge Dahlgren as it flew back on its rails could not have missed him by more than an inch.

Theo dragged an arm across his face, blotting sweat and powder-smoke. His eyes stung. The thick hot air was choking. He'd pissed his trowsers. Yet it was not as hot as the engine room at full speed. Not quite as choking as when toxic gas had filled his lungs. He was exerting strength he hadn't known he had. And so far each hammering blow of ball or shell had left them stunned and shaken but still whole.

Time blurred, drew out, took on many aspects of eternity. Theo checked his watch at a lull. Nearly ten. The men fired, reloaded, fired again. They'd been fighting for an hour and a half.

Two simultaneous hits slammed into the tower. They knocked down Lieutenant Stodder and a sailor who'd leaned against the nut-shield. Theo aligned deck grids with hatches, and they lowered the stunned pair to reaching hands below. A pail of water and a copper cup came up in exchange. They sealed up again and kept firing, the tail man on the port gun carrying the bucket about between salvos. Most of the men didn't drink, just rinsed their mouths and spat the liquid out. Others poured it over their heads and grimaced, features streaming.

Merrimack was aground, Greene reported. Worden twisted the battery in close. They whaled away at her. But the other slewed clear, floated free again, smoke bleeding from her riddled stack. She sidestepped westward, trying to slip past them and attack the frigate again.

The turret whirled now almost without stopping, dizzying as a merry-go-round. They didn't stop for instructions anymore or to shout questions down. They loaded, sighted, fired, without reference to anything outside. The rest of the battery no longer existed. The wind and the sea no longer mattered. All they needed was steam and powder.

Hubbard thought, This is the new era we have brought to men. A terrible novelty in war. This bubble of iron charged with volcanic asphyxiation, stentorian reverberation. Its denizens frantic blackfaced ghouls who hauled with bleeding hands, swabbed smoking barrels, shouldered up great iron shot like Sisyphus his unending burden; who grimaced, palms to ears, as the guns bucked and roared again and again and again.

It seemed to Theo Hubbard then that he saw himself and those around him from the wrong end of a telescope of centuries. With a humorless smile stretching his lips he looked back on history as a long progression of bloody beasts and ludicrous clowns, with intervals of ludicrous beasts and bloody clowns. Perhaps now that sad march of eons would end and the true ascent begin. With machines like that in which they fought, was battle itself possible any longer?

War made too terrible for flesh to bear. Which meant an end to war.

For such an end, anything could be endured.

Theo Hubbard was telling himself he could stand it when Greene turned from the sight-slit. He smiled grimly, black-smeared, blood on his forehead, shaking with excitement. —Brace yourselves, boys, he shouted. —They are coming on to ram.

32

Lashing Down the Safeties ♦ Captain Thom Prepares to Board ♦ Reattack on *Minnesota* ♦ Double Charges Aimed at the Pilothouse ♦ Retreat of the Tormentor ♦ Ebbing of the Tide ♦ Council of War and a Divided Verdict ♦ Withdrawal for the Day

T
HE straining and shaking went on for minutes. Horrendous sounds echoed up from *Virginia's* engine room, blasts of heat, a hair-raising clanging. White stuttered out that they'd lashed down the safeties. Ramsay was throwing everything into the furnaces: cotton waste, lubricating oil, splits of fat pine. The smoke billowed through the scuttles, extruding itself in ribbons between the deck planks. The stack wasn't drawing, that was why the furnaces were smoking, White said. But the boilers wouldn't hold. They were bad to start with, and now they were rusted through from lying on the bottom of the river.

—Then you'd better get up in the chain locker, Minter told him.

—The chain locker?

—As far as you can get from them. That's the place for you if you fear dying so much.

White's eyes snapped from terror to hatred. Lomax turned away. He had nothing but contempt for such cowards.

Jones came down the central aisle. His balding scalp was grimy with smut. All their faces were blackened, sweat-channeled masks. Thom, Wood, Sinclair, Simms, Davidson, Marmaduke, Littlepage. Only the eyes staring through gave evidence of life. Around them the hands still stood to the guns, though the strain was evident in their attitudes too. They flinched as another hit clouted the port shield. More splinters flew off, and the men shrank from an ominous inward bulge.

—We're off, someone shouted.

The shuddering lessened. Looking through a port Lomax saw muddy water scooting past. —I don't think so. That's just the screw wash.

The engines clamored. Jones called shrilly to shift the rudder, swing it from right to left and back again. Lomax didn't see what good this was going to do. Not with the screw reversed.

But perhaps its frenzied minutes-continued thrashing had dug away the mud beneath their counter. A reel of the deck testified they were free once more. A weak tiger-cheer rolled forward, then surged back, fists punching the air as it passed from gun crew to gun crew.

He hurried forward, eager to get his sights back on the thing. On the way he passed Jones, and overheard him asking Eggleston why he wasn't firing.

—Well, sir, the lieutenant drawled, —our powder is precious; and after two hours of firing at her, I find I can do her about as much damage as snapping my fingers every two minutes.

Jones seemed to struggle to find something to say, then turned away. —I will ram, he announced to no one in particular. —Since our gunnery has no effect. Mister White, tell the engineer I am going to maneuver, then ram. When I do so, he must reverse the engines at once, even if I fail to order him to do so.

Lomax sent several shells after the Ericsson as they backed away, then clumsily turned in a sweeping circle. This took a long time. The ship felt different beneath him. Even more sluggish and waterlogged. Meanwhile the enemy ironclad held its position. Shots were still coming in from *Minnesota,* but the range had opened to three miles, and few hit.

After jockeying back and forth for some minutes, Jones gave the order for full steam. She responded like a dying nag but gradually built speed. Listening to the racket below, Lomax wondered how much longer the gears and linkages could stand up. It was a miracle her abused machinery had worked this long. But if Jones could bury her javelin in the enemy's vitals . . . He kept loading and firing as they approached.

But just as she was on it, the little craft's prow swiveled away. *Virginia* jostled to a glancing blow as the smaller vessel spun down her side, slamming another one-two punch that threw the after gun crews to the deck. They pushed up slowly, those closest to the shield bleeding from noses and ears.

From his makeshift observation scuttle he could hear Captain Thom mustering his marines on the spar deck aft of the funnel. All of Company C and half the soldiers from the batteries. He was passing out sledgehammers and iron spikes to jam the turret with. Sergeant Charlesworth was yelling to fire into any sight-holes they came across, then throw their jackets over them to blind the men inside. Lomax eyed the slowly rotating tower a hundred yards away. Waiting for the blast of canister. It didn't come, but each time they edged closer the enemy scooted back. There was no way of lying alongside the more nimble craft unless she permitted it. And she was wary now, keeping her larger but wearying adversary at arm's length. After leaving them for some time exposed, Jones ordered the boarding party back inside.

They battled on into the afternoon, exchanging blow after blow but not coming to close grips again. The men moved as if asleep, loading with bloody hands. The carpenter reported water coming in through the bow. A round carried their ensign away, but Jones sent a party up to rig another. They stood in toward *Minnesota* again and shelled her until the Ericsson barged between them once more.

Wood broached a plan. All the rifled guns to double their charges and aim for the rectangular box on the foredeck. He was convinced it was steered from there. Jones told them to try it and for some time they did, but each time Lomax missed. He mistook his footing and fell from the barrel, knocking down two of his boys. Lay there for some minutes, panting, before getting back enough strength to rise again.

When he did, the Georgians were exclaiming excitedly that the "thang" was retreating again. Taking a sight, he saw indeed it was so. It was steaming away over the flats, toward a burning tug that had been so unwary as to linger in range of *Virginia*'s shells. The flagship was on fire too. As he watched, the Yankee device, smoking more than it originally had, passed both the burning tug and the stranded frigate. It was definitely retreating, and yawed from side to side as if its steering had been damaged.

The cheers this time were weaker. Waves of heat came off the guns, which had been firing nearly without interruption for over three and a half hours. He sent another round after their fleeing foe before the word came to cease fire.

Catesby Jones came down the ladder as the officers gathered around it. It seemed to be an informal council of war. His first words were, —Well, Mister Wood, you seem to have driven off our gadfly. Beautifully aimed. My congratulations to the stern rifle.

The temporary commander glanced around. —However, we are not without damage ourselves. We have serious injury to the outer armor. None of the shots penetrated, but from what I can see looking over the side, another hit at the same point might. Fortunately he never fired at our waterline. The crew is drained. And due to the state of the tide we cannot get close enough to *Minnesota* to finish her off, nor follow the Ericsson onto the flats. Mister Ramsay, our engines?

The chief engineer looked grave. —Unfortunately we can no longer reverse. The reversing link stripped as we were backing off the shoal. Some fool made it out of brass, not iron.

Jones looked grave. —We have power ahead only?

—Nor can I guarantee that much longer.

—Lindsey? What of our flooding?

—A trickle forward, but I stopped it with oakum, sir.

Ramsay said his pumps could keep up with reasonable leakage, but his men were giving out along with the engines. —A hundred and thirty degrees down there. They can't take much more.

Dr. Steele, asked his opinion, said that though they'd had no injured today, the men were suffering the deleterious effects of bad air; they had inhaled far too much smoke; also they had been subject to the pestilential miasmas off a marshy beach when at anchor the night before.

Jones said with immense weariness, —There you have it, gentlemen. The pilots will not place us nearer our enemy. We can't take the risk of grounding again. Especially without reversing gear. And our crew is spent. I propose we return to Sewell's Point, rearm, coal, and make repairs. Then come out again tomorrow.

Lomax felt wild. On the point of complete victory, Jones was proposing to retreat. He thrust up a hand. —Sir.

—Mister Minter. You object?

He said hotly, —I do, sir, in the strongest terms. The Ericsson has turned tail. The flagship is still in reach. If we must destroy it from long range, so be it. If the men must stand at the guns a few more hours, they are willing. We *must* not retire until victory is complete.

—Your enthusiasm does you credit, sir. But the responsibility is mine. We can fight as well tomorrow as today. No, better, once we have our solid bolts aboard. Jones looked around the circle. —Anyone else?

Ramsay spoke up. The chief engineer agreed with Minter, they should not leave before forcing *Minnesota* to strike. Without that the moral effect would be most unfortunate. Wood joined in, though he thought *Minnesota* already damaged enough to put her out of service; they should head for the fort and destroy the transports.

Jones said, words dragging, that he could not agree more with their spirit, yet he did not see at all how these undoubtedly desirable objects were to be accomplished. With each passing minute the area in which they could maneuver was shrinking. If they grounded again, and the enemy steam battery returned, they'd be nothing better than a helpless sacrifice.

—But they're in full retreat, Lomax pleaded. —We've won. Why not take our advantage? Stay here even if we have to sit on the bottom through the low tide. Shell out the men-o'-war and the transports this evening when the flood returns. In front of the French observers.

—That is true. For the moment we remain victor on the field. Jones passed his hand across his forehead. —But we're the only force capable of stopping a naval thrust up the James. We've sunk one man-o'-war and burned another. Put the Ericsson out of action. Damaged the squadron flagship. We're low on coal and almost out of ammunition. It's time to retire.

Minter could not believe his ears. This was the rankest foolishness, the most blatant blind incompetence he'd ever witnessed. After Porter's blunders and laxity, Forrest's dilatory oversight, the laziness in the yard, the slowness on the railroads, and every other betrayal, dereliction, outrage, and neglect, they'd put to sea at last and, in a battle that might have ended in their destruction, still carried the day.

Or *all but* won it. For leaving this task half complete would be worse than never having begun. If they left the transports unburnt, the Chesapeake open to federal traffic, and the blockade still intact, they'd wrought no real change in the military situation at all. The British and French could see this as clearly as it would shortly be to everyone. The Yankees would build more ironclads, and what glory they'd won—what *he* had won—would taste of gall and wormwood in the realization this was not conquest but *defeat*. He burst out, —Sir, we *must* remain. Whatever the risk. Burn the *Minnesota*. Sink this Ericsson. Buchanan would never leave now. He'd fight till not one man stood. I—

Jones interrupted coldly, —You have given me the benefit of your *opinion*, Mister Minter. I am grateful for it; and now that is enough. Mr. Ramsay! Reduce your boiler pressure to a safe indication. Helmsman! Set a course for the mouth of the Elizabeth.

The council, if that was what it had been, broke up. Lomax was seething, and he didn't think he was the only one. The others looked taken aback, thoughtful, doubtful. But no one objected further. He was left standing alone, clenching his fists.

33

Attempts at Ramming ♦ Replenishment of Shot ♦ A Word Through the
Gunport ♦ Return to the Confrontation ♦ A Lucky Hit ♦ A Blinded Captain ♦
In Charge in the Turret ♦ The Antagonist Rebuffed ♦ Retreat and Pursuit ♦
The Thanks of the Rescued ♦ Remarks by Mr. Gustavus Fox

THE moments while Theo waited for the impact seemed interminable. Greene ordered them to run out but did not fire. The
exec stood bent, face pressed to the sight-slit. The smoke
streamed steadily up the turret well. It reminded Hubbard that everything
depended on the blowers. If they jammed or the belts broke again, the
crew would have to get topside before they asphyxiated. Which under
present circumstances meant either death or capture. After seeing its effect on Worden, he had no desire to languish in a secesh prison camp,
deep in some buggy quagmire of darkest Davisdom.

—Here she comes, Greene said.

Theo heard the engines go to full power, their clinking and whumping
succeeding ever faster till they merged into a continuous rumble. Newton
must have the main steam valve wide open. The deck trembled. *Monitor*
was no speedster. But surely she could outpace the lumbering, smoke-
leaking colossus with which they were disputing the mastery of Hampton
Roads.

And possibly the outcome of the war.

Should they lose this battle, McClellan's back would be unprotected, derailing the entire campaign against the enemy capital. Should the rebel mammoth run them under, pierce and sink them as it had *Cumberland,* she'd capture both *Minnesota* and *Roanoke,* and no doubt armor them into more ironclads.

And even these multiplications might not be the worst issues of defeat. The reports of the French and British observers would make clear the blockade had been shattered. European recognition of the Confederacy, aid and arms, could place restoration of the Union beyond the pale of the possible.

The deck leaned in a hard turn. Greene stood motionless at the slit. All at once he motioned frantically to the right. Theo grunted at the handle. Perhaps it was the growing heat or the grinding away of the rust in continued operation, but the control rods were moving more easily now. The tower rattled and slewed till he gazed out at a slanted tar-dark barrier, shockingly close.

—Here she comes, Greene shouted again. —Take a brace, she's almost on us. The men grabbed stanchions, gun carriages, the nearly empty shot-racks behind them, praying or blaspheming in their variegated faiths and tongues.

A barely perceptible jolt swayed them from side to side. Theo held on, thinking: That couldn't have been it. He'd been jostled more violently in Broadway omnibuses.

Greene yelled, —Stand clear. He jerked first the starboard lanyard, then moments later the port. The guns recoiled with such terrific noise Theo realized he was hearing their blast thrown back from the mass outside. —Square on the forward casemate, the exec shouted, and the men cheered, hoarse and cracked.

Hubbard rotated away as they reloaded. Greene stepped to the ladder, rose cautiously to present his head above the tower bulwark. —Did it penetrate? Theo asked his back side.

—I believe so . . . perhaps . . . no. Greene dropped back as muskets cracked and balls pinged off iron. —Damage, but no penetration.

—Let us fire one of the wrought-iron shot, Theo urged. —Why else do we have them aboard?

—They weigh more than the cast iron.

—And will have more impact.

—I don't see that. If their weight's doubled, their speed's halved.

—The relationship is not so simple, as I understand it, Theo said. They stared at each other. After a moment he added, —Then double the charge. If you punch through, you can rake her from stem to stern.

—Those are not my orders.

—You can win the battle at a stroke.

Greene's blackened lids blinked. Theo pressed. —Surely that is what Worden, Marston, Goldsborough would do in your place.

—I am satisfied now she cannot run us down.

—Sir?

—Nor can she injure us by her fire. Greene was thinking aloud, glancing back toward the sight-slit. The gun-captain held up his hand in the "ready" signal. —The only thing that can destroy us is an exploding gun. That's why the captain made sure I repeated his order.

—No Dahlgren's ever burst yet.

—Nor will it aboard this vessel. We're the Union's only hope. Greene eyed the waiting gun-captains, voice firm again. —Fifteen pounds, boys, just the standard fifteen-pound charge. And the cast-iron shot.

—Only four left, sir. Running short on powder too.

—Align the hatches, Greene told Theo. He shouted down to Keeler, lingering patiently in his role as runner, —Tell the captain we're out of ammunition. We must haul off and replenish. Master Webber! Powder division, stand by on the berth deck. Get those men on their feet!

Its designer had provided no convenient way to resupply the turret during fighting. Worden sent word he would withdraw into shoal water but to carry out the evolution as quickly as possible. Heads milled below, and after a few minutes the first charges began coming up. Serving the cartridges presented no difficulty. Hoisting the shot, which weighed a hundred and eighty pounds, was a different matter.

Theo was sagging against the nut-shield, rubbing his arms, when he saw a face peering in the gunport. —Ahoy, the tower. He flinched violently before recognizing the captain. Hesitated, then climbed the ladder and looked down.

Worden stood on the foredeck. He looked perfectly fresh, face and gloves clean. —Mister Greene up there?

—He's below, sir, hurrying the powder division along.

—Is everything all right in there?

—Two gunners stunned by a shot, sir. Otherwise we're doing fine. Ten more minutes and we'll be ready to toe the mark once more.

Worden paced around the tower while Theo shaded his eyes against a noonish sun. They lay off a curving beach. It looked strange, speckled, dappled. He could not make out why. Behind them lay the grounded frigate, smoke rearing above her. A mile away their unwieldy but indestructible antagonist lay motionless, hove to. It seemed to sulk, as if resenting they'd withdrawn where it could not follow. Perhaps they were recovering over there too. Passing around juleps. Whatever juleps were.

A sudden wave of dizziness made him clutch the ladder, afraid of passing out and falling. In a few minutes they'd be back at it. His hands shook. His thighs quivered. How long could they keep belaboring each other, like medieval knights clanging on each other with mace and morningstar? They could not go on so. Sooner or later one or the other must suffer a breakdown or a chance hit. Take a spark in a powder-charge, ignite a conflagration.

Despite himself he discovered a grudging respect for whoever manned and conned their remorseless antagonist. Rebels or no, they were fighters through and through. Whoever prevailed in this contest would earn his victory.

As for himself, he'd be happy just to see tonight's dusk.

—I don't see any cracked plates, Worden called up.

Theo tried to steady his voice. —That's good to hear.

—Just this one big dent here. How are the nuts doing inside?

—I heard a couple spall off, on heavy hits. The inner shield contained them.

A distant thud, the whoosh of a smoothbore shell going over. It burst a hundred yards past, and water leapt up under it. As he watched, they began moving again. Back toward the stranded *Minnesota*. Worden took one more cool saunter around the tower as a second round whooshed and burst, this time closer. He strolled to the pilothouse hatch, climbed in, and pulled the iron plate into place over his head.

Smoke jetted from the other ironclad's side. When *Minnesota* fired back, Theo could see her projectiles breaking up on the casemate. If just one happened through a port, this battle might be over. It had to end, sooner or later. Didn't it?

Greene came up shouting into the turret. Theo drew one more breath of clean wind and threw a regretful look at the sparkling calmness of the Roads.

He made out, astonished, that the speckle on the beach was human beings. For miles toward the fort it was thronged with a spectator crowd. Rowboats had put out from shore, and colorful parasols told him not all those in them were tobacco-chewing Virginians or blue-clad troops.

—Hubbard! Get your ass down here!

Their life-or-death struggle had become a circus entertainment. Suddenly enraged, he dropped down the ladder, pulled the pierced-iron cover to, and descended the last few feet to the control.

Returned to deep water and the fray, they lay close to their huge antagonist for some time, giving and receiving the heaviest strokes each could deal. The turret filled with swirling smoke. Invigorated by the news their armor showed no damage, and a cupful of straight whiskey each, the men loaded with renewed energy. Greene continued pulling lanyards as Theo carouseled past his opponent's bearing. It wasn't an accurate way to fire, but no question it was faster than employing the stoppers. His arms ached, but he kept grimly at his post.

Keeler shouted up that a boarding party was mustering atop *Merrimack*'s casemate. Greene ordered the port gun loaded with canister, and kept banging away with solid shot from the starboard tube. Theo caught sight of her again over the gun, only yards away.

A staggering multiple smiting knelled the turret like a cathedral bell. Balls leapt from their racks. He lay stunned on the greasy damp planks, watching scraps of light like burning snowflakes dart about the dim interior. A boot stamped his hand, crunching his fingers. Down was no place to stay. He got to one knee, leaning against the shield though he knew he should not, then back to his feet. Staggered to the control and wrenched it into a spin. The enemy was concentrating fire, and he wondered how much more abuse the spindle clutch could take. The turret wasn't actually attached to the hull. It simply rested on a roughened plate atop the spindle. A heavy enough blow could send it flying off into the water. He didn't think a broadside carried that kind of momentum, but it wasn't pleasant to think about.

—Looks like we're going to take a turn at this ramming business ourselves, Greene shouted. His voice was paved with gravel. Theo's own felt like hot brass rasped raw with a bastard file. He mopped soot and sweat with a sodden sleeve. —Left, left, *left!* the turret officer screamed.

Theo twisted the controls viciously with the exhausted strength of despair. The port gun boomed out. They were so close he heard the rattling lash of grapeshot on iron. Ram and counter-ram, batter, feint, attack. Sooner or later a coupling had to shear, a seam split under the impact of shot, a tiller line part. They couldn't keep on forever.

But apparently they didn't or couldn't ram, and the dose of canister had discouraged the other commander's intent of boarding. The mutual belaboring continued at extreme close range. Again he felt the bump and sway of colliding iron, and saw the riveted revetment crowding the gunport. The smoke murk took on an unfamiliar undertaste, tar with a hint of damp earth. They were sucking their opponent's exhaust in through the blowers. For a moment he looked across intervening space into another man's eyes. A face black as a coal miner's above coppery beard bristle. Out of it blue eyes blazed. He was framed by a square port above a smashed stub of cannon muzzle. Then flame and blizzarding smoke shrouded him, and the port was replaced by slanted iron, blackened and dented and gouged like some ancient, harpoon-scarred prodigy of the deep.

The guns recoiled. Coughing, hacking seamen with gory faces and torn hands reloaded with spheres of iron. Jets of white fire blasted the dimness like solidified lightning. The box of primers was exhausted. They had to send below for more. Greene, seemingly tireless, aimed and fired. Then after some innumerable time straightened, puzzled, pumping a clenched fist. —Cease fire. Cease fire! We're sheering off. Opening the range. What's going on?

Someone was shouting below. Theo bent to hear past the din. Cupped his ear. —What's that?

—Said, the captain's hurt. He wants Mister Greene.

Hubbard waited till Greene fired, then steered back to center line. When the accesses aligned, he snagged his sleeve. —Keeler says the captain's hurt. Wants you in the pilothouse.

—Hurt? Greene straightened from the sight-slit. Rubbed his mouth, staring, leaving a black smear like a child caught with licorice. Then without a word he stepped to the hatch. Started forward on the berth deck, then turned back. Yelled up, —Keep firing. And for God's sake keep hitting. It's all that's stopping them from boarding when they're close alongside.

—Loaded, sir, Stocking said. Lochrane seconded him. The crews stepped back. Theo rotated, but couldn't pick up his target through the port. He hesitated, but everyone was looking at him. He was the only officer in the turret. He squirmed his way to the sight-slit.

The narrow piercing penetrated eight inches of iron to give him a miser's paring of day. The sun spangled off the waves. He saw land far off but no foeman. He pointed to the left, and after a moment Stocking stepped to the controls. His touch was tentative, but the turret engines engaged and soon, rocking, the tower began moving again.

Merrimack came into view. A quarter mile away and nearly directly astern. Theo made out his own flag. It was powder-stained but still intact. Astonishing, considering how thick the storm of shot and shell had raged the last three hours. No banner was visible on their enemy, which was smoking heavily and almost motionless. *Monitor* was steaming directly away from her. Theo ordered the gun-captains to elevate five degrees, hoping that was enough, and fired. He couldn't see where the shot fell. He fired once more, then stopped, unwilling to waste ammunition. Where was Greene? Was the captain dead?

Minutes passed. The range continued to open. He slewed left and to his horror saw they were passing *Minnesota*. Leaving the field. Running away.

—Reload and stand by, he told the gun-captains. He cautioned them not to touch the control—if the turret began slewing when he was going below, it would cut him in half—and dropped down the ladder.

The berth deck was dim, and the powder division lay sprawled about as if dead. They stared at him wordlessly as wraiths. The engine knock was very loud here. The blowers moaned like banshees. He looked for Keeler but didn't see him.

He spun and ran forward.

He met Greene coming out of the captain's cabin. Behind him he saw Dr. Logue leaning over a recumbent form. —Is he dead?

—Blinded. A shell hit the sight-hole while he was looking through it.

—My God.

Greene seemed to see him then, and anger took his features. —Didn't I leave you in the turret?

—We're out of range and getting farther away every moment. Who's at the wheel?

Greene froze. He cursed, then ran forward. Tossed over his shoulder, —Get back to the fucking turret, Hubbard!

He found the gun crew lying about, taking a blow. They scrambled up as he appeared. The battery shuddered into a hard turn a-port. A peep through the slit told him they were far upriver of both *Minnesota* and the enemy machine, almost to the Hampton shore. Even given the battery's meager draft, she could not have been far from running aground. He ran the turret around to point forward again. Peering out at the pilothouse, he saw the hatch had been blown off and lay on the deck. The top of Greene's cap was bobbing about inside. The helmsman's flat hat, and the top spoke of the wheel were also visible.

Perhaps a mile separated them from the enemy. But as he watched the hulk seemed to foreshorten. It was logy and conveyed in some indefinable way that it was moving with even more difficulty than before. Perhaps they'd damaged it. Or the thing had injured itself during its attempts to ram, or when it had run aground. It seemed less fearsome now than at first sight. Awkward. Lumbering. But still, he reminded himself, a most dangerous opponent, driven by men who'd proven themselves capable of giving as hard blows as they received. He remembered the braiders pontificating around the wardroom table on what poor seamen the South bred, how impossible the cottonocracy could build a navy. Well, they'd done so, and might still emerge this day victorious.

But he couldn't figure out what they were doing now. Spewing great clouds of churning fug, the wallowing structure was inching across his field of vision. Steaming away from *Minnesota,* though now and again a shot snapped back at it.

Not until a quarter hour passed, and both craft held their courses, did he let himself understand. The other was regathering its escorts. Steaming slowly, and with many a Parthian shot, back whence it had come. Greene pursued it for a few minutes. They threw two or three more salvos and were the targets of several in return. But then Greene slowed, drifted to a stop. The range opened. Shrouded by an inky, fuliginous cloud, the enemy dwindled.

The men straightened. They looked at him and at each other. Theo felt giddy, then as if he was about to black out. The control was at neutral, but the walls of the turret seemed still to be spinning. The faces around him were spinning and flickering like the nodding, running figures of a zoetrope.

He squatted, suddenly overcome by a relief so great he only with difficulty kept himself from bawling like a child.

In the wardroom that evening they drank silently. Exhausted, of course. But also let down in some indefinable way. The doctor had taken Worden—their only casualty, it appeared—ashore. Greene, left in command, had fallen into a brown study. They hadn't sunk the monster. It had withdrawn, true, but according to the pilot most likely due only to the falling tide. It had taken all they could throw. Theo cursed himself. Why had he not insisted Greene double the powder-charge? Or done so himself when he was left in charge?

Orders, of course. But could they not at least have *tried*?

A stir outside, and a stocky, bearded man in a frock coat pushed his way in. He held his top hat in his hands. As one the wardroom rose, startled, apprehensive.

—Mr. Fox, Greene said, bowing. —Welcome aboard, sir. I was not informed you were in the offing.

—I asked your deck watch not to announce me. The assistant secretary was flushed, beaming. He smiled at the laden table, the stewards bustling forward with port. Accepted a glass. —I watched the entire engagement from the battlements. And I must say . . . I must say . . . well, gentlemen, simply that you don't look as though you were just through one of the greatest naval conflicts on record.

Greene looked surprised. Then bowed in return. —No sir, we haven't done much fighting. Merely drilling the men at the guns a little.

Fox rattled on, terrifically excited. The noise level rose. Another bottle was brought out. Then another. Men began grinning. Laughing. Theo felt himself smiling too. They'd won a victory. A tremendous victory. The greatest yet of the entire rebellion.

Had they not?

34

Preparations to Repel Attack ♦ A Night in the Lines ♦ Marching to
Hampton ♦ Witnesses from Shore ♦ Death in the Daylight

CAL woke to find a cartridge pouch jammed under him, himself curled full length on cold earth under a damp blanket. His right hand gripped a musket, and his bare feet were icy even though he'd rustled them over with dry leaves when he bedded down. It must have been the guard's report that roused him; he could hear it traveling away, down the line, till the response was so faint he maybe was only imagining it.

His clothes were still wet. With the salt in it the wool would stay damp till he got a chance to rinse it out in fresh water. Shivers gripped his body. He was ravenous. He stared at a dark tree-shape against the stars, gripping his musket and listening to the night. A dog howled far away. Sleeping men grunted and snored to his left and right, away down the line.

He lay and told over in his mind's eye the day before. Their helplessness before the Leviathan. Chubb Johnson's head flying off. Rollins wounded and left behind, dead and fathoms down by now. Goran lifeless on the beach, then mysteriously resurrected. The only Cannoneers left with him were Henry, Ewins, Jock, and Williams. And of course the powder-boy, Puncie. The Slabtown orphan was sleeping beside him, curled into his arm. Cal lay cradling him, listening to peepers somewheres off toward the water, the lilting music of a nightjar from the direction of the river.

They were in line with some Massachusetts boys, with their left flank on the river and their right somewhere inland. He didn't know where or how far, only that after *Cumberland*'s survivors had sat dazed on the exposed beach for some hours, Mr. Morris and Mr. Selfridge, who'd gotten a Zouave uniform from somewhere, had shagged them off the beach onto a road.

In that straggle were hungry men, cold men, burned men, and even some of the wounded who'd refused treatment. A lot were shoeless, like him, those who'd had to swim ashore. But they didn't bitch, or at least not much, and they tried to keep up. The commissary sergeant who'd tossed a sheet-iron cracker to each sailor as he filed by the wagon said a rebel column was headed for them. When they'd gotten here, long after dark, unseen voices issued them each a musket, a cap box, and a cartridge pouch with fifty cartridges. Then led them up to the line. The troops said Magruder's boys were on their way, a division or maybe two. The rebs would probably attack at dawn. They knew about the iron apparition. Knew the offensive was off and they'd probably get thrown out of Virginia altogether. And most didn't sound as if they'd be sorry to go, to head home and leave the skirmishing, if there was going to be any more after this, to somebody else.

He was drifting off when an early cockcrow recalled him again. He lay for a long time after that, unable to close his eyes now dawn was near. When he could see the trees against the sky, he got up quietly, leaving the boy to sleep, and went forward and sat with his rifle across his knees waiting for the rebel attack.

Toward nine o'clock, still unfed, ungrog'd, and uncoffee'd, the survivors were pulled out of the line and marched back over what might have been the same road they came up on. The older men and the wounded were stumbling along ready to fall out. To his surprise Cal felt strong and alert. He'd been disappointed when the officer rode along the line on the horse yelling no Johnnies were coming, it was a false alarm and the "gallant tars" could play off.

They heard the first thuds there, on the road. Cal lifted his head, angled his ears back and forth. —Ten-inch, one of the men said.

—Maybe heavier, Cal said. Counting the seconds between reloads, if it was the same guns he was hearing.

—It's come out again. Goin to muss up *St. Lawrence* and *Roanoke* and *Minnesota*.

—It'll never stand up to *Minnesota*'s broadside, one of the old salts said.

—She ain't got no heavier than we had, Cal said.

—Yeah, but she got more of them.

The argument died, and they slogged through the morning light, kicking up dust with bare feet and ruined shoes. Cal missed Goran and the cutups he'd have pulled. The glum silence tasted of defeat. He couldn't help thinking that if O'Leary was right, the war was lost, and he'd never see his family again. The melancholy became crushing as he remembered that even if he did, he couldn't buy them out. Everything he'd saved, stolen, killed for was gone. Though that wasn't why he'd killed the buckra lawyer. Just that he'd taken his own money back out of the strongbox, then seen the rest, and no sense to leave it there to be burned up.

It was so dispiriting, he wrenched his mind back to where he was. He was amazed at the depth of the dust. The roads were inches deep in it, a yellow pollen flour that rose between the ranks of straggling sailors. They were strung out for hundreds of yards, some limped so.

They shuffled into Hampton town an hour later. Lieutenant Morris had borrowed a horse and gone ahead, and fixed for them to draw army rations, hard bread and a joint of meat for every ten mouths. Still there was no grog, and the older sailors were in a bad way. They and the wounded collapsed when the walking stopped. A corporal told them where they could find horseshit and straw behind a cavalry stable, to make fires to cook their food.

But by then the cannonade had built to a crescendo of din, the sky complected with smoke above the trees. It came blowing through them with a pungent call he could not resist. Finally he followed some troops down to the beach to see what was going on.

He and Puncie sat there through the late morning, on past noon, gnawing on and off at the granitelike hardtack and watching the battle.

They overheard an officer telling a lady the little craft out there was called the *Monitor*. A Swede from New York had invented it. Cal explained to Puncie that the little battery was trying to protect *Minnesota,* which, being quite close in to the Hampton shore, and lying motionless despite the efforts of a tug, must be aground. The rebel batteries across the water were firing too, adding to the seething overcast. The combatants circled in wide arcs, cracking away at each other. For long periods those on shore could see neither, the stuff came so thick off them, black coal-smoke and white powder-smoke mingling to a dusky lead in a great ascending storm cloud like the time he'd watched a hurricane approach at sea, black and curving and solid and feeling like death in the hushing daylight. The wind was in their faces, and the bitter smoke blew over them, so they seemed to be fighting in the battle themselves and not just powerless spectators.

The firing stopped. The smoke rose into the heavens, and only wisping remnants of it blew over the shore. He was surprised, as it lifted, to see the little thing still out there between the high sides and tall masts of the stranded frigate, and the black demon that had come out to destroy all that had escaped yesterday. They lay some distance apart, moving this way and that like head-butters groping dazed and blinded for an opening. Turning his eyes he saw the strand was lined with watchers as far as the fort, that its ramparts too were lined with onlookers. He wondered if the rebels were watching too, from the other side.

After some minutes the thunder began again. Once more the expanse curtained with smoke. Though their gazes could not pierce it, the sounds of battle came clearly: the heavy bumping of the big guns, the whiplash clang of shells striking, the whistle of long shots. As hours passed he moved to a tree and sat against it, Puncie between his legs and the boy's curved back against his chest. Cal rubbed the child's woolly warm head absently as now and then they glimpsed shapes in the murk. The bizarre adversaries seemed to touch, then moved apart and resumed circling. Once the smaller, which looked like a cheese on a shingle, moved a few hundred yards off. The monster seemed to want to follow it, but feared to; it backed off and resumed firing at the grounded frigate, which thundered back broadside after broadside till the very sky quaked.

A rent in the curtain showed the rebel's ensign gone. A cheer came from the spectators, some of whom had climbed trees to see better. But it was still firing, carmine tongues of flame darting out from her sooty side. Cal kneaded the boy's thin arms, hating the thing. If only he could have aimed straighter, struck harder the day before. The enemy flag rose again, and the huzzas died away. The double *crump* of the smaller craft's guns, deeper than the ram's, came again and again. Then it ceased. A murmur swept the blue-clad ranks, the tattered hosts of contrabands who'd come to the fight late and squatted on the wet, lumpy brown sand, staring with expressions that might look dumb or unfeeling to a white but that Cal knew spelled fear.

He knew what they were afraid of. The same as he. Peace to an escaped slave didn't sing sweet as to a white man. Peace meant the army'd turn them all back to their masters. Back to—how'd the general put it?—"the Union, as it was."

They couldn't depend on the white man. And he didn't believe in the buckra God, who was just Massa blowed up like a hog's bladder and Heaven his plantation.

The little thing steamed off to the west, away from the untouched monster. Cal clenched his fists, willing it to turn back, to keep fighting. But it didn't. Just kept steaming away.

—What's wrong with it, Uncle Cal? the boy piped up, frightened. He understood too.

—Don't know, boy. He dug his fingers into the thin shoulder.

A renewed fusillade between frigate and ram. A shell arched toward the watchers. It burst with an echoing crack and a shower of spray not far from shore. The Negroes swayed, groaned, but not one ran.

The ram lingered, as if unable to approach her prey closely enough to kill, yet reluctant to leave. Cal figured it must be her draft keeping her so far off; he could see by the fresh-shining sand down where the contrabands sat that the tide was ebbing. And, yes, now it was withdrawing. Slowly turning in a great gradual curvature. It took fully half an hour before her bow pointed back toward the south. Her bleeding stack fouled the sky with black pus.

When he looked back, the Yankee machine was advancing again. It fired at its retreating adversary but made no move to pursue. Instead it came back to its original position off the frigate and hovered there, smoke puffing up from its deck as it regarded its departing adversary. The shadow of which shrank leisurely away toward Norfolk, and gradually blended into the blue headlands.

The last of the battle murk filtered past. The afternoon sun shot golden rays through it. It put him in mind of the searching beams through the depths of the sea, and drowned sailors swaying on the deepy sand. Around them the soldiers began to rise, stretch, talk in low voices. The blacks sat still on the strand, looking out. They didn't move, as if they couldn't believe what they'd witnessed was really over; as if they were waiting for something more to be shown forth.

—Who won? Puncie wanted to know.

Cal shook his head wearily. Neither, far as he could see. Neither one of the strange new machine ships. Neither had lost in any way he could recognize as losing, such as going down or burning or striking her flag. If they'd been fighting over *Minnesota,* why, her flag still flew, though she looked stove up more than somewhat.

But he didn't think this battle had been over the one ship. And he didn't think it was over.

The monster, he was sure, would be back again tomorrow.

35

A Decision to Return ♦ Expression of Doubt Rebuffed ♦ A Joyous
Reception ♦ Pride and Defiance ♦ Invitation to a Celebration ♦
The Bitterness of Triumph Cast Away ♦ Interview at the Atlantic Hotel ♦
Tobacco, Lavender, Rosemary, and Rue ♦ Rencontre in Darkness

THEY were steering for the Elizabeth, at a snail's pace due to the balky engines, when the stern lookout reported the Ericsson was returning. Then that it was firing again. A parting shot cracked out from the stern pivot. Then the range was too great, and the guns fell silent at last.

Lomax clicked open his watch. Not long after noon. The engagement had lasted almost four hours. He was soaked, quivering, coated with powder grit. His throat was raw. When the spirit bucket came round, he bolted whiskey and water. Then exercised his privilege as an officer and took a second jolt.

The great ironclad wallowed on. The troops sprawled, coughing and spitting on the deck despite the imprecations of the seamen among them. As they came abreast of the protecting batteries on the point, the boatswain's pipe signaled to stand down at last.

As if that release unclasped some tensioning spring, his knees suddenly stopped supporting him. Like the others, he dropped on the filthy, sand-gritty planks. His arms and legs jerked as if pricked with an electric wire. After some minutes he forced himself up again. Then got his gun crew back to their feet as well. Their faces, skin, and clothing were pitchy with burnt charcoal.

He was watching them slowly sweeping down and putting away the gear when he noticed out the port that the shore was still inching past.

—Back to Norfolk, the helmsman shouted down when he asked where in the devil he was heading.

—On whose orders?

Littlepage shouted back, —Lieutenant Jones's.

He found Catesby Jones topside. The exec was looking back at their erstwhile opponents. The sun seemed excessively luminous and the March air very cold after the dimness and swelter of the casemate. From their station off Pig Point, where they'd watched the battle, the tugs that had escorted Leviathan from her lair were steaming to rejoin. From over by Craney Island, from Lafayette River, the small craft were swarming again now the guns were stilled. From ashore came a lilting thump as a band launched into "The Bonnie Blue Flag." Lomax lifted his cap, though he was taut with indignation. —Sir, I understand from Mister Littlepage you have directed a return to Gosport.

—Correct, Mister Minter.

—Sir, we have some cracked plates, a slight leak, some walking wounded. Beyond that we're fit to engage again at first light.

—And I say we are not and must withdraw. Nor do I care to have my orders questioned. Is that clear? Jones turned a cool look on him.

—I cannot permit you to do that.

Jones drew himself up. —*You* cannot permit, sir?

—*Honor* does not permit, sir. You *must* engage again, to vindicate our withdrawal from the field. Lomax threw a glance back. —We must moor here and renew the fight tomorrow. We can't turn tail and skedaddle—

Jones said icily, —That is *enough,* sir. I begin to see what they say about you is not undeserved.

—What do you mean by that?

—Go below, Lieutenant, or I will put you in irons for insubordination. From what I hear, it will not be the first time one of your commanders has found that necessary to curb your tongue.

Blazing, Lomax aimed a slap at Jones's face. His cocked arm was intercepted by Ramsay and Davidson, who dragged him back. Davidson hissed into his ear, —For Christ's sake, get control of yourself.

—He insulted me.

—You insulted him first. And he's in command. Once we get our plates fixed and rearm, we'll make short work of that little tub.

Panting, he shook off their grips. Jones waited, chin lifted, daring him to continue. For a moment he almost did. He was growing very tired of Virginians. First Claiborne, then this arrogant fool . . . insufferable, supercilious, self-important . . . *cowards*. He turned his back and walked to the starboard side. Stood there, fingers grappled behind him, erect and unseeing with rage as a barge full of cheering civilians rowed along with them, huzzaing and waving their hats in uncontrollable glee.

The pungies and barges thronged them all the way, joined every mile by more until there were dozens, their occupants cheering themselves husky. The troops on deck returned the cheers with a hi-hi-huzza. As they came abreast of Fort Norfolk, the colors dipped and a salute thundered out to the returning victors. From every pier and water side, applause and singing rang out. Commodore Forrest called up congratulations from his barge, to which Jones replied with a smile and a bow. *Jamestown* and *Patrick Henry* came to anchor as they passed the hospital. As the great ship slowly eased to rest alongside the pier, Lomax heard bands, saw the tossing, excited crowds that thronged the waterfront. Norris was waiting too, the secret service officer's face as transfigured as the others'. Porter was there as well, the naval constructor deadpan as ever though his workers were carrying him around on their shoulders. Lomax couldn't hear what they were singing; the din was too raucous.

As soon as they landed, the crowds rushed aboard and most of the crew bolted ashore, in an unexpected and instantaneous reversal of roles. Wine was soon passing from hand to hand. He was bombarded with invitations. He pushed his way through the mob packing the gun deck, gnashing his teeth. What was this tawdry stagecraft? He was still brutally angry.

Still the celebratory madness mounted. The souvenir seekers began pulling splinters off the walls and plucking up spent primers from the deck. Soon they were removing the bayonets from stands of small arms. One woman, boot braced, began prying the sight-bar off one of the Brookes. The marines began pushing down the aisle, forcing those they caught to replace their mementos. Marmaduke passed the word that ship's complement was free for the evening once they'd submitted a damage report. Lomax wrote one out and took it on the pier, where Jones was deep in conversation with Forrest and Norris.

Presenting it, he asked once more if they'd throw down the gage of battle again tomorrow. Forrest looked aghast; Jones said distantly he thought not. The chief carpenter had just reported that the iron ram-casting was missing, most likely still embedded in the sunken *Cumberland.* They could not think of renewing the engagement without it, and repairing the cracked plating, overhauling the engines, repairing the leaks, and replacing the smoke-pipe. The damaged guns must be replaced, and both anchors had been shot away. Forrest put in that they could not risk her again in her present condition. In fact they'd best warp her into the drydock at once. He would put the yard workers on their honor to whip her back into shape in the shortest possible time.

Before he could protest, Jones dismissed him. He and the commodore walked off, heads close. Disgusted, enraged, sickened, Lomax decided they could all pan-fry in Hades. He spun on his heel and headed for the gate.

He intended to lock himself in his room and get thoroughly liquefied. Instead he was kidnapped off the footbridge by General Huger's junior officers, boys he'd dealt with on the powder matter, and dragged into their boat. High-living, spirited young bloods, they were already in a convivial state due to pocket flasks of a satin-smooth bourbon. In a short time he was elevated too, bawling out "God Save the South" as they lustily rowed across a river blazing with illumination, bonfires, and gun salutes from the shore batteries in the gathering evening. —Y'all done us proud, an Alabamian named Frazar leaned to shout boozily into his face. —Y'all is grit to the bone. Damn, the Navy! We never spected that. Done us all proud.

—It's not the victory everyone seems to think.

—Take a drink, boy. What's that you say?

—They still hold the Roads. The transports are untouched. We're still in the grip of a pincer, from Roanoke and Fort Monroe.

—Don't matter about that. Frazar waggled his head and gave a ululating yell that skipped across the water like a flat stone, was echoed by scores of throats from the approaching shore. —Y'all gave the Yankees what Paddy gave his drum. Kicked some Yankee tail, last couple days. Gave them smug-ass sonsabitches a blow upside the head. That's what we're kissing on you for, boy. Y'all are sure enough heroes, and we ain't *never* going to forget that.

They landed him at Hardy's Wharf, where they found an unattended carriage and dragged him (themselves between the shafts) to the Atlantic Hotel while they brayed like mad donkeys. The streets were jammed with civilians who acted as if they'd won the war that afternoon. The Alabamian shouted here was one of the heroes from the *Merrimack*. Women waved Confederate colors from windows. They tossed flowers and scented handkerchiefs while old men crowded against the wheels, thrusting segars and calling cards at him. At the hotel he was lifted to the top of the bar and forced to recount the story of the fight to what looked to be the entire white male population of the city between fifteen and seventy. Then a reporter from the *Day Book* cornered him, pumping for detail while waiters kept bringing glasses of the finest brandies and champagnes.

By now Lomax was quite drunk, but he retained enough presence of mind to keep back his reservations. The Yankees would read every word the local rag printed. He presented *Virginia* as invulnerable and undamaged. He predicted she'd be back out momentarily to finish sweeping the Roads, then deliver Baltimore from the tyrant's heel.

—And the enemy ironclad? The *Monitor,* they call it?

—A paltry contrivance, a child's tub toy. We had it whipped and running, and will crush it like a tobacco tin next time we put out.

The reporter looked puzzled. As if he wanted to ask something but didn't at the same time. Finally he said, —You had it whipped?

—Most assuredly.

—Then, I beg your pardon, sir, but why didn't you all finish it off?

The question brought back the gloom in crushing force. Lomax parried it with something about the tide, and saw mistrust infiltrate the reporter's eyes. But he wrote down what he was told.

A party of elderly gentlemen took him to dinner, where they had to tell him about their experiences in 1812. Stuffed with roast beef and many more brandies, he found himself at one point without his sword. Head filled with the vision of some crazed keepsake-hunter making off with it, he found it at last back in the quince behind the dining room. He might have left it there himself.

Which might mean he should slow down. He opened a door at random and found himself neck-deep in the black air of a back alley. Hooting and yipping echoed in the distance, and the pops of firearms being discharged—into the air, he hoped.

The goddamned fools! Celebrating a victory that was no victory, that *could have been* one if only . . . But then too they might so easily have been sunk. He reeled five paces and fetched up against a board fence with a crash. He unbuttoned and pissed, long and satisfyingly, easily the greatest sense of accomplishment he'd felt all day. Then tried to pop a match to one of the dozens of segars stuffed into his pockets without setting his eyebrows on fire. The stars sneered, supercilious and unconvinced, and he snarled back at them, getting the corona going, before he took one wavering step. Then another.

He'd intended to walk for a few minutes to clear his head. But one block became another. Here the streets were quiet. Only a candle glimmer now and then, a lamp-flame, showed where someone was still up.

The house on Freemason had not even that. Its windows reflected only the rising moon. He stood before it, swaying. Then, remembering what he'd spied before, went around to the back. Pressed his face against the cool glass but saw nothing within.

Behind him the cow lowed. He deliberated, then staggered toward the sound. His boots sank into the soil, and he realized as he came out from the shadow he was walking in the yielding earth of a freshly turned garden.

Here was the candle flicker. Back in the little slant-roofed shed, which smelled of clean manure and leather and clover hay. The flame burned in a chipped bowl balanced atop the corncrib. Bundles of paper-skinned onions hung from the rafters, with drying sheaves of lavender, rosemary, and rue. Gardening tools, sickles and spades, hung each on its peg and shone with grease. Someone was bent beneath the brown flank, and the hissing of milk into a pail was like, he thought, the hissing of his own urine against a board fence.

She turned her head, and with a start he recognized her.

Catherine had let the servant go to bed when she complained her back hurt, whined she couldn't turn another hand. Knowing she was doing the wrong thing, raising her up to be a complaining girl, but too tired for the weeping and protest punishment would entail. Simpler to do it herself. So she'd rinsed the pail at the pump and taken it back through the gathering night. Sat for a while, mind empty in the drowsing hush of the shed. Filled with the comforting presence and homely smells. Then at last reached to feel the warm teat, the velvety udder taut and swollen. And began to pull, the warm scent of milk welling up into her face.

Now she stared at the man who'd suddenly appeared without warning, without notice. Obviously unsteady. Who just as obviously, by his expression, hadn't expected to see her back here. But then, who *had* he expected? Dilla? Betsey?

—Yes? she said sharply.

Lomax noted her creased brow, her startled-deer expression. As if she'd never seen him before. Her eyes were as searching as when he'd first met her. But along with that was guardedness, suspicion. He rubbed his face. He'd had a washup at the hotel, but traces of powder-soot still came away on his glove. —It's me, he said. —Lomax Minter. I know I am intruding at an unwonted hour. Please accept my ab—my most abject apologies.

He took off his hat, murmuring regrets, and Catherine recognized him. Belatedly, under the soot and rumpled hair. And for just a moment a terrible fear rooted her to the stool. —You bring a message? she whispered.

—A message?

—You have news? But he was shaking his head, looking confused. Even as she said it, she saw he did not. And that he was either exhausted or drunk. Perhaps both. For a moment she was relieved. But then frowned again. If not to inform her of unpleasant tidings, what then was he doing here? If one of her neighbors had seen him enter, the consequences could be unpleasant. She put starch into her tone. —You quite startled me, sir. It is late in the evening to be paying unexpected calls.

He cleared some thickness in his throat. —That is quite true. . . . Altogether it has been a most unordinary day. . . . I am surprised to see you do your own milking.

Catherine faltered, not happy at being caught in so menial an occupation. —My servant milks of a morning. In the evening I sometimes take a turn. Pray excuse me if I continue.

She bent again, and again he heard the hiss, hiss, the seethe of bubbling cream. She was in a housedress and apron. Not the slightest hint of a crinoline. Bits of hay stuck to the skirt. She must have just filled the manger. Earth stained the apron, as if she'd been grubbing in the dirt. The cow shifted its haunches. Save for that all was silence. He could hear her breathing in it.

—I can do that for you, he said.

Catherine sucked a breath. She had no intention of letting him milk, nor of letting him stay. —Really I am nearly finished. And in truth, this is an inconvenient hour, Mr. Minter.

Her face was serious, lips pursed. She added, and perhaps it was his own ear that sensed an undermeaning, —I hear the *Virginia* has won a famous victory. Perhaps that is the explanation for your unseasonable call and your . . . fatigued state.

He debated how to answer and found he could not. Instead he staggered to the side of the crib and leaned on it casually. Tagged his cap on an unoccupied peg. Selected a cob of feed corn and rotated it idly before his eyes. The rounded kernels were flecked with black and red and green. But his eyes were drawn, as if by some invisible magnet, to her bent back, the delicate arch of her neck below gathered hair. Her sleeves were pushed back off pale arms speckled with creamy froth. The warm air was close with earthy smells, of cow, of herbs, of hay. Of woman.

Through lips that seemed unable to mold the words he wanted to utter, he mumbled instead, —Your little lad . . . I suppose he's in bed.

—He is indeed.

—What news of your husband . . . of my old shipmate Ker?

She was growing uneasy. Unless very ill, a well-bred person always received visitors, no matter when they came, who they might be, or what inconvenience their presence caused. But, gentleman or no, the lieutenant had no business here long after the accepted hours for visiting. He was clearly inebriated. Had she not given him to understand he was not welcome? —There is no news, she said at once, hardly any delay between his question and her reply.

Lomax thought she must have been expecting it or likely answered the same question so often she had her response on the tip of her tongue. —No letters? No word at all?

—Not a scrap. She added reluctantly, head down along the beast's flank, —Though Doctor Steele—you know him, do you not?

He touched his breast lightly, felt the bandage beneath. —I know him.

—The doctor called on me after he was released. He told me the prisoners were reasonably fed but permitted no post. I write but have no way of knowing if my letters reach him. I suspect they do not. Now, sir, it is best you left.

He looked down on her bent head. At the parting in her dark hair, the line of white scalp. —I wish you'd let me help. I keep offering to.

Really, the fellow seemed quite impenetrable to suggestion. Her fingers trembled on the bucket, moving it a few inches as the cow shifted its hooves. A dose of truth, then. Perhaps it would serve where courtesy had not. —I'm not sure you really want to help me, Mr. Minter.

—What do you mean?

— I have heard, since you first came, something of what has occurred between you and my husband.

—Who has told you that?

—No one whose name I need give you. No doubt I do not know the entire story, nor do I wish to. That is properly between the two of you. But I have heard enough to know you are not perhaps such a close friend to my husband as you have presented yourself.

Lomax thought this last remark rather too sharp, considering he'd only come here, had he not, to see if she was well, to offer his assistance. —I never presented myself as his *close friend,* Mrs. Claiborne. Only as his shipmate, concerned for his welfare as I should be for any fellow member of our service. It is true, we've had differences. But if I may say so, his relationship and mine need have nothing at all to do with ours—with yours and mine, I mean.

He thought with mingled satisfaction and irritation, Now let's see what she has to say to *that*.

Her pulling under the cow had become more violent; the beast lowed, protesting. —That is quite enough, sir. You will do me the favor of leaving now.

—I don't care to. If you'd let me—

She looked up, eyes blazing at last. —Then you force me to make myself plain, Lieutenant. I don't want you here again. If you return, I shall notify your commanding officer.

—Of what?

—That your attentions are unwelcome. That you are pressing them on me in my husband's absence. I have no doubt what his response will be.

He coughed. —You accuse me of ungentlemanly behavior?

She tried with all her might to keep her voice from shaking. —We are alone; let us speak plainly. I am told by those who should know that you are not only not my husband's friend but his enemy. Or am I misinformed?

He stammered, —Misinformed . . . not exactly.

—Did you not slap his face? Call him traitor?

Lomax said with great solemnity, —He challenged me, madam. I did not challenge him.

—I find that hard to credit, but let it go. What I am asking myself now is, why do you keep calling on us? Making these protestations of concern? Ingratiating yourself with my son? While his father is absent? And why are you slinking about me now, in the dead of night? Why, Lieutenant? Enlighten me. I will not withhold from you, it is far from the way men of gentle breeding act in the circles in which I was raised.

Her tone was disdainful, and hearing it, his upper lip rose. It was the same tone Claiborne had used. And Catesby Jones. Their inner circles. Their fucking aristocracy. He threw down his segar, ground it out under his boot.

—It never occurred to you that you're an attractive woman? he said, more harshly than he had at first intended.

She didn't answer. She kept her face lowered. —Don't ignore me, he said thickly. —All right, I'll say it. Why I am here. I cherish an especial regard for you. Have since I first saw you. If I have annoyed you—

She said nothing, only wiped her fingers on a rag, keeping her face turned away. He saw that her hands were shaking.

When she stood and tried to push past, he cursed and thrust her back.

Catherine stumbled and the milk stool caught in her skirts. Or perhaps his boot was on the hem. She almost lost her balance. Brought her hands up, but he caught her wrists.

The cow lowed in protest at the disturbance. Minter's weight forced Catherine back against the rough slats of the crib. She fought in silence. No protestation would do her any good now, nor would any scream. She got one wrist twisted free as his face approached, half lit and half in darkness. Felt him recoil as the edge of her hand, jerked upward in protective reflex, caught him across the throat.

He felt her lips only for a moment, cold and rubbery as gutta-percha, before the sudden pain made him choke. He staggered back, slow to react. The drink, of course. He should not have indulged so freely. The pail hit the ground, loosing a buttery flood searching out upon the miry ground. His elbow hit the candle bowl. It tipped into the corncrib and went out.

Rubbing his throat, gasping, he heard the flutter of her breath in the darkness. Three breaths in the sudden abyss of night. His, and hers, and the beast's, the last deeper, placid, untroubled. He was between her and the shed door. No way out save past him.

He rubbed his mouth, wondering what he was about. Desire? Lust? Revenge? Disappointment? What would come of this? He did not know. Nor did he care overmuch. The moment was here when he could make her his.

The straw crackled as he moved toward her ragged breathing.

Part V

THE FEAST OF FIRE.

March–June 1862.

36

———◆———

Aftermath of a Battle ◆ Commencement of a Stand-off ◆ Return to New York
◆ The Monitor Bureau ◆ Encomia from Captain Ericsson ◆ The Offer of
a Lifetime ◆ A Discovered Horror

A ND you, Mister Hubbard. *Monitor*'s new commanding officer
turned to Theo the next afternoon. —I understand you are with us
on a volunteer basis, out of the Ericsson offices, and that you rendered signal service during the battle yesterday.

—Actually out of the Monitor Bureau, sir. And I only operated the
controls. Mister Greene was in command in the turret.

—Except you took charge there after Captain Worden was wounded.

The interview in the captain's cabin had been cordial thus far. Theo,
Engineer Newton, Dr. Logue, Paymaster Keeler, and Worden's replacement as commander, Thomas Selfridge. But Theo considered his answer.
It was strictly against precedent for an engineering officer to command
line members. By rights the senior gun-captain should have taken over,
but he'd shown no signs of doing so. And Greene had *ordered* him to take
charge. But that too felt like sticky ground, so he just said, —Up till then
I had pointed the turret under Lieutenant Greene's direction. After he
went below to see to the captain's wounds, I continued doing so, as we
were still in close action.

Selfridge said coolly such was contrary to regulation. Perhaps it might
be condoned in the heat of battle, but it would not be officially logged

and must never recur. Theo nodded, boiling inwardly. Selfridge was well connected; his commodore father was still on active service. Now that there was glory to be had in monitors, the braiders were moving to corner the market.

Well, Bushnell and Company couldn't object to that. If it helped sell more of them.

Selfridge brushed out a magnificent, tangled side-beard. —And the *Merrimack* or *Virginia,* whatever they've renamed her. I have a personal score to settle.

—For *Cumberland,* sir? said Keeler. —What was that like, pray?

—A savage fight, Mister Paymaster, the fiercest I hope ever to see. There were very few left in my division by the time the word came down it was every man for himself. The entire main deck was covered with the dead. I was one of the last to leave it. I threw off my coat and sword, and squeezed through a gunport. Unfortunately just then the gun gave a lurch and jammed my boot heel between it and the port sill. I thought for a few precious moments I should be carried down with a sinking ship.

—But you are here with us.

—I finally succeeded in wrenching off the heel and jumped into the water, which was quite icy. Swam to the launch astern and was picked up. He blinked and compressed his lips. —Yes, that score must be evened. For all our glorious dead. What was the rebel battery's condition when she retired?

Greene said, —She—it—was still afloat and retired under fair headway, though with difficulty.

—Did you observe a list?

—None I could see.

—I have heard a report you pierced her armor.

Green said, —*That* we did. I fired every round myself, sir, until our noble and gallant captain was wounded, and I was called on to take command. I sent at least five shot of a hundred and seventy pounds each through her side.

Selfridge considered. —You had a view of her from the tower, Mister Hubbard?

—A partial one, sir. As good as anyone but Mister Greene.

—And you saw her penetrated as well?

Again he chose his words with care. —As I said, the exec had the best opportunity to observe, sir. I cannot say I saw her shot through. But it may well have happened so.

—At any rate you both agree she was heavily damaged. Precisely why, then, was she permitted to escape?

This was a poser, and Theo raised his eyebrows, glancing at the others. They looked as surprised. Greene stammered, —*Permitted* to escape, sir?

—I was on the strand, able to observe the entire action. The enemy was aground when her shell struck your pilothouse. You steamed directly away from her for perhaps twenty minutes. During that time she freed herself from the shoal, fired several more rounds at *Minnesota,* and destroyed a tugboat standing by the frigate.

Theo saw where this was going. —That was when Captain Worden was blinded. It required time to care for him and to work out the proper course of action. During that period the helmsman was on his own. I do not think any imputation is due Mr. Greene, if that is what you are suggesting, sir.

Selfridge said distantly he was suggesting nothing; if unanswered questions remained, he would recommend a court of inquiry. If the rebel ram should come out again, however, he was not inclined to let her escape a whipping a second time. After a few more questions about the engines, Theo was dismissed.

He stood in the wardroom, rubbing his still smutty face. Too tired to be angry at the games still being played in the midst of war, battle, death.

Late afternoon, the day after the engagement. All the previous night and into the morning they'd stood by the stranded *Minnesota.* As Fox had said in the wardroom the night before, the enemy vessel was an ugly customer. Theo himself had not seen any of the penetrations Greene had described. It would be very good luck to think they were clear of her. Hardly anyone had managed to sleep. Theo had forced himself to lie in his hammock for three hours. Everyone expected the morning to bring a rematch, for the ominous smoke-pillar to reappear.

But the enemy did not come.

At daybreak, after the tugs had worked all night long, the stranded frigate had finally slid off the shoal. Detached from her support, *Monitor* had passed through the fleet on her way to the fort. Cheer after cheer had gone up from the transports, troops on the beach, even the British as the ironclad thumped past. But that afternoon Commodore Marston had sent over a note informing them he was assigning a new commander. Selfridge had arrived shortly thereafter and immediately ordered a thorough white-glove inspection, during which he'd commented negatively on the way the ship was kept.

Theo stalked aft, still fuming. The day before they'd all been shivering in their boots. They'd laughed at the "cheese box," the "water tank." Now they wanted to know why they hadn't sunk the monster. He'd accomplished all he could here. He went down to the wardroom and composed telegrams to Ericsson and Isherwood, reporting on the craft's performance and notifying them that he planned to return to New York by the next steamer.

But no steamers were available, and Ericsson and Isherwood both replied asking him to stay in case the enemy ram should come out again. Lying at anchor under the fort, the battery recoaled and rearmed, swaying aboard powder, shot, hard bread, whiskey, and machinery stores, then took up a blocking position off the mouth of the Elizabeth. Theo saw that his presence irritated Selfridge. The regulations prohibited a chief engineer being assigned to a craft carrying only two guns. He busied himself rebuilding the pilothouse, reverting to a pyramidal design Ericsson had dropped in favor of the more rapidly constructed box.

The next day they lay at anchor as rumors flew and exhausted men tried to sleep between being called to quarters whenever anyone saw smoke. The Roads grew emptier day by day. The last transports, coal ships, and hospital ships were leaving. At last the army's spies in Norfolk sent word the Southern ironclad had gone into drydock. The flag-of-truce boat said Buchanan, in charge of her, had been wounded, was said to be dying. Selfridge asked permission to go in after her and was refused. The president had sent orders the new battery was not to be risked.

Theo went ashore, to the fort, to the telegraph office. When he mentioned his ship, men shook his hand and offered flasks. They asked anxiously if *Monitor* could keep the wasp bottled up. Theo said he hoped she'd come out again so they could sink her. They were not injured at all, while their enemy had been damaged pretty severely. This seemed to relieve them. From there he went to *Roanoke,* then back to the battery.

He was getting anxious to get back to Eirlys and Lily. Which was surprising, as up to now he'd never wanted to get back to anyone. Newton could handle the machinery. Rebuilding of the pilothouse, replacement of the few nicked plates, was in hand. Finally he got first Selfridge and then Marston to agree he was no longer necessary.

Landing at the Brooklyn Navy Yard two days later, he took the ferry across to Manhattan. Ericsson wasn't in at Franklin Street, but Theo saw the telegram report he'd sent lying on the draughting table. Tick marks were pencilled on it, as if Ericsson had checked off each suggestion he'd made.

MacCord came out of the back, wiping his hands on a rag. —Mister Hubbard, back from the wars! Looking for the old man?

—Where is he? Delamater?

—A private dinner, at Eaker's. They'd be glad to have you look in. The draughtsman shook his hand warmly. —He's the man of the hour, just as he always dreamed. The city's awarding him a sword, I hear. You might get one too.

—What would I do with a sword?

—Toast wieners with it in the boiler room. Now tell me the tale, the voyage down and the battle.

Theo broke away as soon as he could, pleading he wanted to get to Eaker's before the party dispersed. He took a hansom to Fifth and sent in his card. He examined himself in the hall mirror, making sure his uniform was not disarrayed or greasy. Fortunately he'd been able to buy new paper collars that morning and get his hair cut.

The butler returned in seconds, wreathed in smiles. —They're in the drawing room, sir. You're to go up at once.

They were on their feet when he entered. A luxurious room, but a man's room; lit not by gas, he noted, but still by whale oil. A coal fire glowed between carved Indian warriors supporting the mantelpiece. A French clock chimed eight. Old Eaker came toward him, hand extended. He'd expected to be greeted, but not with a hearty slap on the back. Behind Eaker the rest of the Consortium raised glasses in salute. Ericsson, the first time he'd ever seen the inventor look pleased with anything. Flushed, beaming, he seemed another creature from the prickly, suspicious misanthrope whose cross Theo had carried for a hundred strenuous and uncertain days. Bushnell, Winslow, Griswold, and a grave frock coat introduced as The Honorable Erastus Corning, their silent but influential partner in the House. Members of Congress were not supposed to hold stock in the corporations they gave contracts to, but now Theo understood how things got done. He shook hands around. When he came to Ericsson, the inventor said loudly, gripping Hubbard's shoulder, —I was called before the Chamber of Commerce of this city yesterday, and a motion was made complimenting myself and Captain Worden. I took that occasion to enlighten the Chamber as to where the true merit of the matter lay. That the presence of a mastermind on board my battery in Hampton Roads alone brought victory, and that mastermind was Chief Engineer Theodorus Hubbard. The glory is his, far more than any captain's.

The gathering burst into "hear, hear"s and hearty applause. Theo wrung the old man's hand. —No sir, you are too generous with the credit that is John Ericsson's alone. It is to you all our thanks are due. The thanks of the Union, the Navy, and, not least, that of *Monitor*'s crew.

He found a pipe of champagne in his hand, a first-class segar, himself being shown to a seat by the fire. They pressed for the news. He gave it to them, complete. The tale of the voyage down, the leaks, blower belts, the steering failure, her miserable nature in a seaway. The desolation and terror they'd found in Virginia. And then the battle. Grave men of affairs hung like schoolboys on his account of exchanging fire at such close range he could describe the eye color of an antagonist. The rusting of the controls and the uselessness of the port-stopper arrangement. He ended by describing the effect of *Merrimack*'s shot, his measurements of the depth and diameter of each dent. —But dents was all they were, gentlemen. Not a single penetration, whilst we inflicted such damage on our opponent she is now in drydock for an extended stay. Our New York ironworkers, shipbuilders, and mechanicians have delivered what Captain Ericsson always assured us it would be: a completely impregnable battery.

As he finished, a glance traveled from one of them to the next. Bushnell cleared his throat.

—Well, sir; well. It is plain we have backed a winner, and that is a great relief. We have news of our own, as it happens. From Washington. We have closed for six boats on the *Monitor* plan, for four hundred thousand dollars each. They are to be a trifle larger, with the twelve-inch guns. This will do, will it not?

—It will indeed, sir. I am very pleased to hear it. Especially if we in the Bureau can induce you to make such trifling improvements as the first trial has pointed out may perfect the captain's design.

Ericsson said, —Not nearly so pleased as you have made us, Mister Hubbard. The imperfections of the structure I saw a long time back. To correct them is child's play, now the principle is proven. And this is but the beginning. What do you say to a twin-turret monitor? A swift ocean battery to carry twenty-inch guns? A shallow-draft model for ascending the Southern rivers and rooting out the last sparks of the rebellion, once McClellan has finished with Richmond?

—It will be fascinating work.

Bushnell said smoothly, —And *very* profitable. We were discussing a moment ago that we require a man of parts to take charge. To be the Consortium's engineering manager, working with the Navy and Congress as well as with Captain Ericsson and ourselves to smooth the path for the rapid production of a great many more improved monitors.

Theo looked from one to the next. —Whom are you considering for the position?

Eaker said gravely, —We're prepared to offer it to you, sir. Unanimously.

—But I work for the Bureau of Steam Engineering. For Mister Isherwood.

Bushnell said, —Exactly so; you have Isherwood's confidence as well. Another reason we should like you to join us, Hubbard. I believe we can promise you a salary and a . . . stake in the enterprise, that will make it well worth your while to write out your resignation from the Navy.

They were all smiling at him. The segar was choice, the best he'd ever tasted, though he was usually a pipe man. —And my . . . debt?

Eaker chuckled, waved a speck of dust away in the warm friendly light. —*That* minim? Sir, *that* has long been forgotten. Think nothing more of *that*.

His mind's grip was slipping, like a loose, wet blower belt. Through his astonishment he heard them go on about their plans. Dozens of ships. Millions of dollars. Sales to Russia. Sweden. France. Spreading production across the North to assure support in Congress.

These men could do it. The driving, powerful, farseeing capitalists who would win this war, then drive ahead like a gigantic locomotive into a majestic future of steam and electricity, of shining rails across continents, shining wires across oceans.

It was what he'd always wanted, to be one of them.

The problem was, he couldn't. And he saw puzzlement write across canny faces as he told them so; that he very much appreciated their offer and would remember the confidence they and Captain Ericsson had placed in him; but that his duty lay with the Service. Saw that bewilderment change, to his relief, to admiration.

—Well, sir, we are disappointed to hear that; but I suspected as much. Captain Ericsson doubted we could win you over from the Navy, though it seemed to me working with us would contribute as much to the restoration of the Union as any seagoing victory. Bushnell slapped his shoulder. —You are young and touched with fire, and we old men all envy you. Now tell us again how they hit you with two shells at once, and knocked everyone in the turret to his knees.

In the night-filled street he looked up at the blazing windows. A thrill of regret sang along his nerves, beneath the comforting soothe of the champagne. He *did* regret it. But at the same time knew he'd made the right choice.

He wasn't doing it for the braiders. To hell with them! They'd fight to keep their privileges, their glorified, pompous images bright in their mirrors of self-importance. He was doing it for those he'd worked with and fought beside: the stokers, oilers, common seamen fresh from the farm, the young volunteers bewildered yet eager from school and factory and engine shed. They needed someone to instruct them, to guide their hands on Isherwood's and Ericsson's engines.

Yet the invitation and the pride of having declined it warmed him for several blocks through the city and over the night ferry to Brooklyn. Till at last he stood looking up again, at another window. From time to time a shadow passed in front of the lamp. She was up there, then. With his daughter.

A night for decisions, it seemed. He only hoped that in later years, they'd seem as right as they did now.

How much could one forgive of another—and of oneself?

Was it possible he could build something resembling a family?

He didn't know. All he hoped was that when he climbed that stair, two souls would rejoice at being reunited with him. Perhaps, with time, the distrust on both sides could be overcome.

Smiling to himself, Theo mounted the stairs. Imagining it: The door opening, and there they'd be: a surprised and smiling Eirlys, and, behind her, playing on the rug, the little girl who looked shyly at him out of his own eyes.

But at the top landing the door was already open. The woman within, the shape he'd seen from the street, was not Eirlys but their half-crippled landlady. She was pushing a mop across the floor. When he stopped, startled, in the doorway, she dropped it in the bucket and stepped back, crossing her arms as if he'd just accused her of something. —So you're here. About time, she said, pushing out her lip.

—What's going on?

—Don't lean on that door. It's broken.

He looked around at the shabby boardinghouse furniture. One of the chairs was smashed. As he took in the room, he saw other things had been altered. Wrecked. Or missing. But what held his attention was the stain on the floor, thickened, hardened, only half mopped out.

—What has happened here, he said in a low, threatening voice.

Obviously frightened, but of the ratlike sort in whom fear becomes indignation, the landlady berated him for leaving his mistress alone. The men had come the day before. They'd asked about the woman on the fourth floor. Whether she had a child with her. What name they went by. Not long after had come the sounds of an altercation. She was an old woman. She could not have interfered. When the Metropolitans had come, they'd found the woman on the floor, bleeding. She'd died before they could get her downstairs.

He said dazedly, —Dead?

—Dead and gone to potter's field. Weeks overdue on her rent. Where were you, mister? What was they to you?

—But I left her money. She had . . . and the girl? He stepped forward, and something in his face must have frightened her; she snatched the mop up and held it before her like a quarter-staff. —*Where's the girl?*

—Little tot's gone. Took her with they, maybe. You can ask Mister Hirschbiel on the third floor. Says he seen one, a big mean Chinee looker, with his arm bound up from a knife slash.

He slumped against the shattered door frame, seeing now the marks of struggle everywhere. The bolt, ripped from its screws. The cuckoo clock Eirlys had bought in the Village, smashed in the corner. He crossed numbly to the chest where she'd kept Lilibeth's frocks. They were gone, though her toys were left. A handful of jacks, a ball, a carved wooden bird with one wing broken. He crossed to the wardrobe. Eirlys's dresses were gone too.

—I didn't take nothing, nothing, the crone shrilled, turning to watch as he went from corner to corner, like a panicked rat himself, some impersonal corner of his mind noted. —Let them stay, niver even said nothing when she had men up to the room. Oh, yes, she did. Can't leave a harlot alone. A tosspot as well. Anyone could see it. Too bad for the kid, though, right smart little sparrow she was. She held her palm out. —Twenty dollars sets it right with the busted furniture. Have anythin' you want to keep out by tonight. I got a Hunky family movin' in termorrer.

At last he stood in the street, panting. The Jew on the third floor had been frightened, but had told him what he'd seen. Theo had no doubt who it had been. The description was too exact. He also said one of the three had been in a police uniform.

He swayed, staring at the window that minutes before he'd gazed up at with such expectation, such anticipation that what he'd yearned after so long was finally in his grasp.

Delayed, as if the very cords of his heart had thickened and slowed, the magnitude of what he'd lost arrived. He clapped his hands over his eyes and drew a quaking breath.

For the first time in his life Theodorus Hubbard's numbed brain could not formulate the semblance, the beginning, even the merest suggestion of a plan.

37

Commander Ker Custis Claiborne. C.S.N., to Mrs. Ker Claiborne

At Fort Warren, Massachusetts
March 11, 1862

Dearest Catherine,

I take up my pen to indite what I trust will prove to be good news. Hoping you will pardon this inferior paper—it being all that is available for purchase from the sutler here.

I have not received anything from you since a single letter which reached me not long after the New Year. I know you must have been writing more often than that & I have either the interruption of the postal service between the states or possibly the spite of my gaolers to thank for my lack of correspondence. I will however take the opportunity to slip this missive to one who may be able to pass it on to hands that will eventually bring it to you. You will understand if I cannot name him, in case it should be intercepted by those who do not believe prisoners deserve even the fundamental right of communication.

Rumors have flown for the past weeks concerning the suspension of proceedings for our trials. As I wrote before, Dr. Steele was released not long after our incarceration; I hope he has been able to acquaint you with our circumstances in this prison off the coast, and the threats posed against us due to our <u>lawful</u> cruizing activities. & that you have been able to forward such news to Aunt Sue & Jamie too if you can send care of his regiment.

And now to my news. Colonel Dimick came in to see me this morning not long after my wash-up with the grudging news that parole & exchange is at last being considered for our officers & men. It is possible even I, the notorious "pirate commander," may be thought eligible. He made it v. clear that such eventuality was in no way related to the Confederate Gov.t's having communicated in a note to Secretary Seward that if we were tried & hung, an equal number of federal prisoners of commensurate military rank & family connexions would be "suspended" in retaliation.

A threat of which I was not aware & which fills me with a most disturbing compound of feelings. How to rejoice at a policy which, though it may deliver me if it succeed, will result in the deaths of innocent & no doubt brave men if it does not? Can one combat evil with more evil? Do not all sink into iniquity together? I confess I should rather have our country take "the high road" & adhere to the letter of the law of war than stoop to the level of Seward & his ilk. I should have liked to have been able to talk to those who proposed this intimidation before it was put into effect, to our everlasting shame.

Dimick also without joy relayed an order from his superiors permitting me to meet and mess with the others henceforth, through I am still to be held in a separate cell each night. So not long after I had the great pleasure of shaking hands with those whose distant forms I had been able to glimpse only now and then on the walls. Mr. Dulcett, Mr. Shepherd, Mr. Bertram, Mr. Kinkaid, and others you may recall me writing of were there. After many explanations and embraces, a solemn toast was drunk to "Bob-Stay" MacDonnell, who perished for the Cause during the battle with *Potomac,* and to Count Zdzislaw Osowinski, a fighter against tyranny in all its multifarious forms, who had passed away during the winter of his injuries during the same engagement.

I am well & most happy to see the coming of Spring, though it is not yet much in evidence hereabouts. The wind comes right through the stone & our fires do little to ward it off. The ground is damp & only a little sun is in evidence today from the ramparts.

Events in the West are worrisome, at least as they reach me through the crimson lens of the Boston papers. As is the gathering of McClellan's army on our soil. I suspect that sometime soon will occur the decisive battle. I do not doubt it will end with our independence, and say with Nelson "May the great God give my country a great and glorious Victory, and may no misconduct in anyone tarnish it."

Alone in his cell the prisoner may have seemed solitary to his vigilant guard. And he has struggled with melancholia and is prey at times to dismal thoughts. Especially since Romulus, charmed by those who promised him the moon, decided to leave his service for the emancipating freedoms of the Pilgrim City.

For some weeks I pondered whether it might not be best to wager all on the chance of escape. There is one embrasure through which I believe I could squeeze if I starved myself down to a shadow. And at one point, I set out to do this. Yet even outside these stone walls I would still be imprisoned by the winter sea, with absolutely no chance of a boat—none land here save those heavily manned by troops—and with such tide-races and miles to swim that to venture it would be nothing more than conscious suicide. At last I set the thought aside. Without help from outside, from this modern Château d'If there is no escape. But I would have hazarded it even so if the order had come down for my execution.

Yet the long days have not been without improving influences. I have read again the New Testament, my imprisoned condition giving new force to the words of Paul. Also Dr. Frothingham has been kind enough to lend me his books on the French Revolution. I have sat at the feet of Carlyle & Condorcet, Headley, Abbott, de Tocqueville's <u>Ancien Régime</u>, Las Cases & Victor Hugo. Pondering the progression through constitutional government, to the Terror & leadership by the Mob, to the restoration of monarchical trappings by the uncle of the present Emperor. How little the passage of laws & upheaval of regimes affect the underlying genius of a people! As you know I have never believed slavery a just system. Yet no observing man can but harbor grave doubts about the ability of all but the most advanced of the African race to participate in affairs. One way or another, slavery will pass away in time. Yet if precociously abolished it will only have to be re-created under another guise. What can they know of us who have never lived among us? Let the South modify her institutions in her own way.

Enough for the present. My rising heart says, away with doubt. There will of course be much maneuvering delay & bargaining connected with our exchange. And as the usurper's hirelings have spattered far more ink on us in the public press than we ever let blood, no doubt it will take place in dead of night & no notice of it released. But if eventually we are to be exchanged, I will endeavor to notify you of my impending arrival. May Providence make it sooner rather than later. I could not guarantee my health through another Yankee winter.

Good-bye, my dear wife. May God bless you & Robert. How I should love to see him if he has not quite forgotten his old prickly bearded Papa. God grant we may all be together soon. I hope Norfolk remains safe & that the forces there are sufficient to hold the city. But if threatened go at once to your parents in Richmond. You can then have the counsel of your Father & Mother for whom I have the greatest respect. If this letter should make its way to you, remember me to them both.

I think of you always & long to press you to my breast once again. With love to my own dearest Wife,

Ever devotedly, your husband,
K. Claiborne.

38

<hr>

Disagreeable Reflections on the Line of the Richmond & Petersburg ◆ Parcel from Commodore Buchanan ◆ Impromptu Declamation from the Platform ◆ Report to the President ◆ An Unpleasant Surprise

<hr>

LOMAX sat slumped in his greatcoat, the canvas-wrapped package beside him on the seat. Taylor Wood sat opposite, segar nearly bitten through by the jolting, squinting out a window through which a brisk breeze swept. The car rocked and clattered, going over a section of plate-rail line, but making good time. He gazed out at newly tilled fields, at darkies trudging behind plodding ox teams. At the station buffet someone had said they weren't planting cotton this year. No point, since they couldn't ship it out. They'd plant corn to feed the army, and to fatten hogs.

He closed his eyes, seeing again the images that rode with him. The wounded. The dead. A ship aflame, men being cooked alive.

The woman, Claiborne's wife—there weren't any images with that. But he remembered the feel of her in the dark. Maybe it shouldn't have happened. He'd been well liquored, that was for sure. If her husband found out, it'd be Hell to pay and no pitch hot. But she'd never tell. Not and have everyone think what they naturally would.

Reporting back aboard the day after he'd found the ship torn apart by a swarm of workers and a note waiting from Buchanan. The old fighter wanted him and Wood to wait on him at the hospital. He had something he wished forwarded to Richmond. Lomax had formally requested permission to depart from Jones, and received it just as coldly, just as punctiliously.

An orderly ushered them into the commodore's room to find him lying supine, eagle nose jutting at the ceiling, his white hair frizzled untidily on the pillow. He looked close to death. His leg was covered by packed lint into which a steady drip was trickling from a monkey jar suspended on a rope. The orderly checked his pulse, refilled his water glass, and withdrew.

Opening his eyes, the old man gestured weakly for them to be seated. If Lomax had expected compliments, he was quickly set straight. —I hear you failed to destroy either *Minnesota* or this Yankee cheese box. I am disappointed at that result.

Wood said unfortunately that was true. —So were we all, sir. Disappointed, that is.

The old man looked as if he wanted to ask more, possibly about how Jones had conducted himself, but pressed his lips firmly together. Of course, Lomax thought. He'd never ask juniors to testify against their senior. Franklin Buchanan's grain did not run that way. Instead he said, —Well, we shall sally again. I intend to recover quickly and resume command.

—If you were to do so, sir, I have every confidence we would return bearing the palm of victory, Wood said soothingly.

Speaking in a strained tone, as if in pain, the old man fumbled a note into their hands. Then nodded to a canvas-wrapped parcel at the foot of his bed. —Take my report to Secretary Mallory. Accompany it with that, if you please.

—What is it, sir? Minter asked.

Buchanan said sharply, —Just give it to him and don't ask so many goddamned questions, Lieutenant.

—Aye aye, *sir.* Wood stood, grinning, and after a moment Lomax did too. —We are cautioned not to tire you, sir. We will be on our way.

They'd stopped to ask the doctor how he was doing. He said the old man had been lucky. The bullet had torn the femoral artery. Still nip and tuck whether he'd pull through, at his age. Lomax had asked when he might return to duty if all went well. The doctor had said it would be months before he could even stand again, let alone go to sea.

Lomax had glanced into his room again as they left. To see Buchanan's envious gaze following them away.

When they disembarked at Richmond station, a crowd was waiting. The telegraph had carried tidings of their arrival, and they were called on for remarks. Since this had also happened at Suffolk, Wakefield, Waverly, and Petersburg, they had their act worked out. Lomax recounted the first day of battle, Wood the second. They concluded to an ovation spiked with pistols fired into the air. When they jumped down, they were besieged by offers of drinks, which they fought off, but accepted the offer of a conveyance to the Mechanic's Institute.

Secretary Mallory received them standing at his desk. Lomax had not met the secretary before. A roly-poly, stumpy fellow with a round red face, he spoke with a Florida accent. He waved them to seats, and sat back while they went through their tale once more. He asked about the Ericsson, *Virginia*'s performance against it, and their opinion of the merits and drawbacks of the two designs. Wood placed the envelope on the desk and Lomax the parcel.

—And this is?

—From Commodore Buchanan. He did not tell us what it is, sir.

Mallory started to open the letter, then jumped up. —No. We must take this to the president. Mr. Tidball! Call my carriage, if you please.

The executive mansion was on the far side of Capitol Square. They descended from the carriage to the muddy street, then climbed from there the marble stairs of a two-story gray-stuccoed mansion not nearly so grand as the White House, but not without neoclassical dignity. It had been the Brockenbrough house. Lomax had been in the city when word arrived that Richmond was to be the capital of the new republic. Not long after, the local papers had carried the news that the city had bought the mansion, at the suggestion of several men of quality, and leased it to the new government as the president's residence.

A colored butler took their hats and coats, in an entryway with bronze statues of Comedy and Tragedy flanking the entrance to a comfortable-looking parlour. He directed them to the second floor. He tried to take the parcel as well, but Lomax held on to it. At the top of the landing Mallory introduced them through a window opening to the president's elegantly suited secretary, Mr. Burton Harrison. The excited shrieks of children at rambunctious play came from back in the house as Harrison ushered the visitors in.

Davis's office was carpeted in a deep red figured pattern. Both an overhead gasolier and a desk lamp connected to it by a gutta-percha extension tube were lit. A fire crackled in the black marble fireplace. A roller-map of North America had been pulled down above a sofa. They'd evidently interrupted a meeting, but the gentlemen who looked up from a round table by the window did not seem upset. Their careworn faces were expectant.

—Mister President, may I present two young heroes direct from the recent battles in Hampton Roads. Lieutenants John Taylor Wood and Henry Lomax Minter, of the steamer *Virginia*, late the *Merrimack*. You know Mister Wood of course.

—How are you, nephew.

The two shook hands, and Lomax, swallowing, remembered that, yes, Wood's mother had been the sister of Davis's first wife. The mystery of why Wood had been sent along, when Buchanan had entrusted letter and parcel to him alone, was solved. Mallory went on smoothly, —Mister Minter is from Mississippi, sir. I believe, not far from your own Brierfield.

Davis welcomed him as well with a hearty handshake and every appearance of joy, which took Lomax aback. His grip was strong, and close up the president appeared vigorous, though tired; he held his back straight and his noble head erect as if still on parade at West Point. His speech sounded more Kentucky than Mississippi. His famously blinded eye was touched with a pearly film.

He'd heard the president called saturnine, distant, but Davis seemed perfectly affable. He introduced them to the others, who offered congratulations with the engulfing handshakes of lifelong political men. Mr. Benjamin, a heavyset, smiling, Judaic-looking gentleman. A queer sickly little fellow whom at first, confused, Lomax took for a child, so smooth and sad was his tiny face, was Alexander Stephens, the vice president of the Confederacy. His emaciated, crippled doll's hand felt like spider silk over brittle twigs. General Cooper, the adjutant general, and a Mr. Seddon, who did not seem to have a title or much of a personality either. Davis asked the secretary to step over to the executive offices and see whether anyone else would like to come over and hear their report.

—Well now, Davis said, still smiling, —let us have your account of the engagement. No doubt what we are reading in the newspapers has little to do with what actually happened.

Minter was glad now they'd had the chance to rehearse, as it were, their report. He tried to make it less spread-eagle than had seemed appropriate shouted from the platform of a train to an excited crowd. Davis listened intently, twisting his goatee with thumb and forefinger. When they were done, he said, —What repairs do you consider necessary? Before she can face this new foe once more?

—We can steam again at once, Lomax said hotly. —In fact we should never have come in, but continued the fight.

Mallory cleared his throat. —The lieutenant shows the ardent intrepidity embodied in our new sea-service. The preliminary report sent to me by Commodore Buchanan makes particular mention of his daring in the affair of the *Congress*. However, telegraphic reports from the yard make plain we have some refitting to do before venturing another engagement.

Davis asked him, not quite ignoring Mallory's intercession but not acknowledging it either, —We old men certainly admire such fire. I would not for the world have it otherwise. What is your opinion of *Virginia's* fighting abilities, contrasted to the Ericsson? Be frank with me.

Minter said, —Sir, I consider ours much the superior concept.

—Excellent. Mister Wood, you agree?

—Essentially, sir, though there are errors in construction. *Virginia's* most serious failing is her deep draft.

—What will be the result of a return engagement?

Lomax said, —With bolts of chilled iron, steel if possible, we can penetrate her. Or else we can run her down, once our ram is repaired.

—And Mister Wood?

—With all appreciation of Mister Minter's opinion, sir, I consider the *Monitor* fully our equal in a ship-to-ship engagement. The result of another battle would be doubtful.

—But you agree we have the superior type of craft, Benjamin put in, smiling cherubically.

—I do, sir. But the present vessel has serious flaws.

—Mister Minter, you and Mister Wood appear to disagree.

He lifted his head. —No sir. I do not disagree with Mister Wood. If anything, he underestimates *Virginia*'s shortcomings. She is a makeshift. And she might have been to sea earlier than she was. But our fighting spirit is so far superior that we cannot help but win.

Davis nodded. He asked more questions about draft, speed, armament; he seemed to be well informed and to have a quick mind. Lomax gradually lost his awe and gave forthright answers. At last the president turned to the naval secretary. —Stephen, your policy of building ironclads was the right one. You have brought us in one bound from a hopeless inferiority to what I should call parity, if not yet absolute superiority.

Benjamin, still smiling, added from the sofa that he was preparing written reports of their victory to forward to London and Paris. —I shall tell them that within ninety days they may consider the blockade lifted and our waters free. Combined with the Lincolnian arrogance over the *Trent,* it will certainly result in recognition and perhaps even military aid.

Davis said in a magisterial tone, —And there you have it. Complete the ram's repairs, Secretary Mallory. Then finish clearing out Hampton Roads. Press ahead with the other armorclads in New Orleans and Memphis. I will also transmit to Congress your proposition for the construction of ironclad vessels in Europe.

—I will issue orders to that effect, sir.

—This spring will see the crux of this contest. If we can maintain ourselves in the east, our losses in the west will not affect the strength of our main armies. Maintaining control of the lower James will slow the enemy's offensive. If we can repel McClellan, then, Mister Stephens, it will be time to advance the peace policy you have pressed me to put forward, and end this unjust war of invasion and subjugation. Despite the cabal, many at the north still remember what it is to be free. They acknowledge our inherent and inalienable right to self-government. That is all we expect from our former brethren, and all that we demand.

Mallory said eagerly, —Mister President, with your permission. Commodore Buchanan has forwarded something of interest to us by way of Lieutenant Minter. If you will permit him.

At Davis's nod, Lomax placed the parcel not on the table, because it was too small, but on Davis's desk. He undid the strings as the witnesses gathered round. Within was a second bundle, made up in a roll, the way seamen stowed their clothing. He read the inscription aloud. —Flag taken from U.S.S. *Congress,* frigate, March 8, 1862.

He pushed it to unroll down the length of the desk. As it unwound, the smoke-stained scarlet and white stripes came into view. The politicians exclaimed. Davis lifted his end, the end with the blue jack. It was large, a battle flag. He had it almost to eye level when the light from the gasolier revealed the gluey puddle that soaked the rest of the material.

The smell of blood filled the room. The entire lower half of the flag was saturated with it.

—The invaders paid for their aggression, Lomax said into the sudden silence. —We only asked to be let alone.

Davis set down his end; Mallory, moving forward, quickly rolled it up again and tucked it under his arm. —I will return this to the Navy Department, then.

—Perhaps that would be best.

Little Stephens was rubbing his eyes. —What is all this carnage and slaughter for? Why this array of armies and all the lamentation and mourning? he murmured.

—For one object, and one only, Stephens, Davis said. —As you of all of us should know. To defend the principle that government derives its just powers from the consent of the governed. It is everything for which free men should live and for which they must always be willing to die. If we can hold to that principle, constitutional liberty will live. If we should fail, it will be lost forever.

From behind, Mallory silently touched their shoulders. After a moment, though he wished still to speak out, Minter too turned, and they walked out into what, to his surprise, was already evening.

39

Abandoned by the Army ♦ A Challenge Ignored ♦ Laboring Like Heroes ♦ Maneuvering on the Peninsula, and a Chance to Strike Passed By ♦ The Flag That Did Not Fly ♦ Some Minutes After Midnight ♦ A Question as to Fitness to Command ♦ The Pitfalls of Professional Advice ♦ Brandy amid the Fall of Troy ♦ The *Virginia* Lives No More

TWO months later, on a soft-aired Saturday evening, early in May. *Virginia* lay to her mooring under Sewell's Point, as she had for several days now, keeping a sharp eye to the mast tops of the distant Federals. Alphaeus Steele and the others were enjoying a leisurely dinner of terrapin, roast goose, and oyster salad when the flag lieutenant got back from his long pull into town. That morning Tattnall had noticed the Confederate flag was no longer flying ashore. Worried, he'd sent his lieutenant to find out why.

The army had vanished, he stammered white-faced to them all. The enemy had landed in force on the bay shore and was reported marching rapidly southward. Sewell's Point, abandoned. Fort Norfolk, abandoned. The navy yard, the great ram's repair base and storehouse, already in flames. General Huger and his staff gone by railroad. All his troops pulling out, without so much as a by-your-leave to the great floating bulwark that had protected them through the spring.

Steele did not like the purplish hue that took Josiah Tattnall's cheeks. Nor was he sure the same choleric tint did not stain his own.

To come to this so quickly after their victorious engagement with *Monitor*! Inconceivable, after the high hopes of March. But dithering and waste had frittered away all the bright opportunities. A cloud of fear seemed to have slid over the summer sun. Fear of McClellan's slow-paced but seemingly unstoppable advance.

No one admitted it in public or to the lower ranks. But Steele had heard the murmurings of doubt. Seen the grave miens of senior officers. Caught Tattnall with his face buried in his hands when he forgot his physician was attending in his cabin.

These might be the last days of the Southern Confederacy.

Two days after the battle, Richmond had sent them another antique commodore. "Jo" Tattnall, a Georgian. A long-armed, snowy-haired, barrel-chested sea dog with a pugnacious lip whose prowess with the cutlass had made him feared in his youth. But that had been during the War of 1812. Tattnall was even older than Buchanan now, and in Steele's opinion not of the same metal. Then, as they awaited repairs, Brooke and Porter had quarreled again over modifications to the armor. Enraged at the delay, Mallory had sacked French Forrest and replaced him as yard commander with Robert E. Lee's brother Sidney.

They'd spent nearly a month in drydock. But when at last she left, she was more powerful than ever, more heavily armored along the waterline. Her broken plates and damaged guns replaced, and her crew resolved to show beyond any doubt their superiority to the Ericsson, which Northern papers were shamelessly trumpeting as winner of their first engagement.

Winner! When it had turned tail and run! This time it would not escape. Steele had provided bottles of chloroform. If they couldn't pierce the smaller ironclad with the new chilled-iron bolts, a boarding party would toss the anesthetic into the turret, cover it and the pilothouse with tarpaulins, and wait for the crew to surrender.

In mid-April they'd steamed out to renew the battle. Steele had waited below, playing piquet for hours with Albright. But the enemy had cowered under the shelter of Monroe. Even when *Jamestown* captured several transports, they could not be lured out to battle. *Monitor* had shown no more fight than the wooden ships. After steaming back and forth before the enemy for hours, the Confederates had withdrawn in frustration. At least they seemed to be delaying McClellan. Since *Virginia* blocked the

James, his troops had only crept forward, unsupported on their river flank and resisted the more fiercely the closer they drew to Richmond.

A few days later the commodore had gotten them under way yet again, this time for an evening attack. McClellan had reached Magruder's lines at Yorktown. If they could pass the squadron and fort and escape into the Chesapeake, they could take the Union generalissimo's transports in the York River. Spread terror and fire, and cut his waterborne supply behind him.

It had been a moonless night. Steele, when he went topside, had not understood how they knew where they were. But steaming darkened, watching the passing lights of the anchored Yankees, they'd actually gotten abreast of the fortress without being detected. In another half hour they would have been in the Bay and free.

But that chance too had slipped away when the old captain had turned back. Jones said there'd been a lantern-signal from shore. Steele could not imagine Franklin Buchanan reversing course. Like Horatio Nelson, he would have claimed he couldn't see the signal.

After that the enemy's force had built as their own position had weakened. Two new ironclads joined the Ericsson. Burnside's troops were fighting their way up from North Carolina. The week before, the rest of the Confederate squadron had steamed slowly off up the James. When word came that the Yankees were bombarding Sewell's Point, Tattnall had taken the great ship out one last time. Yet again he'd taunted the combined federal fleet. Once again they'd refused the gage of battle. Since then, here they'd lain, waiting for orders, decisions. But hearing nothing.

Now the meaning of that silence was clear. The advancing Yankee army was threatening the rail communications between Norfolk and the capital. That was the only explanation, Jones was arguing, for the army's precipitous withdrawal: to avoid being cut off. The others followed the debate tensely. Tattnall sat back, finger barring bearded lips, pondering what each man said. He was not in good health. Alphaeus had bled him the night before, and administered jalap root as a counter-irritant for cerebral congestion. Finally he lifted that finger, and the wardroom fell silent.

—This is unfortunate news, gentlemen. We have been ill served, that is quite clear. But recrimination is bootless. Let me recap our choices.

—Our base of operations has unexpectedly vanished. This ship has proven—no reflection on you, Engineer Ramsay—that she cannot steam more than a few hours without repairs. With the navy yard destroyed, she will therefore shortly become helpless. Limiting our options to very few. He ticked them off. —One: a headlong attack on the reinforced fleet at Fort Monroe, consisting of twenty sail, including *Monitor, Minnesota,* the ram *Vanderbilt,* and others. Two: abandon her to the enemy. (A murmur of "No, no.") —Three: attempt to work up the James to Richmond.

He coughed into his fist and added, —Though death or glory has its appeal, the third is that course of action hewing closest to our orders— which are both to cover Norfolk and to prevent the enemy from reaching the capital by water. The former being lost, we must devote ourselves to the latter mission. If we are to take up a blocking position in the river, we must do so swiftly. In fact tonight. We must pass Newport News and be well up the James before daylight discovers us to our enemies.

He turned to the pilots, who stood leaning against the sideboard. —Gentlemen, the last time we discussed this, you said a draft of eighteen feet would get us over Harrison's Bar. Is that still your considered professional opinion?

Parrish, the chief pilot, with a bow: —It is, Flag Officer.

—Mister Ramsay, Mister Jones: can we lighten her to eighteen feet?

The engineer and the exec said with bleak expressions that they believed it barely possible, though it would unfit them for any fighting. Tattnall pushed back his chair. —Then muster all hands, if you please, and let us set to work.

The crew labored like heroes for the next five hours. Organized into passing parties, they hoisted kentledge from the bilges and pushed it over the side through the gunports. They pried up the deck ballast and tipped it into the sea. Stores, chain, anchors, deck howitzers, water, rum, beef, all went over. Every man was determined to escape the closing jaws. Steele joined in, sacrificing all but the most essential of his medical stores, his porcelain chamber pot, even dismantling his bunk. He didn't understand why they were doing this now rather than when they got into the James.

But since he did not expect his seniors to comment on his surgery, he did not question their orders anent military operations. Tattnall had commanded since the eighteen-thirties, and come through near wrecks and hard-fought battles in Mexico. So Steele hoisted his bunk rail onto his shoulder and worked his way up the ladder.

It was night on the spar deck. In the gutter of pine torches the great ship had grown a bobbing nimbus of barrels, timbers, and clothing. He slid the rail down the casement and watched it join the rest of the jetsam with a somber splash.

—Midnight, Doctor. Or even some minutes past.

Catesby Jones, looking haggard. Steele checked his watch in the torchlight. —If you are speaking metaphorically, sir, I would guess you are close to the mark. If however you are inquiring as to the exact time, it still lacks ten or twelve minutes of that hour.

—Your opinion, Doctor. Is the commodore fit to command?

Alphaeus harrumphed to mask surprise. —In what sense, sir?

—Is his mind clear? I know you are treating him. For apoplexy, is it not?

He bowed courteously. —I do not feel at liberty to reveal either his condition or my treatment, sir.

Jones waved that aside. —I ask because his orders make no sense. Lightening our draft exposes our unarmored sides. It would have been more prudent to preserve our fighting power for the passage through the enemy fleet, and resort to lightening her, to whatever degree necessary, once in the upper reaches of the river.

Which was what Steele had wondered too. But aloud he only said, —Have you shared your views with him?

—He cursed me out of his cabin with such violence I feared he might suffer a stroke there and then.

Steele rumbled, —To answer your question, sir, neither his maladies nor the treatment I have administered are of such a nature as to cloud his mental vision. He is of an advanced age. True. But since our leaders knew this when they ordered him to us, I do not feel warranted in doubting him on that basis alone.

Jones muttered something under his breath. Without a word further he swung away and went below.

Alphaeus was lying on a blanket on the bare damp deck when renewed shouting and clanging woke him from confused and ominous dreams. When he groggily struck steel and lit his candle, his watch revealed two a.m. No doubt they were getting under way to slip past the Federals. As there was nothing the ship's surgeon could do to help, he pinched the candle out and lay back, breathing heavily.

Minutes later he was roused again by a hammering on his door. Albright, the paymaster's assistant, stammered that he must prepare to abandon ship.

—I beg your pardon, he said, raising himself on an elbow and misdoubting whether this was not perhaps another dream. —To do . . . what?

With a lamp flame jittering in his hand, the clerk explained that the pilots had changed their minds. Something about the wind being out of the west. About eighteen feet still being too deep a draft to get over the bar. They refused to take the responsibility of guiding her up the James. —The commodore's beside himself. Like a madman.

Steele didn't wonder. This was awful news. He fought his blanket off, groped for his trowsers. —What is his color?

—His color, sir?

—Is it high? Is his face distorted? Does he seem to have trouble speaking?

Albright said Tattnall's color was high, but he seemed to have perfect mastery of all sorts of picturesque and abusive speech. Half dressed, grabbing his pocket case should exsanguination be called for, Steele pushed by him.

Tattnall's cabin was crammed with men, all shouting, all expostulating. The old man roared loudest of all, flinging his arms around as if fighting hornets. His face was puffy and purple as an overripe plum. Apoplexy could not be far off. Alphaeus tried to take his pulse but was flung away. The old man clapped his hand to his sword hilt when he tried a second time. Judging retreat the better part of valor, he retired to the doorway.

—Don't you think I wanted to fight? the commodore shouted. —Then why did I take you out twice, to flaunt our flag in their faces? We're no longer fit for battle, unless you relish suicide. Ground her and burn her! That is the order. Now carry it out, damn you!

The whistle of "up grog" sounded from above. The bitter faces wavered, then slowly dispersed. Some cursed as they pushed by him. He saw tears of rage shining on more than one cheek. He looked wonderingly at the commodore, who had slumped suddenly into his armchair, wheezing.

—You must calm yourself, sir. It is dangerous to give your passions such rein.

Tattnall stared as if he was speaking Greek. Steele tried again for his pulse, and this time succeeded. The commodore gradually relaxed. His unhealthy hue faded. Holding his wrist, counting seconds by his watch, Steele knew he should not speak. But anger lived in him too, and he could not help saying, —All was in vain, then?

—What?

—The battle. The deaths. The woundings. Not just ours. Theirs too. What did all those boys die for, Commodore? Why more armor, and special ammunition to fight other ironclads? If we're to scuttle and flee, why did we defy at all?

The old man jerked his wrist away. —You'd have me—what? Throw more lives after them? I thought of all people *you* would understand. But even you do not. Answer me, sir!

—But why destroy the ship? I yet do not comprehend. One does not like to run. But if it is to fight another day, why not? This is all too sudden—

—Why? *Why?* Tattnall shook and blowed like a defied bull-walrus. —Because her shield's out of the water now. They told me if we lightened, we could escape. So I lightened. Now they say since the wind is from the west, the tide will be shallower than they first allowed. Even lightened, they cannot take us past the Jamestown Flats, up to which point the enemy is in control on either side of the river. We *cannot escape* and we *cannot fight*. That is the pass to which fate and cowardice and treachery have driven me. I will not sacrifice my people to a senseless slaughter. And I *will not* give such a weapon as this to the enemy.

He was shouting again, and his shaking cheeks were flecked with violet. Steele stood dumb, still groping for what he did not comprehend.

Why had not someone inquired about all this beforehand? If the pilots were so changeable and uncertain, might they not be wrong about getting past the flats? Until Tattnall screamed, shaking his fist, —What are you waiting for? Get out. Get out, you old fool!

And now that fatal moment had arrived. Despite their arguments, the crew's protests, all their efforts—it had come.

Abandon, and destroy.

Below their feet the engines were laboring, taking them across the river for the last time. Steele fingered a stiff beaker of brandy, the outwardly calm but inwardly bemused eye of a tornado, as about him in the surgeon's cabin the loblolly-boys stuffed the precious contents of his medical lockers into canvas sacks. Glass shattered, fumes rose, but he made no objection other than to step out of the spatter of spilled acid. Telling them to take the *hydrargyri unguent*, it was no longer in supply. From the passageway came shouting, the stampede of feet, the smashing of crockery. Finding the beaker empty, he refilled it from a bottle he only just caught in midair. Unable even yet to credit what seemed to be happening, unable yet to comprehend, so abruptly had events gone from already bad to completely unimaginable.

Catesby Jones thrust his head in. His tunic was unbuttoned, face drained pale, and beard smeared with what looked like flour. It was the first time he'd ever seen the exec less than perfectly groomed. —You are ready to depart, Doctor?

—Then it is true? Our unconquerable is to be destroyed, by our own hand?

—I am no happier about these orders than you. We are to run her ashore in the bight of Craney Island, land the crew, and set the vessel on fire.

—There is no hope of escape? I confess I still do not comprehend the situation. Exactly why must we—

—I've tried to reason with him, Jones broke out. —He will not hear me. The alternative is . . . His voice tailed off. He glanced at the enlisted bustling around them. —Never mind that. Perhaps there is no alternative.

Get yourself topside. Put that damned drink down, sir! I want you off in the first boat.

Jones looked like a man tried beyond himself; possibly close to shock, to judge by the tone of his skin and the white showing around his eyes. Steele held up the bottle. —I am proceeding as swiftly as I can, Lieutenant. You would do well to reduce the strain on your heart too. Will you join me in a prophylaxis?

For reply he got a snarled order to pack his traps topside and be quick about it, or they'd leave him aboard when they set fire to her. This did not sound a tempting prospect, no matter how attached he'd grown to the old girl. He hastily swallowed off the beaker, smacked his lips, regarded the third of a bottle remaining; and at last, reluctantly, turned from the shambles belowdecks and made his way up the ladder.

It was not far across the river, even at their snail's pace. She took the ground far off the beach, a gradual slowing surrender to the bottom that had received her once, relinquished her for a time, and, according to the old seamen in her crew, never ceased yearning for her afterward.

Alphaeus walked along the shadowy nave of the gun deck, a turmoil of emotions agitating his breast. All the lamps were out now. The gunners were piling combustibles, pouring out lubricating grease and paint along her littered aisle, between the now-silent guns. Barrels of powder stood by the ladder, guarded by a somber lad with a drawn cutlass. He eyed Steele as the surgeon laid his hand gently on one of the Dahlgrens. A machine to deal death. How could he miss it? Yet he could not, he *could* not leave her without a heart's pang. For a time it had seemed he too might partake of glory. Old as he was. Useless, Tattnall had called him. He shook his head slowly. No fool like an old fool.

Topside on the slick, narrow gridwork men pushed to and fro, falling over bales of records, seabags, cruise boxes. The crew was swinging out the cutters. Blocks squealed as they went down splashing into the dark water. Steele searched about for his boys, for his stores. At last he found them, all the way forward. He looked out into the night. The beach, if there was a beach out there, was completely dark. Not a fire, not a house, apparently. Where were they going? Had anyone planned their reception? Or was it all of a piece of their stopgap, haphazard leadership, always a day late and a dollar short?

He didn't make the first boat. Nor the second. Gradually fires sprang into life ashore. Figures moved about them. Eventually, accompanied by his essentials, he was helped down the casemate and into the cutter. It bobbed alongside the now sharply exposed bottom edge of the iron shield for some time, loading men and their impedimenta, before they finally shoved off. A long row followed. After which he was helped again, over the gunwale to step into shallow water, then to trudge up onto a dark, mucky-smelling beach.

Still long before dawn. He sat on the sacks and chests looking back as the rest slowly came over. Then after a time, one last boat, the men leaning to their oars as they sped shoreward.

Up to now the great ship had been an immobile shadow in the night. Now faint yellow light began shining dimly out the open ports. It glowed upward in a broad, flickering golden ray, through her grated casemate deck.

Over the next few minutes it grew brighter. It outlined her stack, her rails, the bare flagstaff, the familiar slope of the casemate.

The first tongue of flame licked out of the forward port, throwing brightness across the water. Others joined it till they illuminated the faces of those who waited, who watched, unspeaking and unmoving, on the curving beach. A gun barked a cascade of marigold sparks into the night. Then another. The flames soared higher as the officers moved among the men, as the petty officers chivvied them into a loose formation. As the loblolly-boys dug pits in the sand for his medicines. Would they be back for them? No one could tell him. No one knew. In the dark, in the confusion, he couldn't find Tattnall, nor Jones. Someone said they'd gone ahead to search out the road to Suffolk.

The last deep mournful boom reached them as they stumbled along a dark, rutted country track. Looking back, Steele saw the scarlet sky traced with the meteors of exploding shells.

His astonishment was giving way to a cold anger. He still could not understand how swiftly victory had turned to ashes. How completely that which the enemy could not do, they'd done to themselves. It wasn't the men's fault. They'd been brave with the courage of youth. Gallant unto death. Someone above had blundered. Tattnall, Mallory, Huger, Davis himself—he could not tell, did not know. He seethed at the waste of it. The men stared wordless, watching as the glow faded. One by one, as if each marched alone, they turned slowly back to their ebb and retreat.

But no matter *who,* no matter *why.* Their confused, thirsty, leaderless march through the gloom, a blanket and his clothes bag burdening his bent back, made perfectly clear *what.*

The great ironclad *Virginia* lived no more.

40

Transfer to *Vanderbilt* ♦ A Billet for Puncie ♦ Summons to Mrs. Peake's ♦
A Child in Her Father's Arms ♦ Won't We Sing and Shout ♦
A Deity of Endless Torment

LATE that May, Cal Hanks got a letter. He wasn't used to getting mail. In fact it was the first letter he'd ever received. So he carried it around in his flat hat for a couple of days while he mulled what to do with it. Now and then he'd go out on the forecastle, where he could almost be alone, and sit and rub his thumb over the spidery ink scratches, as if feeling them could tell him what it said. The paymaster had told him it was postmarked Hampton. Which was not far from where he sat, perched on a bitt in his whites and freshly made straw hat, looking out over the Roads. It had rained that morning, and the sun pulled wisps of damp-mist curling up off the deck in the hot bright light.

After a few days ashore while the Navy got things sorted out, the *Cumberland's* old crew, and what was left of the Avengers, had been broken up. The officers went home on leave, but the crew got sent to whichever ship had put in for warm bodies. They sent Cal to a volunteer steamer that had been plated up with iron in order to ram the monster when it came out again. *Vanderbilt* had been the largest and fastest transatlantic passenger packet before the war, somebody had told him. A rich man had sold her to the government for a dollar. Cal had asked if Puncie could stay with him. Since the boy didn't have family, he'd managed to take him along.

White sailors took their ratings with them from ship to ship. Blacks didn't, so he wasn't a quarter gunner anymore. Now he was second loader, and Puncie was powder-boy. That hadn't bothered Cal. Just looking out every morning for that smoke down toward Norfolk had gotten him out of his hammock every day.

But as it turned out, he'd never gotten another shot at the monster, though he'd seen it twice more, from a distance. It had come out in April, again early in May. Both times she'd stayed to the west, out of range of the fort's guns, while the Union squadron stayed to the east. As if both sides were more afraid of the other than eager to come to grips. Then the army had thrown ten thousand men across the water. They'd marched into Norfolk to find the rebel army gone, the Leviathan blown up and sunk. So the coast was clear, and their own ironclads had steamed up the river for Richmond. And now he was getting up with the letter in his hand, having spied the ship's chaplain, who'd come out to take his pipe in the lee of the pilothouse.

Dear Mr. Hanks,

Hope you will fergive this brief missive to ask you to call on me and Missus P at our home at Browns Cottage if it is convenent to you. She is very low and wd like to see you.

Your very obedient servant,
Thomas Peake.

A little flower garden in front of the cottage was in full bloom. A tethered goat eyed him, then went back to pulling up oniongrass. With its little foolish beard and treacherous gimlet eyes it looked like the engravings of Abraham Lincoln in the newspapers. The air was dreadfully warm and still. He was soaked with sweat as he hesitated at the front gate. Wondering for a moment, the back door . . . He didn't think so. He went up the steps and stood for a moment enjoying just being on a front piazza. Then knocked.

He didn't know the woman who opened the door, an old mulattress with stains under her eyes and freckled cheeks. He said, —Come to call on Sister Peake.

—She ain't takin no callers no more.

—Mister Peake done sent me this letter tellin she wanted to see me.

—You Hanks?

—Uh-huh.

She opened the door and he stepped in.

To smell at once the close stinging odor of the sickroom. He went through the parlor remembering a Christmas tree, children full of sugar and mischief. Now all was still. He tapped at the door, then pushed it open.

They looked up from around the bed as he edged in, holding his hat before him. Lockwood, the white minister. Mr. Peake, who made him look twice again, so much did he favor a white man. The mulatto woman came in behind him and plumped down in a rocker, taking up her knitting. A nurse, then. He took a step forward, and the woman in the bed opened her eyes.

—Brother Hanks, she whispered through cracked lips.

—Hello, Sister.

—Sit down here by me for a moment. Let him, Thomas.

—Thanks, Peake whispered, touching his hand as he got up. Lockwood reached across and ostentatiously extended his hand as well. Cal slid into the chair, clearing his throat. Glancing at the bloody cloth in the basin, the vials of bitter-scented medicine on the side table. Her hand groped out. It was hot and dry and contracted spasmodically but so weakly he could barely feel it, like holding a dying bird.

—You are well, aboard your ship?

—I'm doing all right.

—Your family? Have you heard from them? The ones still in Egypt?

—I ain't heard, Sister, no. Sometimes I misdoubt I ain't never going to again.

—Don't you have anybody else?

—Just a boy I takes care of.

—You take care of someone?

—Seems like it come to that. How, I ain't exactly sure. He come from Slabtown. Ain't got no fambly. About ten year old.

—But he has family now. And so do you.

He sat blinking into something he hadn't seen before. —Guess I does, he said at last. —Guess I does at that.

—So you're beginning to see. Can you love enough, yet, to forgive those who wronged you?

Cal shifted his brogans. He didn't care about these others, the blue-eyed Negro and the Yankee parson who breathed through his mouth, but he found himself unwilling to come up short in her eyes. So he only said, —I is maybe got a ways to walk on that, Sister.

—I have a vision, she whispered. —Our Saviour has told me our cause will triumph.

—Our cause?

—We are sowing seed that will become a tree to overspread the whole earth.

Cal shifted his boots again. It was very hot in here. Sweat was running down the back of his neck, soaking his woolens under the white duck. —Jesus tole you this?

—Don't you believe He appears to me? She smiled with a sweetness he'd never seen before on a human face.

—I believes you. Just that He don't to me.

—You've never felt His presence?

He couldn't answer no to that, because he'd felt *a* presence. Only he didn't know if it was Jesus or somebody else, different maybe as God from Satan. But even the name of Satan didn't seem enough to stand for the Thing he'd talked to in the fire, and felt behind him during the battle. A shiver squirmed up his back. How could it be God? It felt more powerful than Jesus, older and more evil than the Devil. Shit, he didn't know what it was. Only that it was *there*. And Mary Peake was dying, and he didn't want her to. He desperately didn't want to have her die and leave him even though he'd only seen her three times in his life and only held her hand. If she thought he didn't know what love was, she wasn't watching him very close. But he could see by her sly look she knew that without being told. So he just bowed his head, and she smiled again.

—Do you believe I'm happy?

—You looks happy, Sister.

—I am happy, *so* happy. As joyful as a child in its father's arms. If I could hold back my spirit by lifting a pebble, I would not do it.

—You goin to be all right.

—I *am* all right. He told me that I am where I should be, and that very soon, after only a little pain and trouble, I shall be with Him. I wish you could have such peace.

She started to say more, but broke into coughing. He scooted back as the nurse pushed him aside to help her to a sitting position, to hold the basin as she went through the agony. It was very bad. He saw the shadow pass across the faces of the men, and the old woman too, who cut him a sharp glance as she held the sick woman gently as a baby. He saw suddenly from the cheekbones and eyes whose mother she was.

Mary sagged back, struggled to breathe. It seemed as if she wasn't ever going to be able to get breath back into the tortured frail chest under the bedclothes, and he clenched his fists.

—Oh, Brother, she whispered, and panted shallowly for some seconds. All at once her body arched and she reached her hands up toward the ceiling, hissing in a low voice that was both tormented and inexpressibly happy, —Yes, I shall sing. I shall shout! Won't we sing? Won't we shout? Oh, yes, we shall. We shall sing and shout!

He stood awkwardly, not knowing what to say or do, but feeling tears stinging his eyes and brimming down his cheeks. She said, in that same hoarse, painful, passionate whisper, —Oh, won't we. Now touch my hand and go.

Outside on the same piazza where he'd told her about being a murderer, Lockwood said, —She said good-bye to her husband and her mother and her little daughter last night.

—That was her mother in there.

—Yes. It is not long now. She keeps reaching up to someone only she can see. You will not talk with her again, Mister Hanks.

—I sees that.

—She always felt she'd hear of you, though. She often asked if I remembered you. You're still in the navy, by your uniform.

—Yassuh.

—Fighting for the Union.

That wasn't what he was fighting for, but he just said, again, —Yassuh. An' for the people.

—Of course, of course. One expects nothing less. Will you be here in a few days? If she should . . . leave us?

—Sir, I can't say. There's talk of going out on the blockade. Now that *Merrimack* ram is gone, they don't need as much of a squadron here in the Roads. But if . . . anything happen to Sister Peake, you can write me on the *Vanderbilt*.

—I will do that. I hope we'll meet again, Hanks. May the Lord be with you.

Cal stood on the walk in the little garden, smelling the perfume of lilies and nasturtiums that hung in the hot still air. Suddenly he was seized by an anger so enormous he could not contain it. More overwhelming even than his hate for the marsters. His fingers flexed and fisted. It was rage at whoever had let this all happen. Who let it go *on* happening. Who had created and presided over a world of such pain, such everlasting and eternal pain. A deity who joyed in subjecting his creations to endless torment. Maybe it *was* God who'd spoken to him out of that burning. As to Moses, out of the fire then too. Maybe it was exactly God.

The flowers smelled as sickly sweet as death.

41

A Long Scramble Backward ♦ Seven Miles to Richmond ♦ Thus Far and
No Farther ♦ The Submarine Battery Division ♦ Rejoining the *Merrimack* ♦
Shall Southern Boys Be Brave? ♦ Four Hours Against the Federal Fleet ♦
A Glade on the Reverse Slope ♦ The Fomite of Destruction

H ENRY Lomax Minter reined in his sorrel when the artillery men
shouted for him to stop. Then stood in the stirrups, looking
down a sheer hundred feet at the turn the river made at the foot
of the bluff.

At the brown flood of tide. A steam pile-driver chuffing and thudding.
The antlike frenzy of hundreds of men, black and white, digging desperately on the muddy, riven, bare-stripped hills. More hundreds toiled in
frantic haste on log piles, stone cribs, scuttled vessels whose upperworks
and paddle boxes jutted above the eddying waters. He recognized
Jamestown, which had fought alongside *Virginia* two months before.

Dawn, and his tenth day in the saddle. The army was stumbling backward before the overwhelming weight of the Army of the Potomac. Lomax's special unit, with the rest of "Prince John" Magruder's covering
force, had gradually fallen back up the Peninsula over the last six weeks.
They'd stalled McClellan before Yorktown for a month, then abandoned
the position as the slow-moving Union general began his pre-assault
bombardment. After another delaying action at Williamsburg, Magruder
had scrambled back toward a last stand. Minter had not slept two consec-
utive hours since, nor glimpsed a bed or hot food. He removed his hat

and wiped his hair back. It fell now almost to his shoulders, and under the dirt shone more bronze than copper.

From here they could retreat no farther. A Union naval force had been working its way upstream for four days now. Released by the self-immolation of the great ram, two federal ironclads and several timber-built side-wheelers had churned and smoked their way up seventy miles of twisting, shoal-strewn stream, shelling out each makeshift earthwork and suspicious-looking copse as they advanced. Lomax had nearly been killed the day before, crouching over a telegraph-key detonator in a hastily dug pit. But his charge hadn't exploded, and the Federals had steamed on past.

Now Richmond lay only seven miles upstream, making this bluff the last chance to stop the Union vanguard before it brought the capital, Congress, and the city itself under its guns.

The chief came up behind him. Still sitting the sorrel, Lomax pointed out possible locations for their torpedoes, ahead of and between the stone cribs and piles and other obstacles taking shape below.

He'd been part of the Submarine Battery Division since mid-March. Detached from *Virginia* and ordered to work on infernal machines. He'd protested the assignment. If Buchanan had remained in command, he'd have been continued on the ironclad. But the old man was out of action, invalided to North Carolina, and Lomax had perforce become acquainted with telegraph batteries, insulated wire, and the delicate art of electrical fuzes.

He lashed the mare to the exposed root of a stump sunk in glutinous mud. The tree itself was gone, like every other for acres, chopped down for bunkers and walkways. The grass was gone too, trodden under by mules and men and wagons, and it had rained heavily for the preceding three days. His boots sucking in quagmire, he climbed an earthen rampart and looked off to his right, down the river.

This crest was an excellent position. Any attack must run head-on against the bluff. But there were no more defenses behind this. Only a few small wooden steamers, a paltry force the Union armorclads would crash through with no more effort than brushing off cobwebs.

True to our fatal habit, he thought grimly, no one, army, navy, military, or civilian, had devoted any thought to defending the capital from riverine attack until it was actually on their doorstep. For days now hundreds of artillerymen had been laboring to turn Augustus Drewry's hill farm into an earth-walled redoubt, emplacing heavy guns from Richmond and the scuttled warships.

He spat angrily. Tattnall should be hanged, he thought furiously. And Forrest. And others, all the way up. Only weeks before they'd been masters of Hampton Roads, primed to clear the enemy from their coasts.

Now that enemy was at the gates.

He found mostly army uniforms within the fort. The overall commander here was naval, but most of the troops were from Augustus Drewry's Southside Artillery Volunteers. The captain was directing the denudation and spading-up of his own property. A sergeant told him the sailors were dug in lower on the bluff. He half-walked, half-slid down the muddy steep slope scarred with dragged timber.

The first familiar face he saw was Reuben Thom's. The mustached marine said the *Virginia* boys had come in the day before, from Suffolk, by rail. Some were digging in *Jamestown*'s guns, which had been dismounted and thrown ashore north of the fort. Others were digging rifle pits at Chaffin's Bluff, across the river. His marines were in pits at the river beach, with orders to sharpshoot and harass.

—Who else is here?

—Jones. Wood is on the far shore. Butt's here, and Davidson. Midshipman Littlepage too. He saved our colors, brought them along in his knapsack.

—Where's Catesby?

—You passed him if you came down the hill. Thom pointed, and Lomax, shading his eyes, made out log-revetted positions not far below the crest.

When he reached them, now coated thigh-high with slime, *Virginia*'s former executive officer was supervising a party sandbagging an eight-incher. Jones was haggard and mud-daubed. He seemed to have forgotten any enmity, though, and took his hand. —Minter. You look healthy. What've you been doing with yourself?

—Attached to a torpedo unit. We haven't managed much as yet, but the weapon has possibilities.

Davidson too gripped his hand, blue eyes piercing. —Lomax. Joining us for this fracas?

—We'll be side by side. Lomax kicked the gun carriage. —Is this one of ours?

—You mean *Merrimack*'s? Unfortunately not. From *Patrick Henry*.

—Where are the Federals? Last I saw, they were steaming up Jones Neck.

Jones nodded toward the river. —That's their smoke round the bend. They fired one shell over us yesterday evening, at long range. The projectile struck the ground near the turnpike.

The sun had barely risen, but already a stain eclipsed the eastern sky. Minter gazed at it, heart sinking. So close as that. —Then they'll be here soon.

—We expect their attack in an hour or so. Yes.

He glanced back to the woods, where the torpedo wagons were drawn up. It took the better part of a day to rig the things. Too late now.

A musket popped in the distance. Minutes later a horseman burst over the crest. He yelled at the top of his voice that the Yankees were coming, the ironclads in the lead.

Davidson said gaily, —Well then, a fight it is. Will you second us, Lomax? Some of our old crew yet remain. The second gun over could use a bit of supervision.

—Lieutenant Jones?

—With all my heart, sir. Join us. Who knows; it may be the last time we fight under our own flag.

—Just let me get word to my boys and get them down to help out with those sand-bags.

His gun crew were lads he knew, the blue-jackets who'd been core and soul of the old ship. Gaskill. Donnovant. Eli Johnson, who'd served the bow pivot with him the second day of the battle in Hampton Roads. They welcomed him, and he told them they'd done well to stick. They'd stop the enemy here. The gun was a sixty-four-pounder, an eight-inch. They'd dug it in naval fashion, with a plank deck, the train tackle rigged to dug-in timbers, and a low overhead of stripped pine trunks covered with earth. Someone said there were three guns at the fort, five more in the naval pits. Looking down at the approaching smoke-plume he wished there were more of them. Not overmuch to match against a squadron. Albright came by. Minter asked if the surgeon was with them. He said Dr. Steele was setting up a makeshift operating theater in a copse some distance behind the fort.

They came into sight down the river not many minutes later, steaming beneath a lowering squid-cloud. As the rider had said, the ironclads were in the van. The other craft—gunboat types—hung back. The bumping of howitzers sent birds whirling up along the banks. They were scrubbing out the brush with grape at short range. Lomax didn't envy the riflemen down there.

The leader looked like a steam sloop, bark-rigged, but with a rounded hull. Unsheathing his pocket-glass, Lomax made out a commodore's pennant and iron sheathing. He made out the cheese box silhouette of the Ericsson behind the flagship. They steamed steadily up a river as broad and wide and straight as some triumphal avenue.

Till it reached the bluff.

Commands rang out from the fort. Lomax quietly told his own boys to load. They had no shell. Only solid shot. Well, that was all right, if they were to fight ironclads.

Over the next hour the squadron advanced. The wooden gunboats came to anchor half a mile downstream. But the ironclads came on. Some five or six hundred yards away—in perfect range and full visibility—the flagship sheered hard a-starboard and backed water, flaunting the Stars and Stripes directly below the waiting muzzles. The roar of chain cable echoed between the hills. He had to admit it was finely done. A lovely piece of seamanship, and a fearless confronting of what they must have suspected would be a powerful position.

Which did not mean he did not intend to kill every soul aboard, and to do it with the same savage satisfaction he'd have felt erasing a swarm of vermin from his hearth. He bent to check Johnson's gun-laying. He'd allowed for the downslope and for a heavy powder-charge. It was impossible to miss.

A huzza sounded from the flank; a moment later his boys joined in, three times three and a tiger. Looking toward the fort, Lomax saw familiar colors rippling in the hilltop breeze. Stained, riddled, they were the same Stars and Bars that had flown over the great ironclad those gallant days of March. His heart lifted to see them.

Then all fell into place. He understood.

All his life he'd sought something beyond himself. Unbidden, this sunlit morning, he'd found it at last.

It didn't really matter now whether they won or lost. They'd stand, and die where they stood, defending their country. Inditing with their heart's blood an epic immortal as Thermopylae and the *Chanson de Roland*. What was life for, but glory? To be young and in battle—he lifted his head and felt his spirit loft like a darting partridge.

A burst of smoke below; a warbling howl overhead. The quake of a detonation from behind. A rifled shell. The first salvo long; the second would most likely strike the bluff full on. —Fire, he shouted, and their own weapon rebounded with a bellow of smoke and white flame.

Every gun in the valley answered with them. Columbiads from the fort. The naval batteries. Dug-in field batteries from Chaffin's. The whole long river reverberated with the thunder of a lightning storm, and a continuous rattle of musketry blazed from rifle pits and bunkers all along the shore.

Smoke burst from the gunboats' foredecks. Their fire rose from the river, seemed to hesitate, then plunged downward to crash along, below, and just beyond the crest of the bluff. Solid shot *wumphed* into heaped-up earth. Exploding shells gouted sprays of mud to arch lazily in the morning sun. Fragments zipped and whined. A stump wheeled its roots in the air, then fell into the fort. Saffron fire lanced from banks of smoke, confined by the hills to lie like fog close over the eddying stream. The din was tremendous.

Reloaded, the sixty-four slammed out again. This time Lomax could follow the glowing dot of his projectile receding out and down in an arc that ended at the Federals' hull. The water burst and boiled around her with near misses and sprays of fragments. The bluff batteries were concentrating on her. Focusing his glass, Lomax saw what might be penetrations already, punctures in a thin metal sheath.

But now, steaming around her in the narrow stream, the broad black raft he knew so well chugged forward. The turret turned eerily, a half-blind Goliath searching for its tormentors. Then erupted in flame. The roar re-echoed from bluff and hills. Looking down he made out light perforated metal atop the turret. A ball dropped just there . . . He flung round after round, the men working like maniacs. His target answered. The turret no longer revolved jerkily, as it had the last time he'd confronted it. It seemed under smooth control now, rotating away to load, then turning back to face the bluff. He had leisure to study those open muzzles pointing, it seemed, right at him. To be blotted out by a flashing bellow, then the crash of shells into the hillside.

The duel went on and on as the sun rose behind the enemy. The men's blouses grew sodden with sweat, their faces black with mud and burnt powder. He was certain their shells were hitting the Ericsson's deck, if not the turret. And perhaps they were, because after a time she left her position beside the embattled flagship and drifted downstream again, opening the range.

But this seemed only to focus the enemy's fire, improve their aim, because now a perfect tempest of grazing shot and exploding shell swept over the top of the ridge. A whole corner of the fort heaved upward. Timbers, cart wheels, gouts of earth, whole trees tumbled through the air, fell to earth, leapt upward again like flour shaken in a cook's sifter. The shattering crack of air-fuzed shells racketed across the works, shooting iron-tipped lances of smoke down where the gunners crouched. Men streamed upward from the rifle pits, clutching bloody arms or heads, limping, crawling. Saber-wielding sergeants herded the unwounded back to their posts. Howls and shrieks mingled with the jar of shells, the massive ground-shaking concussion of solid shot ploughing into wet soil.

—Can we stand this, sir? A shout from one of the men, features mud-smeared, distorted with the emotion of battle, equal parts of rage, elation, and fear. He knew it. He felt it too.

—We have no choice. If our country is to be preserved, it is up to us.

A shot slammed into the beams above their heads, dropping the bunker roof onto them in a cascade of dirt and timber. The men turned to at once, hauling the timbers out of the way, shoveling mud and broken sand-bags out of the position. He could not believe no one was seriously injured. They were back in action within twenty minutes, though now without overhead protection.

But the din, the smoke, the daunting accuracy of the onslaught withered his courage and loosened his bowels. Having fought behind armor, he found it difficult now to stand in the open. To punish his body for wanting to cringe, he climbed to the top of the revetment, showing himself at full length, and looked down the length of the reach.

He stood above a river of golden smoke, lit by a burning sun. Tongues of alabaster fire darted within it. Above the smoldering gold, volumes of inky coal-smoke churned above barely visible funnels. The enemy was mere shadows within the glowing pit. The air opened with a shattering crack, and dirt flew up all around him. He swayed but didn't fall. He could hardly believe he had not been hit, so close had the iron hissed past. And at the same time knew himself more truly invulnerable than when bulwarks of oak and iron had stood between him and death.

—Lieutenant! Lieutenant!

They were shouting for him to come down. He pointed into the abyss. —I have heard no order to cease fire, lads. There is the enemy. Shall they show Southern boys how to be brave?

An inchoate howl rose from the gun crew, and with a bellow the iron tube recoiled. Again he followed the flight. This time the projectile vanished into the open bow port of the anchored flagship. For a moment nothing changed. Then, with a rumble audible from where he stood, flame and smoke shot out from every joint and crevice of the armored envelope. The screams that followed were like listening to the tortured in Hell. He clapped his hands to his ears, appalled despite himself. Men leapt from the interior, clothes aflame. They were instantly shot down by the hail of bullets from ashore, fell into the river, and whirled away downstream.

Not long after, the chain cables fore and aft disappeared in a welter of chocolate foam. Turning lazily, the still-smoking flagship began a drift downstream. It passed the Ericsson, which was still firing. Though it seemed without enough elevation to her guns to loft their heavy shells to the crest of the bluff. They crumped heavily into the face of the cliff or exploded over the rifle pits. With the flagship's retreat, the fire faltered. A feeble cheer ran along the crest. It gathered volume and became a roar as Minter too felt a savage yipping yell burst out of his heaving chest.

Half a mile behind, in a glade whose spring-green leaves shivered only now and then to the concussion of a distant shell, Alphaeus Steele drank deep of unwatered whiskey before turning back to the table. Planks set across barrels held a struggling boy. His arm was a ruin of smashed sinew and bone. He wrestled violently in the attendants' grip. Then drooped, the agony draining out of him as he slumped unconscious beneath the cone of sleep. It was Steele's third amputation this morning, and the stretchers on the brown, leaf-littered, muddy slopes were growing more numerous with each passing hour. He and the army surgeons with him were falling steadily further behind.

He lifted his eyes to the brightness beyond the trees. To the clamor of the guns. They echoed and re-echoed like the very voices of the gods. Those gods whose powers of destruction paled to insignificance beside the forces man had arrogated, then unleashed. Upon himself.

Steele no longer cursed those who'd turned this engine of war upon their kind. He understood now it was a disease within the human brain. A fomite that capered and leapt like the plague flea from one to another of those who thought themselves ruler and judge. A cancerous diathesis, a virulent pox immune to learning, to religion, to philosophy. No misgivings of a weary old man could divert it from its grisly harvest of the species that had hosted it time out of mind.

Alphaeus Steele no longer believed in glory. He no longer believed in independence. Nor even in an old man's right to peace. They all were caught up in the crush and roar of such a titanic millstone no human brain could encompass what grist might now result.

—Doctor, one of the assistants murmured.

Steele started. Stared wide-eyed on pallid, naked flesh.

Angling the scalpel, he swept it with all his strength in a sweeping arc. While behind the traveling blade, blood spurted with sudden and tremendous force.

42

The Aftermath of Invasion ♦ Fire and the Sword ♦ Disappearance of a Servant ♦ A Letter from Secretary Mallory ♦ Farewell to a Garden ♦ Encounter at Fort Monroe

CERTAINLY, Missus Claiborne, the pinch-faced woman said. —We'll keep your pretty house neat as a pin, an' send you the rent every month, wherever you say.

She dimpled under her bonnet, but Catherine did not trust her or the looks of her hangdog family. Refugees from up the Peninsula, where two great armies were grappling like huge slow wrestlers in a hold that would bring one or the other crashing down. She suspected they were Unionists. But it was better than leaving her home vacant. No telling who'd claim it then. The enemy army. The "contrabands," as they were calling the servants now.

No telling either whether she'd ever return. She'd sold the cow. Sold what she could of the furnishings. What was portable was in the wagon. Their silver, clothes, what mementos of their life she couldn't bring herself to leave behind.

Norfolk was occupied territory now. The enemy flag hung over the customs house. A Union general and his staff had moved into a house on Bute Street. And she and many others were leaving. For Richmond or farther west. Perhaps it didn't matter where. She knew only that she couldn't stay.

She riffled through the wad of shinplasters, checking the banks they were drawn on. Then tucked it into her reticule. Beside her Robert stood sniffling. He'd been shushed, then finally paddled when he refused to leave his play battlefield in the side yard. He didn't want to go. Even when she told him why. Aunt Dilla stood with her carpet-bag, waiting with the patience of an old servant. Betsey had not shown up for several days. Catherine had applied to the sheriff, who'd hemmed and hawed. A slave gone runaway these days was a slave lost, he finally told her. She was most likely in some camp by now, washing clothes for the Yankees or serving an even more shameful duty.

Leaving the tenants standing on the piazza, she took a last walk through the house. Through what felt now like a cast-off integument. Like the hollow, eaten-out shell of a cicada . . . down the back stoop to her garden. She kicked at a sodden pile of uprooted peonies, brown and withered beneath old cabbage leaves. Looked on the tender shoots of carrots, the nodding sprigs of just-sprouted potatoes. Freshly spaded, not a weed in sight . . . She glanced into the empty cowshed, but didn't go in. Pulled her shawl close, and turned away.

Leaving a home she'd loved and made her own. Perhaps forever. Who knew, these days? Who could see the shortest step ahead? But the lump of winter fixed now beneath her heart did not allow her to weep. She'd moved through the days since the outrage trying to think and feel as little as possible. Thinking led her into such a maze she stood bewildered. Lost.

She did not want to feel anything ever again.

She stood in the side yard, forgetting what she'd meant to do next. Looking without expression at the earth she'd been so eager to plunge her hands into.

Norfolk had fallen six weeks before. The army left overnight, without warning, moving out by rail. The next day the authorities set fire to the navy yard. She'd watched it burn the first time, the April previous. Now a second pillar of smoke towered across the river.

She hadn't understood why they left. Some said it was the possibility of invasion from McClellan's growing force. Others, that the Federals were threatening to cut off their retreat. But surely the *Virginia* could sweep any troops from the banks and sink any invasion force that ventured across the Roads? The first any of her neighbors or friends knew was the rising flames from Portsmouth. Then, later that same day, came the news the enemy had crossed. Landed at Sewell's Point and was even then marching overland, toward the undefended city.

The next day they paraded into town. The townsfolk stood wordless witness to shame and defeat as bayonets swayed above the dusty blue columns. Even the coloreds stood silent, glancing from the troops to their masters. Bands blared raucous tunes as they trooped down James and Bute and Granby Streets. Irish brogues called insulting proposals to stony-faced women. Catherine heard the gabble of strange languages, saw the foreign lineaments on dirty faces. The scum of Europe was being unleashed.

She knew then she'd have to leave. She couldn't live under their flag. Under oppression, tyranny, a hypocritical despotism that in the name of "Union" ground out the last sparks from Liberty's torch under the iron heel of force.

But then Rob's vague symptoms had turned into the chicken pox. She could go nowhere with a sick child. Bad news came like hammer blows. Each day brought fresh disaster for the Southland. The fall of New Orleans. A bloody engagement in Tennessee some called Shiloh, others Pittsburg Landing. The fall of Island Number 10 on the Mississippi. And then, as the last straw, the letter had come. The one she'd hoped for, for months. But holding it in trembling fingers, she'd felt like vomiting. Her eye had skittered across the loops and whorls of official penmanship, slipping from phrase to phrase as if they were fashioned of slick thin ice that gave no footing, that creaked and sank away beneath her weight. That covered a black coldness waiting to swallow those who ventured to trust it.

> . . . *Have the pleasure to convey . . . with the greatest respect . . . order by Secretary Seward for a special exchange . . . will be released upon parole, pending exchange for an officer of equivalent rank . . . to be exchanged at Fortress Monroe, and granted leave prior to his next assignment. . . .*

He was coming home. But to what?

The new tenants were eyeing her from the front yard. She shook herself and went toward the wagon. Aunt Dilla was weeping, tears rolling down her leathery cheeks. Catherine squeezed her hands. —Auntie, you needn't come with us, if you don't want to.

—Lord, Miss Cathery! Who else 'd I ever go with? The cook lowered her voice, glancing at the tenants. —I sure don't care for *these* low peoples. But where are we going? Church Hill? Always been so nice at Wythe's Rest.

—I can't tell you, Auntie. That will be up to Mister Claiborne when he comes back to us.

Robert was crying too. He was still sickly, still prone to lying on the floor when he felt weak. She yearned suddenly to scream. Her skull throbbed, as if something too large for it to hold was growing there. As if her dilemma had lodged in the channels of the brain, blocking all its natural processes.

For she could never tell. Never must she allow the faintest whisper of what had happened to escape. Ker would be bound to fight the man who'd shamed her. But would a scoundrel's death restore her honor? Bring back their happiness? Remake what had been lost forever? Of course not. And what if Ker died instead?

Some things had to be borne in silence. In patience if it could be managed. In resignation if it could not. Women knew this. Yes, women knew this above all.

Her thoughts moved on to the fort, to the truce boat. To what she could say when she saw him again. Perhaps across the water, as it neared. Whether he'd be in good health. What he'd look like. How he'd smile when their eyes first met.

Her mind stopped there. The numbness returned, a rushing in her ears as from a seashell picked up on the beach. The ceaseless reverberation of a terrifying storm.

She gradually realized they were all waiting for her. A little motionless tableau. The tenants. Dilla. Her son. She shook her side curls and snapped, —Very well, it's time to go. Wipe your nose, Robert. Stop sniveling. But remember this day, son, and who brought it on us. This is all part of war.

The driver set a stool. She gathered her skirts and climbed up. When he whipped up the team, she did not look back.

413

And now she stood beneath the terrifying mass of masonry. Looking up at their hated flag. At great guns pointing out over the sea. At a hurry and bustle of wagons and soldiers and draymen that beggared the imagination. She'd asked those who'd been exchanged before where to go and what to do, to see him. To speak to him, possibly, for a moment if his guards would permit.

Robert dragged on her skirts as she begged directions from unsympathetic men in blue uniforms. As she explained what she desired and handed out coins that did not soften hostile scowls. Behind her they were talking in loud vulgar voices of a great battle on the Chickahominy. They said Rob Lee was the new commander of the "rebel" army. She kept her reticule tight in her hand and clamped her teeth together. Ignoring the stares, murmurs, sniggered remarks. The truce boat would leave at two. If she would wait near the pier, she would most likely be able to speak to him as he passed by. If the guards felt lenient.

Waiting there, for a moment she felt faint. She pressed her hands to her corset, to her belly beneath it. A pain, a cramp. Her bowels, most likely. She fanned herself, lifting her bonnet to look out across the water.

—There's Daddy. Her son was pointing.

She crammed her fist to her mouth to keep from screaming. There indeed he was. Wearing his old undress uniform. Walking toward them through the press. A pair of armed troopers in blue behind him. He was so thin she almost didn't recognize him. So stooped and wan he looked older than his years. He'd not yet seen them. But in a few more steps he'd raise his eyes. The moment she'd dreamed of for so long would be here.

Waving her handkerchief, she forced a smile to her lips.

ABOUT THE AUTHOR

David Poyer's twenty-five novels in print make him possibly the most popular living author of American sea fiction. Sailor, engineer, and retired naval captain, he lives on Virginia's Eastern Shore with novelist Lenore Hart and their daughter.

Please visit David Poyer's website at www.poyer.com.